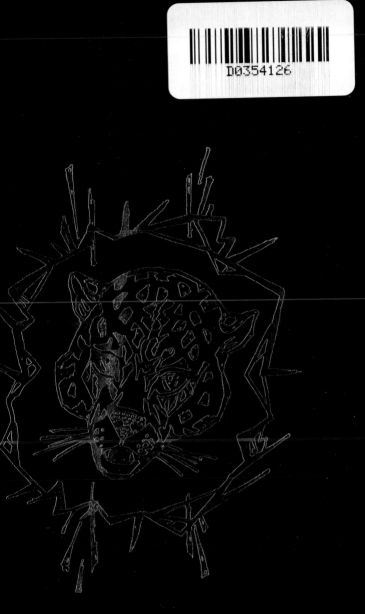

Red Jungle

Red Jungle

A NOVEL BY

KENT HARRINGTON

Dennis McMillan Publications
2004

FIRST EDITION
Published December 2004

Endsheet stamps and maps by
Joe Servello.

ISBN 0-939767-50-3

Dennis McMillan Publications
4460 N. Hacienda del Sol (Guest House)
Tucson, Arizona 85718
Telephone: (520)-529-6636 email: dennismcmillan@aol.com
website: http://www.dennismcmillan.com

To the fallen in the struggle for
human rights and economic dignity

"Swing me way down south,
Sing me something brave from your mouth."

—The Dixie Chicks

Red Jungle

TIKAL

GUETZALTENANGO

PANAJACHEL

ANTIGUA

LAKE ATITLÁN

CIUDAD DE GUATEMALA

HONDURAS

EL SALVADOR

TRES RIOS COFFEE PLANTATION

GUATEMALA

N

W

E

S

PROLOGUE

It all started with the sky, which was immense, devoid of feeling except for a few flat pink clouds that were fierce and pagan looking, the way they can seem in Central America. It started too with a *Fado* song on the jukebox, the melancholy music playing over the afternoon voices of a jungle barroom that was little more than a shack.

"Only the dead are really satisfied," the bartender said to Russell.

Across the road, a small group of Indian men worked under a ceiba tree, the tree's hulking great canopy lording it over them. The men intended to plant a cross where their loved ones had died. A young priest had come with them to bless the spot.

Russell watched as a shirtless, muscular Indian hit the top of the painted white cross with the flat of his shovel. He hit it hard several times; they heard the metal, *clang-blong, clang-blong*. Like a bell rung for the dead.

The third-class bus on its way to market had crashed into that ceiba tree the week before, on a perfectly sunny day. Five people had been killed on the spot. The bus had been opened like a soda can and the poor people on their way to market had died, gripping their vegetables and chickens. Even the chickens in their cages had been killed.

The bartender told him the story of the crash. How it had happened about that time of day. How everyone in the bar had run out to help. They had saved many people. The bar girls had held the dead in their arms.

The ceiba tree, the bartender told Russell, was hard as a soldier's heart. He'd been a soldier during the war, he said, and knew something about hard hearts. "You see things. Then you never forget them," he said. "Things that change you."

The Indian stood back from the cross and signaled to the kid priest to go ahead and get on with it. The Indians all doffed their worn straw hats and knelt down in the clearing under the tree. The kid priest in his black cassock stepped in front of the cross and spread his arms out. He started praying to his God.

Through the ceiba tree's lacy canopy, Russell noticed the clouds gathering above the men. He saw the new, raw-looking white cross standing now, saying what it said, marking where the people had died. The clouds didn't seem to care. They were sweeping in anyway. It was going to rain hard soon. They'd had a lot of rain that winter. Too much here on the Pacific coast, but nothing in the Peten. Even the weather seemed to be conspiring against coffee prices.

Russell Cruz-Price planned to buy a coffee plantation that afternoon from a Frenchman who'd gone bust. He knew it was a foolish act, but he didn't care. He'd gotten to that place in life where you just stop caring very much. You just try to satisfy yourself, and that's good enough. You believe what you want to believe about how it will all turn out.

He'd been playing with a double-0 shotgun shell, rolling it back and forth on the bar in front of him. The bartender took his empty beer away. It was hot in the bar and the air smelled of cigarettes and decaying jungle and the perfume the bar girls wore.

After they planted their cross and said their prayers, the men came across the empty road and into the thatched roof barroom for a cold beer. Even the priest came in. This bar was not used to seeing priests pass through its doors; a lot of people came to *La Ultima* bar, but not many priests. Sudden outbreaks of violence were very common in *La Ultima*. Men from all classes got drunk together here, then shot each other for petty reasons – usually over the young bar girl's affections. Couples danced night and day to the juke box on the polished concrete floor. *La Ultima* never closed its doors. It was a church, someone told Russell once, but for sinners.

"You see the dead, they care for nothing now. They don't care about sex. They don't care about love. Not even about food. Nothing," the bartender said, getting ready to set the Indians up with beers.

Russell had decided to wait here for the American who would guide him to the plantation, for no particular reason other than that he liked the place, and it was right off the Pan American Highway, and the back had a view of the jungle and a river that was entertaining to watch. He liked the way the jungle grew right down to the river's edge.

A psychiatrist might have suggested to him that he came to places like *La Ultima* because he had a death wish. He was ignorant of that particular desire, as he was of so much of his psyche. Some desires he was very aware of. Some were sitting around the back of the bar, wore short skirts, and could, under the right circumstances, make you feel better. But not always. The others were less obvious. He sought out fearful situations and now he had the desire to make a great deal of money. He couldn't explain his seeking out fear, but he was aware of it. It was as if he were trying to prove to himself that he was not a coward, and whatever he did was never enough.

In fact, he thought he was fine. But all his risk taking was a strange way to live, he would have agreed. Other men he knew wanted to feel safe, safe in their occupations and families. He'd always envied those men their children, their wives, their knowing whom they could count on.

Something had happened to him that made the simplest things in life difficult and the harder things easy. He would run towards a fight and away from anyone who said they cared for him. It wasn't right and he knew it, but it was the way it had shaken out.

The men from the road sat at the bar, and the place livened up. They wanted to put the deaths behind them now. Russell bought them all a round; they thanked him, and said he was "*muy Christiano.*" Very Christian. He said he was sorry for what had happened.

Fit and tall, Russell had his Guatemalan mother's thick brown hair and his American father's rawboned good looks and green eyes. He had a quick, knowing smile that put people at ease right away. He was working now as a financial journalist for a famous English newspaper, which suited him. He could have continued with that, but didn't want it anymore. He wanted money now, and was going to buy the coffee plantation from the Frenchman.

The afternoon started to crumble into long dull moments, still appallingly hot but overcast. The immensity of the jungle outside reflected the endless tangled nature of existence. Things floated by on the river.

"You want something to eat?" the bartender asked later.

"No thanks," Russell said.

"You want to talk to a girl?"

"No. Not in the mood."

"You're young. You should talk to a girl," the bartender said. "It's always fun."

"Maybe later," Russell told him.

The men who'd planted the cross proceeded to get drunk. The young priest had one polite drink and left for his church. Russell moved to a table and continued to wait for the American while he watched a parade of impoverished plantation workers – men and women – in black rubber boots, some carrying their machetes, walk past the bar toward the town.

Russell knew from his reporting work that the old feudal world his mother had been born into had ended with the destruction of the coffee economy. And yet the coming brave new world, promised by well-dressed young people at the World Bank, was not in place, either. It was a strange time. No one knew what was coming next. The execrable feudal traditions – abhorrent to him – were at least based on a perverted social contract that guaranteed homes and food to the country's most wretched. To his mother's class, it had also guaranteed great wealth and leisure.

But now, even that grossly unfair contract was being swept aside by Darwinian "market" forces that guaranteed nothing to anyone. The plantations were closing down, and there seemed to be nothing left for the poor to count on. A hundred and fifty years of history was being carted away, as if by magic.

He'd met the old American in a restaurant in the town. The American had claimed to know *Tres Rios*, the plantation Russell was going to buy. The old man had offered to guide him. It would save time, and Russell had eagerly agreed to meet him later. He was a man in a big hurry. He wanted to find the Red Jaguar, the Mayan antiquity he expected to dig up there, which would make him rich and allow him to leave Guatemala for good. And the sooner, the better, he thought.

The bartender walked out from the bar and put a new beer in front of him. "I put it next to my girlfriend's heart," the bartender said. "It's ice cold."

They both laughed. It had started to rain, first softly, then suddenly in a great hostile downpour. The voices in the bar seemed to get louder. Russell could hear the rain striking the building's corrugated metal roof.

He slid the shotgun shell into the pocket of his jeans and turned and watched a couple dance. Suddenly, and for the first time in his life, he admitted to himself that he was completely lost. He put the idea aside quickly, a little afraid of it.

His mother's family had owned one of the biggest coffee plantations in the country. His mother, Isabella Cruz, had been raped, murdered and thrown into a ditch by communist guerrillas, while he'd been sitting in a math class a thousand miles away. He'd gotten a long letter at school from his uncle, who'd written him with the news. His uncle's letter had been very beautiful, but lacked something.

Russell's mother had died when he was ten. They had been very close, in the oddest way. They had an understanding and sympathy towards each other that went beyond the usual mother and son relationship. There was no possible way to describe it; words do fail sometimes. Because of the war, he'd been sent abroad to school. His relationship with his mother had been epistolary for the most part, although he'd come back here to visit her for all his vacations.

Because he'd been trained not to show "weakness" in the military schools he'd attended, he hadn't allowed himself to cry when he got the news of her death. Sometimes, however, when he'd glance at his writing desk, he'd felt like it. He'd seen other boys cry, and he hated it. He wanted to slap them. It seemed a violation of everything they'd been taught about being a soldier.

He was eight when he was told that war would make him a man. He'd believed his teachers, the way young boys do.

The school had been brutal, so he'd learned to cope with brutality and physical violence at a very young age. (Every adult on the staff, short of the cooks, had the right to practice corporal punishment on the students, and they had.) He'd become expert at both psychological warfare and the strange, capricious, and often purely sadistic behavior of adults.

Many of his fellow students would die trying to prove how tough they were. One died in Somalia in Delta force, the toughest of the tough. Russell had seen his name in the newspaper. They had been on the cross country team together. He remembered the boy catching him on a hill once in the rain, and they'd raced along together in silence, sharing the pain of a long run.

His school was shut down when the idea of making "soldiers" out of young boys finally went out of fashion. As far as he was concerned, it had been a good education, and prepared him for a world that was less than fair most of the time.

Russell watched the old American's beat-up, lime green Volkswagen bus pull up in front of the bar, right where the men had planted the cross. The driver's-side door was bashed in. The old American slid out, locked his bus up and waited for the traffic to clear on the road, then ran across in the downpour.

He must be seventy or even older, Russell thought, watching him run towards the door. He was spry, though. The old man came into the bar and, seeing Russell, approached him with a decrepit bonhomie that was common out here when finding a fellow American who might be better off than oneself. The shoulders of his worn cowboy shirt were stained dark from the rain.

"I don't care what kind of beer… anything wet. *Tres Rios*. It's impossible trying to find it, if you've never been up there.

7

No signs. Nothing to go by. You should get some quality coffee out of a place like that. You said you were going to *buy* it?"

"Yes," Russell said.

"Wow. That takes guts, with coffee not worth shit right now." The old American looked at Russell from ancient, keen eyes. "Don' pay too much, that's all," the old man said, after they exchanged handshakes. "You can call me Coffee Pete."

Russell signaled the bartender and ordered him the beer he'd asked for.

"I know the way all right. Don't worry, I can save you a lot of time, I spent years out near *Tres Rios* chicken farming," the old man said. The American's blue eyes darted around the barroom, landing on a young bar girl in a red tank top and white short shorts, sitting alone.

Russell didn't ask the old man his connection to the Frenchman who owned the plantation he was going to buy. He didn't really care if there was one.

"You should listen to me, son," Coffee Pete said. "Get out of this damn country while you're still young. Hell! Better places than this backwater. Why don't you go to New York?"

"I was there," Russell said.

"No shit. Girls there all had good jobs and big tits – when I was there, anyway."

Coffee Pete managed to smile and flirt with the young girl halfway across the barroom. "Don't be like me. I can't leave now." The old American was tall, wore dirty khaki pants, and had a short-barreled .45 shoved into an expensive-looking quick draw holster on his right side. The side arm was the only clean-looking thing on him.

He claimed he'd come to Guatemala to train the Cubans for the Bay of Pigs invasion for the CIA and decided to stay on. Russell could see he'd been big and strong and proud once. He was diffident now, not proud anymore, but still dangerous, Russell thought. Maybe it was even true about the Bay of Pigs. But one heard so much bullshit in these bars.

"I guess you can pay me now. Three hundred Q," Coffee Pete said, putting down his empty beer glass. "If you don't mind. If I had time, I'd take that girl over there and go have a relax out back." He smiled, and Russell saw a great animal cunning in the old man's face.

Russell counted out the money and added fifty quetzales, just because the old man seemed down and out and he felt sorry for him.

"I didn't think there were people like you anymore," the old man said, thanking him. "Generous people out here don't last, as a rule. Only the mean last, kid. 'Cause the mean just don't give a shit about heaven." He slipped the money into his shirt pocket, behind taped-up reading glasses. Russell paid the bill and they left. The old man went to the bathroom, telling him to follow him once he got his VW turned around and pointed south.

Russell went out to the parking lot and loaded his combat shotgun with six rounds of double-0 buck shot. He loaded the little Velcro belt built right into the stock of the shotgun, then put more loose rounds on the seat, where he could get to them quickly. When he was finished, he laid his weapon on the seat next to him and looked out at the road. He'd tried unsuccessfully to buy a hand grenade on the black market. In a firefight they made all the difference. He would try again, he thought, waiting. He didn't want to die defenseless, as his mother had. The war had ended, but not the violence.

Russell watched the old American come out of *La Ultima*, run to his VW bus, and start it up. It belched smoke. The old man flashed him a smile, then pulled carefully out into traffic and took off. Russell kept expecting, as he watched from the

9

parking lot, for the VW to turn around and come back south. The old man drove off, gaining speed, heading north toward Mexico.

Russell watched him pass a truck and disappear. He thought about chasing him, but decided against it. It would be a race into the town, there were a thousand side roads to turn into and hide, and undoubtedly the old man, like any good rat, knew all the good holes. He took off with only the name of the plantation and a curt description of how to find it. He got that lost feeling again as he drove south, but it passed.

He'd written his mother a last letter soon after her death. He wrote it on her birthday and mailed it. In that letter, he told his mother everything he'd never gotten a chance to tell her. He laid out his plans for the future, telling her that he thought that his years of military school had been good for him, and that he hoped to be a doctor or soldier; something "worthwhile." There had been a moment after he'd read his uncle's letter when he'd been gripped with a horrible panic. He thought he might have no future at all.

He'd walked to the duty officer's room and handed him the letter, which was a "dead letter" even before it was mailed. The older boy—a captain—in mufti, because it was the weekend, was on the phone with his girlfriend. The captain nodded to him, took his letter and threw it on a pile with many others; and that was it. He'd gotten on with his life. He'd gone on. Now he'd ended up back here in his mother's country, half crazy and not even aware of it.

ONE

October 1, 1972
Guatemala, Plantation "Las Flores"

Isabella Cruz Price, despite all the people around her, felt very alone. She turned the crank of the old-fashioned black telephone in the morning room, trying to get a line.

The Cruz family plantation, Las Flores, was enormous—ten thousand acres. Even now, parts of it had never been planted or exploited in any way; whole tracts lay virginal and untouched. It was a verdant, tree-filled womb, creating oxygen that would fill the lungs of Californians, New Yorkers, and Englishmen without them ever knowing where it came from. The plantation had been bought by her great-grandfather for—it was said—one thousand dollars, long before Isabella was born and sent to the United States to study at a convent school near San Francisco. A nun at that school fell in love with her, because even as a young girl, she was very beautiful. Isabella had thick chestnut hair, very white skin, and exciting blue eyes that pulled you in. The nun—who lost her faith—would die years later still thinking about Isabella, still completely in love with her.

She got a line. The telephone operator put her through to her brother's apartment in Guatemala City. Isabella heard the phone ring. She pictured the living room of the apartment with its view of Avenida La Reforma, the grandness of that view. The street, a Third World version of the Champs Élysées, had been designed by an architect who hoped Guatemala City might, someday, be the Paris of Central America. He was an intelligent fool, or an extreme optimist; the city would never be anything like Paris.

When they were children, Isabella and her brother would drink lemonade on Sunday, before lunch with the family, watching out for their father's car—a big black chauffeur driven Buick—as it came down the widest avenue in Central America. They would rollerskate through the halls of the apartment, frantic to greet him. They had been very happy as children, surrounded by three generations of the family and the knowledge that somehow they were important and powerful.

Isabella had kissed the President of the Republic on the cheek in front of that big window in the living room. Isabella had had her first period in that apartment, mystified by the bleeding. Feeling as if she were going to die, she'd run into the arms of her Indian nanny crying, very frightened.

Her brother, Roberto Cruz, had changed some things about the apartment, modernizing many of the rooms after their parents died. He'd sold off some of the old-world furniture. Her brother loved everything new and everything American. He wanted, more than anything, to be a modern American swinger. Isabella loved the heavy antique furniture her grandmother had brought with her from France. It was said that her grandmother had been born and died in the same bed. Her brother had sold the bed and bought something out of a catalog from the United States, with an upholstered headboard and a built-in TV set. The advertisement had claimed that this style bed was used by the stars in Hollywood. The TV set had never worked.

She missed the heavy purple curtains that had hung in her grandmother's bedroom. The dark curtains seemed in keeping with the somber visits she remembered from an ancient

12

Spanish priest, who had fought alongside Franco and against the Spanish Republic. The priest came every day while Isabella's grandmother was dying. He would hold Isabella's hand and tell her that Christ loved her very much. She was glad that Christ loved her. It made her feel good. She knelt by her grandmother's bed, her skates on, and prayed to Christ, asking him not to take her grandmother away.

Her grandmother died the month they sent Isabella to the United States to go to school. Her grandmother had said something to her in French the morning they brought Isabella in to say goodbye. Isabella never understood what her grandmother had said. She had simply told her granddaughter: "Enjoy life, dear. It is very short."

Isabella wished she and her baby were in the capital, safe. But they weren't. There was going to be a war. The air was different now. Even the rain was different now, the way it fell against the coffee patios in unforgiving thunderous moments.

She looked down the hallway of the plantation house towards the bedroom where her infant son, Russell, was sleeping. She wondered if he would always love her. Her son had the blood of two countries: Guatemala, the poor coffee country, and The United States, the great top hat country of Henry Ford and Broadway and jet planes and smoking factories. She called him her little Yankee when she fed him, and would laugh while stroking his white skin. She had bathed her son in the same bathtub she'd been bathed in, a bathtub her grandfather had bought and had carried from Puerto Barrios in 1899, through the jungle, to rest here in the plantation house that hadn't changed in more than a hundred years. Indians who saw the porcelain bathtub coming up the narrow jungle track —like some porcelain god— would bow, her father had told her, laughing. The Indians, the story went, would run from their houses just to touch its white sides with

13

the magical words "American Standard."

"Olga. Olga…" Isabella said.

"Manda?" the Indian girl answered.

Olga Montes De Oro stepped out of the bedroom and looked at Isabella. The two young women had known each other since they could remember. They were born two days apart, there on the plantation. If they weren't sisters, they were–in Guatemalan terms–something very close. (Isabella's American husband would never understand these mysterious relationships.) The sight of Olga made Isabella feel a little better. A little reassured. Like the day that Olga's brother found them lost in the *cafetales* when they were children, terrified by the red ants they'd found crawling up their naked feet and legs.

"The child?" Isabella asked.

"Sleeping now, *Doña* Isabella," Olga said. Isabella was ten when Isabella's father insisted that Olga begin using the *doña* when she addressed her friend. The two girls laughed about it; it was as if Isabella had suddenly grown up. Olga was jealous, but never said anything to her friend. She wanted to be *Doña* Olga. Olga told her father. He said that she would be a *doña* when Olga saw pigs fly over their house, and laughed, rolling a cigarette with one hand. When Olga asked her father why her friend Isabella was a *doña* and she wasn't, her father, a worker who smelled of sweat and cheap alcohol, and who'd never had more than three quetzales in his pocket at any one time in his life, said it was because they were poor and Isabella was rich. He told her it would be that way until the sea dried up and God came back to earth to take them all to heaven, rich and poor alike.

"I may drive us. Drive us to Quetzaltenango," Isabella said. The two young women looked at each other in a way they didn't normally. Each had a role to play–each had to give meaning to her society, master and servant. But this morning everything seemed to be different: the air itself seemed charged, dangerous, electric, like the afternoon when they had been lost together. They could hear the rain hitting the roof, and Isabella wasn't sure that Olga had heard her. She wanted to reach for Olga's hand and hold it, as she had when they had been children. She wanted to say she was frightened, but she didn't.

"Did you hear me, Olga?" Isabella said instead.

"Yes, madam." Olga's eyes betrayed the obvious—that she was frightened, too. She had heard gunshots, and the radio said the war had started in earnest and that someone called Jimmy Carter was going to help them. In Olga's mind, she saw Jimmy Carter dressed like a Catholic saint, with a stigmata on his naked side from a Roman lance. He wore a crown of dollar bills.

"I've called Don Roberto in the capital, but he's not answering," Isabella said. "I'll try again later."

The cook came running out of the kitchen, across the wet patio. Also a young girl, the cook was heavy-set, with thick legs. Her stomach pressed against the cheap fabric of her cotton dress, which had cost her exactly two weeks' wages. She stopped under the awning, her hair shiny and very black. If there was a war, she knew nothing about it. The cook would die in a government ambush, her brain pierced by a bullet made in Indiana in a small factory with no sign. Ironically, the bullet was made by a woman, and fired by a woman who was fighting "in the name of the fatherland."

Isabella watched the cook hesitate, pull open the screen door, and then walk in. The young woman, who'd also grown up on the plantation, smelled of wood smoke. They used wood in the kitchen to cook tortillas long after they could have used propane.

"Madam, I have the pork for lunch. Will there be anyone else today?"

"No," Isabella said. "No, I don't think so."

"Don Antonio?" the cook asked. "Will he be coming to lunch?"

They heard more shots then, and there was no mistaking them; they were shots and they were coming from the south near the town, less than five kilometers away. The women could hear them over the rain and the rolling thunder, which had broken twice over the house since Isabella had come to use the phone.

Isabella instinctively told herself not to show fear; that if she did, that somehow it would be the beginning of something bad, something she couldn't control, and the people around her would lose their courage too and they would all be lost. She felt, at this moment, as if she were the center of all their universes. She was the heart and soul of the plantation that her grandfather had left them. After all, she was a Cruz, and had her grandfather's lion heart. She had the boy in the other room. He was sick. He was too small to be sick here on the plantation, with a war starting. He was fragile. *What kind of Yankee was fragile?* she wondered.

"I want you to turn on the radio in the living room," Isabella said to the cook, instead of saying: *"God help us. They're here. The communists are here, and will kill us."*

Her father had died of throat cancer a year before in London. She had loved him very very much.

At that moment Isabella, only twenty-one, felt very young, too young for the shooting and too young for the child. Her father had said he would not die in this wretched country full of communists, and Isabella had cried. He had gone to London and died surrounded by English nurses. He had spoken to them in Spanish, and they had not understood a word of his confession. Whatever he told them went to the grave with him.

16

He had been close to many presidents of the republic, especially Araña. Perhaps it was about that—the things her father had done to keep people in power. He had helped with the Bay of Pigs invasion. He had died wondering why Castro had won the battle. He blamed Kennedy, but was very sorry when he'd heard he'd been assassinated, because Kennedy was a good Catholic.

"Did you hear me?" Isabella said.

"Sí, señora."

"Not the records, Maria … *the radio.* I want to hear the radio. It's noon, and they play the marimba at noon time. I want to hear it the way papa used to. Do you remember, Maria? With a gin and lemonade before lunch."

"Sí, señora," the cook, Maria, said. She passed Isabella, moving into the dark hallway with its yellow wallpaper from Belgium, past the room with the infant and Olga. Maria walked on towards the living room, all of them ignoring the sound of the gunfire. She walked to where the big old-fashioned wooden radio sat in the living room.

Isabella heard the sound of the radio suddenly. A BBC reporter's earnest voice filled the hallway. Isabella had been listening last night, alone, drinking, waiting for her lover, trying to get some news. She had had many lovers since her divorce, but this one was important because he was the first she felt anything for. She was a modern woman and a failed Catholic. Antonio De La Madrid had called this morning and said that he couldn't come to lunch as planned. There was no reason to ask why. It was the guerrillas; they were everywhere, he told her. He'd seen them on the road below his own plantation house. He didn't dare leave his mother alone. He was only nineteen, but was the head of the house because his father lived most of the time in New York, where he raced horses. They had hired some American mercenaries and were hoping for the best, he told her.

"No. Not that," she said loudly. She didn't want to hear the BBC or talk of war. She walked towards the living room and stopped by her father's office door. The door was closed. "Please, Maria, not that. I want to hear *Marimba*," Isabella said, holding the doorknob to her father's study. The music suddenly filled the hallway. *Luna De Xelaju.* The sound of the marimba, romantic and haunting, filled the house.

"Thank you, Maria," Isabella said. She took her hand from the doorknob, then touched it again and opened the door to the office. For a moment she saw her dead father standing over his desk, the way he had been when she was a child. He turned and smiled, holding his lemonade and gin, his shirt sweat-stained from having been out all morning walking with the plantation's administrator, his khaki pants muddy at the cuffs. He wore his never-really-care smile. "Dear, I know you can be brave. You were always brave when you were a girl. The bravest," her father's ghost said, and winked at her.

"I don't know, Papa," she said aloud. "I really can't be, not really, I'm a woman. And you know how we are, pretty and all, but not for this sound of guns. Where is Roberto? Where is my brother? We need him; I have a child. A boy."

"I told you not to marry that American. He was much too dry for you," her father said, touching his blond mustache. He turned his back to her and looked at something on his desk. "He should be here with you. He should have lived here with us."

"Could we dance, father? The way we used to. Remember?" she said. He turned around, smiling again, and she saw her father as she had seen him for the last time, and she closed her eyes. She didn't want to see him like that. She wanted to see her father of 1955. She opened her eyes again and he was there in a tuxedo, looking very fit and handsome and young.

"How's this? The Italians call this monkey suit a 'tight.' Is your mother ready?"

"Yes," Isabella said.

"Would you like to dance? I'll tell you all about the party tomorrow when we get back," her father said.

"And will everyone be there?" Isabella asked.

"Everyone that should be," her father said, holding out his arms. She stepped into the room and she felt her father's arms around her shoulders and she was dancing, and he was talking about how they were going to go to the beach at Tilapa when she came back from school in the States for the Easter holiday.

"I want to go to the party, Papa. Please!"

He held her away from him for a moment. "Look, Gloria! See your daughter."

Isabella turned around, and her mother's ghost was standing in the doorway in a party dress. Her hair, blonde, was done in the style of her day. Her mother had died in a car crash in Fresno, California, when she'd gone to visit her sister in 1962. She was hit by a traveling salesman from Chicago, who managed to walk away from his brand new Cadillac and ask her if she was all right. She said she thought so, but she died anyway in the ambulance. She spoke to everyone in perfect English until the very end. She had been educated at Columbia University, and she had always prided herself on her English. The last thing she thought about was that she'd left her handbag in the car, and that it was such a silly way to die.

"You have a child now. A child of your own," her mother said. That was all she said.

The room went still; her parents abandoned her. There was nothing but her father's empty desk. She went to it and took his revolver from the top drawer; for some reason, he'd always called it "the bottle opener." She opened the action and saw the bullets neatly seated in their chambers. She snapped the action closed and walked out of the room with it in her right hand, the hand she'd used to play tennis at her school in the

19

United States, where girls didn't learn to shoot. She'd learned to shoot here, on the plantation. She was different from those blonde girls she'd lived with so long, the Helen Albrights and Madeline Thompsons of the Yankee world. Helen Albright had asked her incredulously if Isabella's father rode a donkey, like she'd seen in the movies. She said no.

Because Isabella was so beautiful, the other girls respected her. But they were never her friends, not really. She made friends with another Latin girl from Chile, whose parents owned a bank, and who ironically had blonde hair just like the Americans. Once, on a train trip to San Francisco, the two friends listed a hundred things that made them different from the other girls. They never admitted that they were both in love with Jesus Christ, the way young American girls were in love with the Beatles.

I'll kill anyone that harms my child, Isabella said, and closed the door. She never saw her father's ghost again, no matter how hard she tried.

She could hear the rain falling as she walked back to the porch, and thought she would have to speak up if her brother called. But he didn't call that day. He was sleeping with one of his maids, and he couldn't be bothered to answer the phone. (The maid had heard the phone ringing.) Isabella rang him again anyway, hoping he would answer.

The patio outside was drenched in a warm torrent; the yellow trumpet flowers planted near the kitchen house bent over slowly as they were pelted. Isabella finally gave up trying to reach her brother and walked to the screened-in windows to stand and think of what to do.

Why? she asked herself. *Why.* Everything when she was a girl had been so good. Her father was here, and her mother, and there was happiness and no war. And if her brother was a tall, irresponsible, charming boy, it made no difference what-

20

soever. But today it did matter, very much, and she felt so alone.

She had wanted to tell her brother that the guerrillas were seen on the section of the plantation that looked down on the little town of Colomba. She wanted to tell him to come home and help her, because she had the child here and there was no one willing to drive them out to the capital because of what happened to the Asturias family. The Asturiases had all been murdered by the Communists on the lawn of their house, and the bodies were still lying there stiff—first in the sun, later in the rain. No one, not one Indian, no one, would dare drive them out to safety now.

She was alone. Not alone; really; there were 500 people living on the plantation—but she was alone. She felt it now for the first time. She was white, and the rest weren't.

She played for a moment with her long brown hair, and looked out at the water-bombed patio. She could see the green of the coffee bushes at the end of the silent driveway. She'd ordered the gate locked. She wondered, if she prayed to God, whether her father would appear at the gate at the bottom of the garden and take them somewhere safe in his car.

She saw the pathetic little lock and chain hanging from the gate in the rain. No, praying would not be enough. The fact that God had let her father die seemed cruel and impossible. She had never forgiven God for that. God had sinned against her, she told a priest. He had not answered.

The plantation, one of the largest on the coast, was left to her and her brother and their older sister. It had been bought on a Sunday at a dinner party near Guatepecque, at the home of her grandfather's mistress, sometime before the turn of the last century. The mistress had arranged the sale. There had always been questions about the propriety of the sale, and about her grandfather's law practice, which had enriched itself

21

during the flu epidemic of 1898. It was said that her great-grandfather, Ramon Cruz, had started life as a young bank clerk in Guatemala City, the son of poor Spaniards, and finished a very, *very* wealthy man who could and did shout at the President of the Republic. The story of his rise was, according to some family members, the story of swindles and the shameless abuse of widowed women left alone by the flu epidemic. But no one could be exactly sure, now, how the Cruzes had gotten to own so much. As Isabella's aunt liked to say, only the dead know that story, and they aren't in a position to tell it.

TWO

Russell had met Gustav Mahler–the archaeologist, not the musician–when Russell had been sent to interview the young German, who'd become famous after his startling find of a lost Mayan temple at Bakta Halik. Mahler and Russell had agreed to meet at the Circus Bar in Panajachel, on the shores of Lake Atitlan.

Mahler looked like Kid Rock, and had an IQ of one-hundred eighty-three. At times he stuttered. His teachers in Germany thought it was only because he had so many conflicting ideas that came to him all at once. His mind raced; he'd learnt to live with it.

He had been named after the famous German composer, who'd been a distant relative. Mahler's father was a world-renowned Mesoamerica scholar and an expert on Mayan history. He had worked the *Tikal* site in Guatemala during the war years and brought his wife and child with him, despite the danger.

While his father worked, Gustav had played in Tikal's famous grassy courtyard, between the stele *Roja* and the Temple of the *Jaguar Grande*. The local Indians had embraced the young boy, and taught him things about the jungle most white people never learn. He was happiest trekking in the bush alone, singing Rolling Stones songs at the top of his voice. He had wanted to be an archaeologist since he was six years old.

Mahler was only twenty-four when he made the discovery that made him famous. He'd gone out into the jungle and found it without any help or university backing. He told Russell that he'd come to Guatemala to write his Ph.D. thesis, but ran out of money. It was unheard of.

The temple had been full of priceless Mayan antiquities. Mahler had saved them from a group of colonels, who'd planned to clean the temple out as soon as they'd caught wind of his find. He'd gone to the world press, sounded the alarm, and stopped them. The Colonels had been arrested. Mahler's picture was printed in all the German newspapers, who called him a hero. Stanford University had offered him a teaching job in California, but he'd turned it down.

Mahler had brought a Dutch girl to the interview. She was a brainy, thin, glasses-wearing, twenty-five year old from a small country town, who seemed to be a bona fide sex addict. "She just vants to suck my dick and smoke weed," Mahler told Russell matter-of-factly. "You've heard of the Red Jaguar?" he asked.

"No," Russell said over the music, watching the Dutch girl, braless and fetching, stop to talk to friends at another table.

"It's out there. I'm sure of it. It's not a myth, like some people say," Mahler told him. "It's worth a fortune. My father told me about it when I was just a kid. He looked for it, but never found it."

Russell glanced at the bemused Dutch girl as she headed back to their table. Someone at the bar had bought her a brandy, and she was holding it in both hands. Her skin was golden from sunning herself at the hotel pool all day.

"You'd have to give it up to the government," Russell said. "If you did find any kind of treasure."

"Not, not ... if you find it on private property," Mahler told him quickly. He looked Russell in the eye. Russell realized that Mahler stuttered, but controlled the affliction through

force of sheer willpower. The German's face contorted a little with the effort to control his tongue. There was a mean look in Mahler's eye as he struggled to get the next word out of his mouth. Russell decided, looking at him, that Mahler was probably as arrogant as he was brilliant.

"Okay, I'm game. What is it then, this Red Jaguar?" Russell said.

"A… A…great bloody piece of red jade. I *mean* bloody big. Heroic. You know what that means? Right?" Mahler asked. He took a drink of his wine, the flamenco trio on the bar's tiny stage playing louder now.

"Life size. Right?" Russell said, speaking up over the music.

"Might be bigger," Mahler said, putting down his glass. "Might be like the stone jaguars at Bakta Halik. Remember? There at the entrance. You've been there, haven't you? Those are eight feet high, man!"

"Yes. I've seen them," Russell said.

The Dutch girl came back and sat on Mahler's lap. In the lamplight, Russell could see her breasts clearly through her sheer cotton blouse.

"Big," the German said, ignoring her. "Could be *very* big. And those are stone. The Red Jaguar, they say, is made of *jade*. That's the story, anyway, what the Mayan texts say. Can you imagine what that would be worth to a collector? Or a museum? *Millions! Millions, my friend!*" The German reached over and hit Russell on the shoulder, managing to keep the girl on his knee.

"It might be a myth. You know, like El Dorado," Russell said, trying not to stare at the girl's tits, not taking him seriously. "Or the Lost Dutchman's mine."

The band stopped.

"I don't think so," Mahler said quickly. He touched the girl's cheek with the back of his hand and smiled at her, as if he

25

already had sold the thing and had the bank book in his pocket. She got off his knee, but not before grinding a little.

"Jaguars are frightening," she said, getting up and moving to her own chair. "I bought a mask in Chi Chi, but I had to give it away. So dark!" She looked around to see if she had any more friends in the bar. She growled, a little drunk. She produced a joint, and they went out onto the street to smoke it.

"What are you suggesting?" Russell said. Holding the last of the joint, he offered the last hit to Mahler, who shook his head. Russell threw the roach in the gutter. The Dutch girl was window-shopping further up the street. Russell could see her outline in the moonlight. He felt very high from the joint and the wine he'd been drinking. It seemed to hit him all at once.

"I'm suggesting you throw in with me," Mahler said. His eyes glowed behind the roach's ember as it raced past his face and fell in the gutter.

Mahler told him he thought the Red Jaguar might be on a plantation that bordered the site at Bakta Halik. He said the plantation was up for sale because of the coffee crisis. "That's my suggestion. I have no money to buy the place." Mahler said.

A week later, for no good reason, Russell had decided to do it, to throw in with Mahler and search for the Red Jaguar. Sometimes, he thought, you do things and you don't even know why. He was just stumbling through life, and couldn't stop himself.

• • •

In the late afternoon, Russell pulled up in front of a formidable steel gate. Wind whipped at the ragged banana trees along the road to the plantation's main house, their broad green leaves writhing wildly. His windshield wipers couldn't keep up with the torrents of rain.

After eighteen miles of horrible dirt roads and a filthy rain, he'd found *Tres Rios*. He'd made only one mistake, and it had cost an extra hour. An ancient faded sign read, *Finca Tres Rios Familia O'Reilly*.

The plantation house stood a football field or more away, behind the locked gate. He could see that the house was big and very old. If not grand, it was still impressive-looking. It had been built with a very deep veranda on the main floor, and had a stick Victorian façade that belonged to another century.

He honked his horn, giving it a long blast as the Frenchman had instructed. He had been told to wait; someone would let him in.

A young girl in a bright yellow dress, maybe eighteen, darted out of one of the shacks on the road above. Her hair was rain-wet, very long, and very black. She ran towards him like a deer in the forest, beautiful in the rain. Russell got out of the jeep and met her at the gate.

He glanced at an abandoned guard shack to the right. The rain was pouring through a hole in its roof. The girl smiled at him, her beautiful face wet. She had big eyes, the whites startling like snow in the jungle. Thin and tall, her waist was flat against her dress. He offered to help her and reached for the key, the rain pelting him hard in the face, but she didn't give it to him.

"No, yo lo abro, Señor," she said, and bent down to unlock the gate, her yellow dress soaked. It clung to her back and shoulders like a skin. She unlocked the gate, then stood up, managing a smile. The gate, she told him, was too heavy for one person to move. He helped her pick up the steel pole, and they walked it back across the driveway. The entrance to the plantation clear, they set the pole on the ground and ran back to his jeep. Russell picked the shot gun shells off the seat so she could sit down.

"Thank you," he said, looking at the girl once the doors were closed. He was struck by her beauty. He couldn't help but notice the way the water pearled on her face.

They heard a thunderclap. It rolled the way it does there on the coast, forever, and then broke hard in parts, as if the sky were cracking apart. She was a stunner, the kind of girl you see on magazine covers in America.

He leaned back in the seat, wiped his face, and put the jeep in gear. They passed through the gate and went up the dirt road towards the big house.

"Aquí, por favor," she said suddenly. He stopped the car. "I'll leave it open," she said in Spanish, nodding towards the gate. She glanced quickly at him once, their eyes meeting, then opened the door and jumped out. He watched her disappear into one of the wood shacks, its low corrugated metal roof a deep orange-red. The doorway of the shack was black, like her hair. He looked down at the wet empty seat where she'd sat, then drove on toward the big house.

The road turned and moved up the hill as it passed other shacks, some abandoned. Mahler had told him that the plantation was barely being worked, since the collapse of coffee prices.

Another long peal of thunder rolled over him. He saw Mahler's old blue Toyota Land Cruiser, with its ladder and steel baggage-rack welded to the top, parked in front of the big house. The top of the old Land Cruiser was covered with netting and blue plastic. Russell parked alongside it.

A maid appeared on the veranda, came down the steps with a large golf-style umbrella, and ran to his side of the jeep. Russell saw a tall white man, the Frenchman called Don Pinkie, come out onto the veranda. The Frenchman stood on the porch, a solid curtain of rain between them. Russell stepped out of his car, the thunder breaking again, and ducked under the maid's umbrella.

"Buenos tardes, Patron," the maid said to him. She must have heard that he was there to buy the place. He had the first payment in his wallet, a cashier's check for thirty-thousand dollars drawn on his account in the States. He'd sold everything he'd had left back in the Bay Area: a few landscape paintings he'd collected when he'd been a stock trader, a ski boat he'd kept in storage. He'd maxed out his credit cards too, but he'd gotten the first payment together.

The word *patron* slapped him in the face. Always before when he'd heard *"patron,"* it was addressed to some rich Guatemalan. The expression had always embarrassed him a little.

"Thank you," he said. He and the maid moved quickly toward Don Pinkie standing on the porch. As Russell went up the stairs, still under the umbrella, he saw Mahler come out of the house. The two men spoke in French and then Mahler turned toward Russell and smiled, his narrow face white and cold-looking.

"How was the trip, *amigo?*" Mahler asked.

"No problem," Russell said. He shook hands with both men.

"We'll start tomorrow," Mahler said. They were sitting in the living room, which had an incredible view of a garden. There was a giant Olmec head, and three small stone jaguars and a stone lizard, all antiquities found on the plantation over the years and now displayed in the front yard. Don Pinkie had moved out and was staying in the guest house with his wife and children. Russell had agreed to let them stay on until their house in the capital was ready.

"Don't know how I'll make the second payment," Russell said. "You should know that I might not even be able to. I'll try and see if we can sell the coffee to a broker, but with the price the way it is right now, it won't be much. So we don't have much time. The Frenchman will want his place back if we don't make the second payment on time." He was nervous about owing so much money.

"I'll find it," Mahler said. "Don't worry, amigo." Mahler was wearing American army fatigues and dirty boots with red mud trapped in their heavy lugs.

"There's a hundred and ten acres," Russell said. The realization of what he'd done and the stupidity of the search crashed in on him. He looked around the poorly-lit living room. As was customary, all the furniture had been included in the price of the plantation. The French family had bought *Tres Rios* just before coffee prices had collapsed; they'd been in Vietnam before that. The descendants of the original Irish family that pioneered the place had been killed during the war, driving over a land mine on their way to church.

"Let's start right after lunch," Russell said. "I have to go back to the city day after tomorrow. I want to look with you while I can. Maybe I'll relax if I start looking."

"I'll need money for food and for a few things," Mahler said. He was sitting in one of those soft mid-century American easy chairs, mustard-colored. He looked tired.

"How much?"

"A thousand Q should do it," Mahler said.

"Five hundred, partner. I'm not made of money." The German looked at him and shrugged his shoulders. "Yeah, five-hundred. *Das geht.*"

"If we find this thing, we have to sell it. How do we do that? We can't exactly take it to London on a plane," Russell said.

"No, but it's not illegal either. You own it if you find it on private property. I told you. It's not like Mexico."

"Yes, I know. I looked into it. But *how* do we sell it?"

"Carl. He said he'd buy anything we find. You can start with the stuff on the lawn if you want."

"Carl?"

"Carl Van Diemen. The Dutchman who lives in Antigua," Mahler said. "How do you think he paid for his big fancy house there?"

Russell had met Carl Van Diemen once. "I know him. I thought his daddy was rich or something," Russell said.

"His daddy *is* rich, so … why you so pissing?"

"It's, why are you so pissed," Russell said.

"Okay, why?"

"I think I just did probably the stupidest thing I've ever done in my life," he said. The German started to laugh at him.

A clap of thunder rolled over the house and shook them. Russell started to laugh too. It was crazy. He'd gone crazy. It had finally happened. Russell had heard countless stories about people like him, foreigners who went around the bend. Foreigners who had been here too long. He'd been here three fucking years. That was long enough to go crazy, he supposed. The rain hammered the roof.

"We're both crazy," the German said.

"Yeah, but you have a PhD from the University of Düsseldorf–almost," Russell said, still smiling. The laughing had broken his dark mood. Okay, he was crazy. Okay, he'd just bought a coffee plantation in the middle of nowhere because some German hairball had convinced him that a giant red-jade jaguar worth a fortune was buried on it! He started to laugh again, the kind of laughter he couldn't remember since he'd been a stock trader in New York, when he'd lost ten million dollars almost overnight. He looked up, holding his sides because they'd started to hurt. Mahler was looking at him very seriously.

"Fran…Fran…Frankfurt," the German said, dead serious.

"What?" Russell said. He finally stopped laughing.

"Not Düsseldorf. Fran…Frankfurt," Mahler said, very seriously.

"No shit! What the fuck difference does it make!" Russell said.

"It *makes* a difference." Mahler smiled like he'd just found some money lying on the carpet.

"Yeah? Why?"

"Because everyone in Düss... Düsseldorf is a fucking idiot. They couldn't find an elephant in a coal mine." And he started to laugh again.

While they were laughing, the girl–the one who had opened the gate for Russell–crossed below in the garden. Mahler turned when he saw Russell looking. He said something in German. Russell didn't have to speak German to understand what Mahler had said about the girl; it was universal. She was a goddess.

"Okay. Tomorrow we start," Mahler said, turning back around.

THREE

September 1, 1973
San Francisco

"They say you shot a man," Montgomery Price said. Isabella's ex-husband was a tall, blond Protestant from a good San Francisco family, with a fabulous career as an IBM executive in front of him.

He had won an award—in fact, it had been presented to him by J. P. Smith, the grandson of IBM's founder. It had been the proudest moment of Montgomery's life. He had sold more mainframe computers than any other salesman on the West Coast. Only the New York office had outsold him.

The award was an important milestone in his career. The day Montgomery won the award, he knew he would have to divorce Isabella. He was smart enough, at 31, to comprehend the extent of his mistake in marrying her. He was still young enough to fix the one thing wrong with his life. He'd simply married the wrong damn woman; it hit him as he went back to his seat, award in hand, and glanced at Isabella who, contrary to his wishes, had worn a mini skirt. (She had bought it in Paris, with her own money.)

Isabella had been a mistake. Some of his colleagues had stared at her. With the right woman by his side, he knew he could work his way into management. There would be no

33

end to the possibilities, his boss had told him . . . but his boss had also suggested that Isabella was *not* an IBM wife. Not even close. She was simply too Latin, too flamboyantly feminine, and too young and sexy.

She made men uncomfortable. She was an embarrassment. She had parties where liquor was served in abundance, parties where she danced and got drunk in public. She had homosexual friends who called other men "honey." There was a rumor that she used marijuana, which in fact was true.

"Is that true? Did you really shoot someone?" he asked Isabella.

He gave her a peck on the cheek. He thought she looked terrible, and was too thin. Since he'd never been to Guatemala, he had no idea what the place was like, other than the people he'd met—principally his wife's family. They all seemed to be —over-*everything,* over-emotional, over-wealthy, over-fun loving, and lazy. He didn't believe any of them ever *really* worked (Protestants of his ilk associated style with the devil and laziness). Isabella didn't get up until ten in the morning. When she did get up, it was simply to give orders to the maid, Olga, who seemed strangely fond of her mistress, and vice versa. He thought their relationship "unhealthy," and had told Isabella so.

"Yes," Isabella said, and turned away. They were standing in a suite in San Francisco's Clift Hotel, on Geary Street.

"Good God! And the baby was with you?"

Isabella turned for a moment to look at her husband. He was handsome in the way she expected of American men: healthy, tall and strapping. Many of them were a disappointment in bed. Montgomery had been the kind of man who clutched at her, and heaved. Heaving had been his idea of love making. After the disappointment, he would roll over and talk about his office. But it was the heaving that had left her feeling like an animal instead of a wife.

He wasn't a bad man, and she'd been in love with him because he was what her long stay in the United States had taught her to want—a strapping, well-employed, blue-eyed man who looked like Troy Donahue.

She sat down by the window. Below, she could see Geary Street, and a theater marquee advertising "Man of La Mancha." She had shot and killed a communist at the gate of her plantation, with her father's pistol, while Olga, sitting next to her, clutched the baby and screamed. Afterwards she'd driven the three of them to the capital.

"Well, I always said that country was no good. Rotten, isn't it. I'm certainly glad I never went. It's in the papers all the time, the war news. Frightening. How can anyone do any business? I'm glad you're leaving the boy with me. The right thing, of course. . ." Montgomery said. He finally saw the pain in her eyes and stopped talking for a moment, not knowing what to do. ". . . I mean, for everyone concerned."

"It's temporary," Isabella said. "You understand that, Monty."

"Of course. To be honest with you, I don't know how Sally will do with Spanish. I think she studied it in high school—or was it French? Does the boy speak *any* English?"

"A little," Isabella said. She was dying for a drink. Since she'd shot the man, she'd started to drink more.

"Well, we'll change *that,*" Montgomery said. "Can't live in today's world and *not* speak English. Most of my clients from Mexico speak it better than I do!" Monty spoke to her as if she were one of the boys. "You know I've gotten a promotion."

Her ex-husband, in the traditional IBM blue suit and white shirt, went to the opposite end of the suite. It was a suite that her father and grandfather had always used, whenever they were in San Francisco. "Latin America all the way to Punto Del Fuego. Quite a territory for a man my age. Really, I think it was because of you. I suppose they thought I understood the Latin mind." Monty sat on the orange chintz-upholstered couch, put his hands on his knees, and looked at her as if she might give him an award. *I suppose I do,* he told himself.

She realized he was a fool, and was surprised that she'd never seen that until now.

He'd come during his lunch hour to pick up his son. He had hired a nurse to take the boy home and provide for him until his wedding. He was engaged to a girl who had just graduated from UCLA, who, he told Isabella, would make an excellent mother for the child. He was betting on her the way you might on a horse to win a race. He told people, in fact, that she was going to "go the distance."

"As soon as things calm down, I'll take him back," Isabella said. "You understand. It's impossible right now with the war, and I have to make the plantation work somehow. It's all that Roberto and I have. Would you mind if I had a drink? Would you like one?" Her ex-husband shot her a disapproving glance.

"Sorry. It's a Thursday, and quite early at that. I have one on Saturday night."

"Well. It must be the time change," she said, and went to the servi-bar for a gin. She called Olga to get her a glass from the bathroom.

Olga came out from the bedroom. Monty stood up. The two had never said more than "good morning" and "good night." Monty, for whatever reason, was afraid of Olga– probably because she reminded him of the wild Indians he'd seen in the movies. Olga politely came to Monty's side, called him *Don Monty,* then turned to get Isabella her glass.

"Does he have everything, Olga?" Montgomery asked. "Clothes and things?" Monty always forgot that Olga spoke no English. He waited for an answer as she walked towards the bedroom.

"Yes. He has his clothes," Isabella said, looking at the little bottle of gin in her hand. She was afraid of the bottle, and she loved the bottle. It was like most things in her life, a bit of a mystery. When the man had jumped on the jeep to stop her, she had mysteriously fired her father's gun at him. The barrel of the thing drove into the man's brown stomach. His rifle slung over his shoulder, he'd never expected a woman to shoot him. But she had: She had shot him well, as the plantation workers said later.

For the workers, Isabella had taken on almost mystical powers after that. They viewed all outsiders—including the guerrillas—as a threat. After the shooting, she got the kind of respect her grandfather and father had enjoyed. The workers believed the Cruzes had magical powers and would protect them from the communists.

"I hope Robert is helping you with the place. Is he still playing polo? Or whatever it is he does all day?"

"They've killed all the horses," she said, cracking open the bottle. "It was quite horrible, really. Seeing them like that in the stalls, dead. Are you sure you wouldn't like a drink, Monty?" She realized then that Monty was a boy and would never be a man, if being a man meant that you weren't afraid. He was afraid of everything. He'd been afraid of her in bed. He was afraid of his boss and of his company.

This moment was to be the first impression, and memory, Russell was to have of his father. He would recall later that the man was tall, and looked down at him as Olga brought him out from the bedroom where he'd been napping. There was a lushness that he would always remember about life with his mother. She sank down beside him, her long hair falling over her shoulders.

"Mí querido, hoy te vas con tu papá. My dearest, today you go with your papa." She said it in both languages. Isabella rubbed his hair and held him tightly for moment.

37

Nothing would ever hurt her as much as that long moment. Not being alone on the plantation later, with the constant threat of death, or the loneliness of her affairs, or her addictions, or even the dreadful pain of missing her mother and father.

"He's a big boy," Montgomery said, walking towards him, speaking a language that Russell couldn't really understand. Isabella wouldn't have cried, but Olga started, and then Isabella couldn't stop herself. The boy, not accustomed to the two women in his life crying, looked at his mother for an explanation. None, unfortunately, was forthcoming.

He was taken from his mother exactly a half hour later by a "nurse" who smelled of Listerine and called him Russ. The first word he learned in English was "Mother." Russell once heard his father tell his stepmother that Russell's mother was a drunk.

The first thing Russell remembered about life—about being alive—was the gunshot that had saved them. It had been very loud. His mother had shot well. Everyone at the tennis club in Quatepeque said so. The guerrilla had intended to kill them, people at the club said, because he hated the rich.

FOUR

The price of commodities throughout Latin America had collapsed completely, leaving strangled economies unable to breathe. Guatemala's currency, the quetzal, dangled by IMF machinations and a prayer. Violent crime in the country had reached absurd, Hieronymus Bosch-style levels.

The free markets were at work, just give them time, urged his newspaper's editorial writers. But they were in London, and even to Russell—who believed in the system—their opinions on the crisis seemed hopelessly out of touch.

Come to Carl's Party in Antigua, the email had said. The invitation had come to Russell's office computer in Guatemala City, the Thursday after he'd returned from *Tres Rios.* It gave an address and a long list of people, some known to Russell, who were planning on coming. He scanned the list of names. It promised a good time and he immediately wrote back, saying he planned to come.

He called Katherine Barkley, an American girl, asking if she'd like to go to the party with him. She answered her cell phone from somewhere out on a coffee plantation, building housing for poor families.

Barkley was the opposite of the wealthy Guatemalan girls he'd been dating, girls whose main preoccupations had been their hair and their breast size. Katherine worked for a UN-affiliated NGO called "Houses for Humanity." She was serious, intelligent and completely unimpressed by his big job with the *Financial Times*, which she considered an "establishment rag." At the party where they'd first met, they had argued about the IMF's role in the life of the country. She was, she'd said, an anti-globalist. He thought her position ridiculous, and told her so. He'd told her that capitalism *would* make the world richer, but it would take time.

He honestly believed that. It's what he'd been taught at the University of Chicago, and like any neophyte, he believed what he'd been taught with passion. It was a harsh Darwinian system sometimes, he agreed, but it was better, *far better,* than anything else. Leave it to Adam Smith's *invisible hand.* It was the only way, he'd told her. If it worked in America, it could work anywhere. Weren't people all the same? He told her he thought it racist to think only white people had a right to prosperity.

They'd agreed to disagree, and he was surprised when she'd given him her number and told him to call her. On the way home that night, he began for the first time to silently question his beliefs. Stopped at a traffic light, he'd looked at the pedestrians as they crossed in front of him. He couldn't help but see the pain in their faces, really see it, as they stood waiting for buses, holding a child's hand. Their faces were marked by suffering, really stamped by it now. He'd seen it clearly—anyone could—a shared frantic look that said there were limits to patience before people exploded. The communist insurgency had lasted thirty years, and now this strange new enemy, an economic war with unseen generals and unseen armies but real casualties, was being visited upon them.

That Saturday afternoon, Katherine Barkley picked him up in her UN-issued Jeep, and they drove past the groomed concrete collection of shopping centers on the way out of the capital to the party. A red diesel-glow hung over a free trader's dream of a skyline, bristling with gaudy bank buildings and

Big-Business towers. Guatemala City was the biggest city in Central America. The diesel-smoke skyline was the carcinogenic byproduct of secondhand American school buses that had been shipped here, and were ubiquitous. Brightly painted, the "chicken buses," as the tourists called them, spewed a rich black sulphur exhaust one could literally taste.

They passed the American-style strip-malls adorned with corporate logos: Papa John's, Nike, IBM, Gap, PriceSmart. HBO posters hung neatly at every bus stop, telling passengers to enjoy *Band Of Brothers*. "War the way it should be," Katherine joked.

They passed a huge green *maquiladora* with Korean script, saying only a Korean knew what. The prison-like factory was anonymous. The tops of its high walls, wrapped in concertina wire, looked ominous and terrifying. Above the wire, the iodine-colored sunset was fiendish and hysterical.

They listened to a pop station whose DJ kept saying, "We got your *hot mix*," in bad English. *"And there's a shadow in the sky and it looks like rain,"* Nelly warned everyone from Pop Land. They left the buses-crawling highway at San Lucas. It was cooler up there above the city, the little shanty towns dismal and uninviting.

They took the turnoff to Antigua and started to descend on a modern three-lane highway. Katherine smiled at him, her body language seeming to invite him to kiss her. She was dressed in jeans and a white blouse. "We got your *Hot Mix*." It was verging on dark, but they could see the outline of the *Volcan de Agua* suddenly hulking by the road, a bad actor in this country's play. She was talking about her work in the countryside, and all he could think about was taking her clothes off.

Crosby, Stills, and Nash came on, more "We got your *hot mix*." It was a beautiful evening despite everything. He was randy; it had been weeks since he'd slept with anyone.

They passed the last of the handmade furniture places at the bottom of the hill, just before getting into Antigua proper. Now the wan, polluted light had gone dull, like dark water pooling on a stone. A few samples, handmade desks and chairs, were being carted in by young skinny kids pushing against the twilight's swift angles. The boys looked like crude skinny cherubs come to life. *Maybe you'll sell tomorrow,* Russell thought. *Maybe tomorrow* someone will buy them all. He had his doubts, though. Lately he couldn't stop the doubts pouring in. Was he changing? Like all men, he hated change. Had his professors been wrong? It had seemed impossible when he first got here, but now he wasn't so sure. He'd been two weeks in Argentina the year before, and what he'd seen there had scared him. He'd witnessed the complete collapse of a society.

There were red taillights and cars, and the sudden confusion of Antigua's narrow colonial-era streets. The walls of houses and buildings, very close, still glowed from the sunset. The buildings' warm colors felt soft and welcoming. Young shop-girls walked with their black hair pinned up. The town's colonial architecture was a blessing of another century, before the ungodly cheap modernity and buck hysteria of the capital.

They stopped for a drink at the Opera Café. They sat in the back and talked about how it was to be a foreigner in a country, how they never, no matter how well they spoke the language, quite understood all the nuances. The language had its little side streets, didn't it? Katherine said.

He didn't tell her he wasn't really a stranger to the country. Even his colleagues at the paper didn't know about his mother. Or who his family was.

They drank Chilean white wine, good, cold, and expensive. He was not one to save money. If he had it, he spent it. Sometimes he would spend it all just to feel broke, something he'd never understood about himself. To have nothing but his job and the beer in his refrigerator and the wax on his floors. He didn't want to collect things—he'd learned they could disappear as quickly as they'd come. He'd wondered if this sense of futility was what might be wrong with him emotionally. If he wanted *things,* he could have taken another trading job in Paris or London—not become a journalist in Guatemala. Things—TV, new cars, clothes—were somehow silly here, and beside the point. Here you lived by the minute or by the hour, but no more than that.

Somehow, in the tropics, the idea of the future seemed ridiculous—and yet it wasn't enough. He wanted money. He wasn't even sure exactly why. Now, thinking about what he'd done with Mahler, he had no explanation for his decision. He knew it was the adventure. It wasn't the money, not really, he decided.

He liked to look at the movie posters and the cool people who came to the café, mostly young couples drinking coffee. He liked the red of the walls and the photos of famous singers. It was his kind of place, elegant, clean, sophisticated, with something extra, something that made him relax, took him away, a mixture of the right light and the black and white tile floor and the waitresses—in Indian garb, *corte*—who were very professional, never botching things.

They had only one drink, then decided to walk on to Carl's place for the party. They might have been in a café in New York or San Francisco, except there were a few men with pistols strapped on just under their jackets sitting at the café's bar. They were rough-looking. They stared at Katherine as they walked out the door. *Dope,* Russell thought. *Real* killers.

FIVE

Major Douglas Purcell U.S.A.R.
Blackwell Academy
232 White Blossom Road
Palo Alto, California 96601

April 2, 1988
Mrs. Isabella Cruz Price
Plantation "Las Flores"
Colomba, Costa Cuca
Guatemala, Central America

Dear Mrs. Cruz-Price,

We are in receipt of your letter of 15 January, which included full payment for this school year. Thank you.

In answer to your question: Yes, we have spoken to Cadet Russell about the results of the intelligence test he recently took, and we are aware of his concerns. As you may know, because so many of our graduates go on to the various private high schools that feed the United States service academies, we have, as a long standing policy, administered the military aptitude test, which is a prerequisite for entrance into these schools.

I'm happy to write that your son tested very high, and that we were pleased and gratified to report the results to both parents of record. We feel his long stay here at

Blackwell has proven of real value to Cadet Russell and will hold him in good stead in the future.

However, I must take this opportunity to express my concern about Russell's negative attitude towards both having to take the test, which he at first refused, and his troubling attitude towards the results themselves. It seems that he <u>doesn't believe</u> the results—in fact, he says he's quite stupid. Furthermore, he has stated to members of our staff that the test is a "gimmick to make him feel good about himself." These attitudes are certainly unfortunate and of concern to us, as Russell has maintained a sterling record both academically and otherwise, until very recently. Perhaps there is something wrong at home?

I must also inform you that Russell has been involved recently in quite a few fights and that this behavior cannot be tolerated indefinitely. I'm sure you understand. One incident was quite serious, and resulted in his being removed from the pistol team when he was accused of pointing his weapon at a fellow cadet. Should this event have been witnessed by a staff member, it would have led to an *immediate* dismissal from Blackwell. As there was no proof that this event took place (the other boy involved has subsequently left Blackwell) — and as Russell has been with us since the second grade — we have decided to speak to him about his recent behavior and warn him that he is on probation.

I must also ask you to write your son and warn him of the consequences of any further inappropriate behavior. All of us here agree that Russell is a very fine boy – a boy we feel will make a great soldier — who is very much liked by the staff. We all consider Russell a great asset to both our football and baseball teams, and I'm sure he will get back on the right track!

Lastly, all of us here at Blackwell Academy hope that the Communist insurgency you and your country face will be quickly defeated. Russell has spoken often about your struggles out there in Guatemala. God bless you in your fight against this menace to free people everywhere. We are all praying for your safety. Rest assured that your son is in good hands.

God bless you.

> Sincerely yours,
> Major D. Purcell
> Commandant

Las Flores
Sunday April 3

Dearest Russell,

Querido, I've just had a letter from the major at your school and he assures me that you are doing fine and that your chances of going on to a good high school are excellent. (I would like it to be the military academy in Virginia that your grandfather went to, if possible.) Do you still want to go to West Point? I think it would be lovely. We could go to the Army-Navy game and I'll wear something very Gatsby! I have written to your father and he promises me he will contact his congressman at the right time. But it's still a little soon, dear.

Your aunt says that we need military men here, and that you should come home as soon as you are able, to help us defeat the Communists! Right now she is living in Miami and I miss her very much, as I spend a great deal of time alone here working with no one but Olga to speak to. Your uncle Robert has gone to live in Paris—He is producing films!— so I don't have any help. I wish you were all with me here. Maybe someday. But none of us can live without someone from the family being here on the plantation and seeing things are done properly— war or no war.

Dear, about the test they gave you. I really don't think things like this should upset you. Of course you aren't stupid. Why don't we just forget the test. I know that you have always done well in school, and that's really all that is important. As far as pointing the gun at the boy, I'm glad you wrote me and told me the truth about what happened. I don't want my son to be a momma's boy, and if that boy was bullying you, well, here it would be understood completely. God knows your grandfather pointed his pistol at more than one man! (I'm afraid to tell you the stories!)

Always stand up for yourself, my love, and know that your mother loves you and hopes that we can be together here someday. I love you and think about you everyday.

The guerillas came to the plantation two nights ago, but I was visiting a friend and they couldn't find me so they left. They said they wanted our family to pay a war tax! Anytime the communists get close, workers from the ranchos come up to the house to warn me and I hide with them! Everyone here is very loyal to the family— thank God!

Besos y Abrazos
Tu Mama.

PS: Coffee prices are wonderfully high, 106. So I've sent along some extra spending money. Antonio and I saw Elizabeth Taylor in Acapulco last month at the Villa Vera, where she was staying too. She and I had a conversation about our children, sitting by the pool. She's actually very, very kind, and not at all like they say on the BBC.

• • •

Like jails, military schools are run in part by the adults, and partly by the students. Several boys had come to him about the Greek, as he was called. The Greek was an asshole; the Greek was a bully, but worse, the Greek was buggering the younger boys at night, and it had to stop.

The Greek's father was important. The students didn't know what he did, but it had to be big, because Major Purcell was scraping and bowing like an Ottoman house slave every time the Greek's parents showed up in their limousine. Someone had suggested the Greek's father was a gangster; others that he was a congressman, or senator. The Greek wouldn't say. (Russell learned later that the Greek's father owned an independent oil and gas company in Louisiana.)

There had been a vote in study hall. Russell was a lieutenant now, and the younger boys looked up to him. This respect was given not because he'd been at the school since he was in the second grade, but because he was a sports star. And because, as officer in charge of the pool during the weekends, he didn't allow towel snapping in the showers. Younger boys had been terrified of the showers until they'd put Russell in charge.

The towel snapping had stopped. Towel snapping with a well made "rat tail," wet at the end, could leave terrible welts, and worse. It was like being hit with a leather whip. The older boys had hit Russell plenty with the rat tails when he had first come to the school, and Russell remembered how painful and humiliating it was. (Of course, if you spoke to any of the staff about it, just as in prison, it would only make matters worse for you.)

Later, Russell only smiled when people asked him why he'd spent hours in the gym getting strong. As he had learned in his military tactics and history class: superior and over-

48

whelming firepower wins battles. (The rest, said his teacher who'd fought at Guadalcanal, was horseshit.)

The meeting had been called before lights out. Everyone was in pajamas and robes. It was dark. Russell remembered sitting on his bed, looking down at the house next door. He often spied on the family who lived next to the school: two girls, a mother and a father. He loved to watch them have dinner, but didn't often get the chance.

Russell felt as if he knew the family. He had shared birthday parties and many holidays with them, if only from the window of his room. The girls and he were about the same age. The parents were kind. He could tell that. The father was a tall, thin man, and he would speak to his daughters while they did their homework at the kitchen table, as he helped or did the dishes. The four of them would spend the evenings there in the kitchen. Russell liked to imagine their conversations. Sometimes providing dialogue for the family (a habit that would later help him as a journalist and writer), he would stare in amazement at their world, free from loneliness or the threat of physical violence.

Right now the girls had finished their homework, and the parents were alone in the kitchen. Russell had a great desire to be adopted by them, but knew it was crazy. One Saturday he had almost knocked on their door to tell them that he was their son of sorts, their son of the third floor window. Their son of the school next door.

This was the first time he'd had a strange and obviously bizarre thought. He would have many as the years went by and he was always able to control them, but barely. He'd started to act out in strange ways, mostly on the football field at first. He loved the violence of the sport. Then he began taking dares, any dare, any challenge. Lately, it had been shoplifting. He'd stolen records by the Beatles and the Rolling

Stones, even though he could have paid for them.

"We've come to see you about the Greek, Lieutenant," a PFC, maybe nine years old, was speaking for the whole first floor. The younger boys of this floor had elected him to speak for them. Four other boys had come up to the third floor dormitory where the oldest boys lived.

Russell put down his book, closed the curtain, and slid his feet over his bed. The boys were standing near the door.

"Close the door," Russell said. One of the smallest boys closed the door behind him, and they all came closer.

Officers had the best rooms, and only one roommate. Younger boys lived four to a room.

"At ease, gentlemen." There was, despite everything, a true military order to the boys' lives. They respected the Lieutenant deeply, as Russell had when he first arrived. The boys didn't really relax. "What's the problem?" Russell asked. The PFC stepped forward, a real tow-head who wasn't afraid of much and who would one day die in Lebanon. (Several of Russell's schoolmates would die in the armed forces.)

"The Greek's coming down onto the first floor at night, sir. He tries to do stuff . . . to the younger boys." He spoke as if he wasn't one of them.

"What kind of stuff?" Russell asked. He knew what kind, or at least he suspected that he knew, but he had to be certain what he was dealing with.

The boy turned away and looked at his friends. No one who hasn't been through it understands what happens to children who are forced to leave home at an early age. They mature and they make new bonds, bonds that may be even stronger than the familial ones they've been forced to break (this break is very profound). Ironically, this new family was what would make them good soldiers later. The military was their mother and father.

50

The boy looked Russell in the eye. "He . . . you know, wants to touch." The boy started to turn crimson. His friends looked everywhere but at Russell.

"I get it," Russell said. He held his hand up.

"We've spoken to the house mother, Mrs. Crimp, but she hasn't done *anything* about it, sir. She's always asleep when he comes down." Russell watched the boys nod in unison.

Lisa Crimp had been a dottering old shrew who smelled of lilac water and fish when he'd been on the first floor years before; she couldn't have gotten any better with age. Her biggest concern was that sick boys not bother her during the day, when she was watching soap operas. God help you if you ventured into her room then. She'd cuff you and tell you to get out. If you told anyone, it was your word against hers. She was his first lesson in fascism.

Russell stood up and went to the little bookcase he shared with his roommate. He slid his copy of Dana's *Two Years Before The Mast* in with the other books he'd collected. He turned and looked at the boys, and saw the time. Taps would play in a few minutes, and if they weren't in their rooms, their house mother would give them five demerits.

Demerits were not just a silly way of dehumanizing children; they were a real scorecard. If boys got too many during the week, those who lived close enough couldn't leave the school to spend the weekend at home. For the boys who rarely went home, like Russell, demerits meant they couldn't leave the school to go to the shopping center on Saturday, to see a film or meet girls or play pick-up basketball. You would be confined to the school. Nothing was more horrible or lonely than those hours after the movie let out, as they made their way back in groups through the Saturday evening streets, with their sidewalks lined with homes. Each step carried its own kind of disappointment and the promise of a better day, when they would be in charge of their lives.

Russell always felt stupidest on Saturdays, and dehumanized on Sundays by the trip to church to listen to old men prattle on about something they called God. God didn't go to school with them, so who gave a shit about him?

Russell waited for Paterson to get back from playing taps. Paterson and he went back to their first days here, in the second grade. Paterson's mother had died that year, and he wasn't talking much. His taps were lovely, soft, pitiful things.

Russell watched Paterson put the trumpet down on his desk. He pulled the mouthpiece out, as he always did, and stood it up on the edge of the bookcase. He took his hat off and laid it down next to it. Russell and Paterson had lived together at the school through most of their childhood, and now into the first years of puberty. Although they would never see each other after they left the school, they would often think of one another.

"The first floor was here," Russell said. He had been looking up at the ceiling of the room, at the holes in the varnished knotty pine. He looked now at his friend as he undressed. Paterson would go on to become a famous heart surgeon; his father was a surgeon, and his grandfather before that.

"Yeah," Paterson said.

"The Greek is wandering." Wandering was what they called it back when they were on the first floor.

"That's not good," Paterson said, and sat down at the desk. He bent down and unlaced his shoes. Their Spartan furniture was old, from the Thirties, all with art deco motifs and very heavy dark lacquer.

"I want you to leave the pistol case unlocked tomorrow after practice," Russell said. He heard the sound of Paterson's shoes on the closet floor. He and Paterson had had a fight once, years before, and they'd gone into the closet of their room to have it so that no one could hear. It had been wild slugging in the dark, hitting with shoes and hangers, whatever they could grab.

They had come back to their room and it had been torn up by the duty officer; they had left something undone or unclean. Each blamed the other, and they fought like that in the dark, like animals, full of hate for everything around them. They never fought again after that.

"What are you going to do, rob a bank?" Paterson said.

"No. I'm going to go speak to the Greek." There was a long silence. Paterson undid his pants, folding them carefully. He walked to the closet, and Russell heard him hang them up. Then he re-crossed the room, opened his chest of drawers, and took out his pajamas. "Well, will you do it?" Russell asked. Paterson stepped into his pajamas, took off his shirt, and put it in the pile on the floor of soiled clothes that they would drop off at the laundry after breakfast. He turned off the desk light and got into bed in the dark. They used to talk more at night, but since Paterson's mother died, he had stopped that. It seemed he just wanted to sleep, or study, or be busy with whatever.

"Okay," Paterson said, turning over. "You got it."

Russell had wanted to ask him if he was all right, if there was something wrong, but military school isn't like a real family, and you don't ask about things that make you weak. That was the rule: show no weakness. Even between friends.

He hadn't needed light. He'd lived here for over eight years, and knew the school so well he could have gotten around it if he'd gone blind. He went down to the indoor shooting range in the basement of the gym, to the gun cabinet on the wall. The climbing ropes dangled in the dark behind him.

Paterson was in charge of locking the gun case after practice and keeping the key. He had left the metal locker door open, unlocking it after he played taps. Russell felt for the first pistol

on the specially designed cabinet. There were twenty-five
.45 automatics, their barrels buried in wooden slots. He took
one and dropped the clip out, making sure it was empty. He
racked the action twice to make certain, then he left the gym
and went across the grass towards his dormitory. He collected
leaves on his slippers as he made his way back to speak to the
Greek.

He opened the Greek's door. The Greek slept by the
window; both he and his roommate were asleep. Russell
turned on the small flashlight, walked between the beds, and
climbed up on The Greek's bed, putting his knees on either
side of the sleeping boy's body. The Greek was big, six feet
and two hundred pounds. There was no way Russell could
beat him in a fight, he'd known that. He had simply decided
to use the lesson he'd been taught in school: Superior tactics,
combined with overwhelming force, win battles.

He turned the pen light on the Greek's face, then put the
barrel of the gun on the Greek's forehead.

"Wake up," Russell said. He moved the pen light so the
Greek could see that it was a pistol he had resting on his
forehead.

The Greek had blue eyes. Russell hadn't noticed that before.
"I'm going to kill you unless you stop bothering those boys.
Do you understand?" He pulled the hammer back for effect.
It made a big sound. It was a sound the Greek would never
forget. He would never learn empathy, but he had finally
learned fear.

Russell glanced over at the Greek's roommate. He was
awake, and was staring at Russell. He was no friend of the
Greek's either, though, because he was smiling.

SIX

A young Indian woman, dressed in a formal blue and white maid's uniform, opened the heavy antique door to Carl Van Diemen's colonial mansion. Van Diemen, Mahler had told Russell, had spent a fortune remodeling the place. It showed. The maid led Russell and Katherine out to the traditional courtyard, which was full of mostly young partygoers. Van Diemen, in his late twenties, had become one of the biggest dealers of Pre-Columbian antiquities in Europe, and was obviously making a killing, judging from the magnificent seventeenth century digs.

Russell and Katherine followed a hallway along a twenty-foot-high stone wall. Painted plaster saints, their white faces hit by spotlights, hung next to Mayan stone fertility figures. The juxtaposition of the two clashing cultures was dramatic and poignant. At the end of the hallway was a towering, Titianesque painting of the Last Supper—it had been pulled from the ruins of the city after an earthquake. Under the colonial-era painting, young women in tight jeans and exposed midriffs swayed to Dirty Vegas's famous trance tune.

"You come. I'm *so* glad," Carl said, pushing through the crowd to get to them. He was a big man, a little overweight, a little ripe and unctuous-looking, in the way of Europeans of a certain class. Van Diemen wore a black turtleneck shirt—the shirt untucked—and faded but ironed blue jeans. The young man's face was round. He was very blond and very rich, and the two things seemed to come together perfectly

55

in him. At least, that's what Katherine had said on the walk to the house. She'd been to lots of Carl's parties, she confessed.

Carl gave Russell a bear hug, then roughed up his hair. They had spent a week at the same hotel in Costa Rica once, and had gotten to be friends there. Carl was with his Costa Rican lover then, a well sun-blocked kid of maybe eighteen who wore an orange Speedo, even out to the clubs. Carl's lover looked a lot like a girl, except for the package in the Speedo. In the streets people would yell *maricon* at them, real hateful. Carl and the kid were oblivious. Intrepidly queer, they didn't seem to care.

Back then, Carl was always buying everyone around the hotel pool drinks, so Russell had decided Van Diemen had to be a rich kid, a gangster, or a fool. He liked Carl well enough. Most people did. He was the new kind of German, silly, pretentious, pacifist. He was the kind of German who wouldn't go to war unless it was over a fashion statement, Carl had told Russell one night by the pool. His boyfriend stood in the shallow end, holding a fancy blue colored drink and looking at Carl like a girl. Russell had thought that was pretty funny. "Attack when you see Tommy Hilfiger," he had said.

"I'll only use laughing gas, and those little drink swords!" Carl had said.

Katherine said that Carl gave the best parties in Guatemala because he didn't let in the squares. From the look of it, it was only hip people tonight, which in this country meant you could talk politics and art instead of soccer, and drink wine instead of whiskey.

"I didn't know you knew Carl so well," Katherine said, turning to him surprised. Russell hadn't mentioned Costa Rica to her.

"We spent a week in the same hotel," Russell said. "I was working on an article. I think it was called, 'Costa Rica: Switzerland of Central America.'" It was a joke, but neither

Katherine nor Carl got it. "That's the standard line," Russell said, trying to explain. "You see four or five of those articles a year. The Costa Rican Tourist Agency pays for a lot of them. It's a lie, though," he added. "It ain't no Switzerland. They have the biggest cockroaches in the world. I don't know about you, but I've never seen one cockroach in Switzerland."

"What's a lie?" Carl said. He'd missed what Russell had said because he was checking out some kid's ass. Carl turned to Katherine. "Russell, yeah, he work in Costa Rica, he no fun. But he has fun here in Antigua. I see him at the Oprah Café with girls all the time." Katherine looked at Carl, then at Russell a little disappointedly.

Russell was embarrassed because he didn't want to appear a playboy, although–if truth be told–he was, to a degree. Women liked him and he liked women. It was that simple.

Katherine hit him with her hip, just like in high school, but he noticed that she kept holding his arm. Carl got them a drink by whistling with his fingers in his mouth and a waiter, a short guy, hustled over like he was playing for Manchester United. They picked champagne glasses off a silver platter and Carl took them to meet a painter friend that Russell suspected Carl was trying to put the make on. The bottle of champagne cost more than the waiter would make in a year, maybe two, Katherine told him later.

"Did you know that Gore Vidal used to live here?" the painter said. "In this very house." The painter was a handsome American, and Russell pegged him as an upper cruster. The painter seemed very preoccupied with his watch, spinning it around his thin wrist. Russell asked him if he'd come to Guatemala to paint. The young man looked at him shocked, as if he'd been asked if he picked his nose, or ate bugs that landed on him.

"No, of course not. I've stopped for the time being. I'm not doing *anything*. Really. I'm trying to figure out the next thing.

Then I'll paint it. I mean, you have to get a good picture of where we're going and then get that down, man. You know, get it down. Guatemala is next. I think its going to be hot. I'm going to Coban and see what's there. Caves, I've heard." The painter acted as if he'd taken crystal meth. He had that wired anticipatory look. He was thin and had a stud in his tongue. When he spoke, it looked as if the end of his tongue wasn't on quite right.

The music stopped, then started again. Someone put on the sound track from the movie *Stealing Beauty*. With the small yellow lights strung up everywhere, the mansion's wide Mediterranean-style corridors, and the sound of the water from the big fountain in the courtyard, they could have been in Ibiza or the *Costa Azul* in Spain, Russell thought.

If the mountain fell in the sea let it be. I got my old world to live through. The Hendrix cover got turned up loud. Some people nearby got in the groove and started to sway. Two very blonde girls speaking in Dutch were sliding their hips to the music.

"Girls from Holland like to fuck, smoke dope, and read books. And tell you how it's going to be when the Greens take over the world," an English guy told him, staring at the girls. "I been here a month. I want to fuck them all." He smiled happily.

"You want to go to the coast with me? Tomorrow?" Katherine asked him over the music. "We're building some houses on a coffee plantation."

"Sure," Russell said. He mostly wanted to sleep with her. Unlike a lot of the people here, he wasn't a do-gooder; he'd gotten a master's degree in economics at the University of Chicago when he was only twenty three and looked askance on all the do-gooding, only because he felt charity—no matter how well intended—was just that, charity, not a solution for the country's chronic underdevelopment.

"We'd have to leave early tomorrow," she said.

"I don't mind," he said, but he was lying; he would have just as soon stayed in bed and screwed all morning.

"You can stay at my place," she said. "Tonight. That way you don't have to get up so early . . . it will be a lot easier." It was the invitation he'd been hoping for.

"Sure," he said. "Okay."

Mahler appeared with a drink in his hand. When he saw Russell, he took him further out into the garden, and they sat on the edge of the fountain. Mahler gave him a report on *Tres Rios,* and Russell listened carefully. They'd only been able to survey the river on horseback before Russell had to go back to work.

They smoked a joint together. As he spoke about the work, Mahler's blue eyes were intense, the fountain's light catching them. Russell listened to Mahler talk about east of the river, *Amargo.* It was exciting and it was dangerous because he was working alone, he said. They had to keep the search a secret or they would run the risk of losing out to others, Mahler told him.

Russell agreed. He tossed the roach into the fountain and looked around the garden. The whole place seemed straight out of some MTV video.

"If something happens out there in the bush when you're alone, you're fucked," Russell said.

"I'm blessed. Nothing ever happens to me. Let's go talk to Carl before he gets too busy buggering some choir boy," Mahler said. They went, and found Van Diemen talking to some girls. Carl took them into the house, to a library full of Mayan antiquities. The room had green leather club couches and dark red walls. Mayan statues and Olmec heads rested on a huge mahogany coffee table, along with a few tiny solid gold figurines. Mahler whistled out loud as they walked in.

"I'm so glad we can do business," Carl said. "I mean, I buy the Jaguar. If you guys find it. I buy it. We get rich." Carl smiled and looked at them happily. He was a little drunk.

"You're already rich," Mahler said, looking at the stuff on the coffee table.

"Great," Russell said, impressed.

Mahler crossed the room, picked up a huge black obsidian knife from the bookcase, ran it across his throat, and smiled. "Fucking Mayans," he said.

"You'll buy all that stuff in the garden at *Tres Rios?* I need the money," Russell said.

"Yes, of course. I buy all of it. Don't worry . . . just find the Jaguar," Carl said, watching Mahler.

Mahler tossed the knife on the couch. It was a heavy knife, and bounced. Carl picked it up and put it back on the shelf. Mahler was jealous of Carl, it was obvious, and it suddenly made Russell uncomfortable.

He went back outside to Katherine. She'd been looking for him, standing on the edge of the garden in one of the corridors, young men and women dancing behind her in the yellow light, swaying to the trance music that someone had turned back on.

Katherine had a Snoopy doll on her bed. He threw it off, and she got them something to drink. Some men had tried to stop their car on the way out of Antigua. She'd driven through them, not willing to stop and find out what they wanted. Shots had been fired. She was still upset, but was pretending not to be, he thought. They'd barely spoken on the way back into the city.

She lay down next to him, and he felt her shake. It was like a cat shakes when it's scared. Later, they made love between the fresh cold sheets of her bed.

SEVEN

The general's wife is very, *very* beautiful. I'll warn you," Katherine said suddenly. "And everyone thinks she's crazy. She's not like anyone I've ever met. All the guys I've brought up to work on the project can't stop talking about her. I suppose you won't be any different . . . guys are *so* predictable."

On the drive towards the coast they'd passed some of the country's biggest and oldest coffee plantations: *La Bella, La Sultana, La Gloria,* some obviously still grand and managing to keep going, others forlorn and abandoned because of the coffee crisis. The temperature cooled as they went higher into the mountains near Mexico. At times the dirt road was lonely and terribly rutted; at others it was well graded and busy with workers from a nearby plantation. Some plantations were so massive they'd spawned small towns outside their gates.

"I feel like going home to the States for a visit," she said. "You just like to feel really safe once and a while. Go to Nordstrom, that kind of stuff."

"So have you met General Selva?" he asked, changing the subject. He didn't want to say the obvious, that even home wasn't really safe any more, but he thought it would be mean to remind her of that.

"Yes. He's very nice in his way. He's been very kind to me and the volunteers, anyway."

"Selva is head of Guatemalan intelligence," Russell said.

"I know." She turned and gave him a fey look. "I think that's why he's hosting the project. He wants to convince *Time* magazine he's not a monster. It makes him look like a liberal, having his picture taken with people like me," she said. "He's a committed free trading globalist, Russell—just like you!" She smiled at him.

An hour after they turned off the asphalt, they arrived at the general's plantation. Haggard-looking dogs ran out from shabby workers' housing to confront them. Pretty young Indian mothers, some very young, could be seen inside their shacks sitting by the doorway, some making tortillas on wood burning stoves. Small refrigerators peeked white through shack walls. They caught glimpses of flimsy television sets, even once a glimpse of Jennifer Aniston on the familiar set of *Friends.*

Men, unemployed because of the crisis, sat in groups in front of the company store, some holding machetes. Here and there banana trees grew out of the mud, exotic-looking.

"How many families live here?" Russell asked as they drove past the store. Some of the older men waved at Katherine.

"Maybe three hundred. We did a census, but it was difficult to get a hard number because so many people here are extended family, or have family that are just passing through. But basically there are three hundred, a little more," she said. "With the crisis, half of them are unemployed."

There was something sentient about the red clay ground. It was almost the exact color of the people's skin, so that it looked as if God had simply shaped the people from the clay earth and blown life into them, and suddenly they were drinking Coke and playing soccer and having babies and smiling at you. A little girl, held by her mother, waved at them from the doorway. Russell lifted his hand and waved back.

Standing in dirty clothes at the corner of the building site in the hot sun, Russell watched the college kids, mostly from Europe and Canada, work with joy on their faces. He was quiet and found it hard to share in their excitement. Despite his age, he didn't feel young any more. The others were sure they were changing the world, one little building at a time. He saw the project instead for what it was, a public relations stunt. It made him feel jaded. He wanted to believe that building new houses on the deck of an economic *Titanic* was worthwhile, but couldn't. He wondered now if he wasn't suffering from what he'd seen in other foreigners who'd stayed in the country too long: that strange malaise, a spiritual bankruptcy that overwhelmed them.

He was mixing concrete on a piece of plywood. It was a job that even he could do, as he had no building skills whatsoever. He simply added water from a hose and mixed the concrete with a shovel to a cake batter consistency. He hadn't even known how to do that, until a young girl from Paris showed him exactly how. She was all business, tearing open the concrete sacks and showing him how much water to add. He mixed carefully now, following her instructions, while others came with buckets and took the concrete away to pour in the forms that had been dug and built by a previous crew the weekend before.

He met the general's wife, Beatrice Allenby-Selva, that afternoon. All the volunteers had been invited in for tea at the great house. He was sure his mother had known the general's family, and it was even conceivable that he'd been here as a child, given the proximity to his mother's plantation, but he didn't remember it. The original plantation house had been burnt down during the war, one of the workers had told him. The general's new house had just been completed. It was massive and very modern, and looked like it belonged

63

in Connecticut, not Guatemala. No one had seen either the general or his family during the day. But they had all seen a brand new Toyota Land Cruiser, two bodyguards hanging on the running boards, race past the construction site several times while they'd been working.

All the foreigners working on the project were presented to the general before tea was served. Carlos Selva was dressed in jeans and a white T-shirt, like any American executive might have worn on the weekend. Selva wore his black hair combed straight back. He had a high forehead and was white, obviously from European stock. The general was handsome in a very starched way and somewhat younger than Russell expected, maybe only 39 or 40. There was a trace of gray in his mustache. He had serious blue eyes and seemed smug, like so many important men he'd met as a journalist, Russell thought. He'd come to associate smugness with political power, in fact.

The general barely glanced at him as they were introduced. They shook hands perfunctorily, and then Selva was onto the next person.

Russell had purposefully come in his dirty work clothes. A lot of the others had cleaned up more. He had not. It had been his way of hiding, making sure that there could be no possible connection made between him and his mother's family. The moment passed, and there had been no recognition in Selva's eyes.

As their group was coming down the hall towards the garden, Russell saw Beatrice for the first time. She was coming in the opposite direction, flanked by her nanny and her two young children. The moment he saw her, he knew he had to speak to her. There was something about Beatrice, something about her beautiful face that beckoned. It was the intelligence of course, and her great beauty, and the way they harmonized.

All the young men noticed her. She wore trendy slacks that showed her naked stomach, which was muscled. She stopped to say something to her husband. She put her hand on his shoulder. She'd been a dancer, and it was obvious, she had a great grace.

She was smiling and leading the children, joining the group. It was clear she had been told to make an appearance and bring the children, as it made the general and his trophy wife (he'd been married twice before) seem even more affable.

Beatrice was introduced to everyone when they got out to the garden, where the staff had set up drinks tables. She went out of her way to make eye contact with everyone she met. She kept hold of one of her children's hands. Russell noticed she was wearing an over-sized gold cross. He thought she might be winking at the system, because she was dressed so *au courant* and she was so young. The juxtaposition of bare midriff and gold cross somehow didn't seem to fit exactly, unless you took the cross as making a kind of joke of it all.

He was struck by how young she was. She must have been only twenty-five, or less. She seemed to be a child herself. It was the nature of her beauty, he supposed, trying not to stare. She was equal parts siren and waif. The children, both toddlers, were beautiful–a girl and a boy. Both favored their mother, and were very fair.

Standing there looking at Beatrice and her husband, Russell felt jealous for the first time in his life. Nothing had prepared him for the reaction. He had never been the type. He had certainly been around rich people, and he had been for the most part unimpressed by either their possessions or their families. Even during the great bull market when he'd been working at a bank trading stocks, when men his age were suddenly collecting great manor houses and Lear jets, he hadn't really cared. But he was jealous suddenly of this man who seemed to have brought to earth some kind of goddess. There was something godlike about Selva, too: the military posture, the way his bodyguards and the maids seemed to hang on his every gesture.

Russell noticed that all the young foreigners were swept up into this tropical Olympus. They were all made part–if only for an hour–of the fortune, of the beautiful wife, of the thousands of acres out there that were growing for the general's benefit, bearing fruits for him and his beautiful family. Everything, in the end, seemed to revolve around *him*. Looking at the two of them, Russell found it fascinating as well as intoxicating.

Katherine attached herself to him, actually holding his arm as if they were husband and wife. She was asking him if he wanted to meet the general. He was trying to think of an excuse not to, as he was still afraid that Selva might make the connection somehow between his mother and him. He told Katherine they had already met. But she said that she wanted to introduce him anyway.

"He speaks English like an American," she was saying, "really, really well." He was about to answer her when Beatrice appeared. She had been letting her little boy run on the terrace, and she'd come to collect him. Beatrice stopped in front of them and swept the little boy into her arms, then looked up at Russell.

He would never forget that moment. People say that of course, and don't mean it. Unforgettable, because he felt she *trained* her beauty on him purposely. She even told him as much later. She said that when she looked up and saw him, she knew immediately that their lives–hers and his–were going to collide in some meaningful way.

"He's uncontrollable sometimes," Beatrice said to them, her blue eyes resolute, taking them in.

"He's adorable," Katherine said, bending down to hold the little boy. Russell said nothing at first, feeling awkward as a school boy as he watched Katherine. It took him a moment to gain confidence.

"We've met," Beatrice said to Katherine.

"Yes," Katherine said.

"You didn't tell me you were *married?*" Beatrice said, looking suddenly at Russell.

"Oh, no. He's a friend . . . Mrs. Selva, this is Russell Price."

"Just a friend," Russell said again, looking at her. A nanny came and took the child away.

"It's *Rosa De Jamaica,*" Beatrice said, taking a drink from the tray and handing it to him. "You can't find it in the States. I've looked in Miami, but they don't have it."

He thought that if anyone knew other than Beatrice what was going to happen, it was Katherine. He looked at her later, as Beatrice took them for a tour of the garden. Just the three of them. Katherine kept looking at him as if she knew somehow what was going through his head. They followed Beatrice out into the garden.

The garden sloped downhill. Katherine's college kids were here and there, milling about holding drinks, some in dirty clothes like himself, proud to come up to the big house as would-be workers. He knew it was a sham; they all belonged to the same world. They weren't workers; they were the middlemen between those out there and this General.

But the more he listened to Beatrice speak, the more he stopped thinking. It was as if watching her he suddenly had become someone else, a quieter, more relaxed version of what he had been only minutes before.

Katherine's cell phone rang, and she moved away from them. The sun came out. He looked at Beatrice; she was telling him how she had just come from Roatan in Honduras. She was learning to skin dive, she told him. She was describing her first time underwater. He could barely pay attention to what she was saying. He was focused instead on her hips in her jeans; there was something so goddamn sexy about her hips, the way her waist went long to her breasts, which were small. It was as if a Viking Princess had been dropped down in the middle of the jungle.

"I had to take an enormous amount of decongestants. I had a cold, Carlos thought it was so funny," she said. She lifted her glass and took a drink, her eyes watching him. "Do you skin dive, Mr. Price?" Her eyes held him for a moment; then she looked away, to where Katherine was standing holding her phone.

"No," he said. "I don't." He couldn't feel natural with her at first. Later he spoke to other men who said they felt the same way, men who were normally inured to beautiful women, either because they were playboys or because they were happily married. In either case they couldn't get over the impression she made, it was something *profoundly* sexual. Until you saw it, you couldn't describe it. If you were a man, you wanted her. It was very simple.

"You really must. It's an entirely different world down there," Beatrice said, looking at him. "It's where life began. The ocean." She moved her long blonde hair out of her eyes.

"Well, I'll keep that in mind," he said.

"What *do* you do, Mr. Price? When you aren't building houses."

"I'm a journalist," he said.

"Oh, then you'll have to meet my husband. He collects journalists. He gets them to write only nice things about him. He's very, very good at that."

He heard Katherine's phone slap shut. Both Beatrice and Russell turned to look at her. It was their first conspiracy.

Later, when he was leaving, Beatrice appeared again.

68

"You've lost your book, the Delacroix," she said. Completely nonplussed, he looked at her. He was leaving with the others, going down the front stairs of the house. Beatrice was holding her husband's hand. They were both framed by the enormous doorway. It was very, very hot and almost completely dark out now. The maids had been ordered to bring them flashlights. He was trying to get one, and didn't even realize Beatrice was speaking to him.

"Your back pocket," Beatrice said, as if she was reading his mind. He'd forgotten that he'd taken the book with him. It had slipped out of his pocket somehow in the house. The maid handed him the book and a flashlight. Somehow it must have fallen out. He took the paperback book from the maid and looked up at Beatrice.

"I've read it. I had to at school. Oxford," she said. He nodded a thank you. He had no idea how she knew it was his.

He spent that evening reading the Delacroix by the air conditioner, sometimes walking to the window of the little bungalow where he'd been put up and thinking about Beatrice. Katherine came to the door about nine; she'd been having a meeting with the general. She said she wanted to use the shower, as hers wasn't working. They made love afterwards. She was very amorous. She was much more passionate than she appeared holding onto her telephone, or driving her jeep.

Afterwards he continued to think about Beatrice, what she was doing, even while he was lying naked on the small bed and Katherine was telling him all about the general and what he'd said about the upcoming elections. He was going to run for president. He'd told her that he was sure he was going to win.

After Katherine had left—when it was very late—Russell continued to think about the general's wife, what she was doing. What, if anything, she might be saying to her husband about him. He wondered what kind of conversations that kind of man and a woman who'd been to Oxford could possibly have.

When he got back that Sunday night to his apartment in the capital, he emailed his senior editors in London and pitched the idea of a series of articles on the upcoming presidential election. He knew from speaking to his bosses in the past that they didn't like General Selva on principle, and considered him an arch-example of the anti-democratic forces in the country that were bad for business. His editors, he'd guessed, would jump at the opportunity to push Antonio De La Madrid, the pro-business, neo-liberal candidate who was opposing Selva for president. He wasn't surprised when he got the green light for the series. He wanted to see Beatrice Selva again.

EIGHT

He'd come back to *Tres Rios* to start searching for the Red Jaguar. The morning was viciously hot and clear, as if it hadn't rained all night. When Russell walked outside with his cup of coffee, he could see the *Volcan de Agua* in the distance, part of a cruel-looking set of green mountains to the north. By four in the afternoon it would rain again, but the mornings were hot and humid and perfectly clear. The plantation's rear garden was flat and had a fountain the French family had built, and a huge pond with fish. There was a swimming pool too, but it was empty, its white-painted bottom glistening now in the morning sun.

Russell walked to the edge of the pool. Sitting down, he let his legs dangle over its edge. He'd have it filled, he thought. He drank his coffee in silence and listened to the early morning sounds of the plantation: birds, horses being taken from their stalls, sounds of domesticity from the workers' housing. There was a mixture of children's voices and *ranchera* music, too.

He looked into the empty blue sky, cleaned of everything, for signs of rain. *Why shouldn't I feel optimistic?* he thought. It was true he owed a great deal of money now, but he owned all this, and somewhere out there might be a great treasure. Maybe he would stay here after he found the Red Jaguar. He could be a man of leisure. Carl had assured him the Jaguar would fetch millions of dollars. His share would be enough to live on the rest of his life wherever he chose. Could he

71

really be happy back in San Francisco? Or had this country gotten under his skin in some way, its Wild West quality perversely satisfying something in him?

"Don Russell?" He turned around. The girl who had opened the gate for him that first day was standing in front of him, barefoot like a goddess—a brown-skinned Diana.

"Yes," he said. He had to shade his eyes to look at her. She was wearing the same yellow dress. Behind her, the white volcanic sand used to pave the garden was catching the sunlight. It made the sand sparkle under her feet like crushed diamonds.

"May I work in the kitchen? You will need a cook, *Patron?*" she asked in Spanish. "I worked sometimes in the kitchen—for Don Pinkie." The girl was looking down at her bare feet. "I can clean, too . . . if you like?" The French family was going to take their own maid and cook with them to the capital. They'd been staying here, but were finally leaving that morning.

Russell suspected that Don Pinkie, who owned several other plantations, was going broke slowly and would finally be ruined. That morning at breakfast, he'd kept checking his pager, which gave him the current price of coffee at the Chicago Board of Trade. He'd come to have breakfast and to say goodbye to Russell and Mahler.

"Seventy dollars, that's all we need, right!" Don Pinkie had said to him at breakfast, as if Russell were an experienced coffee plantation owner. The fact was he'd never grown a house plant, much less run a coffee plantation. He knew nothing about the practicalities of coffee production. What he did know about the business he'd learnt over three years of covering the commodity as a financial journalist. From what he could tell, the over production in the world's coffee market was going to kill off most growers in Central America. They just didn't stand a chance against the Vietnamese and the

Brazilians, who paid their workers even less.

The Frenchman reminded him of himself when he'd been holding a losing position while trading stocks. Why is it we always believe things will get better, he wondered, looking at the Frenchman. Why do we believe that the stock will go up in an hour or tomorrow? That prices will turn around? That she will love me better tomorrow?

"Right," was all Russell had said. "Seventy dollars would do it, all right. Things would be much better."

"We'll get it by next January, when the harvest comes in. You watch. The Brazilians can't keep dumping coffee into the market. You'll see that you made the right decision, young man. You're at three thousand feet here. That's quality coffee," the Frenchman said. "Don't forget that." Don Pinkie turned to look out the window at his wife and children out in the garden, saying their goodbyes to some of the workers. "I left Europe without a penny thirty years ago. I was a Legionnaire in Africa. . . ."

Don Pinkie's wife, a tiny, attractive Frenchwoman, was much younger. Russell watched her walk to their old Willys Jeep with a box. She'd thanked him for allowing them to stay in the guest house while they made arrangements to move to one of their other plantations. Don Pinkie talked on nervously about the coffee market while his children played for the last time near the fountain the family had built in happier times. Russell listened respectfully while he watched the wife and one of her maids pack the car.

"Could you take our picture?" Don Pinkie said, finally standing up. "By the fountain. We liked this place the best. It was our home." He seemed upset, but was trying to hide it.

"Of course," Russell said, standing too. Russell and Don Pinkie went out on the veranda. Don Pinkie's wife was crying. She was a pretty woman with red hair cut very short, in her early forties, Russell guessed, and her eyes were blue. She

73

looked at them and said, laughing, that she'd been crying all morning. She'd kissed several of the workers goodbye one more time. The workers, mostly old men, had come to the big house and paid their respects, and she'd kissed the old men and embraced them. They had been embarrassed but moved by her gesture. They all embraced her and shook the Frenchman's hand, and wished him luck there by the fountain.

Russell took the family's picture. The Frenchman looked done in, he thought. He'd gotten older, it seemed. Mahler came out and stood on the veranda watching them.

"My wife says that you have a kind face and people like you always have good luck in business," Don Pinkie said, taking the camera from him. They all walked back towards the family's cramped jeep. The two children, boys, in short pants and white, well-pressed shirts like French school-children, were gathered around their parents, looking sad. Their father took their picture again standing by the jeep. Years later, the boys would look at the photo and say that they'd been very happy there.

"I've let go of the administrator, so you'll have to get someone if you're going to be living in the capital. And there are only about ten families left working here. It was all I could afford. We didn't bother to clean this year, or fertilize. I hope you can keep them on? Of course you have the right, according to the new employment laws, to. . . ."

"Yes... I'll keep them on," Russell said, and they'd shaken hands the way men sometimes do, earnestly, from the shoulder. The wife shook his hand too.

"And the ex-guerillas. They have the plantation next door," Don Pinkie said as he opened the door to his jeep.

"I didn't know that," Russell said, surprised.

"I should have told you. I'm sorry. But they're harmless. The government gave them the plantation as part of the peace settlement. I've been over to help them with technical advice.

74

They were very good neighbors, but they don't know much about coffee. They won't bother you, but I thought you should know. Goodbye then," Don Pinkie said.

He and his family got in their jeep and drove away, the children very quiet in the end. Russell realized, after they left, that he had forgotten even to ask to see the office or the books.

He stood up now and looked at the girl. The fountain had brought it all back. He'd wanted to confess to the Frenchman that he had bought the place only to find the Red Jaguar and that he had no interest in the coffee, or the coffee business, but that had seemed cruel. He told himself he was taking an incredible gamble and that he shouldn't feel guilty about paying good money for the place.

"Yes, of course," he told the girl. "If you like. I need someone in the kitchen. What's your name?"

"Gloria Cruz. *Gracias Patron,*" she said. The girl turned around and walked toward the house. He called to her and she stopped, her hair silken and so black on the yellow of her tattered dress, her breasts heavy against the fabric. She reminded him at that moment of a great painting.

"Gloria…? What do you want? Your salary?" he asked her. She looked at him a moment, nonplussed.

"I don't know," she said, smiling, and turned around. He let her go. He tossed out the rest of his now cold coffee on the ground. It made a dark spot on the sand, and he followed the girl to the house. She was born here, he thought. She was afraid he would send her away from the only thing she'd ever known. She just wanted to stay there. The idea of the city probably scared her to death.

"I've ordered two horses," Mahler said. "I take you to where I want to start digging."

"Fine," he said. Gloria cleared away the breakfast dishes. They'd come back to the dining room, with its view of the

75

fountain and gardens. Mahler flirted with the girl as she cleared up, asking her where she was born, about her mother and father, if she was married. Each question drew a girlish smile. Russell stayed out of it. Rather than be sexually attracted to the girl, he felt protective of her. He doubted Mahler felt the same way.

Mahler, shirtless, lit a cigarette. The wife of the Frenchman had put up new wallpaper in the breakfast room. It was bright yellow with white roses, very elegant.

"What are you looking for? I mean, it's daunting isn't it? So much jungle," Russell asked. He watched his partner inhale and settle back.

"Hills, that's what we look for," Mahler said. "That's what we look for. Clearings and then small hil... hills that don't look right. Geo...logi...cally out of character."

"Look, I'm no expert, God knows that, but I've been out here in the bush and I know you can't see shit—much less clearings. There are no fucking clearings... How could there be?"

"You're nervous. Since you came here. Re...Relax... I find the jaguar," Mahler said, letting the smoke pour out of his nose.

"There's a hundred and ten acres. Half of that Don Pinkie said was jungle. Never been planted with coffee and no roads into it. It's virgin jungle," Russell said.

"I said *relax,* old boy."

"I'll need more than that, *old boy,*" Russell said quickly.

"Water," Mahler said, and winked at him.

"*Water.* And what the fuck is that supposed to mean?"

"The Mayans worshipped water. They needed water to irrigate their crops and they didn't build if there was no good source of water nearby. They were very smart people," he said.

"And?"

"There are three rivers on this plantation, one is very small. What you call a. . . ."

"Creek," Russell said.

"Yes. Creek."

"That leaves two. One runs through the *cafetales* and is used for hydro power here. They would most probably ha...have found any ancient building site of size when they were putting in the coffee years ago. The workers would have been all over that river.

"Okay."

"That leaves the other one. *Rio Amargo*. We look there," Mahler said, flicking the ash off his cigarette. "It's virginal, like that beautiful girl in the kitchen."

"Okay. Sorry. It's just—I've never owed $200,000 I can't pay," Russell said. "I have to make a payment next month. Twenty thousand dollars. I've got to pay it to *Banco Industrial* by the twentieth of the month. And I don't have it. I don't even have half of it." The enormity of what he'd done hit him. He had no idea how he was going to raise the next payment.

"Don't worry. Carl says he buys the stone lizards and the Olmec head outside, remember?"

"Yeah, for five thousand dollars. That's not enough," Russell said. One of the old men was bringing their horses. Russell could see him from the window leading them across the road from the stables, across the brilliant white volcanic sand driveway. He didn't feel hopeful the way he'd expected to.

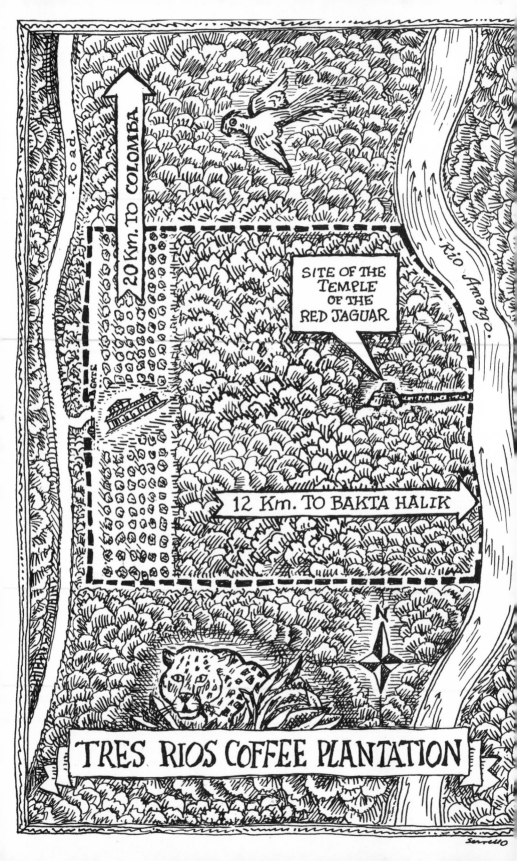

NINE

R*io Amargo* ran wide and not too deep, so they could use it
as a road into the jungle. They'd seen spider monkeys,
so Russell knew they were far from any roads now. He could
hear the monkeys' screams, echos over echos coming down
from the jungle canopy, at times thrilling. It was hot and it
was raining. Drizzle fell from the slot of sky over the river.
The neck and flanks of Russell's horse, a bay, were stained a
tan color by the rain.

He'd strapped his shotgun around his neck so that it sat on
his stomach. He wore a black nylon bodyguard's vest, with
extra shells in the loops. The vest was soaked through. The
sound of his horse's hooves splashing in the river was loud,
the metal horseshoes tromping on the riverstones.

Russell stopped his horse and turned in his saddle. He
looked down the river through the mist and rain. He could
see Carl on his horse a hundred meters behind. The young
man's horse had stopped and was fighting to turn into the
jungle, wanting to leave the river and climb to easier ground.
Carl was having trouble controlling his animal. The man was
completely out of his element in the bush, and was no horse-
man. Russell reined his horse, turning him back up river.

In front of Russell, in the lead, was Mahler, leading a mule.
Mahler rode a small Arabian horse, far ahead of them now,
his shoulders slightly forward as he rode. Like Russell, he

could ride well, and the challenge of riding upriver against the current wasn't a problem for him.

Mahler had insisted that Carl—who'd come to pick up the antiquities in the garden—come out to search with them. Russell had been against it. Carl had confessed that he'd never spent time in the bush, and Russell didn't think *Tres Rios* was the right place to start. In the end he'd relented; he was sorry now that he had.

Russell had gone into the town to buy newspapers and come back late. He'd found Carl in the living room alone, reading. He was wearing his wire glasses and pajama-style slacker shorts. He looked like a college kid on vacation. A big black flashlight sat at his feet. Carl said the power had gone out briefly while Russell had been gone.

"Where's Mahler?" Russell asked, putting his things down.

"I'm not sure," Carl said. For a moment they looked at each other; then Carl stood up, and they shook hands.

"You did a smart thing here," Carl said. "Buying this place. I was just looking up the objects out in the garden. They're worth a lot, especially the snake. Collectors love those Olmec snakes. I can get you maybe ten thousand dollars for that right away. More than what I thought."

"How much are you making?" Russell asked. "Just kidding. Ten thousand dollars, sure. I'll take it." He looked towards the kitchen; it was dark. "You want a drink? I called on the way home and told the girl to cook some dinner. Did she?"

"Sure. I'd love a drink," Carl said. Russell put down his shotgun and walked towards the kitchen. There was a maid's bell. He rang it.

"I'm starving," Russell said. "Have you seen Gloria?"

"She was here earlier," Carl said. Carl sat back down.

"Have you eaten, then?" Russell asked.

"No," the Dutchman said. "We were waiting for you."

Russell looked into the kitchen, annoyed that dinner wasn't ready. The kitchen was tidy but empty. He'd called and asked that dinner be waiting for him. He walked into the kitchen, opened the refrigerator, and looked inside. There was German beer Mahler had bought, lots of it. He took a can and called to Carl and asked him if he wanted one.

Russell walked back out into the dimly lit living room that smelled sweet, like old books. "I don't know what happened to the girl. I just hired her. I told her to have dinner ready by eight," Russell said, handing Carl a can of beer. "You want a glass or something?" Russell asked.

"Yes. Thanks."

Mahler stepped out of one of the hall bedrooms then. Russell caught a glimpse—for just a second—inside the bedroom. A bedside lamp was on. He saw the girl pulling her skirt over her head. She'd been naked.

Mahler pulled the bedroom door closed and came out of the shadows of the hallway. He was smoking a joint. He crossed the room and gave Russell a nod without saying a word. Russell could smell the sex on him.

"Did you get the cigarettes I asked for?" Mahler asked, patting him on the back and offering him the joint. Dressed now, the girl came out of the bedroom, her head down, obviously embarrassed, and went straight past them into the kitchen.

He could see Carl's horse struggling to climb up the river-bank, wanting to leave the hard going of the river. Carl was yanking back on the reins and kicking the animal at the same time. Russell swore under his breath, turned his horse around, and trotted back down river toward him. His mother had had him riding as a child, on the plantation. She'd made sure he'd learned horsemanship with one of the cowboys at a cattle ranch they owned. He'd spent weeks with the cowboys during

81

his summers, learning their trade, everything from roping and branding to shooting long rifles at poachers from horseback. When he fell from his horse in the beginning, when they were roping in the corral, he would often begin to cry, his hands and knees in thick green cow shit. The men would only laugh and tell him to pick his sorry ass up, and quit being a faggot. After a week he stopped expecting sympathy. It hardened him in a good way. In the end, he'd learned to love the lasso, the way he could bring down a calf, the way he could get his horse to step back and tighten the lasso. The war had just started then, and some of the cowboys started carrying M-16's. A mercenary who had come to train the cowboys taught him that automatic weapons torque when you fire them. He was twelve.

Russell knew, watching him, that Carl was doing everything he could to confuse his horse. He wiped his wet face. "Fuck," he said out loud. He shouted for Mahler to stop as he approached Carl. But Mahler didn't hear him. Russell pulled his shotgun over his head and was about to fire in the air to signal Mahler to stop and wait, but stopped himself. He realized that the shot might be enough to get Carl's horse—already frantic—to buck him off.

The girl had been embarrassed when she'd seen Russell looking at her as she stepped out of the bedroom.

"*Buenas noches, Patron,*" she said.

"*Buenas noches,*" Russell said. Mahler was still standing next to him, the joint burning pungently in his hand. The girl came across the room and explained that she'd had dinner ready in the stove, and that they were just waiting for him to arrive.

Russell turned to look at Mahler. "What's going on?" he said in English.

"What do you mean?"

"Don't fuck with me. What's going on? I hired her. I'm responsible for her."

"Don't be ridiculous," Mahler said. "She's in love with me. No one is responsible. She's a grown woman."

"Is she?"

"She's nineteen . . . most girls have two kids here by that age. Shall we eat?" Mahler said.

"She's eighteen, *maybe,* and you know it. She might be younger," Russell said.

Mahler looked at Carl, and then back at Russell. He shrugged. "Is he jealous, Carl? Is that it? What do you think, you're a man of the world. Is she sixteen or is she nineteen? They don't even know, most of the time. Did you know there's no birth certificate for these people? Maybe something in the church. But not during the war. Who knows how old she is? She probably doesn't even know."

"He might be jealous. She's *very* beautiful," Carl said. Carl tried to smile about it, trying to make a joke of it.

"You see, my friend. Even Carl says she's very beautiful, and he's a fucking homosexual. Can you blame *me?*"

"She's a simple girl who'll get hurt. She can't even read. She'll expect you to marry her," Russell said.

"Shove the morality, old boy, will you please? She doesn't need to know how to read for what we do, anyway." Mahler slapped him on the shoulder.

"Wow, you're something else," Russell said.

"You wanted to sleep with her the moment you saw her, didn't you? Tell the truth," Mahler said. "Go ahead. I mean, in your newspaper you tell lots of pretty lies all the time, but here you don't have to. It's just us. Didn't you want to sleep with her?"

Russell looked at Carl. "No, I didn't," he said. "You see, I'm not an *asshole* like you."

They got drunk later and Mahler apologized, but it hadn't sat well with Russell, and he didn't let it go. The girl was in love with Mahler, Russell could see that plain enough. They slept together again that night, he was sure of it.

"You have to stop kicking and pulling on the reins. You're confusing the horse," Russell said angrily. He'd come back down the river, the water gray and turbid from the rain. The constant drizzle had suddenly turned to something harder. Above them, the strip of sky showing through the jungle's canopy was completely gray. "Do you understand?" He could see Carl was scared.

Russell reached over and grabbed the horse's halter, then moved up the neck and took the reins. "Now stop doing *anything.* Just stop for a moment," he said, the rain dripping from Russell's cowboy hat as he spoke. He'd told Carl to wear a hat but he hadn't, and now he was scared and couldn't see very well because the rain was hitting his glasses.

"I think I should go back; the fucking horse is wild," Carl said.

"No, he isn't. He's tired of this river and he just wants out. But we have to go upriver; it's the quickest way in," Russell said.

"I didn't know it was going to be like this." Carl was wild-eyed. Everything seemed to be scaring him now. Russell led his horse out, away from the bank. The water was running off his hat and his clothes were soaked through, but he felt like he was sweating; it was that warm, maybe ninety degrees. He stopped his horse, got his plastic poncho out from the saddle bag and slipped it over his head. He would be even warmer now, but he was tired of getting wet.

"Now you have to stop putting on the gas and the brakes at the same time. It's one or the other, but not both. Do you understand? And stop yanking the reins. They don't like that.

84

Think about it; it's a big piece of steel you're shoving around in his mouth."

"Yeah, okay," Carl said. Russell pulled his horse around until they were directly across from each other, then handed Carl back his reins.

"What's he looking for anyway? Mahler?" Carl asked.

"How the fuck should I know," Russell said. "I hope he's looking for a big jade figure. And I hope to fuck he finds it. How much is Mahler getting of that ten thousand?" He hung his shotgun over his back, so that the weapon rode over the blue plastic of his poncho now.

"He gets a finder's fee," Carl said.

"How much? I want to know."

"Twenty percent," Carl said, collecting the reins and leaning back. He kicked his horse; the animal started stepping forward carefully, its head down. "I have to take a shit," Carl said. "Very badly."

"Go ahead," Russell said and wheeled his horse upriver again. "Go ahead, nobody is watching as far as I can tell."

Mahler was standing in the river next to the bank. He had his machete out. He was using one of those fat-ended ones, heavy and wide in the front. He had tied his horse and the mule, which carried all their equipment, to a tree.

"Here," Mahler said. "I found this little creek. . . ." Like Russell, Mahler had worn a hat, but his was the military kind, a soft jungle hat. It was soaked from the rain.

"It will take us a day to chop ten feet," Russell said, looking at the solid wall of jungle.

"Maybe. But I don't think so. We go inside, we cut a path two-man wide. Leave the horses out here, see how it is."

Russell looked around. He saw the water from the creek rushing out from the jungle, pushing against Mahler's pants leg. The river was very shallow here. But otherwise, from what he could see, there was nothing to distinguish this spot from any other along the river bank.

"Wouldn't there be more of a beach or something? I mean, if the Maya were going to develop something?" He had to hand it to Mahler, he could drink until late, stay up with the girl making love, he imagined, and now he looked fresh and strong here.

Mahler started chopping into the bush. The machete made a pleasing sound as it struck wood, a metallic biting sound that Russell had always liked.

"It was a thousand years ago..." Mahler said without turning around. "I found Bakta Halik, didn't I?"

"Yeah, that you did," Russell said. He climbed off his horse, tied it next to Mahler's, then pulled his machete out of the scabbard hanging from his saddle. He'd chosen a different style of machete; his was long and wicked-looking, and served as a weapon, because it was light, as well as for hacking bush. He'd had it sharpened by one of the men at the plantation. It was razor sharp, the dirty blade silver where it had been sharpened.

Mahler stopped and turned. He had a .45 stuck in a clip-on holster in the small of his back. "We have some coffee first?" He took his thermos out of the pack on his horse.

Carl rode up, his blond hair dark and plastered to his head from the rain. He looked miserable. Carl's horse had settled down now. Russell waded through the water and took the horse's halter.

"Now what?" Carl asked

"Get down," Russell said.

"I'll get wet," Carl said. Russell looked at the man, incredulous. "My feet. The water is cold."

"Get the fuck off the horse before I pull you off," Russell said. Carl said something in German to Mahler.

"He doesn't want to get his feet wet. And he's heard there are snakes in the water," Mahler said in a monotone. He was carefully pouring coffee into the black top of a thermos. His backpack was slung on one shoulder, his machete driven into a tree limb right behind him.

"Four Steppers?" Russell said. A black snake called *cuatro pasos* lived in Guatemalan rivers. As a boy with the cowboys on his mother's cattle ranch, Russell often saw them when the cowboys were herding cattle across rivers. They were called "Four Steppers" because that's how many steps you took, after being bitten, before you died. Russell had seen horses bitten and drop the rider, who'd been bitten too after he fell. The cowboys called that a "lucky shot."

"You're a great big fat giant pussy, my friend," Russell said in English. "Now get off that fucking horse."

"I can't. I'm afraid." Mahler stepped forward and handed Russell first the cup of coffee, then his backpack. He calmly walked up and pulled Carl off his horse as if he were unloading a sack of some kind. Carl squealed and fought like a little girl all the way down. When he stopped carrying on, Russell pulled a machete from the scabbard on Carl's saddle and handed it to him.

"If you see a snake, you let us know," Russell told him. The rain and Carl's behavior had put him in a foul mood.

Ten feet inside the bush, it was so hot they had to strip off their shirts despite the rain. Mahler had pinned his long hair up on his head so he looked like a Sikh. His skin was fish belly white, but he was wiry, and his muscles were visible under the skin. He seemed tireless.

Russell and he worked together side by side, cutting through the thick growth. They'd tried to get Carl to help pull the larger pieces away, but he was useless. Tiny mosquitoes rested on them as they worked, undisturbed by their violent motions.

87

Russell stopped, looking down at his chest that was, at times, covered with them. They'd made jokes about getting malaria and being bitten by a *cuatro pasos* at the same time. They figured one would cure the other.

They went through all the coffee and began to drink river water. It tasted like copper pennies and was very cold. Twenty feet in, they climbed up on solid ground, and the way got a little easier. When Russell looked behind him, he saw a green tunnel, and at the end the river.

Suddenly, they were free enough to see several feet in front of them. Mahler stopped. He was sweating like a pig. They fell on their knees.

"I told you it might not be so bad once we got inside further."

Russell could hear the screaming of monkeys above them in the canopy. They could still hear the river behind them.

"Where's Carl?"

"How the fuck should I know," Russell said. "I thought he was behind us."

He'd had to throw Carl over his horse despite his screaming. He would never forget the way he screamed on the way back. The way it seemed to take forever to do those ten kilometers. The river growing muddy from the rain. The light leaving them in the end. The horses jumpy, because Carl kept screaming and moaning. Even now, in the house, with Carl in the bedroom with the doctor, Russell couldn't get that sound of the screaming out of his head.

He crumpled the beer can. The room smelled of weed smoke and beer. It was pitch black outside. He hadn't taken a shower yet; his clothes were still damp. His palms burnt from the blisters he'd gotten from the hacking.

A jaguar had attacked Carl. It had clawed his face real good while he'd gone to shit.

88

"That was bad," Russell said. "I never want to hear screaming like that again."

"Jaguars up there are bi...big. ...He's lucky it didn't break his neck," Mahler said.

"I need something stronger," Russell said. "Jesus."

"I have tequila."

"Get it," Russell said. "God, this is a filthy country. Something like that . . . Jesus."

"We warned him," Mahler said.

"It's just—*Jesus*. That shouldn't happen to *anyone*." He watched Mahler walk down the hallway. He could hear the steady drumming of the rain on the house's metal roof. He heard the door open, and the doctor from Colomba came out of the last bedroom, where they'd taken Carl.

For the first five kilometers, he'd never heard any kind of screaming like that. Even now, sitting in the living room, he couldn't bear thinking about that trip back, with Carl tied to his horse. Twice they'd stopped, because Carl was begging them to. Russell hadn't even wanted to turn around and look at him.

"You shoot me, yeah. Please," Carl had said, breathing funny from so much screaming and crying.

"We'll be there soon," Russell said, turning to look at him. The way his head hung over the side of the horse. His hair all bloody, his pants down, his face clawed and his ass too.

It was Mahler who had taken Carl's reins, pulled his horse around and convinced him not to listen. Telling him that the only chance Carl had was them getting him back to *Tres Rios* and then calling a doctor.

"You shoot him and then what? We have no one to broker the Jaguar," Mahler said. His jungle hat was wet.

The light was almost gone, so that they could see only the mist and the lighter rocks in the river now. Russell could make out Mahler's face in the twilight. He didn't really give a shit about Carl. He just wanted to sell that Jaguar when they found it. Carl started begging Mahler to shoot him, but Mahler just kicked his horse, and they started again downriver towards *Tres Rios.*

Doctor Calsado was a veterinarian, not an MD. But out here in the bush, Calsado was called a lot of the time in emergencies when people couldn't find the regular doctor.

The doctor was the color of coffee and milk. He'd been born out in Livingston. He was a large man, with a large man's rolling gait, and he carried an old fashioned black doctor's bag, having accepted his status as an ersatz MD.

"Mahler's getting tequila," Russell said.

"Good," the doctor said in English. He'd trained in the States, in Texas. His specialty was large animals, horses and cows. He'd been working when Mahler had called him on his cell phone. They'd had to wait more than an hour for him to arrive.

"Is he going to be all right?" Russell asked.

"Yes. In a day or two, he can get out of bed. Twenty-five stitches in his face alone. I put forty or more in his ass. He'll have to take only liquids for forty-eight hours. But he'll be all right."

"He'll live, then?" Russell said.

"Yes. He just won't look quite the same," the doctor said. "Where's Mahler? I need a drink. You two saved his life."

"I would have brought mescal. I mean, to celebrate," Mahler said, coming back inside. Russell heard the doctor start to laugh. It was the kind of joke they made in Guatemala; Russell understood they helped defeat the ugliness of the place, but he couldn't laugh, not this time.

For just a moment back on the river, he'd thought of shooting Carl. For just a moment, when he saw him like that, suffering, begging Russell to do it. He had thought of doing it, just for a moment. Now he was glad he hadn't. Mahler had been right.

Russell got up and got them glasses. He heard the doctor and Mahler laugh again while he was in the kitchen. *Bloody, bloody country,* he thought.

"And what were you doing up the *Rio Amargo* like that? It's full of *cuatros pasos,*" the doctor said, when Russell handed them each a drink. He didn't know what to answer. He looked at Mahler for help.

"My friend just bought the place, and he's insisted on seeing *all* of it," Mahler said, sitting down across from the doctor.

"Well then, you must be crazy," the doctor said in his Texas accent. He looked at Russell and took a drink. "But you won't last long acting crazy out here. I promise you that."

"I keep telling him that, too," Mahler said. "But he won't listen to me. He's an American. You know how they are."

"Yeah. I do," the doctor said.

TEN

He'd thought about Beatrice constantly during the ten days he and Mahler spent at *Tres Rios* looking for the Red Jaguar. When he got back to the capital, he tried to tell himself that his decision to cover the presidential election had nothing to do with having met her. But he knew it wasn't true. He'd been jealous of General Selva, and was smitten with his wife. He couldn't, in fact, get her out of his mind.

Despite himself, he wanted to understand how a beautiful young woman like Beatrice could have married a man of Selva's type. Had she married him only for his money? The general's family was one of the richest in the country. Had he swept her off her feet?

Katherine had told him on the way back from the general's plantation that the two had met in England when Beatrice had descended from Oxford graduate to stripper. The general had been the military attaché at the embassy. He'd frequented the strip club where she worked. She may simply have fallen in love with him, without knowing much about him.

None of it made sense, because he was jealous but couldn't admit it. He simply told himself he was appalled, without asking himself *why* he should care so much about a young woman he'd met only once.

Russell was looking out his office window at the view of the avenue *La Reforma*. Below him, streams of noon-time traffic poured around the huge roundabout crowned by a statue of a Spanish conquistador who'd captured Central America.

His cell phone lay on his cluttered desk, along with his notes on Antonio De La Madrid, the candidate opposing Selva

92

in the election. De La Madrid's party was called the PAN–
Partido Accion Nacional. The PAN was a staunchly capitalist
pro-business party at loggerheads with the World Bank and
the IMF. Russell had just interviewed an old liberal senator
who told him that Carlos Selva was going to be the next
president of the country because Antonio De La Madrid
scared everyone, including the American embassy.

The senator, Rudy Valladolid, had been slightly drunk when
he showed up at eleven in the morning at the café at the
Camino Real Hotel. The well known left-leaning senator
ordered a drink immediately, despite the early hour. The
senator smoked Marlboros incessantly, and looked as if he
might keel over from a heart attack at any moment. He was
sure that General Selva's opponent would be assassinated, he
told Russell matter-of-factly. "He'll either be shot at his home,
or killed with one of his mistresses in bed," the senator said
as he lit a cigarette. "But it won't really matter how they do
it."

"Why kill him?" Russell asked. The senator smiled, put his
cigarette in the ash tray, and took a swallow of his drink,
studying him.

The old man's eyes were jaundiced and the color of scotch
whiskey. Russell couldn't help feeling that Valladolid was a
political dinosaur. Cuba and the rest of that socialist mess
had already been thrown on the junk heap of history, as far
as Russell was concerned. He was sorry that he'd made the
appointment. He'd hoped that the Senator, who had a
reputation for being the country's most astute political
observer despite his left wing leaning, could have helped him
sort out the political players. But what could this old man
possibly know about the new world that his generation
represented? Russell suspected that he didn't even have a
computer. He asked him as much.

"I have a pen," the senator said. "It's worked fine for sixty years—no, *longer*. It's was my great-grandfather's fountain pen. He signed the constitution here. You know our constitution was patterned after yours. After America's. Do you know why President Ubico had my father killed?" Ubico had been the military dictator during the 20's—a little Napoleon, and really no more than the United Fruit Company's representative in the country.

"No," Russell said.

"My father had decided it was a good idea for the United Fruit company to pay some kind of tax here. They never did, you know. They never paid a dime of tax. They were here over a hundred years and never paid a cent. Now was that capitalism, or just old-fashioned imperialism? Don't you see that Europe and America need us to be underdeveloped? Can't you see that, young man? We buy their cars and their computers. That's the way it's always been. And they've made sure of it by hand-picking our leaders."

Russell swallowed. He was tired of hearing about the "ugly Americans." It may have been true in the past, but it seemed so beside the point now if you didn't also admit that capitalism was the only way out for Latin America, or anywhere else. Most of the *new* industries in the country weren't even American; they were Korean, he pointed out. The "United," as she was known, had left the damn country before he'd been born. It was ridiculous to blame America for all Latin America's problems.

"But surely you understand that there have been momentous changes in the world," Russell said, trying to hide his disdain. He wanted to explain that he didn't necessarily disagree about the way Americans had once abused their economic power, but that was then, during the cold war, and that was over. Capitalism had won. End of story.

94

"Capitalism is bigger even than the United States," Russell said.

"Young man, you sound like a priest," the senator said.

"Anyway, you haven't answered me. Why would the military want to get rid of De La Madrid? He's pro-business. He's a capitalist."

"The military is terrified of him. They've never faced a pro-business reformist party before. They're used to left-wing types like me, but not neo-liberals. Christ, Madrid studied at the University of Chicago with Milton Friedman! He's getting all kinds of good press in Europe. They're afraid he might actually clean up all the corruption here. That's the last thing the military wants."

"So who are you supporting?" Russell asked him.

"Madrid," he said. "Are you surprised?"

"Yes."

"Carlos Selva, by the way, is my nephew. I'd say he's too churlish to be president... And there's his unfortunate reputation."

"Human rights violations, you mean?" Russell said. Valladolid had a large swallow of his vodka and grapefruit juice.

"His mother, my sister, calls them 'lapses of judgment.' But yes... and his wife."

"What about his wife?"

"Well . . . well . . . she isn't perfect. She has a reputation," the senator said. "Not that it will matter. Nothing matters here except that the Americans either like you, or they don't. They love Selva, and that's why I'm supporting Antonio."

"She, you mean his wife, has a reputation?" Russell asked.

"Yes. But it has nothing to do with politics, and I wouldn't mention it to *anyone,* or you might have an accident," the senator said. "You understand here, the first rule is never, *ever,* write about a man's wife. Especially my nephew's."

"Is there something that might come up in a campaign, then?" Russell asked.

"God, no. But she's a bit of. . . ." The senator searched for the English word. He'd been speaking Spanish, and it was the first time Russell had heard him speak English. His English was perfect. Ironically, he sounded like an American. "She likes to enjoy herself," the senator said. Russell doubted he would have said anything if he hadn't been a little drunk. "She's the same age as my granddaughter, and apparently they frequent the same nightclubs. I believe her favorite is the Q Bar. *Zona 10,*" he said. "You've met her then, I take it?"

"Yes," Russell said. "I've met her."

"God did a bad thing there, young man. He made someone who was *too* beautiful."

Russell smiled. It was true, and he suddenly liked the old man. They were different in so many ways, too many years between them to really understand each other. But he liked his humanity, and his being drunk at eleven in the morning, and his clean blue shirt and his Yale ring and his manners and his having Fidel Castro's cell phone number. Russell asked him if it was true what he'd heard, that Fidel Castro called him for advice on occasion.

"Only about women," the senator said, joking. "You look familiar, young man," he said as he stood up to leave. "Something about you is very very familiar."

"All Americans look alike," Russell said, trying to make a joke out of it, afraid Valladolid saw something of his mother in his face.

"Do you believe in God, young man?" Valladolid asked, not laughing at Russell's joke.

"No. Of course not. Why? Is it important?"

"Here you have to understand God, to really understand— I mean, the notion of God. The Catholic God, and the Catholic church. If you understand that, you can understand

96

Latin America." The old man leaned forward, putting his big hands on the table. "You see, we aren't really interested in *money,* not in the end. That's what makes us Latins. We're feudal, really, it's all feudal here, the family structures, the business structures. It's never been just about money," he said. "You should explain that in your newspaper. We're medieval."

ELEVEN

It is very late," Katherine said.

"Yes, but it's Thursday," Russell said. "Thursday night you're supposed to start the weekend in Guatemala; it says so on your visa. Haven't you checked?"

"You're awful," she said.

They'd been having an affair. It amounted to afternoon screw sessions and political discussions. Katherine was trying to convince him that his neo-liberal agenda for the world was wrong, and he hadn't been convinced. They disagreed about everything, but both of them were lonely and happy to have each other, even if it was called casual sex in the women's magazines. They'd made a joke about it, saying that sex, if it was casual, had to be good for you.

He suspected she was falling in love with him, because she was earnest and loving when she really didn't have to be. They would find each other for coffee at the *"Cafecito,"* leave her UN Jeep there, and go off for a tryst. He wasn't in love with her, he was sure of that. They were, strangely enough, too much alike, he thought.

"Anyway, I want to go to the Q Bar and I can't go without a girl—a cute girl, besides, or the doorman won't let me in; I'm too fucking old," he said.

"Get yourself put on the list," Katherine said. "I used to know the owner; he was a Spaniard, and he'd put you on the list. Anyway, you aren't *forty* yet," she joked. "Unless you've been lying to me."

It was that kind of club. Even at his age, he was too old for the Q Bar. It belonged to kids in their mid-twenties. And the doormen kept it that way, he'd been told—unless, of course, you brought a very pretty girl along.

They met at eleven, had a drink across the street from the club. As everywhere in Latin America, you could hear the dance club from a block away. He'd asked Katherine to wear something sexy, afraid the doorman wouldn't let them in unless she looked very "hot." He normally associated the word with frat boys and businessmen, and it surprised him. She'd surprised him because she'd paid attention, and met him in a Spanish bar in a small black dress that he didn't think her kind of girl owned. He ordered tequila and listened to the trance music coming from across the street.

Katherine thought his calling her on the spur of the moment had something to do with their affair getting more serious. She looked animated and happy to have been thrown a curve by his request.

"I thought you'd be working on Thursday night," she said. "I didn't expect an invitation."

"Spur of the moment. I had to let go. It's been a killer week," he said, and smiled. Katherine gave him a sweet smile back.

They ordered a second round of drinks. He was thinking about Beatrice, so he found himself speaking in easy prefabricated sentences. He couldn't help it. He was lost. The feeling of being lost struck him with tremendous power, and he was excited by it. He was doing something he knew to be crazy, even absurd, and yet he couldn't stop himself.

Katherine leaned forward and gave him a kiss. She flicked his tongue and rubbed his leg. He looked at her, shocked. She was falling in love with him; he was sure of it now. She wouldn't have come on the spur of the moment if she wasn't serious about him.

She looked into his eyes. They were excited shining girl's eyes, sexual, feminine, and happy. She kissed him on the cheek. He tried to conjure up some appropriate look, but didn't know what it might be. He kissed her back. People at the bar tried not to stare at the American couple making out.

"I have to go to Chicago for that wedding," Katherine said. "My friend. Remember?" she cooed in his ear. "I could get you a ticket." He didn't answer; he touched her thigh and stopped, as people were staring. He pulled back.

"I can't. Busy," he said. He shouldn't have said it. The moment passed, but he noticed something else in her eyes, just for a moment: a profound disappointment.

"Only for a few days. It *would* be fun. I *promise* you. You haven't left the country for—?"

"Years, it seems like," he said.

"Well—come on then," she said.

"When?" He didn't want to disappoint her; he liked her. He glanced across the street and saw the queue of kids trying to get into the club. He saw the doorman pointing at young girls, lifting a blue satin rope to let them pass. He looked at Katherine. She was pretty. She had a nice figure, buxom. She wasn't stunning, though. He wondered if the doorman would let them in. "All right… I'll ask my boss," he said, lying. He just didn't want to disappoint her, as he was grateful for her coming. Perhaps he would even go to Chicago. What difference did it make, a few days, he told himself. "Could you do me a favor?" he said.

"What?" She picked up her drink

"Could you take off your bra?" She looked at him a moment, then smiled. "Why, are we going to have sex ?"

He didn't answer. He was just afraid the doorman might not let them in unless she did. She finished her drink and went to the bathroom. When she came back, she was spilling out of the dress.

He waited for a sign from the doorman, pushing Katherine forward towards the front of the queue. Bodyguards lined the sidewalk, as they weren't allowed inside. Rich kids, some already drunk, waited, holding up their hands trying to get the doorman's attention.

He put his arms around Katherine's waist and moved them forward in the crowd. He heard a Pink track start. He glanced at the bodyguards on the street. They were from another class, and looked at the mob of kids with a certain disdain. The men tried not to let it show on their faces. It was just another stop. Pistols bulged under vests. Indian faces with day-old beards lit by night lights. He felt the bottom of Katherine's breasts against his arm; a sexual blast ran through him. He remembered her on the floor of his apartment, the look in her face as she straddled him in complete abandon.

He held his arm tight around her and pushed forward. He wondered if he would ever see Beatrice the way he had seen Katherine exposed sexually. He felt the sense of pursuit and the need to pursue. It seemed uncontrollable for a moment. He had to clear a path through this jungle of his desire. He had no idea how he would react if the doorman didn't let them in.

Over the music, he told Katherine to raise her hand. She turned to look at him. Maybe she caught something in his voice, or perhaps it was the pressing of their bodies together –the crowd around the door was turned into one body–but he could tell she wanted to do whatever he asked of her. That fact only put his desire to see Beatrice into relief. He realized he was doing something wrong, something stupid and something he would regret, even be ashamed of. He had this woman in his arms who would do anything he asked. She'd proven that. She was sexy. She was in love with him, even. Why was he chasing a woman he'd barely met, who was married, and had children? Because he wanted her, he told himself. He wanted to hear her voice speaking to him.

Katherine shot her hand up. The doorman looked at her. Russell put his hand around her waist. The doorman looked at him, smiled, and pointed to them. They were suddenly past the ropes and moving inside the club. Russell was stopped for a moment while a guard frisked him quickly. He noticed the guard managed to pat Katherine's ass as they walked by.

Inside the club the crowd was packed tight. The room wasn't very large and held only about two hundred people, but seemed like a lot more. The deejay was on a stage, flanked by dancers. He was startled to see Beatrice on the stage dancing, flanked by one other girl. They were both in gold lame retro outfits. He looked at Katherine, but she hadn't seen Beatrice yet. He yelled over the music that he was going to move them towards the bar. For some reason, he didn't want Katherine to see Beatrice. He was shocked—he hadn't expected to see her performing—but tried to keep the shock out of his voice.

He guided them towards the bar. At one point, they couldn't get any closer to the bar. What had he expected? he wondered. *I'd expected to be disappointed,* but he wasn't. *She was there.*

From where they stopped, he could see the catwalk above, and the deejay. He left Katherine's side, pushed his way to the bar, and ordered two tequilas. The bar was a moving throng. Girls with rave bars were wiggling in the confined spaces. Young men in well-ironed shirts stood staring at the girls: some had taken off their shirts because of the heat. Their young bodies reflected the multi-colored lights. The bartender was rushing to fill orders.

A break came in the music. The room felt as if the air had been sucked out of it. A girl bumped into him, obviously high on something. She ran her hand over her boyfriend's naked chest. Still dancing, she held the light stick against his stomach. Suddenly the music started again.

He felt someone grab him from behind. He thought it was Katherine; he turned, and it was Beatrice. She was holding another dancer's hand and she didn't really look at him as she shimmied to the bar, her hands raised in a kind of dance move. She broke free from her friend and she began to dance to the music. Wherever she'd been, she knew how to move in a way that only dancers, trained dancers, have. It was a feeling that she controlled her body perfectly, yet was out of control slightly, so that the energy moved across her and then back again in a wild let-it-all-go step that was meant to go with the trance music.

There was a break with just the beat. He tried to catch her eye, but she was completely absorbed. People made room for her and her partner.

He looked around as best he could to see if her husband was in the place, but he couldn't see him. So much older than the kids here, he knew the general would stand out easily. But Russell didn't see him.

The music picked up speed. Beatrice was sweating. He could see the sheen on her face; her blond hair had been braided, the braids flew.

The barman tapped him on the shoulder. Russell turned, paid for the drinks, and left with them. He saw Katherine nearby. She'd seen Beatrice and clearly recognized her. He moved through the crowd and handed Katherine a drink. She turned to look at him. He tried not to register shock. Or was it something else on his face? Excitement? Lust? All of them?

"That's *what's*-her-name. The general's wife. Look at her!" Katherine said. She leaned into him and yelled over the music, obviously surprised to see her here.

He turned and looked at Beatrice again. He thought she noticed them. He wasn't sure. "Jesus, she can dance," he heard Katherine say. He felt her put her arm around him. Another

103

powerful break came in the music; all the turntables were playing now. A James Brown tune dominated the mix; it was propped up by sitar music.

Beatrice spun. Her midriff flattened. She started a new series of moves, more controlled, shaking her hips to the sitar music then undulating. All the young men at the bar were transfixed now by her dancing and her beauty. It seemed as if she were getting bigger, but it was just the lights that had moved. Someone on the catwalk had turned a spotlight down on them; a purple light hit Beatrice and her companion.

There was a complete stop to the music. You could feel the silent beats building as everyone expected the music to come back. It didn't on the first beat, or the third. The lights started to come on as if the night were ending, five beats... He watched Beatrice slow, then slow again. She was looking at him on the seventh beat. On the ninth, the house lights went dark. Only one single spotlight was left on. Then suddenly, the music came back on, thundering. The famous break in "I Feel Good" came up. *So good . . . so good, that I gotta yoouuu."* The crowd went wild. The breaks worked their magic. Everyone in the place yelled excitedly.

Beatrice had looked directly at him then, as if she'd been dancing all along for him. They played "Make it Funky." He took a drink and for a moment he thought they would move away from the bar, because Katherine was pulling him to a place where they could dance. He turned to look at Beatrice; she was coming through the crowd toward them, as James Brown sang "Like a Boom-er-ang."

Beatrice stopped in front of him and draped her arms over his neck, and they started to dance. It happened like that. He didn't think he stopped dancing for the next hour. By the time he remembered Katherine, she'd left.

Later he checked his cell phone messages; she had left him several. "You're a shit," she'd said angrily. Of course she was right. But there were others, too. She said she was sorry. She said she didn't mean it. She said he should call her.

He did, a week later, but she'd gone to Chicago. He left a message at her office, telling her he was very sorry. He felt guilty for using her. He was truly sorry about that. His affair with Beatrice Selva started that night at the Q Bar.

TWELVE

De La Madrid's press secretary, an ingratiating American called Nesbitt, called Russell's office the next morning to set up an interview.

"Antonio is dying to speak to you about the crisis. He has a free hour in the afternoon around what they call tea time here. These people–" Nesbitt said in an exasperated tone. They were meant to share a moment together–savvy Americans handling the inept Latins. Russell said nothing, and Nesbitt went on, in a more reserved tone. "We could send a car?"

"Fine," Russell said. "Four o'clock, then."

"See you then," Nesbitt said.

Russell put down the phone and tried to collect his thoughts. He'd been doing his homework on the economic crisis. His newspaper had been doing most of what serious reporting had been done on the crisis in Latin America. They ran some kind of story on it almost every day. The U.S. papers were writing about it, but only sporadically.

In the meantime, the regional economy was falling apart. Governments and businesses had borrowed too much from the developed countries and now, with commodity prices having crashed, they couldn't pay the interest on their massive loans. Guatemala was no different. Russell suspected that the currency might collapse altogether; it was only a matter of time.

He stood up and searched the office for his briefcase, found it, and pulled out his notes on De La Madrid. But he found himself staring out the window at the traffic. *Why did Beatrice's husband allow her to go out at night alone? How could she possibly manage to stay out until four in the morning, as she had with him?*

He hadn't wanted to think of her husband at breakfast, or later on the way to his office. He had dwelt on the coming weekend instead. Beatrice had agreed to meet him. He told himself only that the general was bound to find out, sooner or later, that Russell was having an affair with his wife. He expected Selva would come to his office, or apartment, and try to kill him. He didn't really care.

Death didn't scare him. The only thing he thought about being killed was that the desire to lose himself—this inexplicable search—would finally end. He wouldn't have to feel driven anymore. It would come to a conclusion in the street, or at his desk, or in a parking garage, with Selva pumping bullets into him.

He spoke with Nesbitt for a moment in an outer office. They were on the twentieth floor of one of the tallest buildings in the city. De La Madrid's family owned the building as well as the bank that it housed.

The upper floor was grand, its wood floors polished like glass. Secretaries glided past them like specters dressed in Chanel and Ann Taylor. Nesbitt was natty, married and twice divorced. Somehow Russell learned all this in the matter of a few minutes, as they waited for Antonio to appear. Apparently, Nesbitt said, his boss had snuck his barber into the office for a quick haircut.

They made small talk. Nesbitt droned on about his Guatemalan problems: the maids, the water, his bowels. It was the predictable conversation. Outside, through the windows, Russell could tell it had gotten very windy. In the distance was the *Volcan de Agua,* barely visible through the mist of diesel smoke. Behind the volcano was the lake where he and Beatrice were to meet.

He longed for the weekend.

"I've found that Pepto-Bismol works if you. . . ." Nesbitt was telling him.

He worried about the hotel room. He wanted it to be nice. He was worried Beatrice wouldn't like it.

"He'll see you now," he heard Nesbitt say. Russell stood up automatically and followed the American down the hall.

Experience had taught Russell that interviews with very important people, very wealthy or powerful people, usually started in one of two ways. The interviewee was either distant and seigniorial, wanting to commit to barely anything–even a handshake seemed to compromise their stature. Or they were blustering, finger-jabbing types, trying to get you to reveal yourself *first,* so they could then lay down their defense.

De La Madrid's barber was still working on him when Russell followed Nesbitt into the grand office. De La Madrid seemed chagrined about the snafu in communication. Russell decided to ignore the moment and pretend that he interviewed men getting their hair cut all the time.

They'd put a chair out in the middle of an enormous office where the barber was working. The would-be president was covered with a short blue nylon sheet. He was getting his neck shaved. The barber was using an old-fashioned straight razor. The barber was an older man who looked at Russell and immediately seemed to disapprove of him. The barber rested his razor in the air for a moment, then went back to work, deciding to ignore the interruption.

Nesbitt and Antonio spoke a minute about a call from the American Embassy that Antonio was to return as soon as he could. While they spoke, De La Madrid kept looking at

Russell in a curious way, as if they'd met before and he was trying to place him.

They were suddenly alone except for the barber: two men with a secret. Madrid's was a small one, probably to do with the embassy, Russell guessed. His was a big one: he was sleeping with De La Madrid's opponent's wife. Antonio divulged his right away.

"It's the bloody US ambassador. She's quite childish; if you don't call her back within an hour, she thinks you are mad at her. I think she's charming; hell of a golfer too. Some people are like that, too sensitive." Madrid smiled. "I don't dare go to a barber shop anymore; my bodyguards get very nervous."

"I understand," Russell said. The barber was cutting De La Madrid's sideburns with one flick of his wrist.

"Well, are you one of those red meat Americans?" Madrid asked, joking. "But then, you couldn't be. If you work for the *Financial Times*. They're all. . . . What do the Americans call them? Brainiacs. Who eat salads."

"Bookish, the English would say. And I eat meat," Russell said.

The barber looked up. He was doing the other sideburn now and said in Spanish that Antonio wasn't to move. "There have been two attempts on my life, Mr. Price, did you know that?"

"Yes. I read about them both. You were quite lucky."

"No. It's my bodyguards. I have the best. They are fearless. I think they actually enjoy the attempts because they get so damned bored standing around the rest of the time." The barber smiled, and Russell realized the barber spoke English.

"You'd think they'd just pay off Nico here. He comes up and uses a straight razor and there's no bodyguard in sight. Right, Nico? You could buy a place in Miami," Antonio said.

"I don't like Miami," the barber said in English. "Too many fucking Latins. Now if they said New York, maybe I'd do it."

They made small talk until the barber finished. By the time the barber finally left, Russell had decided that he liked Antonio. He was relaxed and affable. There seemed to be no particular agenda. Russell had thought De La Madrid would somehow disappoint him, and instead he found him charming and intelligent. Their conversation ranged from Greenspan to Tiger Woods' sex life.

"And are you enjoying yourself? I mean, it's not *all* work. Is it? Any girl friends? Latin women are on you gringos like flies at a barbecue," Antonio said.

"An American girl," he lied.

"What's she like?"

"Altruistic. Anti-free trade, you know the type. Tall and charming," Russell said.

"You know what I like about American women? They feel guilty when they cheat on their husbands. Really. Latin women don't feel guilty. Everyone here is expected to have affairs and just keep it quiet. But American women, they really suffer . . . I should know." He chuckled. "Is she intelligent?"

They went to a wall of couches and a panoramic view of the city and sat down.

"Yes," Russell said. "She wants to save the world. I think she just might. Someone should, I suppose. It's long overdue."

"Those young NGO girls that come here have the energy of twenty men," Antonio said.

They looked at each other for a moment. Russell was about to make light of his remark, but caught Antonio studying him again in that strange way.

"Would you like to help me save the world, Mr. Price? Save Guatemala from itself?" Antonio said unexpectedly.

"I'm sorry?"

"I'm running for the presidency of the country."

"I know that. I think most of the world does by now," Russell said. "You've done a good job getting name recognition."

110

"I've hired a PR firm in New York."

"That's where you got Nesbitt, I suppose?"

"Nesbitt is a fool," Antonio said. "He's no good for what's coming."

"I don't understand?"

"War."

"I'm sorry."

"Elections are wars in Latin America, Mr. Price. It's the way it's always been. The difference is that I actually want to do something for the country. I want to drag it out of the dark ages and make it run like it should have been run from the very beginning."

"I'm a little lost," Russell said.

"No, you aren't. You know exactly what I mean. I need your help. I need the support of all the important decision-making papers in Europe and America. You write for one of the most important. I need your help. I need you to support me. That dumb thug that's running against me is a danger to the country. The military here are bought and sold like so many cows. I want you to help me win. What do you say? I read your editorial concerning the privatization option. I was very impressed with your ideas."

"I'm a journalist," Russell said. "Not a politician."

"Don't pull that objective crap with me. I've looked into you, Mr. Price; we are very similar. Anyway, none of you journalists are really objective. You *all* have your agendas. It just so happens that you and I share one. I want to bring financial stability and prosperity to millions of people who have known nothing but war and corruption for almost a hundred years. Are you going to help me do that or not?"

Russell had taken out his neatly typed list of questions. He had his pen in his hand, and he opened it. For some reason he thought of Flora, his secretary, the way she'd come to his office so lost, looking for a job. He thought about the hundreds

111

of thousands of peasants that every day were being thrown off the land because coffee prices had crashed and plantation owners were turning their plantations over to the banks. No one knew how those people were going to eat. There were no jobs in the cities; the *maquiladoras* were all shutting down and moving to China and Vietnam, where they paid half of the miserable wage they paid here. He, better than most, knew the extent of the crisis and its aftermath of misery.

"I'd like to ask you these questions, if I could, about the crisis," he said calmly.

"But you're on my side? I can tell. If you weren't, you'd be giving me the asinine speech about objectivity, and the Fourth Estate, or some other plate of bollocks," Antonio said.

Russell didn't answer, but he knew that he was going to help him. By the time they'd worked their way through his questions, he knew that De La Madrid probably could, with a little luck, and help from people like him, get the country going in the right direction, and avoid becoming an Argentina. There wasn't much time; the forces of economic chaos, both men agreed, were moving in on the country in a hurry.

"General Selva is the man I have to beat. He wants to kill me. We went to the same high school," Antonio said. "We were friends once. He's already tried once to kill me, we think. The little shit. You know he bought Sylvester Stallone's house in Miami, just the other day. His army pay is thirty-two thousand dollars a year. The house cost twenty million. What do you make of that?" Antonio asked, smiling.

"A difference of significant proportions," Russell said.

"You know, Price, you're funny. You don't try to be funny, but you are."

They shook hands as Russell was leaving. He wanted to ask De La Madrid everything he knew about Selva's wife. He wanted to ask him if it was true that the general had met

112

her in a strip club in London. He wanted to ask if he, Antonio De La Madrid, was truly a good man Russell could believe in—a man he could trust—or if he was just having him on about bringing real change. He wanted to ask him if he'd ever been lost. He doubted it. Antonio was one of those men who, because of their class and their advantages, are never lost, Russell supposed. He wanted to ask him if he was afraid of being assassinated.

"I told my wife I was meeting a very unusual American this morning. She remembered you. She met you at a party at the French embassy. She said that you weren't really an American, you were too smooth to be one. She thought you might be lying," Antonio said, and laughed. "If you write about me favorably, and say bad things about the general, you know that Selva won't like it."

"Yes, I understand," Russell said.

"Often times people that the general doesn't like have big problems," Antonio said. "The kind of problems it's hard to recover from."

"Yes, I know."

"A difference of significant proportions—those kinds of problems," Madrid said. They both smiled.

Antonio slapped Russell on the back. It was a significant slap and hug, the kind Latin men give someone they want to be their *compadre*. He'd seduced Russell into a conspiracy against the general, whom they both knew was a shit and a mass murderer.

Russell didn't really feel frightened about it. It was the first time he'd felt good about himself in years.

THIRTEEN

He'd gotten the hotel room he wanted, only after he'd complained when he'd checked in late. He'd driven up to the lake by himself. At night it was never a good idea. His shotgun rode on the seat next to him. Kidnappings were constant on the road to Lake Atitlán, especially at night. And being white, he knew he was a target. White people—foreigners in general—were all thought to have money.

He woke up Saturday morning and threw open the curtains of his hotel room. Lake Atitlán sat quiet, like some kind of blue goddess among three volcanoes, reflecting a few cotton-white clouds. Below his room, the hotel's beautiful lakeside garden spread out along the shore. Everything had been watered by the gardeners first thing, and was sparkling in the morning sun. Huge azaleas bloomed red and white, exotic white roses spilled over a trellis by the elegant black-bottomed pool. A pool boy was busy laying out white cushions over lounge chairs.

He lay on the bed and read Delacroix's journal while he waited for Beatrice. Delacroix had lived in a time of promise and hope, a vibrant time that felt itself going forward toward the modern, the rational, the harmonious, the beautiful. Paris had symbolized all the hope that was lying just ahead for mankind. The painter saw his art as a gift to this new rational world, a world no longer dominated by superstition and

114

religion, when nation-states themselves were the ideal of modernity and sanity. Paris had become civilization's high-water mark. Democracy and Art lived for each other in an atmosphere of rationality and reason. What had happened to all that hope, Russell wondered.

His cell phone rang at ten. He sprang up from the bed, dropping the book.

"How are you?" she said.

"Okay." Speaking with her still seemed strange.

"I'm going to be late. Maybe eleven-thirty; is that okay?" she said.

"Yes. Eleven-thirty," he said.

"You saw the boat dock? In front of the restaurant."

"Yes," he said.

"Have you missed me?" she asked. The question took him aback.

"Yes. Very much," he said.

"I'll see you at the dock then," she said, and hung up.

He closed his phone and sat on the edge of the bed. He was completely drained, and didn't understand why. It was as if he'd run several miles. His heart was pounding with both desire and fear.

"Shit," he said out loud. "Shit. I don't know if I can do this." He went to the tray and tried to pour himself another cup of coffee, but the thermos they'd brought with breakfast was empty. He put the cup down and looked stupidly around the room, then walked to the window.

He saw fishermen's canoes nestled together. The *pangas*– small wood canoes–rode nose to nose out on the small lagoon below his window. The fishermen were talking together, eating breakfast. Their boats made the shape of a brown star on the water.

115

"What's wrong with me? I'm out of my mind. I can't wait to see her. I can't wait." He said it out loud, as some kind of affirmation. Everything seemed wild. He was frightened of her for some reason. Her beauty? Her intelligence? Her station? Her role as mother? He didn't know. He couldn't answer. All he knew was that he wanted to have her again, all to himself. He wanted to make love to her. He wanted to see her climax. He wanted her to be that woman-girl she'd been in the Hotel Procedes, after they'd left the club. He hadn't been afraid then. He'd been an equal. He'd been a sexual partner. It was better when she didn't speak, when neither of them spoke. *That was impossible.* Perhaps people like them shouldn't speak, but exist only sexually.

He went into the shower and looked in the mirror. He looked every bit of his age, he thought. She was much younger. She never looked tired.

He looked tired. He'd been up late at the office finishing the article on De La Madrid, and then emailing it to London. It might run as soon as the next weekend. He'd gotten very little sleep with Mahler in the bush. They had cut through to a place Mahler thought they might find the Jaguar. The work had been hellish. It had rained all day. They found nothing, again. Exhausted, they'd ridden back to the plantation without saying a word to one another. He'd had to come back to the capital, as his job was the only thing paying for their search.

Waiting for Beatrice to show up, Russell was slightly confused about the arrangements. He decided not to take his day pack, as he had no idea where they were going. He had a cold drink at the hotel's bar, nursing it.

He was at the pier waiting for Beatrice at eleven-thirty. As he stood there in his jeans and T-shirt, his sunglasses very dark, he watched a helicopter land on a pad built for the wealthy when they came from the capital to eat lunch at the hotel. A young couple got out of the helicopter with one suitcase and made their way up the steps toward the hotel. The pilot cut the engine. Russell watched the propeller blades slowly twist to a stop.

He wondered about the couple. She was a beautiful blonde, her boyfriend was very dark. He decided for some reason that the boyfriend was a narco-trafficker. There was something about him, something– *the fancy cowboy boots.* That was it. They didn't belong to the elites; at least, the young man didn't, as he was dark-skinned. The young man had fought his way to this hotel through the underworld. The young man made Russell think of his own great-grandfather, who had also been self-made. You got dirty on the way up, it seemed, whether it was selling coffee or selling dope. But everyone on the bottom wanted out. That was the rule. It applied to everyone in every time. Everyone wanted a luxury berth, even if it was on the *Titanic.*

Beatrice was late. Russell was sitting on the dock looking at the blurring horizon when he finally saw a small boat, a Boston whaler, coming towards the hotel. She was alone behind the wheel, in a two-piece suit with an orange sarong. Her hair was wet and the color of honey.

She pulled up to the dock and cut the engine. She moved up to the bow and threw him a rope. He grabbed it and looked at her.

"You have to tie it off. I thought we'd have a drink. I've been for a swim," she said. He did as she asked him, although he wasn't too good at knots. She looked at it as he helped her up from the boat.

"You weren't in the Navy," she said, joking.

"No," he said.

"We can't show any affection here," she said. "So pretend I just kissed you."

117

"All right," he said. She looked at him, then knelt down and re-tied the boat off. He realized he'd been monosyllabic since they'd spoken on the phone. He had been even in the hotel, when they'd been alone.

"I'm sorry. I just—well, it's new to me, the intrigue," he said, watching her work.

"No married women in the repertoire?" she asked. As she knelt, her back to him, he saw the beautiful curve of her ass. He wanted to touch her, to feel her wet hair, but couldn't.

"How are we supposed to act right now?" he said

"Well, not like lovers, that's for sure," she said, standing up. "The place is crawling with my husband's friends."

"How are you going to explain me being here?" he asked.

"You are doing a story on my husband, and wanted to speak to his wife. You called me, and we decided to meet here. I've already told Carlos that. I'm here for the week at the house. We have a house on the lake."

"But I'm not doing a story on your husband," he said. "I've finished it."

"I suggested the idea to him yesterday. He agreed it was a good idea, and said I should call you. He wants to be seen like Al Gore. I'm supposed to be his Tipper," she said.

"So, I'm here to interview you?" he said.

"Yes. And to see the lake house, and the children, and have dinner tonight."

"Is Carlos with you here?"

"He flies in this afternoon. Here, to the helipad; I'm to pick him up."

"What about me?" he asked.

"What about you? You're staying at the hotel. We'll have some friends over to the house tonight. He wanted you to come. . . . It's up to you."

"Just like that," he said.

"Yes. Just like that," she said. "I'll make it work . . .our affair."

118

"Are we going to have an affair?" He looked towards the hotel. Some tourists were coming down the stairs towards the dock. They were middle-aged, their well-pressed clothes giving away their age. They seemed out of sorts, having an argument.

"If you like," she said. "I want to, very much."

"I think you've made me a little crazy," he said. He tried to smile, but didn't know how convincing it was. "But I suppose you've heard that before?"

"How about that drink?" she said, not answering his question. She turned and started up the dock.

They passed the older couple who'd been arguing. The woman, stopping them, asked in English where they could rent a boat. The couple turned out to be English; Beatrice was very kind, and spent several minutes talking with them. She seemed to be happy in the company of her countrymen. They slipped into a working class patois. Russell was left out of the conversation for the most part. At one point she touched his shoulder, as she was pointing out Panajachel to the couple. He realized that she was talking to him, saying something to him that had nothing to do with the couple or with the town. There was something about her touch, reaffirming, the way her hand caressed his arm, her finger tips electric. She was saying, *"We're together; we're together in a way that doesn't need all that talking, does it?"* She looked at him carefully as they were walking up the stairs. The older couple, left behind, were staring out on the lake.

"Are you happy, Russell?" she asked him. "Are you happy you came?"

"Yes, very much," he said. And meant it.

"I'm not going to be easy," she said. "It's very hard for me, too, all this, in case you thought it wasn't, or that I was some kind of bitch on wheels."

"No, of course not," he said. "I understand."

"I'm not that . . . a bitch who sleeps around," she said. He didn't answer. They crossed the patio and went into the hotel's bar, which seemed very dark after their time in the sun.

They went over the ground rules of their affair over lemonade in the bar. Beatrice had studied all the problems, she said. She thought they would be fine if they followed them. He agreed to whatever she said.

She explained that she would never call him at the office. He could call her on her cell phone to make dates. She said that she paid her cell phone bill herself out of the household money, and no one checked it. She gave him the number as they sat there. There were other rules: no signs of affection in public, no matter where they were in the country, because people from all social classes knew her and, of course, her husband. It would never be safe.

He wasn't to get too familiar with the children, as they would start to speak about him, she said.

Russell ordered a beer. The owner of the hotel appeared. It was their first test under fire, as it were. Russell stood up very straight as they shook hands, and tried to look relaxed but seem businesslike. Beatrice spoke to the man in Spanish. The owner glanced at him once after they'd shaken hands. It was a questioning look. Any man seen with her had to suffer that look, Russell supposed. But his story sounded good, and he saw the man's interest stop short of suspicion. The owner had been a school chum of Carlos's. He told Russell to call him directly if he needed anything. The owner asked him to mention the hotel in his article, if he would be so kind. Russell said he would.

"No promises," she said after the owner had gone. "That's another rule."

"About what?" he said, trying to look indifferent for the sake of the other people milling around.

"No promises about what will happen. You understand. . . Nothing can happen. I have children. They need their father. We can't fall in love," she said.

"Have you done this before?" he asked. He was getting a little angry suddenly, listening to her give him rules like a schoolboy. Perhaps it was just the heat and the tension of all the eyes that might get him killed.

"I'm sorry," she said. "I just . . . it's my way. I tend to be analytical in the extreme. It was a problem, the affair in the abstract, like a math problem. I was trained as a mathematician at Oxford."

"Yes, I know," he said. He'd read her official bio more than once since they'd met. She'd gotten a first at Oxford.

"I got a scholarship. I'm not from money, if that's what you were thinking. That Carlos knew me as a child because my father owns Costa Rica or something. We were poor. My mother was a waitress. I am just like those people on the dock. Nothing special about me. I'm working class."

The young couple he'd seen land in the helicopter came down from their room with a beach bag and went by them en route to the pool. The man looked tough. The girl was elegant-looking and long-legged.

"That's what all gangsters want. A model," Beatrice said, looking at them pass.

"How do you know he's a gangster?" he said.

"Just look at him. Isn't it obvious? And she's probably a whore of some kind."

He was surprised by the accusation. The young woman didn't seem like a whore.

"So you aren't wealthy," he said, trying to get back to her life. He was curious.

"God, no. My father was a coal miner. We lived in one of those dreadful row houses in the north before he left us. It was just like D.H. Lawrence wrote about, nothing there had changed for a hundred years. Except that the pit closed down when Maggie Thatcher had at us. My father left us right after that. I grew up with my mom and my adopted grandmother. I have a sister," she said.

"Is she as pretty as you?"

"Absolutely not," Beatrice said, smiling.

"Is she as smart?"

"Oh yes. She's a genius, but she can barely leave the house. She has some kind of disease where she thinks she's left something important behind. Then she gets that and goes out on the porch, and then thinks she needs something else she couldn't possibly do without. It can go on that way for hours."

They finally got up to leave. He didn't feel as if he'd gotten through somehow. He felt as if there was something very big between them that went away only when they were touching.

"You'll need a hat. On the water. I thought we'd go for a ride before I take you to the house. I want you to see it, the house, it's very beautiful. There's a cove nearby . . . we could swim."

"I have one, a hat. But it's awful. I feel stupid in it," he said.

"It's all right; I think you're very handsome, so it doesn't matter, does it?" she said.

"Okay. I'll go get it," he said. He realized they were talking like strangers because they were strangers, for all practical purposes.

"I'll wait," she said.

"Right. I'll be right back then."

She looked at him.

"I'm sorry if I've been a bitch. I didn't want to start that way. Honestly." Her face was so beautiful that for a moment he didn't answer her. It was something about the way her hair had dried and the movement of her exposed, tanned belly as she spoke.

"No, you aren't. Don't say that," he said.

"Go get the hat then," she said.

His room was on the top floor, and he had to negotiate a series of terraces to get there. He made a wrong turn, got lost for a moment, and found himself on an unfamiliar corridor. A maid with her cart passed him; the corridor felt very cool. Below, to his left, was a garden with a parrot cage. The corridor was very clean, and bougainvillea grew up the columns, their orange flowers mixed with white ones.

Russell wondered what would happen to them. He felt a sense of dread as he tried to find the way back to his room. *I'm lost,* he thought. When he did finally find it, he saw Beatrice standing by his door.

Surprised, he walked towards her, thinking that he'd taken too long, or that there was something wrong, that she would have to leave or had come to tell him that they'd better forget it. Drop their affair now, while they still could. He got closer. She was facing the door, knocking; he surprised her. She wheeled around, threw herself into his arms, and kissed him.

He didn't understand. After all the talk of rules and ways of hiding their affair, she was doing just the opposite. He heard her begin to weep. She was holding onto him very very tightly. He tried to get the room key out of his pants pocket, but couldn't at first. He had to pry her hands from around his waist to get to the key. He tried to get her to step away so he could open the door. He finally got her to let him go, and he opened the door. They stepped inside, and she kissed him before he could close the door again.

"I was a bitch to you. I'm so sorry. I'm so sorry," she said.

He closed the door, slamming it, looking down the hallway as he did, terrified that someone had seen them. He pushed her down on the still-unmade bed and lifted up her sarong. It came away in his hands. He peeled her bathing suit down her thighs and put his face in her blond crotch. She was still weeping; he heard the weeping stop, felt her open up, and he made love to her that way—still frightened. He felt that he was finally the master of this catastrophe as she came, her back arched on the rumpled linen.

He knew then that he was the one that would have to make them follow the rules, that she wouldn't be able to, that passion would get the better of her. He felt the milky feel of her, the brush of her thigh, the pulling of his hair, the moaning and rocking as she came again. He was a little shocked by her eagerness as she pulled his pants down and made love to him, looking up at him with her blue eyes full of lust while he looked at the volcanoes, the window wide open, the fishermen gone, just the flat water and the feeling of her mouth on him using quick little strokes, the sound of it. The three volcanoes, each one watching them. Before he climaxed, he realized—in the ecstasy—that it was this thing, this affair, that was the last great jungle in which he could lose himself. This was exactly what he'd been searching for, without realizing it. It was the kind of madness that made him trade stocks until he'd lost everything. He'd wanted to give up his self, the great monolith of his personality; he'd wanted to smash it, to pulverize it and walk away somehow different, or dead.

They both heard the helicopter. He'd fallen asleep. He panicked. For a moment, he couldn't move.

FOURTEEN

He made the mistake of standing up. The helicopter flew low over the lake in front of his window. He knew it must be Carlos. He looked and saw the little Boston Whaler sitting down on the water, looking tiny by the dock. The lake was suddenly whipped up into a green-blue froth. He sat down again immediately.

He was naked. He turned and looked at Beatrice; she was only in her bathing suit top. They'd lost control completely. He didn't understand it. They'd known he was coming.

She reached for him. He could see real terror on her face.

"I told him you were staying here," she said. She wouldn't let go of him. He had to pull her arms from his shoulders. "He's going to find us. He'll shoot us. Oh my God! My kids."

He pulled her arms down and slapped her. He didn't know what else to do. She looked at him a moment, and nodded. Her cheek was bright red where he'd hit her.

"Get dressed," he said. He stood up and pulled the curtain closed. The room was plunged into semi-darkness. His mind was racing for an idea, any idea. Nothing came. They both dressed frantically.

"What's he usually do when he gets here?"

"He calls me. I come and pick him up. He's going to–"

One of the cell phones on the dresser rang. It was hers. They looked at each other. She was wrapping the sarong around her hips. He was pulling his pants on.

"He'll have seen the boat," she said.

"Pick it up and tell him you'll meet him in the bar. Go ahead! Tell him you went for a walk in the garden." She looked at him.

"He'll know something's wrong. *I'm frightened.*"

"Don't be," he said. "Everything's all right. It's going to be fine. He isn't going to find out. He is going to get in the boat with you. Then you are going to take him wherever it is you go." Her phone stopped ringing. "Now call him back."

"Shit. I'm shaking, Russell."

He walked across the room, picked up her phone, and took it to her. She sat down. "Please call him back. If you don't, he might think something is wrong." He held the phone out to her. She took it, finally.

She stood up, went to the curtains and opened them slightly. He walked up behind her and looked down on the heliport. Two Bell helicopters were parked near one another. He saw Carlos Selva on the stairs, heading toward the pool. In full dress uniform, he was talking—briefcase in his hand—to one of his bodyguards. He could see the general's cell phone cradled in his shoulder. Beatrice's phone rang again. She opened it.

"Hello. Darling... Yes... I'm in the garden in the back by the parrots. Yes... I know it's silly, but I like them. No, I'll meet you in the bar. Right now. Yes—No, I wanted to be here when you came. I don't know... I can check. Why don't you? The American. No. Yes, he's here. Yes, right now," she said. He watched her husband move up the stairs, flanked by his two men. He was walking slowly. Russell knew that if he decided to look for her outside, they were going to be caught.

He rushed out of the room and started to run down the corridor. He looked down at his feet; he hadn't put on shoes. He ran, tucking in his shirt. He didn't think that he'd closed the door to the room. Carlos was going to surprise her in the garden; he felt it. It was the way Carlos had looked around

126

as he spoke. It was only natural for a man to do that. He flew down the corridor. *God damn it, all the rules and now this.*

He stopped for moment in the lobby. He was breathing hard and sweating. He wiped his face. He looked for Carlos on the terrace and saw him doing exactly what he'd feared. He waited a moment, pulled his shirttails out again and wiped his face off. He told himself that he had to be calm, that he would walk out the side door and intercept the man.

He was lost. His room was on the other side of the hotel. *I was lost. My room is on the other side of the hotel.* He repeated it again and again as he walked across the lobby and out the door to the garden. He saw Carlos coming down the path towards him. He was alone now.

Russell smiled at Beatrice's husband. Carlos looked at him, nonplussed at first, then smiled back, recognizing him.

"Damn Guatemalans," Russell said. He didn't know why he said it. Pure nerves.

"Mr. Price. I was just asking about you."

"I'm lost. Can you believe it?" he said, and smiled. "I thought my room was this way. But I don't think it is."

"I'm so glad you could come," Carlos said. "Have you seen my wife?"

"Wife? This morning. We had part one of the interview. I'm afraid I was feeling a little under the weather. Damn food here. Your countrymen are always poisoning me. I had to lie down, don't know where she is. She said you were coming by helicopter. Wish I had."

He told himself to shut up. It was difficult; he was trying to bury Carlos with bluster.

"Are you all right?" Selva asked.

"Well, if puking your guts out is all right, then I suppose I'm fine," Russell said.

"I'm so sorry. Can I get you something? I can send one of the men down to the town for you. To the *farmácia.*"

127

"Would you? God! Yes, I was just trying to buy something here, but there's nothing," Russell said.

"Yes. Of course. I can send a doctor too, if you like?" Carlos said.

"Doctor? No. No. Just something that will put a cork in it."

"Of course. Let me call my wife and tell her."

Russell held his stomach. "If you don't mind, I think I could use something right away."

"Of course. I'm sorry. Sit down . . . or go to your room. What's the room number?"

"1211," Russell said.

"1211. I'll have my wife go up and see what they can bring you. Why don't you go to the room, and we'll have some tea sent up. *Yerba Buena* is excellent for the cramps. I'm sure they have it."

He'd come up and stood by Russell, genuinely concerned. Carlos put his briefcase down. They shook hands, then Russell watched him call Beatrice. He asked her to go to room 1211, and told her the American journalist was with him in the lobby and had fallen ill.

Russell could finally breathe. It had worked. Carlos went out to the hotel's entrance where he'd stationed his body-guards.

"He's coming here," she said. Russell walked back into the room. The curtain was pulled open. He pulled the bed cover up and looked at her. "I'm so sorry. I don't know why I came up here. I was afraid you would leave," she said. "I need you so much."

He looked at her. He didn't understand the last two hours, the way they had both flouted the danger, but he knew they had to get through the next thirty minutes. He looked around the room.

128

"Do you understand? I've had no one to talk to, no one, for three years. Do you know what that's like, for people like us?" she said.

"*Beatrice.* He's coming up here, right now. Are you ready for that?" he asked.

"Just tell me you love me."

He looked at her again, in shock. He wanted to open the door to the room, and decided it was best he did. He could see the empty corridor, its brown tile floor gleaming in the sunlight.

"Please tell me you won't stop seeing me," she said, standing behind him.

"I won't stop seeing you. We met and had an interview at the bar. I told him that, just now," he said. He turned around, went to the bed, and sat down facing the hallway.

They didn't say anything. Russell just kept glancing up and looking at the corridor. It seemed like hours before he saw the general and one of his men coming towards them.

"Well, old boy, I've ordered you some Lomotil. I sent one of the men down to *Pana* for some. It's wonderful for the cramps," Carlos said. He crossed the room and kissed his wife.

"What do you think, *Gorda?* Will he live?"

"Amoebas, I suppose," she said. Beatrice's voice was a little distant.

"Yes, I suppose so," Carlos said. "You can take the test. I'll have a kit brought in to you."

"Yes, I know. I've taken it before, unfortunately," Russell said.

"You haven't gone swimming in the lake, have you?" Carlos said, joking. "It's all the shit that gets in. The water looks beautiful, but I'm afraid they've spoilt it for swimming. You'll get amoebas swimming in the lake."

Russell turned on the bed and looked at the two of them standing together. He smiled weakly at them both.

"No, I haven't been swimming," he said.

"Americans are always getting something," Beatrice said. She put her arm around her husband's waist and drew him close to her.

"I'm afraid she's right. It's the curse of the United Fruit Company," the general said.

Beatrice hit Carlos playfully on the shoulder. When she did, Russell knew they'd escaped this time. He looked up at the ceiling, relieved.

They left a short time later. The bodyguard brought him some medicines in a plastic bag. The man seemed suspicious by nature. Russell took the bag, thanking the man profusely, and closed the door. He'd told them that if he felt better later, he would come to their dinner party.

He opened the window. Their little boat was gone. He threw the plastic bag on the bed and went in to shower. He drove back to the capital an hour later.

FIFTEEN

Don Russell?" the woman said. She seemed to know him. An Indian woman was standing at his front door. She was crippled, something terribly wrong with her hip. Her name was Olga Monte de Oro, she told him. She'd grown up with his mother, she said. She had been born on their family's plantation.

He didn't know how she'd heard about him, or gotten his address. He'd come to the door, ready to go to the office, and she'd appeared. She was very dark-skinned, her hair gray. Her shoes were cheap-looking and dirty with mud. He'd noticed her shoes right away.

He didn't know what the woman could possibly want with him. He hadn't recognized his nanny.

"*Sí*," he said. She had that Mayan face, the thrusting jaw. She was ugly, he supposed, looking at her. He felt immediately bad for thinking it. The shoulder a little frightening, the way it sloped to compensate for her bad hip.

The porter had called from below and asked if he could let in a *muchacha*. The word *muchacha* here meant a domestic. He thought one of his colleagues from work, who happened to live nearby, had sent him a message via his maid.

"I'm from *Las Flores*," the woman said. "I knew you when you were a little boy." She thrust a photograph into his hand. He looked at the old photo; it was a picture of his mother as a young girl and an Indian girl, their arms around one another.

131

He took the photograph, not knowing what he should do. He invited the old woman into the apartment. She was carrying a small cardboard box wrapped with dirty-looking twine.

"*Don Russell, no tengo donde irme.*" I don't have anywhere to go, she said. She said it evenly, without emotion, as if all her emotions had been used up and there was nothing left.

"I'm sorry, *señora,* but I—" For some reason, with his mother's photo in his hand, he couldn't lie to her. He'd lied and he'd lied about his family, but he couldn't lie to this woman.

"I breast feed you," she said. "When your mother was sick." She was looking at him hopefully.

He moved away from her. She stepped towards him and knelt down on the floor at his knees.

"I want to go back to the plantation, but your aunt says I can't go," she said, pleading. "Please, *Don* Russell, please take me back. I was born there. I gave you the milk." She held one of her breasts.

He was shocked by her kneeling. He turned the light on in the hallway; his finger had been on the switch. The foyer lit up. He saw the top of her head, the part of her black hair.

"*Señora,* please get up. Please," he said. He bent down and made her get up off the floor. He would never forget her on the floor, in that position. He remembered so well, in the church at Colomba when he was a child. The Indians would sometimes prostrate themselves in front of the altar. It frightened him as a child, and she'd brought it all back. She'd brought back the afternoons coming onto the plantation with his mother. The way the old men would stop, their machetes in their hands, the way they'd doff their caps, the way the children would stop playing as he and his mother rode by, the way the Indian women would bow silently as they carried enormous loads of firewood on their heads, and all of this as they sailed by, he not realizing his mother was a little drunk, and her automatically giving the nod. The nod that said conquest and tradition. The nod that said: This is my land and you will be my people, we are never to touch, but I am the princess and you the subjects. We have a *social and historical contract.* He had understood it all, and he had buried it so deep that he didn't know where it had been until now.

It was the afternoon, with the shadows of clouds and no rain coming, and him thinking only about seeing Beatrice again, when he opened the door to confront this woman and his past, and he didn't want any of it. Nothing.

He wanted to tell her to leave. But he couldn't, because suddenly he realized that the woman and he were connected; that he had a place here, a responsibility to her, whether he liked it or not. He couldn't run away from that. It was his duty to do something for her. He embraced her, and heard her start to sob.

"Olga. Yes, of course I remember. Of course," he said again, holding her. "Of course you can go back."

For a moment he stood looking at her, at her poverty, and her dirty plastic shoes and her helplessness, at her raggedy ignorance and her inability to read, at the ten children she'd had, at the war that had killed half of them, at the husband who had beaten her, at the warm rain that had soaked her as she'd wandered the streets of the capital looking for jobs as a maid, and the rejections she'd gotten because she was crippled. All of it sickened him, making him look at his briefcase by the door and then the phone and the door again as he closed it and led her to the kitchen, her cardboard box in his hand as she talked about his mother. She was home; he could tell it in her voice. This was where she belonged, with him, her voice said.

He turned and wanted to tell her to please stop crying. Instead, he told her that she needed to rest. She looked at him and said, "*Sí, patron.*" The contract that had been lost was found again: the contract that had been written the day his great grandfather and some *pistoleros* cleaned the land and said, "We are the whites, you are the conquered, and we will take care of you." It was a filthy contract, written in Indian blood, and it had been honored for a hundred years–only interrupted by the war. Now this woman had come with her torn end, asking for her meager rights. That the contract had been unfair wasn't the point, he realized. It had been signed, and he had to live up to it for better or worse, because she had nothing else.

He walked silently towards the maid's quarters that he'd never wanted filled. He could have hired a maid, but none had come like this, with the contract and his mother's photo.

He glanced at the photo again. His mother in the photo was maybe ten years old. She had her arm around an Indian girl of the same age. His mother was well-dressed, the other girl was in dirty clothes.

Russell threw Olga's cardboard box on the little bunk bed and looked around the room. Some other maid had left a picture of Jesus Christ on the wall. He'd never taken it down, as he thought it quaint and ridiculous: The bleeding heart of Jesus Christ. He'd come in drunk with friends and shown it to them, and they'd laughed about the saccharine quality of it, with its pretense of authority. He looked at it now, ashamed for laughing, and thought about all the women who had lived in this room and been the conquered. He thought about all the times their names had been called with no love, only with the cold hard reality of their position. How lonely had this room been at midnight for those wretched women?

"I take breakfast early, Olga. And I eat very little. Toast and coffee. You'll find everything in the kitchen," he said quietly in Spanish. "We'll see about you going back as soon as I speak to my aunt. Back home," he said.

"Sí, *Don* Russell," she said. He remembered her then; she'd been so much younger then that he hadn't recognized her. Suddenly he remembered her very well, at the hotel in San Francisco, and the way his mother and she had cried over him.

He handed her the photo and walked out of the room.

Later, he called his aunt. She told him she had no idea how Olga had found him, or what had happened to Olga over the years. She said that during the war one of Olga's children had turned out to be a Communist. Olga and her family had been driven off the plantation by the administrator because of it.

• • •

They'd met in Hangar 28 at Aurora airport. His boss was writing a series of articles on the state of the drug war in Latin America, and he'd moved his office out to the DEA's hangar to be closer to the action.

The hangar had offices on the second floor that looked down on the cavernous ground floor. A DEA pilot had once caught fire by accident on the shop floor when he'd lit a cigarette, forgetting about the bucket of fuel nearby. Someone else from the DEA had jumped from his office during a meeting with Russell, who was then writing the *de rigueur* article on the drug war; they managed to put the man out. Russell remembered now how everyone for a moment had sat frozen and watched the man's jacket go from black to orange. That was Guatemala out of the blue, something like that. The DEA officer broke his leg but managed to put the pilot out, although his hands were left terribly burnt.

The hangar door was partially open; Russell could see the lights from the airfield at night. The airport was busy at this time of night. A commercial jet and two private planes were queued up waiting to take off, out on the tarmac.

They heard the roar of the commercial jet as it started down the runway, the jet's engines pouring out hot air.

"You've been away a lot the last few weeks," Russell's boss said to him. They looked at each other. The good thing about their office was that there was so much extracurricular activity that no one was beyond reproach. It made for a relaxed environment. Everyone seemed to be carrying on a double life of one kind or another. His boss—a drug addict—had his. Now, Russell had Beatrice.

"I know about your girlfriend," his boss added. "I saw the two of you at the Q Bar the other night. So did a lot of people. You're out of your mind, you know that. If her husband finds out, you'll be killed. Normally it wouldn't matter, but in his case, of course, it has to. If he found out, he might hold it against us—this office. You know these Guatemalans, he's liable to kill us *all*. Only natural, don't you think? The cuckold can be a mean race of people," his boss said. "He's killed a lot of people. A couple more wouldn't matter."

"Yes." It was all Russell could say.

"If you promise to leave her alone, I could forget about it. It would have to stop immediately, though; otherwise I'm afraid it will all go off in an email to London. I would hate to lose you. I don't have to tell you that, do I?"

"Yes. Thank you," he said.

"Yes *what,* Price?"

"Yes. I wouldn't want to go home right now. Not if I can be of help." It was the first honest thing he'd said.

"Schmitt was writing an article about General Selva. I want you to finish it. It's to run in next weekend's series on the elections here." Schmitt had been murdered in some kind of whorehouse out on the coast, Russell had heard.

"What kind of article are we talking about?" Russell asked

"Not sure, now. Schmitt didn't like the general. I know that."

"That's it then?" he said. "It's up to me to finish what Schmitt started?"

"*No.* Just cover the general's campaign. Boilerplate stuff. He's not worth dying over. No more mention of his past human rights record. I don't know about you, but I want to leave the country standing up. . . . So what did you decide about her? I like you, Price. You're quiet. And I've always admired that in a journalist. I actually have confidence in you."

His boss looked up from his laptop. For the first time Russell saw the man, and not the over-worked journalist with the drug problem. The man's eyes were jaundiced; he was unshaven, and he was frightened. "I have children. Did you know that? In London, two, a boy and a girl," he said. "That's why I decided to have you cover the general, Price. Everyone else in the office has children. Do you understand? You can refuse, and we can drop it. We'll say that Schmitt died in mysterious circumstances. We'll let the murderers get away. We won't really cover the election, not really, and no one will care anyway, as the general is slated to win. And *really,* who cares about what happens in this backwater? Everyone is interested in Iraq. So what's it going to be? Her or the job?"

"The job," Russell said.

"Are you lying? We can't do both, write about the bloody little man, and have the man covering him playing titties and tummies with his wife. Wouldn't be the right thing, would it?"

"No. Of course not," Russell said.

"Good. Very strange, the power of beautiful women," his boss said. "I've met her, Price. I understand. Extraordinary woman." His boss started to type again, and Russell left.

For some reason, as he left the office, Russell remembered the pilot, the way the flames seemed to possess him like some kind of religious martyr. And really, that man had just been drunk when he lit a cigarette in a hangar where everywhere there were signs that said not to smoke.

Warnings were everywhere, but no one paid any attention to them. He certainly hadn't. And now he too was on fire, albeit a different kind.

He went back to his office and turned on Schmitt's computer. The screen saver came on. Schmitt hadn't bothered with passwords. The computer screen showed a country lane somewhere in Maine, in the fall. There was text written on the pavement in white: "God grant me serenity and allow me to accept the things I cannot change," it read.

His phone rang. It was Mahler, saying that Carl was going to Europe for a few days and was taking the things he'd bought from Russell with him to sell.

"How's it going?" Russell asked. He looked at the beautiful picture on the screen, the fall trees so different than the trees of the jungle.

"We've cleared a hundred square meters, maybe more. I've hired two men to help dig," Mahler said.

"Anything? Anything at all?"

"Not yet," Mahler said. "But I feel we're close."

"Well, I feel like I'm going broke," Russell said

"It would go faster if you were here."

"I've got a job. Remember?"

"Fucking General Selva's wife?" Mahler said. For a moment Russell didn't think he'd heard him correctly.

"What?"

"Her . . . her maid is Carl's maid's sister," Mahler said. "If the servants know, man, it won't be long until Selva knows." Mahler hung up.

SIXTEEN

There was a drought. Every day for weeks now, the sky had stayed viciously clear and blue. Someone at his office said that it was the result of global warming and that Mother Earth, who had been seriously screwed with, was now, finally, getting back at everyone.

It was very hot outside, thirty-five Celsius. Russell and the bellboy walked through the lush grounds of the hotel, the air redolent, the glare at noon unbearable even with sunglasses. Russell was wearing a white cotton suit and blue tie. The bellboy had insisted on coming with him to show him the room, insisted too on carrying his briefcase.

He'd gotten a five-hundred-dollar-a-day suite at the Hotel Santo Domingo in Antigua. Beatrice had come to the hotel for a tennis tournament; she'd called him at his office and pleaded with him to leave work and meet her there. He shouldn't have come, as the well-known hotel was the play-ground of the country's rich, and therefore very dangerous. He'd come anyway, because he couldn't stop himself.

The room was huge, with a view of the hotel's fabulous walled gardens. The bellboy opened up the minibar, then checked the bathroom, flicking on lights. He didn't have to say what was obvious: that the American was here to meet a lover. He'd brought no luggage other than his briefcase. The bellboy asked Russell where he would like him to put the briefcase, as if it mattered.

"I'll take it," he'd said. He gave the boy a huge tip and told him to bring a bucket of ice. The boy came back with two buckets and put them on the dining room table.

"Will there be anything else, sir?"

"No," he said. The bellboy smiled knowingly.

"Enjoy your stay," the bellboy said.

The room was huge. He'd spent too much, but he wanted to impress Beatrice. He wanted her to believe that he could compete with her husband somehow. It was stupid; of course he couldn't. But he needed to try. That's what men do when they love a married woman whose husband is very rich. Russell felt in constant competition with Carlos.

There were several big windows off the main room. Some looked on the quiet manicured patio with its topiary and spilling fountain, pink bougainvillea painting the rough volcanic rock walls beyond. Across from that window was a cavernous bedroom. Out the bedroom's French doors was a small private patio shaded by trees. It was just the kind of room he'd wanted. He was pleased, but uneasy.

We shouldn't have agreed to meet here. I'll have to tell her about her maid. Outside there was a breeze. moving the tops of the trees.

He watched Beatrice approach from the patio. She'd come from the tennis courts. She was wearing a short white tennis dress and white blouse, and carrying her racquet over her shoulder in one of those rakish nylon carry bags. Her blonde hair was pulled back in a ponytail, her face flushed from the tennis. A gardener stared at her, holding his rake. She made all other women in the world seem drab. She hurried across the big open patio that the hotel's restaurant looked out on.

Russell watched her turn her face away from the tables. He wondered how many people eating at the restaurant would recognize her. She was—because of her great beauty—impossible to miss. No other woman carried herself like that. How many would be on their cell phones, making dangerous gossip about the general's wife? He hadn't bargained on being frightened every time they met.

De La Madrid's words from an e-mail came back to him as he watched her: *Thank you for the article. We've put the general on the run. Everything's getting better. I look forward to discussing the campaign with you again. We should have lunch and talk about the privatization of the phone company. I'm convinced that privatization is the way to go and I should get your thoughts on how it might best be done, one economist to another.*

When she knocked, it dawned on him that it was only the third time he'd been alone with her. It seemed he'd known her much longer. It had, in fact, only been a few weeks. They didn't speak; they kissed. Maybe it was all the fear and the tension, but he felt that he'd never been more excited or more in need of a woman's touch. *You want to possess Beatrice.* She'd been on his mind constantly since the moment he'd left her at the lake.

He held her tightly, felt her sweaty skin slip to the grab of his hands. He kissed her neck and tasted salt. He started to speak, but she didn't let him. She covered his mouth with a kiss. He saw her tennis racket's black case drop at her feet. He kicked it away from her, and reached under her blouse.

She seemed to come completely unglued, as if she'd not been fondled or kissed in years. As if he were shocking her body with his hand. He felt her ass move herky-jerky under his palm.

"I thought about you all last night," she whispered. There were noises outside the door. Men's husky voices. "I kept waking up and thinking how much I needed you." He felt her kissing his hand as he looked into the hotel room. He stopped for a second. He heard the voices pass in the corridor outside. She dropped to her knees and undid his pants. He heard the jingle of his belt buckle. "I dreamt I'd been doing this to you." He felt his pants come down, the awkwardness of it. Her hand on him there suddenly.

"Are you afraid of him? Afraid it's Carlos?" she asked, looking up at him, her face still flushed. She pulled her blouse off and looked at him, her expression somehow managing to be angelic, her eyes two jolts of blue. She seemed so out of place here in the tropics, her white skin, her English girl's voice. She began to fondle him as he listened to the voices of the men outside the door. He looked down and watched her. It was like a dream, better than a dream, but with the extra intensity of a dream. She stroked him. He became erect. He heard her laugh and then the sound of that kind of lovemaking. He wanted to stop her and kiss her, but he didn't. The voices outside got louder, very masculine voices coming back towards them. Suddenly laughing too, then they stopped, and it was very quiet again.

He suddenly felt the heat and the country in the room. *No rain,* his mind said. He'd been covering the drought that week in the Petén. He closed his eyes and saw the empty roadway in the jungle, the broken corn withered and blown down.

"Oh god, fuck." He said it without thinking. She began to move his hips with her hands. The word *lost* came to him, with the vision of the road in the jungle as he watched Beatrice's face. She stopped, looked up at him, and smiled. There was something so extremely intimate about the way she was looking at him. He was embarrassed. It was as if she weren't the woman he thought she was. She was losing herself too, he realized. She was losing herself in the sex and the fear of what they were doing.

"Are you frightened?" she asked again. She had a look, happy, excited too. He was sweating now. He could feel the sweat trickling down his armpits. (He'd forgotten to have the bellboy turn on the air conditioning.) The men outside in the corridor started to move away from the door. He heard a cell phone ring and someone out there answer. Who were they?

"Are you?" she asked. He couldn't speak. "I love to see you like this," she said. "I do, but I could stop if you're afraid." She was teasing him, he realized.

"No," he managed to say. He tried not to sound stupid. But it sounded stupid, as if he were a high school boy. He was too excited to joke. He just wanted her to keep doing it, and he wanted to watch her do it.

"No what?" she said, her voice garbled.

"No…I'm not frightened," he said, desperate for her to go on. They both started to laugh. She began again. He wondered what the hell he'd gotten himself into, but he couldn't stop or think. Nothing about her let him think straight, nothing. The way she made love, the way she looked, the way she moved. She had a regal, efficient, animal quality. The way she spoke English. The way she called him and the way she sounded on the phone when she called him. It felt as if his erection started all the way back in the middle of his head.

He looked down at her. Female, crystalline pure, somehow all pure blonde power refined down to this girl/woman thing giving him a blowjob on the floor of this hotel room at three in the afternoon in an antique city.

He wanted to come now, but didn't want to come. Each time they met he was lost in a slightly new way. He'd never been lost psychologically like this, unbalanced, and it was getting worse. *God I want to come.* He was unable to see things the way they should be seen, he knew that. He was on this boat moving away from the dock of rationality, and he was glad of it. *I've always been in control. I'd come to Guatemala to lose myself in that detached way, but I'd stayed in control all the while. Until now. I was the most in-control person you could imagine. I want to come.* But she'd made him *cede* control.

Even today. He'd left work. He'd driven to Antigua when he knew he shouldn't have. He'd called her cell phone to see if she'd arrived at the hotel. He'd spoken to her on the tennis court. All these things he knew he shouldn't do, but did anyway. Then he was leaning against the wall on the two lane jungle/sex road, trying to hold back from giving longer thrusts in the warm room. Her mouth warm. She stopped and stroked him.

"I'm going to come," he said. *Please.* Did she ask him if he was afraid again? He started to shudder, the climax starting from the middle of his head going down his throat, down to his navel, his hips. He heard himself cry out. Her blue eyes looked up at him, bemused. The sudden silence of the darkened room in the aftermath of sexual gratification, their hands clutching each other. He didn't even realize he'd been holding her hand so tightly until he finally let it go. He'd gone somewhere very far away and come back. She had possessed him completely. She owned him. She wiped her face, grinning at him.

"He may kill us both," she said. "We can't really be safe. That's what I've decided. We can't be. He knows too many people. Where could we really go? I don't care—"

She was right, of course. Carlos would find out. How could he not find out? "Make love to me," she said. And he *would* kill them, he decided, falling down beside her. He had never felt so free as at that moment, holding her, feeling her body as he laid her down on the carpet and moved her legs apart, pulling her panties down, kissing her there, feeling the sun between her legs.

"I didn't care, darling," she said. "I don't care anymore. I don't care." She picked up her hips and pushed.

144

He'd told the desk clerk that he would bring his passport down later. Of course he couldn't, he thought, picking up his tie. Why should he cooperate with any of the systems? He felt outside all systems now. He had to protect them.

They were getting dressed. Beatrice was in the bathroom, the door open. He felt strangely alive, as if he could walk through walls. She'd given him a kind of bizarre strength. He decided, walking to the mirror, that he would find the Red Jaguar and take her away from Carlos. He could do it. He would find the Red Jaguar if it killed him. He had to, now. He had to have money to get her away from this place.

"He bought it for me," she said, stepping out of the bathroom. "I own it. The club." Her hair was wet. It had turned honey-colored again.

He wanted to know. He wanted to know why her husband would let her carry on the way she did, so he'd asked her.

"Yes, but I still don't understand. Doesn't he mind you being there?"

"Why do you have to understand?" she said. "It's between him and me." She said it in that very proper-sounding English manner/tone she could muster, which could freeze boiling water. She was just in her bra. She leaned forward and pulled on her panties, moving her hips.

He reached out and touched her. She was warm to the touch. The warm shower he thought. It was a lovely feeling, her skin warm and clean and red from the tennis-lesson sun. Did she know what she'd done to him? She'd collapsed any will he had to stay away from her.

He watched her dress as he stood, tying his tie standing in front of a big mirror. He saw behind her the trees outside, gathering themselves in the patio and letting themselves go in the breeze, the way she had when they made love. A hungry, not-much-time lovemaking at first. Afterwards, they'd

145

ordered room service, eaten, then they'd started out again.
This time she was desperately slow. She told him she wanted
to see how long they could make love before they had a
climax. They would stop and talk, or just stare at each other.
It was harder for him; he had to let her talk him away from
that moment, and she had. Until finally—in a twisting of sheets
and strange music from the little clock radio—he'd reached a
place he'd never ever been. And it had changed him. He
wasn't afraid of anything or anyone now.

"I wanted to disappear," she said, looking at him as he came.

He started to wonder about her. She suddenly had a strange
angry vacant pathetic look in her beautiful eyes. She's a sex
fiend, he thought. *That's it. The woman I'm in love with is a sex
fiend. Okay. Fine.* He remembered the Hemingway character
who said there wasn't an answer for everything. There was
no answer for Beatrice. There was no answer for most things,
he thought, when you really got down to it.

"I want to be like this forever. No London. No Guatemala.
No anything. No anything but this. Right now. Nothing," she
said. "Just making love."

He could see her in the mirror. Her back was still wet. She'd
come and put her arms around him as he tied his tie.

"Are you in love with him?" he asked

"Why?" she said. She let go of him.

He had replayed the lovemaking. He wanted to pin her
down. He wanted to get to who she was. Mother? Lover? Sex
fiend? Oxford graduate? Stripper? Who the fuck was she?
He wanted to stop the manic driving passion that had gripped
him since the moment he'd met her, even slow it down for a
minute. He realized she'd been pushing him back from really
knowing her. Every time he was on the verge of getting a
glimpse, she would push him back from the door. Only when
they were making love did she stop defending.

Beatrice, that country, there behind the blue eyes, the country that was youthful, but distant. He wanted in. Like Cortez, he wanted to steal it all, take everything she had. Sex only the tool of his colonization.

"Because. I don't know. Maybe I'm just trying to get my bearings. You know… in this Beatrice country I've parachuted into. I haven't much to go on. You are good in bed. You are a beautiful woman. You're from England. You went to Oxford on a scholarship. You stripped for a living because you didn't want to become an investment banker. You married this big shot. You came here to the jungle. Now you're fucking my brains out in this hotel room. I'm trying to catch up, that's all," he said.

"You have me. You have this afternoon to go on," she said. "You can start there."

"Does that mean I'm a fuck toy? Is that the answer? I don't mind. I just want to know, as I believe I'm risking my life."

She looked at him. He hadn't meant to joke like that; it had slipped out. But they both knew it was true. They were risking their lives. "Besides, isn't that what someone does who's in love, get to know the beloved?" he added quickly. "I want to know *you*. Why won't you talk to me about yourself without getting angry?"

"You don't like Carlos. I can tell. You should like him. He's a good man," she said, ignoring his questions, turning away from him. She went and picked up her Nikes by the bathroom door. "And he loves me." She sat on the bed and put on her shoes, looking like a teenager. Moving her hands quickly. Her shoes looked brand new.

"I was frightened by what you did on Saturday, at the lake. And now today, when you called me at the office," he said. "It was so . . . I don't know, I didn't know what to make of it. I don't know what to make of *you*."

147

She'd ignored what she'd done at the lake. She hadn't spoken of it again.

"You made rules and then you proceeded to break them right away. You broke them again today, this morning, when you called me at work from your house. We were supposed to meet at my apartment on Friday. That's how we'd left it, remember?"

"The rules won't save us," she said. "Nothing will keep us safe. Do you understand? This is doomed. It's a small country. You have to accept that. Anyway, I don't care if we're caught. I need you." She hadn't gotten up off the bed.

"The fact is we barely know each other," he said.

"You know that's not true." Her eyes searched his. "Not true. You. . . . We know each other, people like us. The moment we saw each other, you know that's the truth. . . . The moment I saw you with that book. I knew we were alike."

He thought for a moment about what Katherine had said about *Nineteen Eighty-Four,* and about Orwell. They had discussed Orwell on the way down from the city that day. Were *they*–he and Beatrice–Winston and Julia from *1984?* Was Guatemala's New World Order–its *maquiladora,* its uncontrolled diesel spew, its secret policemen–the future? Was *that* waiting for everyone now? Hadn't Winston, in fact, been a journalist? Was he, Russell, now part of the memory hole and the newspeak? Of course not, he told himself. How could he be? He was fighting *for* something now. It was why he'd agreed to support De La Madrid. And he was also going to steal a treasure, which might not be morally right. What was he exactly? Adventurer? Journalist? Fuck toy?

He was all those things. How could anyone be only *one* thing in life?

"I want you to leave Carlos," he said. He'd finished combing his hair, and he went to the chair in the other room and picked up his cell phone.

"I can't," she said.

He left a few minutes later. On the way back to the city, he knew he was being followed. It was a white Toyota with two men in it. He was sure of it.

SEVENTEEN

He'd agreed to meet Katherine at a tapas bar in the *zona viva*. She'd called him several times since she'd come back from Chicago; seeing her number, he hadn't picked up. He'd been avoiding her. She'd called him that morning at work and he'd answered without looking to see who it was.

"I have to see you," she'd said. "Please."

"All right," he'd said.

The few tables on the front porch of the restaurant/bar in the *zona viva* were packed, but Russell knew the owner and had called ahead for a table. Not seeing Katherine, he sat at a table in the corner near the entrance and ordered a glass of wine. Right away young boys—glue sniffers—descended on him, selling roses. The children leaned over the low railing of the restaurant's deck, the kids' pale faces disturbing. Russell bought some flowers and laid them on the table. He doubted the boys would ever learn to read, but they would hear about Harry Potter and dream of other children's lives.

Two boys stared at him. He gave them a ten Q note, hoping they would leave him alone. One of the boys grabbed it before the other could. The smaller boy with no T shirt, just an open wool jacket, stared at Russell for a moment, stunned at the size of the bill, then turned to grab it away from his friend. The boy with the money was already halfway across the empty street by the time the other one realized what had happened.

The running boy dropped his roses as he made for an alley, the scattered red flowers ominous and beautiful in the street light.

"You haven't returned my calls," Katherine said, sitting down.

"I'm sorry," he said. She looked at him for a moment. The waiter, who knew Russell as a heavy tipper, was there in a flash, his starched white apron food-splattered.

"What will you have?" the waiter asked.

"A glass of wine," Katherine said.

"The Chilean for the young lady," Russell said. He took a sip of his drink.

The street was quiet now. It was a time of night he liked. During the day he was nervous, waiting for Carlos's men to pick him up from his office or wherever he ate lunch, and kill him without saying a word. He was being followed everywhere now. He wondered if he would be brave when the time came, or if he'd spill his guts and cry and carry on like a coward. He wasn't sure he could be brave after a beating.

"How about the shrimp? They're good here," he suggested.

"I'm not hungry," she said. She was dressed nicely, and he wondered where she'd come from. A white blouse and black skirt. Her hair glistened in the harsh light from inside the restaurant. The waiter left them.

"Carlos will kill you. You know that. I wouldn't like that," she said.

"I'll get a better gun," he joked.

"Don't be a fool," Katherine said.

The waiter brought her drink. Suddenly Russell was hungry; he'd had nothing to eat since lunch and suddenly he was hungry. He ordered a plate of shrimp and a plate of Serrano ham and Manchego, and another glass of wine for himself.

"I'm waiting for the click. Remember Paul Newman in *Cat On A Hot Tin Roof?* Newman's character was right when he said there's a click, and then you feel better," he said. "It takes me three drinks. Just like in the movie."

"She's just using you. I've heard stories about her. She's crazy. The drugs she took in London. She's not all there, Russell," Katherine said.

The waiter brought their food. A car came slowly down the street. Russell turned to look at it. It was a green Chevy Suburban, its windows tinted dark. The passenger's window cracked open a bit as it drove by. Russell felt his heart rate jump. He touched his hand to his chin, feeling the stubble of his beard.

"I'm aware of her reputation," he said. "It doesn't really matter to me."

"Why were you so mean to me?" she asked. He hadn't expected that question. "That night. Why didn't you just come out and say what you wanted from me?"

"I'm sorry," he said, and meant it.

"You're sorry?"

"Yes. I am, believe it or not. I apologize."

"You're a prick," she said. She looked away for a moment. The other tables on the little porch were empty now. Russell didn't answer. "I think you're crazy. Why are you doing this?"

"Look. I don't know what good this is going to do. I said I was sorry." He started to get up.

"Sit down, Russell." She took his hand. "Please."

He glanced inside. There were a few people at the bar, three men and their girlfriends. The women were talking together. One of them glanced outside at them. He wanted to go, but he told himself he owed Katherine this for what he'd made her do that night at the Q Bar. The fact was he was ashamed of himself, deeply ashamed of the way he'd treated her.

"All right," he said, and sat down.

"I'm in love with you," she said. "And I'm worried about you. What you're doing."

"Don't be. I know what I'm doing. I'm the last person in the world you want to fall in love with. You said so yourself once. I'm a prick. Remember? A capitalist free trader."

"*Do* you know what you're doing?" she asked.

"Yes. It's all under control. We're having a quiet affair in Central America."

"You think so? I saw you at the hotel the other day in Antigua. I was in the restaurant with the general. *She* had lunch with us."

"You're lying," he said, shocked. "Carlos was in Honduras that day." The idea that Beatrice would lie to him had never crossed his mind.

"You met her there at the Santo Domingo, didn't you?"

"Yes. If you have to know. But I'm an adult, and I didn't. . ."

"Stop it! Don't you see, that woman's *crazy*. He was there. *Carlos.* We had a meeting. She got up from the table and made some lame excuse about a tennis game. I knew right away where she was going. I knew you must be there waiting for her," Katherine said.

"I don't see what business that is of yours," he said defensively.

"I'm making it my business. I don't want anything to happen to you," she said. "You have to stop this. Do you want me to beg you?"

"Nothing is going to happen to me." He picked up his drink and drained it. He reached for his cigarettes, pulled them out, and lit one. She watched him light it. He felt the third drink's effect, but it didn't stop his heart from racing now that he knew Beatrice had lied to him.

"I didn't know you smoked," she said.

"Listen. I've been thinking, my mother's place. The place on the coast. Maybe you could go build some houses there."

"Don't change the subject. Why do you want to die?"

"I don't," he smiled, trying to put her off.

The shrimp came, a huge platter. He wasn't hungry any-more. He put out his cigarette, and picked up a shrimp, and put it on his plate. He could feel her watching him. Katherine ordered another drink, and the waiter left.

"You must want to die . . . or is it because she's so beautiful? Is that it? Is that what you want? Is it because I'm not?"

He put down his fork. She had a pained expression on her face, on the verge of tears, her narrow face cut by the shadows of the candlelight mixing with the shallow wan lights of the street. He hadn't believed her when she said she was in love with him. He'd heard that before from women who just felt bad that they'd lost out to someone else. But suddenly, looking at her, he thought it might be true. She seemed changed.

"I don't fall in love every day," she said.

"I'm sorry," he said. "These things, they're not reasonable. You know that. Attractions are not predictable." He didn't know what to say.

"Okay. But I can't stand the thought of what you're doing. Why don't you help me with that?"

He picked up his fork, stabbed a piece of cheese, put it on some bread, and put it in his mouth. He wanted to go home. He didn't want to hear any more questions he couldn't answer. He didn't have any answers for her. He knew now he was going to leave the paper and search for the Jaguar. And when he found it, he would take Beatrice and her children away to Europe or America. He wanted to marry Beatrice and make her his wife.

"Waiter!" She ordered another drink by holding up her glass. The waiter inside nodded. He'd been leaning against the bar, relaxing. Russell watched him move behind the bar, grab a bottle of red wine, and come out to them.

"You've gone crazy. You didn't strike me as the crazy type," she said. "I know a lot of gringos come here and go crazy. Let go, I guess you'd call it. Let go of their self-respect, but I didn't think you were the type. "

"All right. You're hurt. I understand that." He decided he wouldn't get up and leave no matter what she said. Maybe she was right. Maybe he was losing himself. Was that it? Was he losing his mind? Did he want to die?

The waiter filled their glasses. He noticed the look on their faces and asked if everything was all right.

"No, it isn't. The *Americano* is crazy," Katherine said. The waiter looked at Russell and smiled.

"He's fucking someone's wife, and they will probably kill him," Katherine said in Spanish. The waiter, trapped now by their argument, didn't know what to say. It wasn't funny anymore.

"I think we'll have the bill," Russell said.

"Which one?" Katherine said. "This one? You mean mine or his? I'm not finished yet," she said. "I'm going to lose my self-respect, too. Maybe that's what you like? Or maybe you just want to fuck me in the ass, or put a gun to my head while we do it. Is it danger you're after? Is that all it is? I can do that too. If that's what you want. Is that what you want?"

"I think we should go," he said, shocked. "I think you've had enough to drink."

"No!" she said. "No, I don't think we should go. I think you should explain why I have to fall in love with a worthless shit like you. Can you?" She started to cry.

Russell almost didn't see the green Suburban stop and discharge a short Indian man, very young and natty-looking, wearing a gunman's vest. The man walked toward them, then past them and into the bar, his right hand holding a pistol.

Russell watched as he approached one of the men at the bar. He put the pistol right to the back of the man's head and fired. The man's skull seemed to come apart. And then the gunman turned and jogged past them, not looking at them.

Katherine had stopped crying and stared, as Russell had, as the Suburban pulled away from the curb. All they heard then was the screaming behind them in the bar. Just one woman, framed in the window, screaming at the top of her lungs.

They got a cab down the street in front of the Camino Real before the police came. Katherine hadn't spoken since the moment the shot was fired. Even in the cab, when he was asking her the exact address of her place, she didn't answer him. So they'd gone to his place instead.

He'd put her in the guest bedroom, but in the middle of the night she came into his room and asked if she could get in bed with him, because she was scared. He said that she could.

She slipped into his bed and put her arms around him. He liked it. He liked her, and he wondered why he couldn't let Beatrice go. Was it, he wondered as he held Katherine, the fact that Beatrice was so beautiful? Was that *all* it was? Or was it that he was stealing Beatrice from someone else, someone he'd been jealous of? He wasn't sure anymore. Or had he simply come back to this country to die? Why else had he come back here after all those years?

He'd never really asked himself that question before. What possible reason had he to come back? He felt Katherine's arms around him, and she kissed the side of his neck, touched his stomach. She tried to kiss his mouth. He didn't let her at first, not wanting any more trouble. And then he did, because he wanted to, and she wanted to. They made love tenderly, like young kids, but he didn't love her. He knew that.

EIGHTEEN

"Carl hasn't sent me the money," Russell said.

"He will," Mahler said. "It takes time to sell these things."

"I'm quitting the newspaper. I'm going to work for De La Madrid's campaign full-time," Russell said.

"Why would you do that?" Mahler said. "He's going to lose. Any fool can see that."

There was heavy static on the line. Russell could barely hear Mahler, who'd called from *Tres Rios* to ask for more money.

"Why the fuck should you care? You told me you don't give a shit about politics," Russell said.

"I don't," Mahler said. "That's true."

The fact was, Russell was going to be fired. His boss, having discovered that Russell had lied about giving up Beatrice, had told London about their affair. It was only a matter of time, he knew, before he would be either sent back to New York or London or fired altogether. He didn't intend to leave Guatemala without Beatrice. He was in love, and it was impossible to think of leaving without her.

He knew that in order to have her he would need a great deal of money. He had to be able to offer her something better than what she had here. He had to be able to offer her a fine place for her children and a future worth having. If he had money, he could ask her to leave Carlos; without it, how could he? He was counting on finding the Red Jaguar now, not for the thrill of the search, but as a way of having Beatrice.

157

"Tell that little motherfucker I need ten thousand dollars, and soon," Russell said. "I owe that Frenchman another payment."

"All right," Mahler said. "I'll tell him."

"I'm not joking, Gustav." He felt a new urgency, a violent need for money. He had never felt like this before. He knew he was capable of anything. He felt himself going over the edge.

"All right, I'll tell him," Mahler said again.

"He's got the fucking snake; I want my money."

Mahler didn't answer him this time. There was just the static of their phone connection.

"We need food, and I have to pay these men I've hired," Mahler said after a moment.

"How much more have you cleared?" Russell asked.

"Another two hundred square meters. Maybe a little bit more. It's been raining so hard, it makes it difficult."

Russell calculated that they'd cleared almost a football field now, and they'd found nothing. He'd tapped out his credit cards and had no idea where he was going to get more cash to live on, much less give to Mahler.

"Do we have anything but a hole in the jungle? Have you any more reason to believe the fucking thing is actually *in there?*"

"You have to have faith," Mahler said.

"Faith costs money, *amigo*. So far, we're working on a very expensive soccer field."

"The American girl has come with her students. They're building houses," Mahler said.

"I know that. I said she could come," Russell said.

"The students are a nuisance. They ask a lot of questions," Mahler said. "About what we're doing out there, why I come and go."

"Tough shit. She's my friend and I own the place."

"Someone might talk. That would be very bad if others were to start looking, too. . . . If. . . ."

They lost their cell connection. Russell held the phone for a moment and then angrily threw it down on the car seat next to him.

"Talk about *what?* Our soccer field?" he said aloud to himself. He was angry because he had to make the Frenchman a payment the following week, and he didn't have it. He was angry because Carlos was undoubtedly going to win the election and take the country further down a financial rat hole. He was angry because he was sure that right-thinking people could, at the very least, prop the country up and keep it from becoming another Argentina.

He parked his car in front of Jake's, one of Guatemala City's trendy new restaurants. A white-jacketed valet gave him a ticket, then jumped into the driver's seat and pulled away. The restaurant had been built in one of General Ubico's palatial homes—in his day, Ubico had been the United Fruit Company's man. The United Fruit Company's lawyers happened to be Allen and John Foster Dulles, who also just happened to head the CIA and the State Department at that time. The line between the United Fruit Company and the government of the United States of America became very blurred.

The house was all green marble and high ceilings; Russell remembered the house from childhood. He remembered coming here for parties with his mother.

He walked through the restaurant's garden and looked for Carlos. Selva had called him at the paper and said that he thought they should meet. He told Russell he wanted to outline his economic plan for the country. Afraid not to, Russell had agreed to have lunch with him. What else could he have done, he'd thought when he'd put down the phone.

Carlos was sitting in a beautiful room off the garden. A waiter led Russell to the table. Unlike in the States, the smoking section had the best tables, as everyone here smoked. The windows onto the garden were wide open, offering a view of the considerable rose garden, from which the country had been ruled during Ubico's time.

The sky was parched blue, no clouds yet. It was hard to believe it was raining at *Tres Rios,* Russell thought. It was very hot. Several ceiling fans turned the hot air, not doing much good.

Carlos, in uniform, stood up. They shook hands. There was a white table cloth and flowers. It was all very civilized, Russell thought as he sat down. *Did he know?* Was this meeting about Beatrice? Did Carlos invite him here to tell him he was a dead man?

Carlos took off his coat and laid it on the chair next to him. They talked about the weather for a moment. The heat was truly stifling. The marble floors seemed to radiate it.

"Have you gotten used to it? Our weather?" Carlos asked, sitting back down.

"Not really," Russell said. "It's so different than the winters back home."

"Yes, very. I went to school in New York. In the Sixties," Carlos said.

"I know," Russell said. He'd read everything he could about Carlos's career.

"Of course. You've been doing research on me."

"Columbia University, a degree in political science. Graduated 1983, came back here and entered the military academy," Russell said.

"It was difficult for me to come back. Most of my fellow officers had gone straight through, but the Americans wanted a different kind of army. They wanted people who had studied abroad."

"You graduated with honors and then went to the School of the Americas for further training. Twelve months. Then some more at the US Army's jungle warfare school in Panama. You came home, then went to some kind of war college in Italy. The war broke out here before you could finish, and you came home again. They sent you into the field as a second lieutenant," Russell said.

"Very good. Yes. I wanted to finish, and I didn't want to leave Italy to go to war in Central America." Carlos smiled. "I had a girlfriend in Italy, and didn't want to get my balls shot off. If you'd have seen her, you would understand."

"I can't blame you. It's better with balls," Russell said. The waiter appeared. They hadn't had a chance to look at the menu.

Carlos ordered a steak. Russell took a moment to peruse the menu, then ordered a salad.

"Are you a vegetarian? Your generation seems to have taken it up. My wife is. It's excruciating watching her eat sometimes. What she calls eating, anyway."

He'd thought it would be hard hearing Carlos talk about Beatrice, but it wasn't, surprisingly; it was almost a relief.

"No, not really. I'm just not very hungry. I can never eat when it's like this. The heat puts me off."

"Your mother was a Guatemalan," Carlos said. Russell looked up, surprised. He knew he shouldn't have been, but he felt naked nonetheless, as if the General had called him a name. He didn't understand this feeling of guilt about his mother.

"Yes," Russell said. He wanted to look away.

"I knew her," Carlos said. "She was very beautiful. You come from a famous family. Why didn't you mention it when we first met?"

"Is it really important?"

161

"Of course it is. Everything is different when you're one of us. You know that." He looked at Russell, and they made eye contact. The general took a piece of bread out of the basket in front of them.

There it was. A simple statement. He had been trying to run away from the truth, and the general had simply stated the obvious.

"Did you know your mother was my sister's best friend?" Selva said.

"Look, I don't care," Russell said.

Carlos looked at him and continued buttering his bread. He did it carefully and accurately, the butter very soft in the heat, the ice under it melting away quickly.

"I've been told by my sister to look out for you," Carlos said, ignoring his rudeness. "This is off the record and has absolutely nothing to do with the article I want you to write or with anything else. I made my sister a promise that I would look after you. It can be dangerous for journalists here. You won't have to worry now."

"It won't influence what I write," he said quickly.

"I don't expect it to."

The two men looked at each other again. There was something else. Russell tried to see it in the general's dark eyes, in his perfectly ironed white shirt, in the black military tie.

"Your aunt and my sister are still close, the three of them grew up together. But you must know that. Your aunt Carmen is very hurt that you haven't gone to visit her more often," Carlos said. "My sister told me to tell you that."

Russell didn't know what to say. This was the last thing he'd expected from Selva. He picked up his ice water and drained it, then caught a waiter and ordered a glass of white wine. He needed a drink. Were they to be *friends* because of his mother?

"All right, I'll go see my aunt," Russell said.

"Why do you run away from your blood family?" Carlos looked at him.

It was an expression he'd never seen on the general's face before. It was truly the expression of a man who didn't understand. Family, to Latins, was *everything*. The country itself was a kind of family to them. He tried to find his hate for Carlos, but it was gone. It wasn't there. He reminded himself that he wanted to steal the man's wife, and it wasn't there even then.

"My mother died when I was very young," he said. "After she died, I couldn't bring myself to come here. Not for a long time. I held it against the place. Can you understand that?"

"You are part of this country. Your great grandfather owned most of the *Costa Sur*. He pioneered the coffee business. These are things that you can't escape. You're a Guatemalan by birthright. Your cousin was president of the country during the war. You're one of us," Selva said.

"Okay," Russell said. "Okay." He put his hands up, sat back in the chair and smiled. It was a relief to hear it. *He was one of them. Okay,* he thought. He gave up.

"I told my sister I would invite you to Tilapa for *Semana Santa*. You must come. Everyone is going to be there," Selva said. "Your aunt is coming, too. You remember Tilapa, don't you? It hasn't really changed."

"Yes, I remember it," he said.

"I bought your mother's house there," Carlos said. "Your mother had wonderful taste."

They had lunch. They talked about the coffee crisis and the balance of payments issue. Since September 11, the U.S. had blocked cash transmittals from illegal Guatemalan immigrants working in the States, as part of the crackdown on wire transfers. The illegals in the States didn't have social security

163

numbers, and could no longer easily wire money back to their families in Guatemala. Those dollars, over the years, had grown into a very important source of foreign exchange. They both agreed the Americans had to come up with a solution, that it was only making matters worse.

"I suggest you go to Washington and tell them to back off on this. They'll have to allow illegals without social security numbers to wire money," Russell said. "It's imperative." He found himself more and more stepping into the role of adviser instead of dispassionate journalist. He saw the general was listening to him carefully.

"And the privatization of the telephone company?" Selva asked.

"You have to do it. You should do it with the electric company too," he said. "It will create more jobs in the long run. And it will stop the corruption and lack of productivity."

"It's not a popular idea," Selva said. "The unions don't want it."

"Of course it isn't. Half the journalists in the country have been on the telephone company's payroll. Why would they want to see it privatized? The company is a den of thieves. It needs to be cleaned up."

"Antonio can't win," Selva said, changing the subject.

"I know that," Russell said.

"There is a rumor that you are going to go work for him."

"I am," he said. "I'm quitting the paper . . . after I finish your profile piece."

"Why don't you come work for me?"

"Because I don't support your economic policies," he said. "There's something I have to ask you. In your capacity as head of Guatemalan intelligence services. For the record, and for the article."

"All right," Carlos said.

"Am I being followed?"

"I can't answer that on the record," Selva said.

"Can you answer it off the record?" He wanted to say, as a favor, but stopped himself.

"No, because then you would be in danger. And I would have an angry sister. And I can't have that."

"I see."

"I knew you would. I told you it's a dangerous country for journalists," Carlos said. "Will you come to Tilapa? We would love to have you."

"I've been very busy. I don't know."

"You don't want to hurt your aunt. I told her you would come. It doesn't matter in the least that you'll be working for Antonio, if that's what you're worried about. Your aunt is supporting him too, for God's sake! She's practically a Communist," Carlos said, and laughed.

They drank port after the meal. It had gotten cloudy; the garden, which had been bathed in blazing light, its flowers beautiful in full sun, was now quieter. The corners of the big garden had become shaded. The waiters started to close the windows in anticipation of the rain.

They finished their drinks and left together. Carlos stood up and put on his hat and coat. He caught everyone's attention as they left. He was going to be president; it was on everyone's face. He had great power as chief of the intelligence services, but he would have even more soon. People looked at Russell differently too, as if he were a rock star.

Two bodyguards in mufti were waiting for the general in the garden. They had been there all along, watching over them unseen. They had been trained by the Americans, and were much more professional than the run-of-the-mill type. One was an American, probably an active duty Ranger or Delta Force soldier. The embassy didn't want to lose their man before the election, Russell imagined. It was a clear sign the Americans were supporting Carlos.

165

They walked together out to the patio, the bodyguards trailing after them. Russell was a little high from the wine and the port. Carlos was talking about Ubico. He had met him at Russell's grandfather's plantation as a child, he said.

"Ubico liked to dress like those soldiers in a Gilbert and Sullivan musical," Carlos said. They stopped at the fountain, the bodyguards in front of them and to the side. The American looked at Russell, then looked quickly away. Carlos had led him toward the fountain. It was a large one, and it was making a pleasant noise.

"I want to trade you something. Can we do that? Off the record?" Carlos put his well-shined shoe on the edge of the stone fountain and lit a cigarette. "Maybe you'll understand the importance of family then, and we can be friends." He inhaled and threw the spent match in the water.

"What is it I have that you want?" Russell asked.

"I want you to have an open mind about these human rights issues I've been accused of, in the press." The general looked into the water. He turned around and put his hand on Russell's shoulder. "An open mind is all I ask, Russell. . . . Now I'm going to tell you something. You have a friend, an American girl named Katherine Barkley."

"Yes?"

"There are people here that don't like her. She should leave the country as soon as possible. It's no longer safe here for her. Do you understand?"

Carlos turned and smiled at two businessmen who were leaving the restaurant. Carlos, with the formality singular to Latin men of a certain class, motioned them over and introduced Russell to them, not as Russell Price but as Isabella Cruz's son. It was the first time it had happened since he'd been back.

"One last thing, Russell," Carlos said when the men had left. His guards were anxious to leave before it rained. The temperature was dropping quickly, and it was almost cool now. "I expect, when I'm president, that your project out at *Tres Rios* will not be bothered by the ministry of culture. However, I'll expect to share in whatever you and that lunatic German find out there." And then, as the first rain drops were falling, Carlos was escorted from the garden.

NINETEEN

He'd called Katherine and left a message on her cell. She called him back almost immediately.

"Where are you?" he asked.

"You don't care."

"Where are you?"

"I'm working."

"I want you to come back to the city," he said. "Now."

"No. Why should I? I think it's over," she said. "Goodbye."

"Please." She hung up.

He didn't know what to do. A bus honked and pulled around him. He moved his jeep closer to the curb. A street urchin who'd been doing magic tricks in the intersection approached and tapped his windshield. He ignored the kid's painted clown face, the eyes big, the nose orange. Small raindrops started to hit the windshield, exploding against the dusty glass. *They were going to kill Katherine and anyone with her. It wouldn't matter how many students were in the car with her; he knew how they worked. They would all die.*

He picked up his phone and dialed Carlos's cell number. He looked out on the street as he heard Carlos's voice ask him, in Spanish, to please leave a message. *She's innocent. What had Katherine done to deserve this? She'd only built houses for poor people, for God's sake!*

Outside, on the street, people were beginning to run for cover as the rain suddenly began to pour down. An explosion of rain hit his windshield, and everything in sight seemed to melt and blur. The young boy stood by his window waiting for money, staring in at him, his glue sniffer's eyes red, his white painted face hideous. The paint on his face had started to run, so that Russell could see streaks of brown skin underneath the white. He dug in his wallet while rolling down his windshield. He could hear the rain hitting a long row of ragged store awnings across the street. The boy reached for the worn bill with filthy wet fingers.

"*Gracias, Señor!* May god bless you," he said, unfazed by the rain.

"It's me," Russell said. He had called Beatrice at home in the city. "I have to talk to Carlos. It's important. Is he there?" He had dialed her number despite his promise never to call her at home. "I'm sorry; it's an emergency." He could hear the maids in the background, and a child crying. "Beatrice, is he there? Is Carlos there? I have to speak to him."

"No," she said finally. "Where are you?"

"I'm in the city. Where is he?"

"At the office . . . I think. What's wrong?"

"I'll explain later. Give me the number."

"I can't."

He was stunned.

"Beatrice! For God's sake, give me the number!"

"He said I wasn't to give that number out. Ever."

"Beatrice. Do I have to beg you?"

"He'll know if I gave it to you. He'll know," she said.

"I don't care if he knows or not. I have to speak to him *now, damn it.*"

She hung up. For a moment, all he could hear was the beating of the rain on the top of his jeep in a sick unison with his own heart. Everything outside was obscured, otherworldly, the traffic, buildings, and pedestrians melded into a loose wet fabric, roughly laced together by the rain's great tension.

He drove a block in fear and desperation. He'd wanted to ask Carlos to send some men to protect Katherine immediately. He was going to beg him. He would write whatever Carlos wanted him to write about him.

The avenue spilled him out onto *La Reforma,* in front of a hulking gray statue of Ubico on his marble stallion, crowded with pigeons. He was trapped by the traffic, which swept him into one of the massive circular roundabouts. He saw the U.S. embassy on the corner, its roof bristling with communications equipment, its huge white satellite dishes pointed at the dark sky. He instinctively moved towards the building, catching a break in the traffic. He pulled back onto *La Reforma* and drove toward the embassy like a madman.

He knew from experience that in the afternoon the embassy was quieter. Guatemalans, soliciting visas for the United States, were only allowed access in the morning, and at a special door. The main entrance to the embassy was protected by two checkpoints. What had once been, in the mid 20th century, a home away from home for Americans, designed for their convenience, was now in the twenty-first century a fortress, designed to keep everyone at bay. Manned by Marines, the embassy had turned into a stronghold housing the DEA, FBI, CIA, NSA and their support staff. Ironically, the smallest contingent was State Department workers. The CIA delegation had gotten so big that it had spilled out and taken over its own building nearby.

Since 9/11, parking anywhere near the embassy had been forbidden. Traffic cops in black ponchos were out in force, making sure no car stopped anywhere near the building.

Russell drove along for several blocks, then parked. He ran back towards the embassy pelted by the rain, feeling stupid, and yet hoping that someone inside could stop Katherine's murder. Like a child running home, he made his way towards the cold, menacing building.

The first checkpoint was a simple guard shack, the second a larger guard house, with a metal detector. The Guatemalan guard asked him for his ID and made him empty his pockets as another policeman ran a metal detector over him. He was stopped again and made to sign a piece of paper giving his full name and address in the country and his business at the embassy.

As he filled out the form, a group of young DEA agents he recognized, beefy, collegiate and boisterous, moved through the checkpoints, skirting the metal detectors without being challenged, simply holding up their ID's. They were armed and all carried police knives, their metal clips tucked into the front of their jean pockets.

Russell handed back the form and rushed finally up the marble stairs and into the lobby. The embassy's enormous lobby was empty. There were two doors leading into the interior of the building. When he'd been here before, there had always been elaborate plans made so that when he arrived he was met by whomever he had an appointment to see. Now, unannounced, he realized that the lobby was as far as he was going to be allowed to go without dealing with the Marine guards. The Marines manned a booth that controlled the lobby, which they'd turned into a kind of no man's land. The white shaved head of a Marine wearing a bullet proof vest acknowledged him with a suspicious nod from the other side of the glass of the guard booth. Russell could see stacks of bulletproof vests lying on shelves and stacks of helmets on the floor.

"I'd like to speak to someone," Russell said, trying to act calm. He was wet. His jacket was soaked, and he could feel his shirt sticking to his skin.

"You can speak to the duty officer," the young soldier said.

"No, I need to speak to someone inside. Someone from State." The young man looked at him stupidly, as if Russell were speaking a foreign language, or were mentally deficient. "From the ambassador's office." He searched for the state department's press relations woman's name, but had forgotten it.

"What's your business?" The soldier picked up the phone, said something quickly into it, and then looked at him again through the thick glass. Instinctively, Russell's hope began to retreat.

"It's. . . ." He searched for the right thing to say. "I just need to speak to an embassy official," he said, repeating himself. "As soon as possible."

"You have to have an appointment," the Marine told him.

"Yes, I realize that, but certainly there's someone on duty who can speak to an American citizen with an emergency."

"No, not without an appointment."

"I'm a reporter. I have a press credential." He felt for his credential, but they'd taken everything from him at the guard shack—his wallet, cell phone, everything. He moved his hands foolishly over his pockets. An older Marine officer, in his thirties, stepped into the lobby and approached him.

"Can I help you, *sir?* I'm the duty officer." Exasperated and realizing he'd been a fool to expect help from the embassy, Russell looked blankly at the duty officer. Disdain scrolled across the officer's face.

"I want to see someone in the embassy. Any embassy official will do," Russell said. He tried to sound calm and sensible.

"You'll have to make an appointment," the officer said. He gave him a quick courteous smile that said "Fuck off."

"I would categorize this as an emergency," Russell said. The duty officer shot a glance at the soldier in the booth and stepped closer.

"Are you reporting a threat to the embassy?"

"No! I'm not."

"Well then, you'll have to make an appointment. You can use the phone on the wall. You'll be connected to someone upstairs. They'll make the arrangements."

"I'm here to report an intended crime against an American citizen," he said. The officer looked at him, stiff-jawed.

"Why not tell the Guatemalan police? That's what they're for."

"I don't think they'd be much help in this case," Russell said.

"Well. I can understand that," the officer said with a smirk. "I wouldn't call them either." The man glanced up at the booth and smiled at the young soldier.

"I've met the ambassador, Mrs. Stamp. I work for the *Financial Times;* I'm a reporter. I have a credential if you'd like to see it. And I'm an American citizen," Russell said. He couldn't keep the anger out of his voice now; he could feel his face getting red with anger.

"Tell that to the operator on that phone on the wall," the duty officer said. "She'll be glad to help you, *sir.*"

For a moment Russell was about to give the name of the man he knew from gossip in the office was probably the CIA's station chief in the country, but he realized that it wouldn't make any difference. *Why would the CIA help Katherine?* he thought, looking in the duty officer's steely blue eyes. *She was no one of consequence.* And even if the spooks decided to help, by the time they masticated the problem—as they most certainly would—she would be dead. He went to the house phone hanging on the wall anyway, and lifted the receiver.

"I'd like to see an embassy official," he said when the operator came on. "It's an emergency."

"Certainly, sir. You can come in next Tuesday at ten," she said happily. "Is that a good time for you?" Russell hung up the phone and walked quickly through the lobby.

Katherine called him back as he drove to his office.

"I'm sorry," she said. "I'm sorry I hung up."

"Go to *Tres Rios*. I want to see you. Tonight. I'll meet you there tonight."

"Are you still seeing her?"

"No. It's over," he said.

"All right. I will . . . I love you . . . you prick," she said.

TWENTY

She can't stay here," Mahler said. "It's too dangerous. They'll kill us all."

"She can go out with us to the bush," Russell said. He put down his pack.

"I won't take her," Mahler said.

"Yes you will," he said. "You'll take me, and you'll take her too." Mahler looked at him.

"Or what?"

"Or I'll go without you," Russell said. He picked up his pack and walked down the hallway. He was exhausted from the drive from the capital. "I know where to look now. I don't need you. Remember, I own the place."

"You'll never find it without me," Mahler said. The look on the German's face changed. He'd been sitting in the kitchen, and he stood up. His hair was loose at his shoulders. He'd taken his shirt off. It was hot in the room. Mahler wore just jeans, without shoes. "Don't be a fool. They'll kill us too. Send her away.... I'm close now. Since you left, I found something."

Russell could hear the fans in the room turning, feel the warm air hit his face.

"Why didn't you tell me," he said.

"I wanted to surprise you. I tell you, we're close. And it may be a very big find. . . . A city, maybe," Mahler said.

"What?"

175

"An entire Mayan city," Mahler said. He walked out into the living room. "Do you know what that means? You'll be richer than you can possibly imagine. It's all there, gold, silver, jewels. You see, I think Bakta Halik was just the outskirts. I think this site is big. Like Tikal. The jungle swallowed it all. But it's there," Mahler said. "And we own it."

"I don't care. She's still coming with us," Russell said.

"They'll kill us all. You know what they're like. It won't matter. They'll follow us out there." Mahler put his hand on his naked white chest.

"Maybe," Russell said. "But she can't stay here, can she?" They saw headlights in the driveway. "That's her." He walked towards the door.

"You're a stupid fool," Mahler said before he got to the door. "Typical American."

Russell let the remark go and walked out into the night. He saw Katherine's white UN jeep pull up next to his car and park. The night was warm and humid. Her headlights went out as he descended the stairs. The white volcanic sand driveway was still visible in the weak, bug-infested porch lights.

"Okay, I'm here," she said, hugging him as she got out of her jeep.

"We have to talk," he said. "Come inside." He turned and saw a second set of headlights, yellowish and bright, on the road coming toward the house.

She was still holding him. He moved towards his own jeep and opened the driver-side door. He groped for his shotgun.

The vehicle came up the road and stopped just below them. A Ford Explorer, dark colored; two men got out of the front. A third man emerged from the open sunroof. The sunroof man pointed some kind of weapon at them. Russell couldn't tell what it was.

The two men came towards them, wool balaclavas pulled over their faces. One of the men was holding a Steyr machine pistol. Russell could see it clearly in the light from the house. He glanced back towards the porch and saw the living room lights go out. The awful fear he'd had for months, the fear of being helpless, was suddenly playing itself out.

The smaller of the two men stopped in front of Russell and told him to put his shotgun back in the jeep. The man with the Steyr grabbed for Katherine as Russell tossed his shotgun into the still-open door of his jeep.

"Russell?" Katherine's voice, terrified, called him. The short man, without a weapon, took her by the hand and started to lead her towards the Ford's open passenger door.

"I know General Selva," Russell said in Spanish. "I can call him now." He didn't know what else to say or do. The man who had the Steyr trained on him was going to shoot him, he realized. What Russell had said stopped him. "He won't like this."

The man with the gun looked back at his shorter companion, who continued to lead Katherine away.

"Now what?" the man with the Steyr said in Spanish.

"I'm an employee of the UN. And I'm an American citizen," Katherine said angrily.

"Let me call him," Russell said. The tone of his own voice scared him. He saw Katherine looking at him in fear. He saw the short man hesitate, then stop. The man who had them covered with some kind of automatic weapon from the Ford's sunroof didn't move. Russell took his cell phone out of his pants pocket and dialed the general's home number. A maid answered, and he asked for the general.

"Yes." Carlos's voice finally came on the line.

"It's me, Russell. They have my friend… Will you talk to them? For God's sake." There was a pause.

"All right," Carlos said. Russell looked towards the man holding Katherine's arm.

"General Selva wants to talk to you."

The man with the Steyer turned around. He called to the man standing in the sunroof and told him to get out of the car. The sunroof man climbed out onto the driveway. Russell could clearly see an AK-47 in his hand. The sunroof-man walked over to where Katherine stood and took her by the hand.

"What's this about, Russell?" Katherine said. He wanted to run to her side and beg the men not to hurt her, but he knew it wouldn't do any good.

"I don't know," he lied.

The short, unarmed man walked towards him and took his cell phone.

"*Digame.*" The short man—obviously the leader—said into the phone. Russell caught a glimpse of his eyes. They were not cold, but they were menacing. He listened for a moment. "*Sí. Eso, sí,*" the short man said. "*Pero ella, no. Ya está echo.*"

The man tossed the phone back to Russell. Unable to grab it fast enough, it bounced off his chest and it fell onto the ground. He picked it up.

"She's going with them," Carlos said. "I told them you were a member of my family and, if he did anything to you, I'd find him and have him killed. That's all I could do. I can't do anything for her. She's already dead. But if you do anything to try and stop them, they will kill you, too. Do you understand?"

"Yes," Russell said.

"I'm sorry," Carlos said and he hung up.

When he looked up, Katherine was already inside the Ford, which was slowly turning around. Its headlights painted the porch. Russell dropped the cell phone on the ground and walked back towards his jeep. He threw open the driver's side door and lifted out his shotgun. The Ford continued slowly down the road towards the gate.

As he was coming down the road—staying far to the right, hoping to stay out of the driver's line of sight—he saw, with disbelief, Mahler step out into the middle of the road just down from the house. Mahler waved the Ford down. It stopped in front of him. He could see Mahler smiling at the driver, his shirtless body in the headlights.

"Hola, amigos!" Mahler said. He raised his hands—palms out —high above his head. Mahler walked towards the driver's side window, hands in the air. "I'm sorry I had the gate closed. I'll have it opened immediately," Mahler told the driver. He continued to walk towards the Ford's driver, still smiling, both his hands held high in the air. Mahler finally stopped at the driver's window. He started to lower his hands, making sure he kept his palms out.

Russell—as he walked quickly—wondered if the men in the Ford could see him. He unslung his shotgun and approached the rear of the car.

Mahler, leaning in towards the driver, put one hand on the driver's side door. Russell saw Mahler's other hand move quickly behind him as he spoke to the driver. Suddenly he saw Mahler fire his weapon, point blank, into the car. Russell heard the first shot, then a second. The gunman, sitting again on the sunroof, tried to fire back at Mahler, but was hit in the legs, which were dangling inside the car. Russell, running now, opened fire on the sun-roof man, hitting him in the back with a blast from his shotgun and knocking him forward. There was more firing as Mahler, yelling in German, ran along the side of the now slowly rolling Ford. Russell could see Mahler's right arm thrust inside the Ford's cab, firing his pistol.

Russell jogged down the dark road, his shotgun raised, but unable to fire indiscriminately into the Ford. He watched

179

Mahler—everything quiet now—jump on the Ford's running board and grab the steering wheel. All Russell could hear was the sound of the Ford's tires on the sandy road. Russell saw the sunroof man he'd shot lying across the roof of the Ford. He jogged behind the car, staying to the left. He watched Mahler struggle with the steering wheel as the Ford started to pick up speed, heading down the hill towards the gate.

"Get in!" Russell yelled. He was running, catching up. Mahler, riding the running board, turned to look at him. He still had his automatic in his hand. Mahler dropped it and climbed into the Ford, first pulling open the door and yanking the dead driver out of the cab. Russell had to jump over the driver's body as he gained on the car.

Mahler, behind the wheel now, began to slow the car, then stopped it abruptly. Russell ran to the driver's side window and looked in past Mahler. Katherine was sitting in the passenger seat, her face blood-splattered. He could see the dangling legs of the sunroof man. Russell looked into the back seat, where another body was lying, the dead man's balaclava shot up, the backseat cushions bullet-smacked and torn. Mahler pulled the Ford's emergency brake on.

"I thought you were in here," Mahler said. "I thought they were taking you. I couldn't have that. Not now." Mahler looked up at him. He was smiling. It was the smile of a crazy man.

Russell turned and watched Katherine climb out of the car. The sunroof man's foot hit her shoulder. He ran around the front of the Ford to help her. She was wiping her face with the back of her hand; she hadn't said a word. She put her arms around him.

"What do we do now?" Mahler said from the car.

"I don't know. I'm taking her up to the house."

"We can't just leave them here," Mahler said. "What if their friends come looking for them?"

180

"I don't know," Russell said. He slung his shotgun over his shoulder and walked Katherine back up the road in the dark.

There was the sound of howler monkeys high in the canopy above their camp site. Mahler threw cold coffee on the fire, and it began to smoke. They sat in a jungle clearing, the air above them hazy, tinted blue by the smoke and the humidity.

Russell looked at Katherine. She had spoken very little since the death squad had come for her the night before. Mahler looked at her, and then smiled. The automatic he'd used the night before was stuck in the front of his jeans.

They'd taken the weapons from the dead men before they'd driven them and the Ford to the outskirts of Colomba and left them. They were better armed now. They'd found an M-16 with a grenade launcher and several grenades, as well as the Steyr and the Kalashnikov with a hundred-round drum.

Russell looked up into the canopy, but there was no sky. And there was no sound now from the river, either. They knew what time of day it was only from the half-light that penetrated the greenish-blue canopy. He looked at his watch; it was six in the morning, and it was warm already. He pulled off his filthy T-shirt

"I would go back through Belize. That's the way I'd do it. *Rio Dulce,* and then cross over to Belize. Then it's easy. It's lightly manned, that crossing," Mahler told her. "You'll be okay."

"The airport is out of the question now. Maybe he's right," Russell said.

"If I leave, they win," Katherine said. It was the first thing she'd said since they'd woken up and fixed breakfast. Mahler had been going on about the reach of the death squads and how they worked. He didn't seem to care that he was scaring her. Katherine had just stared at him. She was grateful, Russell

181

imagined, because Mahler had saved her life, but she was obviously horrified by Mahler's insensitivity.

"Thank you for what you did. . . ." she said. She put her cup down on the ground. They'd brought cold coffee in a Thermos.

"I didn't do it for you. I didn't even know you were in the car. I thought it was Russell. I thought they'd come for him." She nodded. "I couldn't afford to see my partner leaving with a death squad just now," Mahler said, cigarette smoke pouring out of his nose. "It wasn't convenient."

Russell stood up and walked to where they'd hobbled the horses. A jaguar had attacked one of the horses during the night, and its leg was scratched up. Five red claw marks ran along its rear flank. The red stood out in the early morning light. Russell had woken up and heard the commotion. By the time he and Mahler had lit a flashlight–Mahler firing his pistol in the air–the jaguar had gone, looking back at them once. It had been a very big male.

Everything on the ground smelled of rot. They were leading their horses back down the path that had been cut through the jungle down to the river. Russell could hear the river first; then suddenly the ground went soggy, and he was staring out at it through the tunnel they'd cut that first day.

Katherine was behind him and Mahler behind her, with the injured horse. They had left for the jungle late the evening before, deciding that the safest place was here in the bush. There would be hell to pay for killing those men, Russell thought, watching his horse drop its head and drink from the pewter-colored river. He swung up on the horse and rode out into the river. He saw the banks of the other side, bright green and higher, and overhead a strip of sky, soft-looking, marred by clouds. He felt safe here. Even if they came looking for them, it would be almost impossible to spot the hole they cut in the bank that led back to their camp, he thought.

He made way for Katherine's horse. She glanced at him.

"You can't stay in Guatemala now," he said almost automatically. "It's suicide. They were going to murder you."

"I didn't know you were so chummy with her husband. What about you? Do you think Carlos isn't going to find out about you and his wife?"

"That's got nothing to do with this. You have to leave," he said.

"How about I leave, if you do?" she said.

"Jesus Christ."

"I'll leave, if you come with me. You can't stay with him." She nodded toward Mahler. "He's obviously crazy."

Mahler came down the path with the injured horse. He was good with horses. The German seemed to have a special sympathy for them. They made way again; Mahler waded out into the river and bathed the horse's injuries, then took out a topical antibiotic and spread it carefully over the horse's deep scratches. The animal, sensing it was being helped, was still.

"Well, aren't you going to ask what the hell we're doing out here?" Mahler said. He stood up, capped the ointment, and shoved it into his army pants.

"It's none of my business," Katherine said defensively. "But I suppose it has something to do with antiquities. Bakta Halik is only over those mountains," she said, "and I met you at Carl Van Diemen's house. It's not difficult to put it together." Her horse brought its head up, its withers shaking. The sky— the bit they could see above the river—was already starting to cloud up.

Mahler looked at her and made a Jack Nicholson ain't-this-all-grand face, and then looked at Russell.

"I don't really give a damn. I mean, about whatever it is you're doing out here," she said quickly. "Stealing from the country, I suppose." She shot a glance at Russell.

"Oh!!!! You see, Russell. . . . We're stealing from the country!" Mahler's voice boomed across the river and echoed back. *STEALING FROM... STEALING FROM... STEALING.* "Do you really think anyone in this rotten country gives one shit about what we might find? Do you think they would have found Tikal? Or any of it! They're always too busy killing each other, or didn't you notice last night?

"If it wasn't for *me,* everything at Bakta Halik would have been carted away by the military and sold off. Everything! Who do you think went to the world press and stopped it? Huh?" Mahler yanked the injured horse around, its hooves clomping on the rocks. He came back out of the river, leading the horse, and faced her. "Let me tell you something. You've been here how long, a few months? Maybe a year? You don't know anything about this country. *Nothing,*" he said angrily.

When it began to rain in the afternoon, they got only drips at first, then a kind of filtered dew-like rain, very soft, that clung to their skin and clothes. The floor of the jungle where they worked became a kind of insect-infested steam room, where even breathing was difficult. Russell looked back to where they'd brought the horses, far below him. They had climbed a hill where Mahler said he'd found something. There was a wall of green in front of them. The hill seemed especially overgrown. Mahler had said it might be something. So they'd begun, after a breakfast of cold tortillas and farmer's cheese, to hack into the hillside.

Because of the heat, the three of them were working without their shirts on. Stripped to the waist, the sweat pouring off them, they hacked away. When it happened, they all heard it. Russell's machete struck something. They heard the hard sound of steel on stone.

The machete handle vibrated in his hand. He pulled the blade back and saw where it had been bent. He thrust his hand into the wall of vines, and felt the damp stone.

"I found something," was all Russell said. Mahler scrambled towards him, his long hair undone and wild.

"What did I tell you!" Mahler said, reaching into the hole with him.

TWENTY-ONE

A huge, blood-red neon Coca-Cola ball revolved perpetually above Guatemala City's main traffic roundabout, where *Avenida Revolución* turned into *Avenida De Las Americas.* Russell had promised De La Madrid he would be at an important meeting at Madrid's house at midnight. They had an announcement for the world press in the morning. It was going to be a real shocker, one that would either win the election for Madrid or send him into political oblivion. And it had been all Russell's idea. They would propose pegging the quetzal to the dollar, to stop the hyperinflation that was destroying the country.

Russell pulled his car around the statue of Pedro de Alvarado, the infamous and brutal Spanish conquistador who'd been with Cortez. He drove into a tony neighborhood of high-rise luxury apartment buildings belonging to the rich, not too different from neighborhoods in Sao Paolo or San Francisco. At this time of night, the empty boulevard was impressive and cold looking, the high-rise buildings looking down on the world they commanded.

He pulled down a driveway and was stopped by a tall metal gate. He spoke into an intercom. Two men with shotguns stood in the shadows by the gate, making sure no one rushed the steel portal.

"It's me; it's Russell," he said into the speaker in English.

186

"Okay." He heard Carl's voice. In a moment the gate swung open; he drove down a steep driveway to the parking garage and parked. The garage was full of expensive, late model cars, even a brand new yellow Ferrari. The building, with its posh condominiums, was home to several big-time drug dealers and bankers. They lived in the same apartment buildings, Russell had heard from his boss, so that it would be easier to launder all the millions of dollars a week the drug business was bringing into the country. Guatemala had become one of the most important linchpins in the international cocaine trade.

He stepped into the elevator. The Muzak played Donna Summer's "Bad Girls." He hit 12. As the door closed, he noticed two men in dark suits leaning against a wall of the parking garage, one of them with an Uzi in his right hand.

Carl's maid opened the door. The Dutchman kept the apartment in the capital when he didn't feel like driving down to his palace in Antigua. Russell followed a tiny Indian woman in a spotless black-and-white uniform into the all-white living room, with its view of the city. Carl and his lover were sitting around a white onyx coffee table, drinking wine out of long-stemmed French crystal glasses and watching "TRL" on MTV.

"Is Katherine ready? Her plane leaves in an hour," Russell said.

"She's getting dressed," Carl said, lowering the sound on the TV. The jaguar scratches on Van Diemen's face were red, and would leave an ugly scar. They'd gotten infected, and part of his right cheek had been cut away. There was a plan to rebuild his missing right cheek. In the meantime, Carl looked a little monstrous. Russell tried not to stare as he sat down across from him.

"I'm going to Europe again for my surgery," Carl said. He looked over at his boyfriend. The kid looked sad, like a little boy whose mother was going to leave him.

"Good," Russell said. He didn't know what else to say. He didn't really give a shit about Carl's face. "Thanks for looking after my friend."

"Of course. They say these claw marks are nothing. The surgery will fix my face," Carl said, holding his wine glass. It looked like the son of a bitch had lost half his face, Russell thought. The jaguar had gotten him good.

"Of course, they're nothing, dear," the kid said. Carl had been keeping his right hand near his missing cheek; he dropped it to pat his boyfriend on his bare leg. The boyfriend was wearing pedal pushers and a tank top.

"I want to thank you for what you did for Carl out there," the kid said to Russell.

"No sweat," Russell said, trying not to stare. "Listen . . . can we talk?"

"Of course," Carl said.

"We want to cut you in for a third. We found something. It might be *really* big," Russell said. He stopped himself for a moment and looked at Carl's boyfriend, then back at Carl. "Maybe a whole fucking Mayan city." Carl leaned forward.

"*What?*"

"A city, a whole Mayan city," Russell said. "On my property."

"You're joking," Carl said.

"No. And we need money. I don't have any. I've quit my job. We'll sell you a third of the deal for a hundred thousand dollars cash. That's what we figure we need just to keep going. We need cash. I have to pay off the Frenchman. And then we'll need to hire a small army to guard the site. If the word gets out before we've had a chance to look into the temple we found . . . well, you know. The site will be stripped clean in a few days."

Carl–obviously in shock–leaned forward so that he had one hand on the huge white onyx table in front of him. He was so excited it looked like he was going to get up and do a fifty yard dash.

"Can I have a drink?" Russell asked.

"Of course," Carl said. He was still staring at Russell. "You know what it could be worth. . . . If it's true," Carl said.

"A fuck of a lot, I guess," Russell said. "We'll be like fucking Cortez."

"Even if we only took out the best. We'll all make a fortune. No . . . more," the Dutchman said. His eyes were animated. He'd forgotten all about his mangled face.

"Yeah, that's what we think," Russell said. "So are you in?" Van Diemen nodded his head quickly.

"Poppy, does that mean we're going to be rich?" the kid asked. Russell turned to the kid.

"Keep your mouth shut about this, or. . . ." Russell glared at the kid. He wasn't feeling right in the head. Maybe it was the days they'd spent in the jungle being bitten by everything there was to bite a man, or the heat as they worked cleaning off the first temple, or the excitement, or whatever. But he was feeling strangely angry since the gunfight. It was too much, he supposed, too much to try to pull down from the shelf, a whole fucking Mayan city. But he was game. He knew that with that kind of money, he could convince Beatrice to leave her husband. He would be rich, and he would simply take her and her kids and disappear into some apartment like this one, somewhere in the world. He'd steal the throne from under the Pope's ass to have Beatrice.

The kid glanced at him, terrified.

"Poppy, he's scaring me," the kid said, huddling against Carl, his brown face pressed with fear.

"That's okay. . . ." Carl put his arm on his boyfriend's shoulders. "Pablo isn't going to say anything, don't worry."

"Good. Because if anyone fucks with us, I'll kill them." He couldn't believe the words coming out of his mouth. But he

189

meant it. He was sure of that. He wanted Beatrice, and getting her wasn't going to be easy.

"*Dios mío,*" the kid said, shutting his eyes. He spilt some wine on his pedal pushers.

"No one is going to talk, Russell. You have my word," Carl said again.

"I'll need a hundred thousand dollars by tomorrow for the Frenchman. I want to pay him off. Get that over with. That way, I own the place outright. No question then."

"How can Mahler and I be sure you won't . . . how did you put it? Fuck *us,*" Carl said, smiling.

"Yes . . . Yes! How can Poppy be sure you won't fuck *us?*" the kid said, looking at him sideways now.

"You can't be. Can you have the maid get Katherine, please? I have to take her to the airport. And thanks for letting her stay here. I appreciate it. I won't forget it," Russell said. "I mean that."

"You look tired," Carl said, ringing a bell for the maid.

"Yeah, well. We've been busy." He took out his cell phone and dialed the general.

"I think you should take a rest, a few days off," Carl said. "You look exhausted."

"We'll all get plenty of rest when we're dead," Russell said, listening to the general's phone ring.

Katherine came down the hall as he closed his telephone. She was dressed in clean jeans and a black mid-length coat. Her hair was pulled back. She crossed the room and gave him a kiss, and he kissed her back on the lips. He'd made love to her out there in the jungle, and he'd lied to her, and it was all designed to make her believe in him so he could get her on a plane and out of the country. He didn't feel bad about it. Maybe, he thought, as he held her, it was all the lying he was doing that was making him strange in the head.

"Are you ready?" he said.

"Yes. Let me get my suitcase. Are you bringing much?" she asked. "My sister is picking us up at the airport, but she only has a VW."

"No. Not much," he said. "I'm sure it will be fine."

Selva had sent him a big chase car, an American Suburban filled with his bodyguards. That was part of the deal. The Chevy Suburban was following him to the airport to make sure nothing happened. It was a short drive from Carl's apartment.

He listened to Katherine make plans for their future. She said they would stay with her sister in New York until the paper reassigned him. Then they would see. She might quit her job, she said. She reached over and held his hand as they drove. He wanted to tell her then. But it felt mean, putting her straight about the way things really were, so he didn't.

"What about the car? Your car?" she asked.

"I'm leaving it there at the airport," he said. She nodded. "I checked my stuff in early," he said. "That way we could get two seats together." More lies.

He'd lied when he told her he had no intention of going on with Mahler. He'd told her the night they made love out there that he was going to give the plantation to the government and leave. Get away from it all. That it was all crazy. How could anyone try to hold onto a Mayan city, he'd said, holding her naked in the heat of the jungle night. The fire burned high to keep the mosquitoes away, the light falling on Mahler's head as he slept across from them. It had all been a lie—everything he'd told her. *He* was going to try to hold onto a whole fucking Mayan city. Why not? Hold on long enough, anyway, to get what he wanted out of it.

Once he had her in the airport, it would be over. He'd gotten Selva to mark Katherine as *persona non grata;* if she tried to come back, she wouldn't get past customs. She would never see the country again. It was a mean thing to do, he knew, but he'd felt he had to do it for her own good. Carlos had promised him she would be safe at the airport.

"I'm so glad you love me," she said. "I don't think I've been in love before. Not like this, anyway."

He couldn't look at her. Instead he looked into the rearview mirror and saw Selva's chase car following close behind them.

• • •

He wondered, as they made their way across the black tile concourse at Aurora airport, if he didn't love her more than he thought. It wasn't like Beatrice. He knew that; what he felt for Katherine was different. He cared about what happened to Katherine, about the men she would have in her life back there in the States. About who she would become, about another country she might go to, and his not being there to protect her. For a moment, as they approached the ticket counter at American Airlines, he wondered what his life would be like if he left right now with her.

But the craziness inside of him wouldn't let him do that. He might love Katherine, but he wanted to possess Beatrice. He wanted to prove to Beatrice he was just as good a man as Carlos. He realized that part of his love for Beatrice was tied up in stealing her from the General.

Aurora airport was surprisingly busy. The red-eye flights for the States were leaving soon. An American, a United, and a Taca flight left for the States almost simultaneously every night. They'd bought her a ticket for Miami. The general's brother-in-law ran Taca Airlines, so it was all set.

Russell saw the Taca ticket counter on his right. He glanced behind him. Two of the men from Selva's chase car had followed them into the airport, and were behind them.

He put her suitcase down. Katherine stopped and looked at him. He knew she was expecting them to go to the

American Airlines counter, because that was the only flight to New York.

"Look . . . I'm sorry, Katherine. You're going to Miami. After that, you can go wherever you want," he said.

"What are you talking about?" She reached for his hand. He pulled his away. One of Selva's bodyguards went on to the Taca counter and picked up the ticket that was waiting for her.

"You have to leave. I can't go with you," he said. He couldn't look her in the face. A customs official came up to them and asked for Katherine's passport.

"I don't understand, Russell. You said you loved me." She sounded like a little girl.

"I do." And he realized he really meant it.

"What's this mean?"

"*Señora, pasaporte,*" the man said. The other bodyguard stood beside her now.

"It means I can't go with you. Not right now," he said. He watched the customs man take her passport and walk towards the gate. The other bodyguard, holding her ticket now, came up to Russell and nodded.

"*Listo?*" Ready? the bodyguard said to him.

"You have to go with him. He's going to go with you to Miami, just in case. I was worried that on the plane—someone —I don't know, I just was worried. This way, you'll be all right," he said. "He'll watch over you all the way there."

"Russell, *please* don't leave me. I love you." Katherine was looking at him, tears in her eyes now. He hadn't expected that. He thought she would get angry, but not that. "I love you. I know you love me. She's not good for you. I want to be your wife. She can't ever do that, Russell, can't you see that? She belongs to *him.* Why can't you see that?"

"I'm sorry I lied to you," he said. "Don't you see, I had to. You weren't going to leave." He nodded to the men. One of them picked up her suitcase. She started to sob. He couldn't stand it, and turned around.

"Please . . . Russell! Please." He heard her sobbing, and kept walking. There were all kinds of people coming for the red-eye to Miami. He forced himself to keep walking across the busy, well-lit concourse, and then out the big sliding glass doors and out into the night, which smelled of diesel and decaying city. The smell hit him in the face. He noticed that Selva's backup car was gone. He stopped for a moment by the taxi stand. He heard the drivers asking him if he wanted a taxi.

"Taxi, Señor?" He wanted desperately to turn around. Somewhere in his gut, he knew Katherine was right. Beatrice wasn't the right woman. But he couldn't help himself.

"Taxi, Señor?" He closed his eyes for a moment and remembered Katherine the way he wanted to remember her: the way she had been that first morning driving down to the coast, her hands on the steering wheel, so sure of herself and her place in the world.

"No, thank you. Not tonight," Russell answered, and walked on.

TWENTY-TWO

There's going to be a devaluation of the quetzal. I just heard," Antonio said.

They had all met at De La Madrid's house, the entire would-be cabinet, including Senator Valladolid. The senator was scheduled to be De La Madrid's foreign minister. Probably a mistake, Russell thought, glancing at the old man.

"Are you sure?" Russell said.

"Yes. My brother just called." Madrid's brother was head of the Bank of Guatemala. "It gets worse. It's going to be eight to one," Antonio said, looking at him.

"Jesus!" He was still reeling from leaving Katherine at the airport. Russell went to a space on the couch and sat down between the would-be minister of the interior and a young woman who was slated to be minister of defense. If Madrid was elected, she would be the first woman in Guatemalan history to hold the post.

Russell didn't think they had a chance now. The political situation—if there was a devaluation—would be chaotic at best.

"Why now?" Russell asked as he sat down.

"The government can't make the payment on a dollar loan coming due next week—five hundred million," Antonio explained. "They don't have the reserves, and they can't borrow any more because of the coffee crisis. The World Bank will provide a bailout package, but only if we submit to an IMF restructuring. Devaluation of the currency is the center-piece of the plan, of course. It's supposed to make our coffee more competitive."

"The whole country is bankrupt!" Senator Vallodalid said cheerfully. "Pretty soon we'll be paying them to buy our coffee." He raised his glass and smiled at Russell. He was drinking scotch out of a Waterford tumbler and wore a pink cravat. He looked like he was going to Cap Ferret, not facing a political and financial crisis.

"We were wondering what you thought we should do, young man? You seem to know all about these financial matters," Valladolid said. "I just think they want cheap coffee." All the men and the woman shook their heads in agreement. "After all, Europe and America are having a recession," the senator said. "They want a bargain."

"It's criminal. It means we get even less for our coffee," the young woman next to him said. She was a young human rights lawyer whom Madrid had selected because her good liberal credentials would steal votes from the more radical left elements. "It means the price for hard bean superior would be. . . ."

"About ten dollars a kilo," Russell finished her sentence.

"That's impossible. It can't be allowed," Madrid said.

"The unemployment rate will go to fifty percent if the IMF gets its way," Russell said. "It will open the door again to the Communists."

The devaluation would create a financial death spiral, Russell knew. It was essentially the same thing that had just happened to Argentina. Once the international currency speculators got wind of the IMF plan, they would drive the currency down even further. The government's bonds would be worthless, and interest rates would skyrocket. Dollar reserves, so crucial to any modern banking system, would leave the country almost immediately as the rich pulled their dollars out of the country's banks.

"My brother says that President Blanco has already approved," Madrid said.

They were all looking at Russell. None of them had trained as economists.

"There has to be a solution," Madrid said. "We can't let the country slip away again."

There was silence. Everyone in the room, including Russell, had lost someone in the war.

Russell looked at the faces in the lamplight. They were frightened. No one wanted another Argentina. No one wanted the Communists to come back as a political force. No one wanted more violence.

"The government could declare a debt payment holiday while they try to renegotiate with the creditors. Then maybe they could build reserves, defend the quetzal. But if you declare a debt holiday, Guatemalan bonds are going to collapse. And new loans will be impossible to get, because the IMF will blacklist you. You can't win…. There is no solution. The IMF and the World Bank hold all the cards. On the other hand, if they devalue there will be massive inflation and unemployment. I think the war will start all over. The reds are already making noises," Russell said. "They're probably talking to Castro in Havana right now. It's their big chance to make a comeback. They're probably praying for a devaluation."

"It's what the Americans want, isn't it?" Valladolid said. "I mean, they want Selva to win. They don't care if there's political chaos. In fact, I think it serves their purpose. When has peace and prosperity served the colonists?" the old man said. "We're finished. We were finished a long time ago."

"Why don't you stop blaming the fucking Americans for everything? They didn't borrow the fucking money from Citibank and then steal it. They didn't send it to accounts in Switzerland. And they didn't stop you from investing here instead of sending your money out of the country for the last hundred years," Russell said angrily. "That's the problem with you people. You haven't taken responsibility for your own damn country. Where are the factories, the highways, the railroads? You're as much to blame as the Americans are, for Christ's sake!"

The young woman lawyer stood up angrily. Madrid told her to sit down.

"He's right," Valladolid said. "He's right. All of you have bank accounts in Miami. I know I do. That's the horrible truth. We, the class that mattered here, when did we really believe in the country? The boy is right."

Russell poured himself a glass of wine and went to the window. He felt ashamed of his outburst. The others started to talk about party politics. He listened for a while. Their internecine squabbles seemed ludicrous in the face of the economic crisis that would sweep them all away.

It was late. He drained his second glass of wine and walked back to the couch. Everyone had left but the Senator and Madrid. There was no consensus on how to face the devaluation. It looked as though Madrid's coalition would break apart. A privatization of the telephone company, which had been the centerpiece of their platform, seemed impossible now. Who would want to buy it now, with the country in chaos?

"There's one solution," Russell said, coming back to the couch.

"Well, go ahead boy, don't keep us in suspense," the senator said.

"A coup," he said. "We get rid of Blanco and take power. Ignore the IMF's suggestions. Do it before the election. Then you privatize the telephone and the water and electricity companies. With the money you get, you defend the quetzal. It's a gamble, but it might work. The international capital markets will love the privatization, and might just not sell

198

the country's debt off once they hear the plan. They certainly won't care much about the coup, given how bad things are anyway. As long as we make it clear the new government is pro-business. . . . Interest rates might actually go down," Russell said. "It's a big gamble. But you'll have to move quick. President Blanco has to go. And the army has to be brought to heel." The two older men looked at him, open-mouthed.

"It might work, Rudy," Madrid said finally. *"Jesus* . . . it just might work. We'll hold elections in a year after the coup."

"The embassy will come to Blanco's defense," Valladolid said. "But I like it. Blanco is a prick. I never liked the man," the senator said.

"I think the telephone company alone is worth maybe a billion dollars. Let's say in four months, you have five or six billion in the treasury. That's enough. You wouldn't have to devaluate," Russell said. "You could start paying on the defaulted loans."

"All we have to do is overthrow the military government," Rudy said. "It's child's play . . . really!" They all laughed.

"Of course—because it's Guatemala—they'll try to kill us first," Madrid said. "Because nobody in this fucking country can keep a secret!"

"We're all like old ladies," Rudy said, slapping Russell on the back, clearly excited by the idea of a coup.

"And what about Selva?" Madrid said. "He's not just going to lie down and take this coup. He expects to win the election."

"No. He'll be a problem," Russell said. "He'll have to be arrested. . . . And I suppose sent out of the country. Or put in jail." Russell looked at the old senator, who had sat back down. Valladolid was looking at Russell differently now.

"That would be very unfortunate for his wife and children," Valladolid said cryptically, looking at Russell.

"Yes. It would, but these things happen in politics," Russell said.

"You know if we decide to do this, we might all be killed," Madrid said, looking at him. "You realize that, young man?"

"Yes. But we might also save the country from a civil war and financial collapse," Russell said.

"Jesus. I love young people!" Rudy said. "They always are ready to die. Personally, I love life too much, I think. The older you are, the more you love it."

Russell looked at Madrid.

"He's right, Rudy," Madrid said. "We have no choice now. Do we?"

"No, I suppose not. But I certainly hope we don't have to *die*. I suppose we can't do this from Miami, young man?"

"No," Russell said, and smiled. "You can't do it from Miami."

"I didn't think so. It was just an idea."

"Well, welcome to the government," Madrid said, looking at Russell. "I'm appointing you to the provisional central bank as of this evening. You'll have to run the privatizations. . . . And help us plan this coup."

"Me?"

"It was your idea," Madrid said. "Anyway, we can trust you, I think. I don't even trust Rudy."

"Young man, if we manage to get ten billion dollars in the treasury, you won't even be able to trust God himself," the senator said.

• • •

Russell cut the engine. The boat, a brand new Boston whaler, glided through the brackish water of the lagoon in Tilapa. Beatrice suddenly yelled his name with delight. She was wearing a sky blue bikini. She'd taken off her top, and her small breasts looked very white in the bright sunlight. Her cry startled a group of parrots. The birds exploded from a tree top on the far bank. The bright green birds, flying just over the water, headed down the lagoon.

"There! There they are!" she yelled. Russell had come down for the Selvas' party in Tilapa. Beatrice sat in the bow, clutching the gunwales. Alone, they'd been hunting for crabs in the lagoon that ran behind the beach.

"Stop here!" she said. "Look. There. Do you see them?"

Russell looked down over the little boat's gunwale.

"See. Blue crabs," she said. She turned around. She'd never looked more beautiful. He held on to the gunwale and tried to look into the blue-green water of the lagoon. On the other side of the narrow spit of land behind him, he could hear waves hitting the unseen beach. "Can't you see them?" she said.

It made him feel uncomfortable that she'd taken off her top; there were other families on the spit for the weekend, and they couldn't be sure that they wouldn't be seen. He had asked her not to, but she'd ignored him. It was as if she wasn't hearing him, or as if she were at times alone. Beatrice had spoken to herself twice as they went up the lagoon. At first he thought she was speaking to him, but when he realized that she was talking to herself, it was as if he'd caught her doing something unnatural, and she had turned away.

"Yes, I see them," he said finally. He'd had to put on his other sunglasses, the very dark blue ones. With their dark tint, he could make out the strange exotic crabs on the floor of the lagoon. They were a species that lived only in central America, in the mangrove swamps along the Pacific. He saw a group of crabs scurrying over the submerged roots of the mangrove trees, ten feet under the water. The crabs, smallish, were dark blue, the color of steel when you heat it up.

"They're beautiful," he said, and looked at her. "Are you all right?" She'd pulled her hair out of a pony tail.

"Of course I am. Why?"

"You haven't answered me about Carlos. I asked you twice when he was expected."

"This afternoon," she said vacantly. "I thought I told you. He's flying in. . . . The helicopter."

"Put your T-shirt on," he said. "Please."

"Why?" She turned back and looked down into the water. "I'm going in to get one." She dove over the gunwale of the boat before he could stop her.

"Jesus." The lagoon was dangerous; sharks came in from the ocean, and there were alligators. He quickly looked up into the mangroves, looking for splashes. He'd brought his shotgun and reached for it, slinging it over his naked shoulder, and then saw her as the water cleared. He couldn't stop himself from smiling, or from wanting her. The sight of her slender figure underwater, the blond hair trailing. "Jesus," he said again. "Jesus, you're so fucking beautiful." He saw her grab at something, then swim towards the surface, her shoulders moving aggressively. She grabbed the gunwale and tossed a crab into the boat. It landed at his feet.

"Are you going to help me? We can have them for lunch. There's hundreds down here," she said excitedly. In the sunlight the crab's color was darker, almost black. The crab struggled to climb the side of the boat and escape.

"Beatrice. There're sharks, for God's sake!"

"I know. Come on before they get here," she said.

He knew he shouldn't go into the water with her, that it was unsafe, that someone might come along and jump them, or tell someone the general's wife was swimming topless with the American. He un-slung his Mossberg and laid it down next to the red gas tank. He glanced for a moment at the crab, at the way it struggled violently, its jewel-shaped claws desperately opening and closing. Already the creature was being affected by the sun, its shell already dry-looking. Russell dove into the warm, dangerous water.

Tilapa was really just a spit of land—a long island between the ocean and the lagoon—studded with the vacation houses of the very rich, tucked away on Guatemala's untouched Pacific coast. Russell thought it was one of the most beautiful places he'd ever been. His mother had owned the Selva house, in fact. The general had bought it from his aunt after Russell's mother died.

Russell remembered the house very well, from his childhood. He sat in one of the compound's several guest cabanas. The worn red-tile floor was sprinkled with white sand. He and Beatrice had tracked it in from the beach. The sun, fierce at mid-day, shone through two small windows high on the wall. A new fan with wooden blades turned swiftly through the warm air, making a pleasant noise that mixed with the sound of the ocean.

"I want to make love," Beatrice said. He'd let her come into the cabana only because she said she wanted to talk. He'd left the door open so that the maids could see what was going on.

He glanced out into the yard. One of Beatrice's children was playing in the large enclosed backyard behind the main house.

They'd made love in the bottom of the boat. He'd taken the crabs they'd caught and wrapped them in their towels. It had been a crude and unsuccessful trap. At the end, when he'd been rocking her, there had been the sound of the water as they drifted, and the sound of sea birds and the heat of the morning sun on his legs and chest. It hadn't made any difference when he felt one of the creatures bite his leg. He'd simply stopped for a moment, reached down and batted the crab to the back of the boat, noticing when he did that all the crabs had managed to push their way out of the towels.

Laughing, he told her their lunch was getting loose. She said she didn't care, her face tense with the sex. They were sitting so that she was astride him, his hands exposed to the crabs. She must have seen them as they worked their way free, but she wanted to keep riding him, making the small boat move in the calm water. He watched the sweat run down from under her arms, the red strap marks clear where she'd been sunning herself the day before, when she'd been alone with the kids. He noticed the lovely smallness of her breasts. He could feel the nudging of the crabs as they moved along his legs.

He'd come like the shimmering of the eleven o'clock swampy sunlight on the lagoon, fast and electric, In small boat-rubbing spasms, her lips on his neck, the crabs on his hands, their cold dying creature-touch odd and pleasurable, like the lovemaking. He heard her laughing and saw small puddles of sweat on his stomach as she came. He could smell gasoline, see the black rubber hose that led to the outboard motor from the gas can, hear the silence of her lifting herself. She was so, so deliberate and sexual in the way she got off him, loving him even while she was finally leaving. She touched him there, with her hand, her wet hair lying on her shoulders, thick-looking. He would never have another time like that with any other woman. Nothing would ever be like that again. It was as if the whole world had shrunk down to just the inside of this little boat, and it had been making love with them, the lagoon going breathless and contracting and then releasing with them. He told her he loved her, that he couldn't live without her.

He'd said it while he'd gathered up the crabs and tossed them into the center of the expensive pink beach towels she'd brought for them. She'd listened quietly. He told her he wanted her to leave Carlos, that he wanted to take her and the children away, maybe to Europe, that he could afford to take care of them, that he was doing something that would make it possible.

She'd sat there naked on the bench as the ocean's current pushed them into the shade of the mangroves, where huge roots, big ones like claws, hooked into the water.

He told her he would do anything to have her, that he had to have her forever, and he promised to take good care of her. There was nothing else he wanted in the world but her, he said, both of them in shadows now. He spoke at the end standing up, looking at the crabs as they silently struggled inside the knotted towel. He looked into the mangroves, their black trunk-shapes a delicate and seemingly endless abstraction.

"Will you come with me? When I'm ready?" he asked. "That's all I want to know."

"I'm scared, Russell. I'm not brave," she said. "I'm scared for the children. You know what he will be like if I leave him. You haven't seen him when he's angry."

"I don't give a fuck what he's like," he said. "This isn't about Carlos."

"He's murdered people, Russell," she said. "Near here. He's taken people out and shot them. On the road to Tilapa." She looked away into the swamp, where they said big jaguars lived and hunted at night. The people here said that they were the biggest jaguars in all Central America. Sometimes, people said, they would swim out to canoes and drag fishermen into the swamp.

"All right, he's killed people," Russell said. "Do you want your children living with a murderer?"

"I don't know what I want. I want you, but I don't know, Russell. I don't know about taking the children from him; it seems so unfair, doesn't it? He loves them. He's a good father. And they have a place here. What will their place be with us?"

"I promise you, I'll have plenty of money," he said. "If that's what you're worried about." He knew it was. He knew she didn't want to live her life the way she had lived it before. She'd been poor, the child of a single working mother.

"It's not the money, it's their country. They're Guatemalans. They speak Spanish. They don't speak English that well, Russell. Do you understand? They're not English children, not at all. I'm English, but they aren't."

"Then leave them," he said, pulling at the motor. "We'll have our own." And he meant it.

He had let her come into his cabana only because she said she wanted to talk. But she'd gone into the bathroom, shut the door, and showered. He had sat on the bed waiting for her to finish, his sunglasses still on, nervous that she was again doing something she shouldn't be. *She shouldn't be in here using his shower.* The maids had looked at one another when they'd stopped to talk in the courtyard, handing off the crabs they'd caught to the cook. He heard the shower running and wondered what the hell he'd say if anyone came to the door looking for her.

"You've got to go," he said when she came out. She had wrapped herself in a fresh white towel. "Now," he said. "Please. I'm serious."

"I can't do it," she said. "I can't leave the children. Don't ask me to do that. But you can't ever leave me, either."

"He'll find out, Beatrice. Look at you, you're in my room showering. The maids are talking. We made love today and could have been seen by anyone out there. He'll kill me when he finds out. It's only a matter of time."

She walked to the cabana door and kicked it shut with her foot. It slammed shut. He went immediately to open it again, but she stopped him. She dropped the towel. Even then, afraid and angry, she still took his breath away.

"Stop it, Beatrice. They're just *outside*," he whispered.

"I can't live without you. You don't understand!" she said. "He can't make love."

"What?"

"Carlos. There's something wrong with him lately."

"What are you talking about?"

"I don't know what it is." There was a knock on the door. *"Señora?"*

"Sí," Beatrice said. *"Sí, dígame, Carmen."* Russell recognized the children's nanny's voice on the other side of the door.

"Your cell phone, *señora* . . . the general's mother," the nanny said.

"Go get the phone and bring it here to me," Beatrice said, calling to her. She bent down, picked up the towel and walked towards him. He had no idea what they were going to do now. She put the towel around both of them and held him. He felt his pants get wet from touching her.

"I want to marry you. Do you understand? I'm taking you away. I don't care what you say."

"All right," she said. "All right . . . all right."

TWENTY-THREE

He'd spent the afternoon in his room at Carlos Selva's beach house, trying to put on paper the economic plan Madrid and the coup leaders could use for the privatization of key industries. After securing power, they would have to go to New York immediately to cajole the U.S. bankers to extend credit. They would have to convince Citibank and the rest of them that they could defend their currency if they sold off the national telephone company. The New York bankers, he knew, would be eager to get the investment banking fees from the privatization of the country's utilities, and could be convinced to cooperate if the Madrid government persuaded them they were pro-capitalist. That was step one.

He couldn't know what the American State Department would think of the coup, or what kind of response they would get. But because Madrid's forces were all pro-business, it would be difficult for the Americans to denounce them publicly. After all, he reasoned, they would be doing what the World Bank and the IMF had been asking Latin American countries to do for decades: Open up their markets. The U.S. State Department, he calculated, couldn't come out and say they supported right-wing generals over capitalist, free-market businessmen who promised to hold elections as soon as the "economic crisis" was over. The Americans would be forced to swallow the coup, he gambled.

Russell wouldn't be going with them to Washington. He no longer had any interest in anything but Beatrice and the Red Jaguar. He would help Madrid and his party organize themselves, tell them what they needed to do, but that was all. He would take Beatrice out of the country as soon as they secured what treasure he and Mahler could. When Madrid took power, Russell would be in the jungle with Mahler. The confusion in the capital, he hoped, would allow them to get away with their treasure unnoticed. If Carlos were arrested, so much the better.

Was it why he'd suggested the coup? he wondered, stripping off his bathing suit. No. He'd been appalled by the idea of the devaluation. But he realized, turning on the shower, that the country would be too busy fighting with itself—at least for a few days—to be able to stop him and Mahler. He stepped into the shower and let the tepid water hit him. He tried to feel guilty about stealing the Red Jaguar, but couldn't. The country owed him that much for taking his mother from him.

He saw that Beatrice had stupidly left her bikini bottom on the shower floor. He bent down to pick it up. As he bent to pick it up, he remembered something he'd read at university, something Sartre had said about Algeria. *There comes a moment of boomerang when the oppressed become the violent, wild men the colonizers insisted they always were.* Would his plan engender a great violence?

It was almost five o'clock in the evening when a maid tapped on his door saying that drinks would be served on the veranda. Russell closed up his computer and left his room. He could see guests coming from other houses down the beach, some of them on fat-wheeled motorcycles. He hadn't expected it to be so pleasant, seeing his mother's extended family, all of them excited that he'd come to the party. Several older women spoke to him about how wonderful and elegant his mother had been. Everyone reminded him that she'd owned the house they were standing in. They all spoke to him as if he had never left. He was accepted—this was his place, their expressions seemed to say.

He'd sought out his aunt, a tall, elegant woman who had lived most of her life in Miami. He sat next to her on the veranda, both of them looking out at the sea. They talked about the family plantation. She'd already forgiven him for not going to see her. She seemed to understand that it was too difficult for him.

"I'm glad you came," his aunt said. She was wearing pedal pushers, despite her age, and an expensive-looking blouse. He imagined that his mother would look like her if she lived now, an attractive older woman. In his memory, his mother was always young. She would be, God, what—in her fifties? What would she think of her son? He would never know.

A few young teenagers played in the surf below the house. One of them had dragged out a large inner tube, riding it into the surf. The waves reflected the orange-red of the setting sun. He turned to look at his cousins and Beatrice, who had come out with the children from the beach. The slight glow of the sunset colored everything, even the faces of his family. He saw Rudy Valladolid sitting with one of his aunt's daughters. The Senator, in shorts and a sleeveless T-shirt, nodded to him, and he nodded back. It was so Guatemalan that they would be planning a *coup d'état* while being entertained by one of its chief victims.

He reached over and put his hand on his aunt's knee. She smiled at him. They had been talking about the Empire Room at the Clift Hotel in San Francisco, how it had been his mother's favorite place when she came to visit.

"I want to know what happened," Russell said, suddenly interrupting her. "The whole story. Please. Uncle Pedro wouldn't tell me the whole story." His aunt turned to look at him. Russell saw the teenage boy, out in the surf, lifted up on a wave and then disappearing behind it. His aunt glanced at him, then picked up her drink.

"It was the Communists. It was an afternoon like this," she said. "It happened on the road to *Las Flores.* We wanted you to believe it was a car crash. Your uncle lied to you. I'm not sorry. How could a little boy understand war?"

"What happened?"

"They left her by the side of the road like an animal." His aunt reached for his hand. He didn't really want to know the rest of it.

• • •

Spring 1988

Even Isabella's brother hadn't had the heart to change their grandfather's bedroom in the apartment in the capital. It looked exactly the same as the day in 1939 when her grandfather had died, asking for reports about his empire in the jungle. They said he was on the phone with General Somoza in Nicaragua when he died. Sometimes, in the dim light of a rainy afternoon, Isabella could see herself and her brother as children running in the dark corridors, unaware of what was waiting for them.

It would be, Isabella hoped, the same apartment her son would someday inherit, an apartment that said so much about their family and yet told little about the individual men and women who had passed through it. Like all the Cruz homes, it was redolent with the country's very smell and the family history, which was one man's fear of poverty, and the achievement of great wealth. Conversations that had changed the history of the country seemed to linger in the dining room, a room that had absorbed all the blood and lust of an entire century.

"Are you my love?" Antonio asked her. Antonio was in love with Isabella, but he was in love with a lot of girls, and she knew that. He was younger; his parents would never, *ever,* let him marry a divorced woman who was ten years older and had a child, even if she was a Cruz and owned the biggest coffee plantation in Central America.

Isabella looked at him for a moment. They were listening to *"Ojala que te vaya bonito"* on the stereo. Isabella had bought the record in Mexico, and it was her favorite right now.

There had been a lull in the fighting. The roads were a little bit safer, everyone seemed tired of the fighting, even the communists. She'd driven up to the capital from the plantation, just she and her driver and Olga, her father's pistol in the glove compartment, the one she'd used to save them nine years before. She'd still been a girl then; now she was a woman. Running the plantation had given her a *gravitas* that most men found threatening. She'd faced the war without flinching. Her brother had gone to Europe.

She was wearing a white sleeveless dress and white shoes. At 32 she was still girlish, slender and tall. The years of trying to be young were almost over, and the years of running the plantation alone were printed on her beautiful face. There was an authority in her eyes now. Sometimes she'd been able to stand the war, and sometimes, missing her brother, she'd run to Paris to stay with him for months at a time. She was both good and bad. In Paris she took lovers and did drugs, because the young were doing drugs and taking lovers. Her brother, who loved her, made her feel at home in his world—the *demimonde* of the cinema and pretty people whose coin was sex—but it was still the world of Paris, and not the world of the jungle and the fighting that she'd come to know and rely on to give her strength. She was a very attractive woman who found in sex a power she wasn't afraid of.

Her son was coming in a week to spend his Easter vacation, and she was planning a wonderful time for him. She'd had the apartment in the capital cleaned, the sheets pulled off the furniture. She'd had the beach house painted, the boat repaired, and hired two American mercenaries to go with them, because Tilapa was as dangerous as it gets. But the Cruzes had always gone to Tilapa in April, war or no war. She'd been there as a child on the beach, and she wanted Russell to go one more time before he was too old. He was almost a man now, and she hoped he was going to be a soldier, something the country needed. Someday, she knew, he would come home and take over the plantation and be ready for whatever life threw at him. He would be a Cruz; she felt it. A powerful man, like her father and grandfather. He would be strong. She had wanted her son, more than anything, to be strong, a man who could take the Cruzes into the new century.

Isabella listened to the melancholy strains of the song as Antonio followed her into her bedroom in the capital. The room smelled of perfume and the old waxed floors. She looked up at the photo of her grandfather and grandmother on horseback. Sometimes her grandfather would come to her like that, on horseback, while she was out with the administrator, the sounds of gunfire coming from further down, towards Mexico. She and her administrator would go out by horseback in the early morning light when it was still cool, riding out to a distant part of the plantation, not knowing who or what was waiting for them.

From where she rode she could see miles and miles of blue green hills, and here and there the red roof of a plantation house in the distance. She'd been called a whore by the men of the country club and the city. People she'd grown up with, all married, couldn't respect her because she wasn't married, and because she used men, they said, like a man. It was on one of those mornings, the administrator sliding from his horse and going to talk to one of the shirtless workers clearing the bush, when she turned and saw her grandfather coming up the road on horseback in his frock coat, with his high Spanish forehead and his stern look.

"Mija ven aca," her grandfather said to her as he rode up into the *cafetal.* "Is it true you're sleeping with men in my house?" He slapped her in the face and demanded an explanation. He said she wasn't a good Catholic. She held her face and told her grandfather that she was holding onto the plantation he'd given them, but she needed men to be happy. She was a woman. She couldn't stand always being alone. I'm no different than you were, she told him.

"You have a son," her grandfather's ghost said.

"I do."

"What will he think of you?"

"I don't know," she'd answered. "I don't know."

"I had many wives," he said. "Some I married, some I didn't. Maybe you got this from me. I'm burning in hell for it. I don't want you to. . . . You're as strong as a man, I can see that. God bless you, my daughter." He rode away.

Isabella started to cry, spurring her horse toward him to ask him if he'd seen her father. But her grandfather was gone, disappearing into the *cafetales* with their white flowers.

The administrator was looking at her. Later, he told his wife that Dona Isabella was talking to herself, and it had frightened him. Everyone was going crazy, he said; it was the war. He blamed the war. His wife said Isabella was a whore and would burn in hell for all the men she'd sinned with. The administrator said nothing. Three days later, he stepped on a land mine. He heard the click of the thing before he died. He saw a *Piui* bird in the sky. And then he was gone. Isabella went on without him.

"Olga. I'm leaving for the party." Isabella had come into the kitchen. She didn't always come into the kitchen. It was Olga's place.

The two women, more like sisters than master and servant, looked at each other. Perhaps it was a premonition. "I don't know what time I'll be back," Isabella said.

"*Sí, senora.*"

"Olga?"

"*Sí, señora.*" Isabella had stopped by the doorway

"Are you happy?" she asked Olga. It was an odd question. Isabella wasn't even sure why she'd asked it. Olga had been married now for a year, and the change in her had been pronounced; Isabella was jealous. She'd never thought she would be jealous of Olga. After all, Olga was deformed, and short, and an Indian; and yet Isabella, the day after Olga's marriage on the plantation, couldn't look at her exactly the same way. She loved Olga, she knew that. It was a love she couldn't have explained to anyone; it was profound, like her love for the land her grandfather had left them.

"*Sí, señora.*" Olga gave her a rare smile. She was normally serious, and had been that way since they were little girls.

"I'm so glad." Isabella went back and hugged her. "I'm so very glad," she said.

For some reason, she decided at the last moment to take her father's pistol out of her purse. Antonio looked at her as she took the old-fashioned heavy revolver out and laid it on the table by the phone. She had carried it everywhere since the war had started.

Then they left. Five minutes later, her son called from his school, saying that he'd just heard that he was going to the military school he'd applied to in Virginia and he wanted his mother to have the good news. He'd missed his mother by five minutes.

Later, as Olga was making tortillas out in the courtyard, squatting alone, she smelled Isabella's perfume mixing with the smell of the corn and the wood smoke, and felt uneasy.

Isabella had been at embassy parties before; many, in fact. Mostly they were rich Guatemalan boys from all the best families and American women who worked at the embassy, gold diggers in their thirties from Tennessee and New York. Women who, like Isabella, were certainly not innocent, and were of a certain age that called for certain girlish attitudes to be put aside if they wanted a man. Like the other women at the party, Isabella understood that they were alone, as women of the world are alone. It was the first time that she had an inkling of the idea she was now a woman, not a girl or a male adornment. There was something in the intense expression of one woman she met, a redhead from Chicago; the redhead was a little drunk when Jose introduced them. It was clear from the woman's body language that she "knew" Antonio very well.

"She helped me with my sister's passport problems," Antonio said. Like most men, he was a bad liar. Isabella knew then it was over between them, not because of the woman from Chicago, but because she was too old now for this, and she was tired of chasing her youth. It was over. It ended there in that living room, listening to the Rolling Stones on the stereo.

The war had changed her. She was tired of men like Antonio who saw the war as only an inconvenience, and were anyway spending more and more time out of the country. She felt very alone, looking around the rococo-style mansion that belonged to the Minister of Health.

She felt as if she were meeting herself after a long absence, and the Isabella she met was a stranger. She saw herself for the first time that evening. It was bizarre. She'd never had a really clear picture of herself, not since she'd been a child in boarding school in the United States, when a store clerk–hearing her Latin accent, but not seeing her–called her a Mexican. She wasn't a Mexican, but she understood what it meant. She was different, and would never forget that the United States wasn't really her home. The only home she had was out there in that strange place of volcanoes and coffee and warfare and Indians and rain and ghosts. She wanted to tell her son to be something, anything but what Antonio and his kind had become–empty rich boys. She wanted to leave the party then, but Antonio begged her to stay. So she did.

It was late, and there were the loud voices of people who had drunk too much. The stereo was playing rock music from the States. It sounded foreign to her. She preferred Latin music.

She didn't know where Antonio had gone. She sat in the living room, impassive. The Minister of Health, only forty, was going on about horse racing. Men and women sat on the couches around her. There was a great deal of blue cigarette smoke. She was drinking vodka and was slightly drunk now, and wondered how she would get rid of Antonio, because she had no interest in ever sleeping with him again. Oddly, she was thinking of what she would eat in the morning when the American girl from Chicago hit her on the side of the head with a heavy Mayan stone god. It had been sitting on the coffee table; Isabella had even picked it up and looked at it, only minutes before.

She died instantly, as Mick Jagger began to sing. Everyone who was there would remember the terrible sound of her body falling on the glass table.

Her son was asleep. He slept well and rose to the sound of a bugle, as he had for the last eight years of his life.

TWENTY-FOUR

Beatrice had gotten drunk. At times she would look at Russell across the dinner table, from her place next to her husband. He'd deliberately sat far away from her, between his aunt and Rudy Valladolid.

Alone in his room after dinner, he could hear the sound of an electric generator. The generator's distant whir had been a pleasant sound over their dessert. They had flan and sweet German wines, the weak lights of the pergola dimming at times. The dinner conversation had been about the World Cup, and how well the American team had done, then turned to children away at college and boarding schools. Russell had barely spoken.

After hearing his aunt's story about his mother's death, Russell couldn't help but spend dinner wondering what his life would have been like had she lived. His aunt told him that the guerrillas had wanted to make an example of her because of who she was.

His aunt and uncle hadn't wanted him to know that his mother had been murdered. They were afraid that it would be too much for him, so they had made up the lie about a traffic accident. Because they had been Cruzes, the story was easy to fix. They'd even had a newspaper article planted with details of the accident, in case Isabella's ex-husband made inquiries. He never did, of course. The only thing Russell's father ever said about his mother's death was that he'd heard

218

the roads in Central America were dangerous and he wasn't at all surprised, given how fast his mother drove, that something had eventually happened to her. Russell thought his father seemed relieved that she was gone for good.

His uncle had explained, the day he'd called Russell from Paris, that the war was making it too dangerous for Russell to go to Guatemala for the funeral. "Your mother would want it that way," his uncle had told him. Russell had decided that his uncle was a coward. He would have gone. He hadn't been afraid. He felt ashamed. He knew that his mother would want him to go, to be there for her.

After that call, he'd crossed the empty lawn back to his dormitory. The rest of the students were in class, the classroom doors shut. Russell could see the boys bent over their books through the windows as he made his way down the middle of the parade ground, past the flagpole with its plaque dedicated to the boys who'd died "defending" their country. The tips of his shined shoes picked up bits of grass, because they'd just run the mowers.

He'd gone up to his room, taken off his Sam Browne belt and his coat, and lay on the bed. The facts of his situation came and went as he stared out at the winter elm trees. He said "coward" out loud several times. Later, he tried to recover the pistol his mother had used to save their life when he'd been a baby. No one—including his aunt—seemed to know where it had gone.

A few minutes before, he'd heard a plane flying low over the general's beach house. It was very loud for a moment, then the sound of the engines moved out over the water.

There was a knock on his door. He was reading. It was very late, and he was pretty sure that Beatrice was too drunk, when she'd said good night to the last of her guests, to sneak off and come to his bungalow.

"Yes?" Russell said.

"It's Carlos." He heard the general's voice.

"Come in," Russell said immediately. It was after one in the morning; he was surprised that Selva wasn't in bed. The general opened the door and stepped into the room. Russell caught a glimpse of the moon through the open door.

"I'm going out on the lagoon. I thought you might like to come." Carlos was dressed in shorts and a *guayabera.* "Just you and I," Carlos said. "Do you have a pistol? Or something, just in case?"

"*Señor* Mossberg," he joked, referring to his shotgun. "It's rather late, isn't it?" Russell smiled and closed his book.

"Yes. But I saw your light on," the general said.

"It's warm in here," Russell said. "I suppose it would be cooler out on the water."

"Good. . . . We don't want to be caught with our pants down. There's all types out at night here. You'd better bring the shotgun. I get so tired of bodyguards all the time. I thought we'd go alone," the general said. Carlos looked at him for a moment. Russell slid his book onto the table next to his bed and stood up.

"You know what the people around here call Tilapa now," Carlos said.

"No."

"They call it the Red Jungle. *La selva roja,* because so many people are murdered either on the lagoon or out in the mangroves."

"Why?" Russell stood up. He felt odd. The general was looking at him closely. "I suppose I should put on long pants. For the bugs." The general nodded and sat at the end of the bed. *Does he know something?* Carlos's eyes were bloodshot from drinking. Heavily brilliantined and combed straight back, his hair looked almost wet.

"The locals are all doing something illegal with their boats. Cocaine. The planes from Colombia fly over about a mile out from the beach and drop the drugs. The boatmen pick it up and take it by sea to Mexico; it isn't far. Sometimes bandits come and try to take the coke from them on the lagoon. It's interesting," Carlos said. He glanced at Russell's shotgun in the corner of the room. "Come on. I'll meet you out at the dock. I'll tell Beatrice we're going out. . . . She worries."

Russell nodded. He went to his pack and took out extra shells for the Mossberg, then slipped on a pair of running shoes and a T-shirt. It dawned on him, as he bent over tying his shoes, that Carlos had learned about him and Beatrice, and was going to kill him.

She might have simply confessed. She had drunk too much at dinner, and with the strange way she'd been acting since he'd arrived, it was certainly possible, he thought.

He walked into the dark bathroom and switched on the light. Beatrice's bathing suit bottom was gone from where he'd hung it. *Damn it.* He'd meant to hide it.

The lagoon was moonlit when Carlos yanked the cord on the outboard. He'd kept Russell waiting as he stood on the beach speaking on his cell phone, his back turned. Russell sat in the boat with his shotgun on his knees, looking out at the lagoon that went for miles towards Mexico. He could hear the occasional jaguar, and once or twice heard the loud sound of twin outboard motors heading towards the narrow opening on the lagoon that opened onto the Pacific.

Coming towards the boat, the general tossed a Steyr machine gun to Russell as he climbed in. It was the same boat that Russell and Beatrice had taken out that morning.

"There's something going on in the capital," Carlos said, standing over the boat's engine. He checked the gas tank, opening it and shining a small flashlight down into the reservoir. "That was the U.S. embassy." He turned and shone the light into Russell's eyes. "My friend, a friend on the third floor. CIA. . . . They say Madrid is planning a coup." Carlos began pulling the motor's cord; the boat, floating out into the lagoon now, rocked under Carlos's weight as he pulled. His voice was punctuated by the outboard motor's attempts to start. "Have you heard anything about this, Russell?" As if answering his question, the motor started.

Russell was holding the Steyr on his lap along with the shotgun. He thought for a moment of shooting Carlos immediately, but realized that the sound of it would draw Selva's bodyguards, and he couldn't possibly get away. He would be dead before he could cross the lagoon.

"No. Not a thing. But then, how would I know that?" Russell said. "It's hardly something they'd tell me."

Carlos sat down. The engine was idling. They looked at each other. Russell could see the beginning of a smile on the general's face.

"My embassy friends asked me what the fuck you had to do with this. They can't figure you out, apparently. You've appeared on their screen and now you're a great mystery to them. They don't like mysteries. They say you're advising Madrid in regards to the economy, but maybe more," Carlos said. He turned the throttle up and they moved away from the dock, the lagoon calm. Russell could see that a few of the houses on the spit still had their lights on, the house lights dim and yellow like yellow oil paint.

"The tide is coming in," Carlos said. It was cool out on the water, much cooler. Carlos was still looking at him. "I suppose I should have the gun now," Carlos said, smiling at him. "Just in case."

"I want to thank you . . . for what you did for Katherine," Russell said. He was gripping the stock of the Mossburg. He slid his hand on the pump end. He wanted to shoot Carlos

Selva, who stood in the way of the country's progress; he was sure of it. He'd cleaned the shotgun and oiled it before leaving his apartment. There was that feel of the oily metal he'd first experienced in military school. He heard the sound of the outboard, felt the water give way under them as the boat speeded up.

He remembered the Greek. *He's just another bully.* He turned and looked at the dark shadows of the houses, along the beach.

Don't I have to? Carlos knew now about their plan and he would, being a good army man, tell President Blanco. He, Russell, could start the coup right now. Carlos was head of the intelligence service. *Why not kill him?* Russell let his eyes move along the shore. Could he shoot a man in cold blood? *Fuck him,* he thought. He knew Carlos wouldn't hesitate to kill him if he knew the truth about him and Beatrice.

"Where are we going?"

"There's a bar on the town side of the beach. It stays open . . . for the smugglers," Carlos said.

"How many people have you killed?" Russell asked. He said it over the sound of the motors. He couldn't just shoot him. He wanted to know. He wanted to tell him that he had to die, or the country would never change.

"Why do you ask?" Carlos said. He didn't seem shocked by the question.

"I just want to know," Russell said. "For myself."

"During the war, you mean? Is it for your article? Not a good idea."

"No . . . I want to know. Just for myself."

"Are you going to interview me now? Why not . . . I don't know how many. Many. You can write that. I killed many communists. People will like to read that in Europe, especially in America. Why not, I'm not ashamed of it. The Americans would have been next. We aren't that far away from Texas, you know. They're like cockroaches—the guerillas, you see one, and you know you'll see more," Carlos said.

Russell's cell phone rang. It was surreal, the sound of it now, when he was on the brink of shooting someone. He let it ring. Carlos sat facing him, his right hand steering.

"Can't get away anymore, can you?" Carlos said. They were going fast, and Selva cut the motor down so he could take the call. Russell glanced at the screen and saw it was a number from the States. He opened the phone.

"I'm coming back." It was Katherine. He looked at the general.

"Don't," Russell said.

"I have to," she said. "I love you."

"I can't talk right now," he said.

"I'm leaving tomorrow," she said. "I've gotten myself on the human rights delegation, a UN plane. Tomorrow. They wouldn't dare keep me out of the country. I'm coming with the commissioner herself."

"Please don't. It would be a mistake," he said.

Katherine hung up. He could see the lights now of the little town of Tilapa. They were near the mouth of the lagoon, where it met the ocean. They couldn't be seen from either the wharf at Tilapa, or the houses on the spit. If he was going to kill Carlos, he had to do it now.

"Who was that? You look upset," Carlos said.

"It's the girl. The American girl. She's coming back. With the UN Commission for Human Rights. She had herself put on the commissioner's staff."

"She's a smart girl. They won't stop her at the airport. And they won't dare touch her as long as she stays with the delegation, either."

"And if she doesn't stay with the delegation?" Russell said.

"That would be a bad idea," Selva said. "But love makes people do dangerous things," he added. "You have to admire her."

The place where he should have done it passed. It was where he could see the current moving out towards the mouth of the lagoon, towards the ocean. Maybe the body would have been taken out to sea, Russell thought.

The dope boats saved Selva. The first one Russell watched coming through the boiling surf, the men standing very still because they were so overloaded. Two others with twin outboard motors followed the first. They were all overloaded. The lead boat was a big twenty foot *tiboronaera* with three men aboard, and the words *Dios Es Amor—God is Love* in red letters on the prow. The gunwales of the boat hovered near the waterline as they approached. Russell could see the bales of coke wrapped in black plastic. One of the young men in the boat, an AK 47 strapped high on his chest, gave them a sardonic wave. The heavy wake rocked them violently as the boat cruised quickly by. They had all recognized Selva, and wouldn't have dared to touch him.

"They meet the twelve o'clock from Bogotá," Carlos said. "You could set your watch by that plane."

I should have killed him, Russell thought. He glanced towards the dark mouth of the lagoon, where the full moon lit the white breakers, which were carrying two more dope boats.

• • •

Sunday, May 23, 1988

Olga had sat in the kitchen for hours. Her mistress gone— although she had always thought of Isabella as her sister, never her mistress. This was the strangeness of it, the perversity of their relationship. In Olga's eyes, they were sisters despite all the differences so obvious to the outside world.

The conquest should have made them enemies; the guerrillas had come to the plantation one afternoon. They'd come to find Isabella and kill her. They'd come in two trucks

225

they'd stolen. The trucks had had some passengers who had been born there and knew everyone, so that later they could have been identified but never were, because they were the sons of the plantation. It was the sons of the plantation who had come to kill the owner and it was the sons of the plantation who had been talked out of the killing by their own brothers and sisters, who told them that killing was wrong and that Doña Isabella was their *patrona.*

They told the guerilas that killing her would be a sacrilege. Some of the other guerrillas, who weren't born there, laughed when they heard this. They'd been to Cuba, or they'd been educated in Russia and come back to Guatemala, and they knew that the old bond between master and servant was ludicrous. But when they faced it that evening, in the twilight, with the woodfires and the people's faces looking at them, they knew that ludicrous or not—absurd even as it was—the oppressed *believed* in the very system that had enslaved them. Somehow the system represented something eternal and Christian to them. It was as if God himself had come to Guatemala and written down the feudal arrangement on a tablet.

The guerilas patiently argued their case. They reminded the people that the whites had never thought twice about slaughtering them or cheating them, or raping them, or exploiting them, or keeping them ignorant. Some agreed, but none of the arguments worked. It was God's will, the peasants said. The guerillas were mystified. They finally left, confused by what they'd witnessed.

After they'd left, the people opened the doors of the plantation church, lit candles and prayed to God that they would never come back.

At 9:00 A.M. Olga had gone to Isabella's bedroom with a breakfast tray, looking for her mistress. The bed was empty and still made. At first she thought that Isabella had come in

226

so late that she hadn't gone to bed at all, but was in the living room and somehow Olga had missed her. She smiled at herself and carried the tray into the living room that over looked *La Reforma,* but the curtains were still closed. The room, full of Victorian furniture, gloomy and smelling of wax, was empty.

"Doña Isabella?" Olga said, slightly bewildered. Olga put down the tray and wiped her hands on her apron. It was something she would do again and again that day and for years to come, every time she thought of Isabella.

Isabella's naked body had been left on a dirt road that led to Antigua.

Antonio and the Minister of Health had made a call to the chief of the Guatemala City police, who happened to be the minister's brother-in-law. The American woman, sober now and frightened, was on her way to the embassy. The idea of holding an American embassy worker for murder was out of the question, of course. No one, not even the president of the republic, could afford to offend the American embassy. The minister and Antonio assumed the woman would be protected.

They waited for a call from the embassy, standing by the phone in the minister's study while Isabella's body lay on the floor of the minister's living room. The study's door was closed, so they couldn't see it. No one wanted to look at it. It was horrible because Isabella's face looked stunned, as if she knew what had happened to her but couldn't quite believe it.

"I'll have someone come for the body," the minister's brother-in-law said. "We'll have to list her as a Jane Doe." The minister, too shaken to go on with the call, passed the phone to Madrid.

Madrid had been drinking heavily, and was just now feeling somewhat sober. The sight of Isabella with half her skull bashed in had made him vomit out the alcohol.

"It's me, Antonio." The two men had gone to school together.

"Antonio?" The police chief said.

"Yes. Felix, what do we do?"

"You have to take her identity, her purse, and destroy it. I'll send someone for the body. She'll be a Jane Doe when she's found. It's the best way."

"I don't understand," Antonio said.

"She'll be found and be unidentified. The unidentified are cremated in two days. That will be the end of it," the policeman said.

"There's an autopsy, certainly?"

"Sometimes, but I'll take care of that," the policeman said.

"What about her family?"

"I'm afraid this has to be kept between us. That's what the embassy wants. They've already called."

"They called you, too?"

"Yes. Just now. I spoke to them. They're sending the girl back to the States tonight. . . . Antonio, it has to be this way. You understand . . . they don't want an incident. Not with the war on. Isabella's family is famous. People here would be insulted."

"Yes. Of course. I understand."

"I'll send someone right now," the policeman said.

"Please." Antonio put the phone down. It was a very old-fashioned phone, from the twenties, black and heavy. "They're sending someone right now. He wants us to take . . . Isabella's purse."

"What do you mean?" the minister asked him.

"We have to take her purse," Antonio said again.

228

"What about the family? We have to call her brother. I know him. You know him. We have to call Pedro, for God's sake. Antonio, she has a son," the minister said.

"We have to do what Felix says. The embassy has already called him. They're sending the girl back to the States tonight." He watched the minister fall into a brown leather club chair that had been bought years before, in London, and shipped to Guatemala.

"She didn't deserve this," the minister said. They had both known Isabella since they were children.

"It's my fault," Antonio said.

"What do you mean?"

"I was involved with the American girl. I should have taken Isabella home when I saw she was here. It was stupid. She told me she was jealous . . . I thought . . . I thought it was just *talk*," Antonio said.

The minister got up and left the room. He said that he was going to leave, that he didn't want to be here when they came for the body, that it was too gruesome.

"He said we have to keep our mouths shut," Antonio said.

"Yes, of course. Of course," the minister said. "It's the American Embassy, after all. They're helping us win this war." He said that almost as if he were talking to himself.

"Yes," was all Antonio said. "The war."

TWENTY-FIVE

The currency had collapsed the week before. President Blanco declared a state of emergency and shut down the country's banks, amid rumors that Blanco had precipitated the crash by emptying the treasury of dollars. The army had been called out to keep order in the capital.

The state of emergency had driven the foreign tourists out of the Camino Real hotel. The hotel's pool, usually crowded by this time of the morning, was quiet when Russell passed. Military filled the hotel's famous coffee shop. A few Americans from the embassy, in Gap pants and well pressed shirts, shared a joke with a group of high-ranking officers. But the laughter had a mirthless tone, Russell thought as he was shown to Mahler's table. No one in the army knew exactly how it might go in the next few weeks, only that the Americans would re-shuffle the deck and come out winners. The generals had simply come to the café to sell themselves, as they always did, like whores at a bar.

"Listen. I can't talk for long," Russell said as he sat down. Mahler was wearing the same dirty clothes he'd left the jungle in. He hadn't shaved, and looked oddly glamorous because of it. A gaggle of well dressed bodyguards, waiting for their military employers, stared at them.

"Carl's given me the money we needed. I . . . I just left him," Mahler said. A waiter came, and Russell ordered. "You have to come back with me. *Now.*" Mahler handed back the menu.

"I can't. Not right away. You have to go back without me," Russell told him.

"We haven't much time. Selva is going to win, or just take over. You know that. He'll nationalize *Tres Rios* and take it all for himself. We have to take advantage of this chaos," Mahler said. He ate scrambled eggs quickly, jamming them into his mouth.

"Blanco suspended the elections because of the crisis," Russell told him. "I just heard it on the radio."

Mahler snorted with contempt.

"Don't be a fool. Blanco is on the way out, and Selva will be the next president. It's pre-ordained. It's what the Yankees want." Mahler nodded towards the corner table of military men. "Selva's their man. And that's the way it's always gone here. The generals always win."

"Maybe not this time," Russell said, trying to keep his voice down.

Mahler fished in his dirty vest and threw something on the table between them. "I found that before I left," he said.

Russell picked up what appeared to be a small Mayan figure of a woman, solid gold, weighing several ounces.

"And some other things. We're close to the Red Jaguar, I tell you." Mahler's blue eyes were electric. "You have to come back with me *now*. I can't promise you I'll wait. If I find the Jaguar–I can't promise anything if I find it," he said, wiping the plate with a piece of bread.

"But you haven't found it. Or you wouldn't be here," Russell said, looking at the antiquity.

"No. I haven't found it–*yet,*" Mahler said. "But I'm warning you. You've fucked around too much as it is."

"I have a meeting," Russell said, standing up. "I'll see you at *Tres Rios* in a few days. I told you." He tossed Mahler back the gold figure. The two men looked at each other.

"I'm trustworthy," Mahler said. "If that's what you're thinking. And I saved your life, remember."

The elevator opened and the IMF country team Russell had met earlier in the week trooped into the cafe, all very well dressed. They were all Russell's age, or even younger. Mahler turned to look at them.

"Who are they?" he asked when he turned back around.

"IMF officials. They're here to try and save the currency."

"You mean they've come to arrange the deck chairs on the *Titanic,*" Mahler said.

"I've got to go. I have a meeting with Antonio," Russell said. It was, he suspected, his political connection with Madrid that was keeping Mahler from stealing what he could and disappearing. For all he knew, Mahler had already found the damn Red Jaguar and was afraid Russell might be too important now to cheat.

"Madrid can't win. If that's what you think," Mahler said, as if he'd been reading Russell's mind. "Your man was finished before he ever started. The liberals here are a pack of fools."

Russell sat down again.

"Don't be a fool. Don't you understand, Madrid has a good chance of becoming President. If he does, we'll be able to do whatever we want at *Tres Rios.* Can't you understand that!" Russell leaned forward and spoke in a soft voice. "Do you really think I'd back a loser?" He looked at Mahler carefully.

"What are you saying? Is there going to be a *golpe,* is that it?" Mahler said.

"I'm saying finish your breakfast and then get the fuck out of here before I decide I don't need *you,*" Russell said.

• • •

Monday May 24, 1988

The dawn had been red and sour-looking when Olga pulled the living room curtains open. She had sat patiently in the kitchen, looking at the clock on the wall, a white shawl around her deformed shoulders to keep off the cold. Sometimes she would get up and go to the hallway if she thought she heard something. Twice the phone rang and she ran to answer. But each time it was someone calling for Isabella. Each time she had to say her mistress was not in. When the callers asked when her mistress was expected back, she didn't answer.

The third time the phone rang, she didn't bother to answer. It was a strange reaction. It was her job to answer the phone, but she couldn't. She was frightened by then, and didn't know what to tell people. She could hear the clock tick by her simple wooden chair, in a corner by the stove.

She finally picked up a cup of cold coffee she'd poured herself hours before and put it in the immaculate sink. She touched the dish towel with both hands and bit her lip. She would have to go to the police. She didn't know what else to do. If Don Roberto were here, she would tell him, but he was far away and she had no idea how to reach him. The child was far away.

It was so different than when they were girls together, Olga thought. There had been so much family on the plantation. If there were a problem in those days, it was just a moment until you were home and safe. But now? Where were Isabella's people? It seemed so strange, she thought, getting her coat.

It seemed so strange that such a beautiful girl could be so alone, without her family. Olga realized that she was better off than her mistress. She had two children back on the

233

plantation. It was true she didn't get to see them as much as she would like, but she had someone of her blood. It was a shame.

She went down the cold white marble steps to the lobby. When she opened the door to the street, she realized it was raining. She thought of going back and getting a better coat and maybe an umbrella, but she didn't. She trudged off instead to *la Reforma,* and headed towards the central police station—just another deformed Indian in cheap black shoes, walking in the rain, her gait uncomfortable to watch.

She'd been hit by a truck the month Isabella was sent away to school. She hoped for a card from Isabella while she was in the hospital, but no one had bothered to tell Isabella what had happened to her childhood friend. Isabella was shocked the day she came home from school to see Olga limping horribly up the driveway.

"I'm looking for a white lady," Olga told the pockmarked sergeant at the central police station. Her deformity had a bad effect on people, making them oddly apprehensive. They didn't really want to look at her.

The sergeant glanced at her, then looked at the two young soldiers standing guard at the doorway. The war had moved to the city. Sandbags protected the front of the building, and a wire mesh covered the door in case someone tried to toss in a grenade.

The sergeant pushed a form at her, after making her wait for several minutes before he turned to her again. Olga could smell gun oil and leather and a Xerox machine.

Two American men with short haircuts walked through the doorway, unchallenged by the guards. They were having a heated conversation. They pushed a young man in front of them. The young man's face was swollen from the beating he'd gotten when he was arrested; he was barefoot. Olga

watched the two white men walk the young man down a
long hallway, then turn and disappear. No one had paid any
attention.

"You'll have to fill that out," the sergeant told her.

Olga tentatively reached for the form, looked at it, and then
laid it down on the counter again.

"I can not read, *señor*," she said. "I'm sorry."

"Then *how* in God's name can I help you, woman?" the
sergeant said. He looked at her, waiting for an answer. She
was ugly, and he didn't want to deal with her anymore. She
didn't know how to answer. But she didn't move, either.

"Perhaps, *señor*, if you would be so kind, you could write
the name for me?" Olga asked politely.

"We charge people for that," the sergeant said. He looked
across at the two young soldiers standing guard at the door. It
was raining harder now, and the water was hitting the
building's protective fence and dripping off. The two soldiers,
very solid young men and as dark as Olga, looked coldly at
her.

"Isabella Cruz . . . Doña Isabella Cruz," Olga said, digging
in her pocket. She put the few quetzales she had on the counter
without looking at the sergeant. He took her money and
grudgingly picked up a pencil. He rushed her through the
inquiry.

The two men in raincoats were not spotted on the road.
Their Cadillac came to a stop near a wide ditch, full of
rainwater and debris. It was so early that the dawn made the
ditch seem almost like something else, something natural, but
it was just a ditch with dirty brown water.

The two men took Isabella's body from the trunk. Neither
man wanted to do it. Neither man was a bad man, or a
heartless man, but they were about to do a heartless thing.
The chief of police had called back and told them they would

have to dispose of the body themselves. There had been an attack by the communists in the center of the city, and he could do nothing for them right now.

Antonio De La Madrid reached for Isabella's legs. He remembered, as he did, how pretty she'd been. He thought he might not be able to do what they had to do.

He stopped and looked down the deserted dirt road before them. They were a half hour exactly from the capital.

Someone named Hugh had called from the embassy. Antonio had answered the phone. Hugh said that it was important that the embassy not be involved in what he called "the accident." It was too sensitive a time, he said. Hugh asked them if they could do the United States government a favor. Hugh said that it wouldn't be forgotten. Hugh said they wanted the problem to "just disappear." That was all he had to say.

"Help the needy and show them the way," Antonio said as he put down the phone.

"What?" the minister said.

"It was a silly song. I remember when we were in the States. Isabella and I. . . . A song on the radio. She used to sing it," Antonio said, looking at the minister. "I *have* to tell her brother."

"Get a grip on yourself!" the minister said. "We can't tell her brother."

"Don't be ridiculous," Antonio said. "We *have* to tell her brother."

"No. You know Roberto. He's a lot of things, but he isn't stupid. He'll come back from Europe and look into this. He has a hundred friends. They'll all help him find out what happened. He'll kill us," the minister said.

Antonio sat down in one of the minister's club chairs. For a long time the two men sat like that, without speaking, because neither man wanted to be the first to go into the room and take the body away.

"There's a boy. A son. She has a son," Antonio said finally. "In the States."

"Had a son," the minister said, picking up his car keys. "Look, you know if Roberto finds out, he'll kill us, or at least try to. He's that type."

Antonio nodded. He knew it was true, because he would do the same if it had been his sister.

On the way through the city that morning, they both promised to help Isabella's boy when the time came for him to come back to Guatemala. They made a solemn pact. The minister, Rudy Valladolid, became senator the next year.

All this went through Antonio's mind as he reached down into the trunk and grabbed Isabella by the legs. Rudy took her by the arms. It was horrible, and Antonio tried not to look down, but he had to. He couldn't help it. He wanted to look at her one more time; even in death, she was a beautiful girl.

After they'd driven away, the rain caught the angle of Isabella's pretty cheek.

She'd had a dream as she died, watching the faces in the living room. She'd seen her father come out from the dining room. It was the exact moment of her physical death. Now alone, her legs tucked up awkwardly under her body, she joined a long list of missing people back on the counter in the police station. The sergeant tossed the missing person form the Americans had insisted they adopt. It seemed ridiculous, but like so many things they had to do now, they did them for appearance's sake.

At that last instant of her life, Isabella understood something her father was saying to her. She was sure she caught it. He was standing across the room and he stopped, not to warn her but to say it before it was too late. The cold collection of molecules that sat in her brain still had the thought as the rain pelted her in the face and her legs bent toward the coming sun.

"Isabella, we're ready. Aren't you coming? We have to go. The plane leaves for the States at four, and you know how your mother hates to be late."

"But I wanted to say goodbye to Olga," Isabella said, her cosmetic bag in her hand.

"You'll see her again," her father said. That's what he'd come to say, just as the thing penetrated her brain, did its damage, and ended it. "You'll see her again, dear." She didn't hear the dear. But it was there, and he'd said it, and that's all that was important. He'd called her dear and she'd loved her father so, it was good that he'd said it.

Perhaps it was that cold message in a dead brain that Olga heard as she left the police station and looked towards the south, distraught and frightened, rudderless as she would be now for the rest of her life.

TWENTY-SIX

Russell rang the bell on the landing. He remembered it from his childhood, a brass lion's paw with a large mother-of-pearl button. It was considered very modern when his great-grandfather had had it installed. He rang it twice.

He remembered very well coming up the stairs to the apartment with his mother. Sometimes they raced up the white marble steps together, more like brother and sister than mother and son. He realized, waiting for the door to open, that his mother had been just a girl then. He moved his finger off the button.

Olga answered the door. His aunt had sent Olga to take care of the family's apartment, agreeing to take her back.

"*Buenas tardes, Don* Russell," Olga said. She touched his arm as a sign of her affection for him, and her gratitude for what he'd done for her. She knew it was his doing that the family had taken her back and allowed her to resume her old duties.

He was shocked, but he didn't pull his arm away. Instead, without knowing exactly why, he embraced her, then patted her on her shoulder, the one that scared people, the one that had been smashed under the tires of the truck on the road to the Cruz plantation. She had foolishly run after a cheap plastic ball; the truck driver had been drunk.

"The streets are dangerous now," Olga said. "You have to be careful, *Don* Russell." She smiled at him, showing her bad teeth.

239

"I hope my aunt called, Olga, and warned you I was coming?"

"Yes, *Don* Russell. I've cleaned your mother's room, and everything is ready."

He didn't know what to say. No one but Olga seemed to mention his mother to him.

"Or you could have your uncle's room, if you prefer?" she said.

"No. . . My mother's room. Yes. That would be fine." He'd told his aunt that he wanted to use the family's apartment, without explaining why. He hadn't intended to stay there, but wanted only to use it to meet Beatrice. He'd thought of the family's apartment as safe – at least, safer than the Camino Real, or the Hilton where they'd been meeting.

Olga led him to his mother's bedroom. The ceilings were high. The wallpaper hadn't been changed since she'd died. It was yellow, with fleurs-de-lis. The room had big, beautiful French doors that opened out on to a narrow wrought iron balcony with a view of a statue of Ubico on a white marble horse.

Olga threw open the heavy curtains. The room smelled of wax and decay. He put his briefcase on the bed. Across the room was a blond bird's-eye maple chest of drawers, with glass top and hair brushes.

He heard the bedroom door close behind him. He'd meant to tell Olga that he was going to meet a friend here, but she'd left. He turned back and walked to the chest of drawers, and looked at what were probably his mother's hair brushes.

• • •

1988

"Do you see, Mother, why I had to do it? I mean the Greek," he said.

It was the last time he ever saw his mother. They were having lunch in Palo Alto. He had told her the whole story very calmly. He'd gone and put the pistol back with the others, and afterwards, when questioned about the incident, had denied everything. Even the police had come to the school, since the Greek's father had insisted that they investigate.

But all the boys had backed Russell. No one—not one boy, not even the boy who had shared the Greek's room—had said anything to the police. Russell had lied, telling the police he was asleep and hadn't heard or seen anything.

But he told his mother everything that day at lunch. He wore his dress uniform, sky blue with a gold cord he'd gotten for academic achievement. His father had come to the lunch too, and he was sitting open-mouthed, not knowing what to say or do. His father thought that Russell was a criminal and probably insane, and that it was all Isabella's fault. Now what would they do with him? (Later, he concluded it was the result of bad blood—those savages and outlaws Isabella was descended from.)

When they were walking back to his father's car—his father still inside the restaurant, paying—Russell's mother put her arm around him. They walked down the sidewalk alone together. The trees were shedding their leaves; the big wet golden leaves, with their dark spines, looked like etchings pressed into the sidewalk.

"You did the right thing, my love," his mother said. "I know you're a man now, and that's all I ever wanted for you, to be a man. Someone who wasn't afraid. Your great-grandfather was never afraid. That's why he was a great man, and why we have what we have." She said this last part proudly. "And my father was that way too. You have to be brave in this world."

"Well, I'm not afraid, mother," he said. "Not at all." And he wasn't, it was the truth. Later, though, he would have to

241

go back and constantly redefine himself as fearless—pushing himself to risk everything, money or life, just to double-check, never satisfied with what he found. No proof of courage would ever be quite good enough.

"Well, it's all settled then. Nothing to worry about," she said.

"I love you," he said. He didn't get to say that like other kids did, but he said it now, holding her around the waist, because he considered himself a man now. At school, he never said it because he had no one to say it to. He never said it to his father, and his father never said it to him. It was true: they had, in the end, different blood. But he and his mother shared the same blood. Russell knew his father thought he was too much like his mother, too Latin, too "hot-blooded." His father was a fool. Russell had known it from the moment he laid eyes on him.

"Mother, will we ever get a house here in the States? Maybe here in Palo Alto, and I could walk to school," he said. But then his father caught up with them, and his mother never answered. His father was worried that she'd overtipped. He was always scolding her when she was spending her own money, as if he had the right to simply because he was a man.

• • •

Russell touched the edge of one of his mother's hairbrushes. He heard the doorbell ring, and turned away from the chest. He stopped for a moment and felt something odd pass over him, something that came to him in the sound of the bell, a loneliness finely defined, a longing that he'd pushed away until now. It was the feeling he had always considered a malaise, but now he finally realized what it was: it was the loneliness he had felt as a child. Was that what it had been all these years? Was it that sense of loss that had come to him so strongly when he came back here? Was it simply missing her? Was it just that this country reminded him of his true

242

psychological circumstance, which had been so papered over back there in the States?

He realized, going to the door, inhaling the smells of the Cruz apartment, that he'd had an essential nature, and it had something to do with this country. Maybe his father had been right, always accusing him of being too much like his mother. As he walked down the hall and stopped in front of Olga, he knew that he would do whatever he could to help his mother's country out of this crisis—it was what his mother would have wanted of him. All of his loneliness, his training and his education had been for a purpose. *Finally,* he saw his purpose and his destiny. He was a Cruz, and his mother's son.

They sat in the living room. Russell watched Olga open the room's curtains, filling the living room with a slanted pulverized light. Beatrice, not sure how to act around Olga, smiled, and Olga smiled back at her.

"My friend Beatrice Selva, Olga," he said. Beatrice nodded. "Olga was my mother's friend," Russell said in Spanish. Olga smiled in a pleased way.

"Can I get you something, *Don* Russell, *Doña* Beatrice?" Olga asked.

"Coffee. Please," Beatrice said. She'd come from playing tennis, and was wearing a brown velour track suit. Her hair was down. She looked like a college girl, not a wife and mother.

The wood floor creaked as Olga went towards the kitchen. As soon as they were alone, Beatrice fell into his arms and they kissed, going to the couch. It had been a week since they'd seen each other, and they let the kiss go on.

"Will she say anything?" Beatrice said finally.

"No. I don't think so. She's loyal to me. To our family. She was devoted to my mother," he said. "I'll ask her not to."

"Good, then we can be as we really are." Beatrice smiled and cuddled up in his arms. It was surprising, how small she felt. When they were making love, she felt bigger.

"I'm going to join the government," he said.

"Why?"

"Because I think I can help," he said.

"But you're an American."

"Technically. Antonio is getting me my Guatemalan passport. They say I'm entitled to it, because of my mother. Then he's announcing my joining the party. What's so strange about that? *You* have two passports."

She looked at him, her cheeks rosy from the tennis. She put her hand on his chest.

"I'm glad then, if it means you will stay here with me," she said. "I worry that one day you'll leave and not even tell me." She smiled. "Would you leave me? Could you?"

"No. That's what I want to talk to you about." He heard Olga coming back. Beatrice moved slightly in his arms, but not much, so when Olga put the coffee tray in front of them, it was obvious to her what was going on.

Beatrice smiled at her and took a cup from the tray. Olga left them without saying anything.

"Was she shocked?" Beatrice asked when they heard the door close, holding the cup and saucer on her lap.

"I think so. She's seen you on TV, I'm sure. She knows who you are.

"I want to marry you," he said. "I want you to leave Carlos and come with me." He'd been planning to tell her, and now he knew he had to, before the crisis got any worse. "I had to tell you now . . . there's going to be a fight. I don't think the crisis can be resolved peacefully." He noticed the zipper of her running jacket was pulled down to where he could see the white of her bra.

"I don't understand?" she said.

"There's nothing to understand. I want you to leave Carlos. I don't want to sneak around anymore. I want us to get married. This can't go on the way it has been. Anyway, he'll find out soon. People are already talking. It's only a matter of time now."

"He'll kill you," she said. She sat up straight, moving away from him.

"I don't think so. Why? I'm not that important."

"You don't know him. He's liable to kill us both." She put her cup down.

"He's not going to kill the mother of his children," Russell said.

"He's a monster," she said.

"I love you. I know living here is out of the question. We'll leave. I thought, New York. . . . I've planned it all. I'll have money, too, if that's what you're worried about. I *understand,* if you are. I know what you expect. I mean, I'll be able to take care of you. And the children, too . . . of course," he said. "I promise you." She looked at him. "I wouldn't expect you to live . . . I mean, to leave this for something *small.*"

"I don't care about money," she said. "Is that what you think of me? That I married Carlos for his money?"

"Well . . . I do care. It's important. Money, I mean. I don't care why you married him. I could care less."

"I could never take the children from him," she said.

"They aren't his property."

"You're a fool," she said angrily, and got up and went to the window.

He knew it was going to be a shock, but he couldn't go on the way things had been. He was in love with her, and he wanted a family. He wanted to have children with her, *their* children. He wanted to have a home, and he wanted to be her husband, not her lover. He wanted to take care of her.

The clouds broke. Bits of late afternoon sunlight hit her velour jacket and her hair that was so blonde.

"Look. I know it's a shock, what I'm saying. But we haven't exactly been discreet, not really. And you know . . . sometimes you don't seem to care if he knows or not. It's better my way," he said.

"I'm not well," she said. She turned from the window and looked at him.

"What do you mean?"

"Something's wrong with me. My brain, the doctor says." She came back from the window and sat down, her knees pressed together at the far end of the couch. "The doctor says that it's the drugs I took. The ecstasy, when I was dancing. In London. There's something that makes me impulsive. He says that there's some kind of scarring, or something. I don't know. I'm scared. I wanted to tell you. I went to someone in Miami, Carlos insisted. He said that there had to be something wrong with me . . . that I'd been acting strange." She turned to look at him. "It's true . . . I have been. I know that."

"Everyone takes that drug. I've taken it. Countless times," he said.

"Well, some people get *this*," she said. She touched her head.

"I don't care. I love you."

"You shouldn't." She dove into his arms. "You shouldn't—" she said.

He kissed her. She smelled of perfume and coffee. They held each other. He could hear the afternoon traffic outside on La Reforma.

"It doesn't matter. At all," he said.

"I can get better," she said.

"Of course."

"I know I can. I'm young." He didn't answer. "I want to be with you." She stood up. "I want to be with you. Everything you want, I want," she said. He looked toward the kitchen. "I want to be with you now."

"All right. But Olga..."

"I don't care about Olga," she said. "Please."

"I have to say something, even if it's for her not to bother us," he said.

"Well then, tell her a crazy English girl wants to sleep with you. Where's the bedroom?"

He nodded down the hall. "The second door."

She went down the hall, turned at the door, and held her hand out. He got up and turned towards the window. He could see a tank crawling down the avenue, cars trying to pull around it. He heard the phone ring. It was Beatrice's cell phone. She'd left it on the table by her coffee cup.

"Don't *touch* it," he heard her say from the hallway. "Just come here."

He knew it didn't matter; the fact that she might be sick, or whatever, didn't matter. He loved her. It was a simple love, really.

When he got to the bedroom, she was standing next to a pile of her clothes on the floor. He closed the door quickly, afraid Olga might see.

• • •

It rained again that afternoon, and more tanks came out on the street as General Blanco was preparing himself. He'd been in politics a long time and knew someone out there wanted him dead, he said to an aide as he watched the central plaza from the palace office. Three tanks stood guard. The traffic outside was lighter than usual.

"The thing about this country is, when it feels quiet, like this, that's when things happen to you," Blanco said. He picked up the phone, acutely aware of what had happened to one of his predecessors in this very palace. He was too old for this intrigue; he called Carlos Selva.

"Carlos? It's Manuel Blanco. I'm stepping down. I've just appointed you President of the glorious republic, *et cetera, et cetera*. I wish you all the best in the upcoming election.

247

"By the way, the currency just collapsed in New York. Completely gone. You couldn't buy a bus ride from the Miami airport with a million quetzales. The IMF said they won't lend any more. Can I help you get your dollars out of the country? No, mine are already gone. Yesterday. Yes I'll see you at the club *Alemán*. Why not. Squash? Why not? And a good lunch afterwards!" he laughed.

Blanco called his contact at the American embassy and told them he was retiring. They had expected it.

Carlos called Beatrice immediately after getting the news, but she couldn't be found.

• • •

Mahler shot the two men who had found it. Really, he thought as he ejected the round from his shotgun, he'd had no choice. He heard the parrots noisily cawing as they escaped through the jungle canopy, frightened by the shooting. He looked up into the enormity of sunlight and tree limbs; it was a beautiful green lace, with just the tiniest bits of blue showing here and there. A howler monkey chased across the tree tops above him. Tree limbs sagged violently under its weight.

He looked down at the two dead men, and then stepped forward to look at the head of the Red Jaguar. Gloria, the girl from *Tres Rios* who had fallen in love with him, came running from the campsite. Mahler had bought her jeans and a new shirt. She'd tied her hair back.

He turned, and could see her coming up the hillock towards the temple. He could see the smoke from their cooking fire. He was pleased with how much they had cleared. It had taken weeks, but they'd cleared a lot of jungle. He'd always liked the feeling of uncovering things, ever since he was a child in his parents' garden and they'd given him a toy shovel and beach bucket.

He watched the girl run toward him. He felt for a shell in his jacket pocket. She was a good girl, and he loved the way she looked naked. And he knew she loved him. He liked Indian women; they were quiet. He'd spent so much time in the bush these last five years, they were the only women he knew anymore. This one running towards him was the prettiest he'd ever had.

He knelt down and wiped his brow. He'd been hacking nearby with a fat machete, caught in a daydream. He was back in Germany, teaching. The students were listening, and he was telling them that he was probably the greatest living expert on Mayan culture anywhere in the world.

Gloria was getting closer. He turned to look at the dead men.

They had yelled something, and he'd dropped his machete and come around to this side of the hill, the temple only partly uncovered. The two Indians he'd hired were standing looking at the jaguar's red jade face, inside the temple where the jungle had invaded.

For a moment, no one had said a word. The electric light they'd rigged off a portable generator shone on the Jaguar's partially uncovered face. Even though he believed he'd find it, Mahler had had his moments of doubts. Everyone had. But when they'd found the temple, he was sure the Red Jaguar was close.

"That's it," he said in German. He'd run to the men, and all three of them began clawing at the thing with their fingers. He told them in Spanish to be careful, his voice echoing against the stone walls. They worked frantically. In a few minutes they'd uncovered the left ear, then the whole jaw, then the entire face started to show through the vines. It was then, after he was sure it was the Red Jaguar, that Mahler stepped away from the two men, picked up the shotgun, and killed them.

249

Mahler looked back at the girl, who was standing where he'd stood when he'd first seen it. She said something in her native language. He answered her in Quiché, saying that it was the Jaguar and that the head was much bigger than he'd expected. He said then, in German, that it was at least ten tons. It was twice the size he'd expected. He had no idea how he would move it alone.

"I'll have to use the horses to pull it out," he said in English. "That's the way to do it now. I'll be alone, and how else can I do it?"

The girl turned to look at him, not understanding what he just said. She read his intent in his eyes. It was suddenly very clear to her that he was going to kill her, too. She instinctively turned and ran down the hillock towards the camp.

Mahler watched her run. He noticed she was barefoot. It didn't matter, he thought, watching her. She was running towards the river, and he would catch her easily, he told himself. He watched her run in a desperate, almost falling way. She did fall, and when she got up, Mahler calmly trotted out of the temple and down the hillock. The temple entrance loomed behind him, its dark gray stones hit by the rain. He carried the shotgun over his shoulder casually.

He called Russell on his cell phone with the good news on the way back to camp from the river, where he'd caught up with the girl.

TWENTY-SEVEN

Russell raised himself on one elbow and glanced out the tall windows, their glass thick and blurry. It was raining violently. Cars sped through the downpour, their yellow headlights signaling late afternoon.

He turned and took his wristwatch from the nightstand. It was almost six. They'd both fallen asleep. It was the first time, he realized, that they'd felt safe enough to fall asleep together.

He sank back into the pillow. Beatrice was facing him, her face angelic. She had a girl's face, something about it precious and cherubic, like a nineteenth-century print of an idealized young girl.

He had an important appointment that evening with the IMF country team. Antonio was to accompany him. But he didn't want to get up. Somehow he felt that this was the last calm that he and Beatrice would know until he took her away.

He pulled up the sheet and looked at the ceiling. Lines in the plaster made odd-shaped countries, turning the ceiling into a map of some lost world. *And if she was sick?* he wondered. *Disturbed.* The idea frightened him, but it didn't change the way he felt about her. After all, wasn't *he* mad? He was planning to assassinate the president of the country.

He rolled over and held Beatrice. Her body was warm and delicious. He had no desire to leave her, but knew he had to.

It was he who had suggested, out of the blue, that someone put a bullet in Blanco and get it over with. It was just like the Greek when he'd been a kid. It was the obvious choice. Blanco

251

was a murderous thug who stood in the way of progress. It had just come to him. *Was it wrong?* Antonio, Rudy Valladolid, everyone had stopped speaking and just stared at him. They could see he wasn't joking.

"You sound very sure of yourself, young man," Senator Rudy said after a long silence.

"I am," he said. "I'm certain it's what should be done. If you let Blanco appoint Carlos Selva president, it will be a catastrophe. He plans on doing everything the IMF suggests, and you'll have another Argentina here. Selva would like nothing better than a return to war with the communists. That's all he knows." Everyone was looking at him; Russell didn't know whether it meant that they agreed, or that they were afraid. Then it dawned on him why they were still staring.

"I'll do it myself, if that's what you're asking," Russell said. "I'm not afraid. It's what you want, isn't it? A solution, for God's sake."

"You know what that means?" Antonio said.

"You probably wouldn't survive, boy," Rudy said. "You must be suicidal."

He supposed he lay in this very bed as a child. He wondered what his mother would think of what he was going to do. He would assassinate a dictator, and perhaps die in the process. Would she approve? Would she try to stop him? Would she tell him he didn't have to risk his life? Would his great-grandfather, the great risk taker himself, be proud of him?

"What are you thinking about?" Beatrice said, looking at him.

"Where we'll live once we leave this miserable country," he said, lying. She moved her body completely against his.

"I fell asleep; it's late," she said.

"So did I."

She reached for him. Her hand felt warm on his chest. "Do you really want me?" she asked. "To marry me?"

"Very much," he said.

"I'm afraid."

"So am I," he said. "But you haven't told me yes or no."

"And if I say no?"

"Then I'll become a priest. Or maybe a circus performer in Poland. . . . You have to, because we love each other," he said, holding her.

"All right," she said. "I can't have you dancing with bears, or whatever they do . . . the circus people." She lifted herself out of the blankets and kissed him. He felt her breasts press against his chest. "You tell me what to do, and I'll do it," she said.

They made love again. It was different than before. He felt safe. He was no longer afraid of losing her. She was going to be his.

He walked into the kitchen. It was dark now. The lights were on, and the room seemed very bright to him after the twilight of the bedroom. Olga was doing the ironing. She seemed to love the work, or at least get some peace out of it. When she'd been with him, she'd been very deliberate about it. She was standing on an old wooden box and using the old marble counter as an ironing board. The iron was a huge mid-century thing.

"Olga?" He continued to tie his tie. She looked up at him, her face slightly wet from the heat of the iron. "Olga, I . . . could I ask you a favor?"

"Of course, sir," she said, concentrating on her work.

"I don't want you to mention to anyone that *Doña* Beatrice was here with me today. Or that she was *ever* here."

Olga smiled like a pixie.

"Why, *señor*." She was teasing him. He was grateful and felt connected to the woman in a way he hadn't before. Seeing her now, as she must have been with his mother, somehow made his mother's memory more real to him. "The *señora* is very, very beautiful," Olga said.

"Yes she is, Olga."

"I've seen her in the newspapers," Olga said. She touched her index finger to her tongue, then touched the bottom of the iron quickly. It hissed. "Beautiful, like your mother."

Olga served them sandwiches in the dining room. It was an elegant room, with the original furniture. His uncle hadn't gotten around to changing it before he'd left for Paris.

They spoke very little as they ate. Already Russell could see the fear in Beatrice's face. She'd promised him something that she might not be able to carry out, he realized.

She brought her cell phone out from the living room.

"Carlos has called me six times," she said, looking at the screen. "I hope it's not the children. I shouldn't have stayed so long."

He watched her punch in her husband's number. He put the cup down and listened. She stopped talking. A strange expression came over her face as she listened to Carlos.

"I can be there in half an hour," she said finally. "Yes, of course. No. I'll just drive myself. Don't send anyone . . . I'm at the club *Alemán* and I don't want a fuss. Besides, it would just take time." She closed the phone. "He's the bloody president," she said, picking her things up from the couch.

"*What?*"

"Blanco's just appointed Carlos president. Blanco's leaving for Miami this weekend, and he's appointed Carlos president until the election. I've got to go." She picked her handbag up off the floor. "It's impossible now. How can I leave him *now?* He'll never give me a divorce now," she said. "Not now."

. . .

"It's so good to see you, Carlos," Rudy Valladolid said. He was in his bathrobe. He'd been drinking a brandy, watching Larry King speak to Governor Connally's widow about the Kennedy assassination.

Valladolid's butler brought Carlos into the room and asked whether the general would care for anything.

"What would you like, Carlos? It's late; how about a brandy?"

Carlos looked at the old man. The general was in uniform, and Valladolid realized that he wasn't there on a social call.

"Please sit, Carlos. How is your mother, my dear sister? And your beautiful wife?"

"Oh, God, my mother won't leave Miami *now*. I mean, with the news," Carlos said. He smiled, finally, and sat down in one of the senator's chairs.

Rudy didn't sit down again. The room felt suddenly hot. He looked at the big screen TV, and at Larry King. He'd always wanted to meet Larry King and ask him how he could be so perfectly blasé about everything.

"Well, if you don't mind, a scotch on the rocks then," Carlos said. "Beatrice is fine; she's in shock. I mean about the news."

"Bring the general a scotch. The Glenlivet," the senator told his butler. "Of course she is. We are all very proud of you."

"Yes, I suppose so. My sister has got something on for the weekend at Puertos. Horse jumping. We'll go, of course," Carlos said. "President or not, she'll kill me if I don't come."

"Of course," Rudy said. He turned to look at his man, who looked worried. "Well, Manuel, go on. The president of the republic is thirsty." The butler, after hesitating, turned and left the study.

255

"I've had him since he was a boy. Loves me like a father," Rudy said. Carlos looked at him, his head slightly cocked to one side. Rudy put his cigar down on the large ashtray. He took the control to the TV and hit the mute button. "Do you like Larry King, Carlos?"

"Of course. Everyone loves Larry King . . . Rudy, I'm afraid there's a situation," Carlos said. "A delicate affair."

"Congratulations, by the way. I'm jealous, of course."

"Yes. I was as surprised as everyone."

"I think Blanco has been ready to leave for months. He has so many *interests* abroad now." Rudy sat down on the beautiful brown leather couch. He felt old, ancient in fact. He was slightly drunk; he really didn't feel good any more unless he was slightly inebriated.

The trouble was that he'd never been able to click off his intellect, he thought, looking at Carlos. He'd known Carlos since Carlos was a child, and he'd never liked him. The problem with so many of his countrymen was that they had no conversation. Not really. They were talkative, but said absolutely nothing.

"Situation?" Rudy asked.

"I'm afraid so, uncle."

"Well, there's always a situation in this country, Carlos."

"It seems the embassy thinks that there's a plot against the government."

"Really? That would be silly."

"They seem to think that you're in the middle of it."

"*Me?*"

"Yes. I'm afraid so," Carlos said.

"Oh, dear. Well, the Americans have very active imaginations, don't they? I mean, they're worried about everything these days. I hope they don't think I'm al-Qaeda or something. I think we had an Arab in the family somewhere. No—a Persian, but then, they don't count, do they?" He tried to smile, but Carlos wasn't smiling now. The old senator allowed himself to realize what his intuition had told him the moment the general had walked into the room: *you're in trouble.*

"They said that you had cooperated with them in the past. I was a little surprised by that, Rudy. I mean . . . given your attitudes."

"Well, I have lent the embassy a hand once or twice," Rudy said. "Of course, they always pay one for that." The senator looked at Carlos in a level, all-business way.

"Yes. Well, they want to know who is plotting against the government. They said that they could make another arrangement with you."

"Did they? They're always so kind to me. Did they say what kind of arrangement?"

"A hundred thousand dollars."

"Good God!" Rudy said, and picked up his cigar. "You don't smoke, do you, Carlos?"

"No. It's bad for the health," Carlos said. He seemed to stress the word bad in a way that Rudy couldn't help but notice.

"Well. That's a lot of money, I suppose."

"I think I can get you more," Carlos said.

"Could you?"

"Yes."

"One would be a fool not to take it. I mean, look at Blanco. All those houses he has in the States. I've heard he bought Stallone's house in Miami?"

"No, actually that was me," Carlos said.

"Must be hard to get that done on a soldier's pay."

"Rudy. They're very anxious to know what's going on."

"I can understand that, old boy. So am I. With all that's gone on in the last week!"

"Can I call them now, uncle, and let them know that you'll tell them what you know? About the coup?"

"*Well*. I wish I could!" The old man leaned forward. "But really, I don't know a thing, Carlos. They don't tell old people much, Carlos, you know that. Why would they? And certainly not about something like *that*. If they did, I would tell whoever it was that it was a very foolish idea. It's always foolish to try to trump the embassy. Ever since I've been a child, that's been the case. Jesus, my mother was married in that goddamn embassy. Did you know that?"

"Uncle Rudy, why don't you tell me something. Something I can tell them. That way, there wouldn't be any unpleasantness."

"Oh. I see. They really are upset, then."

"I'm afraid so, Rudy. They've sent me over instead of someone else from my staff because they understand that because we are blood family. . . ."

"No, Carlos. I'm glad it was you. But honestly, you'll have to tell them that this time I can't be of much help."

"Uncle Rudy. I need a few names. That would be enough."

"Otherwise there will be unpleasantness." The senator finished the sentence for him.

"I'm afraid so. I'm afraid you would have to come with me if you failed to give me some names."

"You know, I'm so glad your aunt isn't here to see this, Carlos. She always hated politics. She told me to stick to the law. But I wouldn't listen. I've always been a romantic, Carlos."

The drinks came. The butler put the scotch down in front of the general. He saw that the old senator was pale.

"Manuel. Mr. Price left his pen the other day. You'll make sure he gets it." He handed the man his fountain pen. They looked each other in the eye. "I think the general and I are going out. I'll dress first, of course." He shot a glance at Carlos. "If that's all right with you, Carlos?"

258

"Of course," Carlos said. The butler took the pen. The man was about to say that the pen was the Senator's most cherished, but Rudy stopped him before he could say it. "Of course you'll see he gets it. Manuel never lets me down." The old man watched his butler take the pen and leave the room.

"You'll have to hurry," Carlos said, taking a drink.

"Yes. Of course. Just a moment. Is it raining out?"

"Yes," Carlos said. "Very heavy."

"This unpleasantness . . . where do you think it will take place?"

"It doesn't have to be . . . all they want are some names, Uncle Rudy."

"How about Larry King? Or, let's see . . . *Pancho Villa,*" the senator said.

He knew he was going to die, that it would be unpleasant, and that in the end he would tell them what they wanted to know, because he wasn't a brave man, not physically. But he was trying—even old, he wanted to try to be brave, if only once in his life. He thought of Isabella and how he'd been a coward that night.

"I'm afraid those names wouldn't do," Carlos said.

"No. I suppose not," Rudy said. "One hates unpleasantness, though."

TWENTY-EIGHT

They were in Katherine Barkley's room, on the seventh floor of the hotel Camino Real.

"It's just like that movie, *Grand Hotel*. But I don't want to be alone," Katherine said. "Like Garbo, I mean."

"It's true, everyone stops here when they come. The IMF, the gangsters, the UN. Everyone comes to the Camino Real," Russell said.

"We all have lunch together in the dining room. Everyone is quite charming to one another. I'm telling you, it's just like that movie."

"You shouldn't have come back, Katherine," Russell said.

"You're *very* mean," she said. "But I forgive you. I know why you did it."

"Promise me you won't try to stay when the commission leaves; you'll go back," he said.

"I came to see you," Katherine said.

He'd seen her in the lobby and thought she would be mad at him, but she wasn't. It was obvious she was still in love with him. He could see it in her eyes the moment she saw him.

"How was Chicago?" he asked.

"Boring." They laughed, and the tension left the room. "I mean, you can get anything you want. But I wanted my UN jeep back, and my mosquito net, and the fear about being stopped on the road—and you." She was barefoot, wearing a pair of jeans and a t-shirt. Her hair was damp from the shower.

260

"I mean, I even keep track of coffee prices. It's all a mess here, isn't it?"

"Yes, and it's just gotten worse," he said.

"Is it going to be like Argentina?"

"No," he said. "No, I don't think so. I hope not."

"You sound so sure. That's not like you. Would you like something to drink? A beer?"

"Yes," he said. She went to the servi-bar and got him one; they had to open it on a counter top in the bathroom, because they couldn't find a bottle opener. They stood in the bathroom talking, leaning against the counter.

"I'm not comfortable anymore," she said. "I tried to be, but I'm not. My mother doesn't understand. She says I need a psychiatrist. It was all right for a few years to try and save the world, but she says I can't go on like this. No man is going to want to marry me if I get too *rough.*" She put her hand on his shoulder. "What do you think I should do?" She tried to kiss him; it was an awkward moment. He knew it wasn't right to kiss her now, that it would only make things worse.

"Go *home.* Or somewhere else. There are other countries that need you. If you stay here, they'll kill you," he said.

He put his beer down and took her by the shoulders. "I need a favor, Katherine. It's dangerous, and it's wrong of me to ask you, but I have to. There's a good reason for it, but you have to trust me, and not ask questions."

"I think I've been here before," she said.

"It's not what you think. . . . It's nothing to do with her."

"Are you still seeing her?"

"Yes."

"Are you in love with her?"

"Yes."

She looked at him a long time, then walked back into the bedroom. He watched her go and sit on the edge of her unmade bed.

261

"I don't believe you really are. Not really," she said.

"What do you mean?"

"Just what I said. You have nothing in common with her. It isn't about *her* at all."

"What are you getting at?" He knew instinctively that she was right. They didn't have anything in common, while Katherine and he did share something—a certain view of the world, a sense of responsibility for it, even if their politics were different.

"It's about what she represents. It's about the danger. If it wasn't her, it would have to be someone like her," Katherine said. "I've thought about it a lot. There wasn't a lot to do at my parents' house. I thought about you. I thought about you and her. And I decided that you were attracted to her because she could get you killed. You want to die, like all those friends back home you told me about. I don't really understand why, exactly. . . . But it's a waste, if that's all it is. If you just want to die, I mean."

"That's not fair. You don't know her."

"I know she married a monster. What kind of woman has children with a monster? Not fair? I think it's not fair for you to want to die. And I think it's not fair that you don't love me, because I'm not married to a killer and I want to have your baby and I would go anywhere with you and do *anything,* and I don't have to be rich. You don't have to prove you're a big man for me. You don't have to do a fucking thing. She's all about the money. Can't you see she has to be rich, to be *anything?* That's all she can be, a rich man's wife. A beautiful, charming, rich man's wife. It would all be spoilt if she couldn't be that. Can't you see that? I can't understand why you can't see the simplest things. . . . But you think you're so smart, and no one can tell you anything.

"Now, please go," she said. "I really love you, and you can't even see we could be truly happy."

262

"I need to go with you to see President Blanco. When you and the group go tomorrow. Can you get me in? I'll need a credential," he asked.

"Is that all you want?" she asked. She stood up and went to the bathroom. She started crying; she wet her face in the sink and picked up a towel from the counter. He felt guilty, and didn't know why. He'd saved her life, after all.

"Yes," he said. "That's all."

"I'll do what I can," she said.

"Don't ever make a decision like that for me again," she added. "What you did at the airport. Never do that again."

"I'm sorry," he said. "I care for you. I didn't want. . . ."

She turned on him, her face still wet.

"You have no right! Do you understand? If I'd been a man, you wouldn't have dared do that." He didn't answer her; he knew he would have done it regardless.

· · ·

It was dusk. Even under the jungle's canopy, Mahler could tell it would be dark soon.

He seemed to exist in a netherworld of smoke from the campfire and the mist/rain that fell quietly around him. Mahler's shirt, now almost a rag, was wet. He drank a cup of coffee, squatting on his haunches. He'd shot the girl while she was running in the river. She'd been getting away; he'd run after her, his boots heavy in the shallow water, firing. The echo of the shots scared the birds in the trees, the sound repeating, banging echoes over the moving river. He wasn't sure he could hit her, in the dimming light. But then he saw her fall, and he'd stopped. He watched her body move along in the current, and finally disappear.

He didn't like doing it, he'd told himself, but she was going to run away. He said it out loud in German: he wouldn't have done it if she weren't going to run away. The Mayan

263

temple loomed hoary in the mist behind him. Why would he? He wasn't a murderer, he was an archaeologist after all, *from a good family.* The men he killed would have certainly killed him once they realized what the Jaguar meant. The statue was bigger than even the most optimistic reports from the Spaniards. It was huge. It was worth... *Only God knew what it was worth,* he thought, holding his cup.

He turned slightly and looked towards the temple they'd uncovered. He remembered those early sketches from *A Journey In Mesoamerica,* which he'd read as a child. The rain was falling through the canopy. The temple door was clearly in view; if anyone happened along now, they would see the freshly-cut jungle around the entrance.

He stood up and walked across the camp, stopping to pick up one of the dead men's waterproof ponchos and pull it on. He walked back to the fire. *If she only had been frightened,* he thought, looking back towards the river. He would have taken her to Germany. The girl would have liked Germany. He would have shown her snow and the Alps. He closed his eyes for a moment and saw her fall. She was heading out to the deep, thinking she could swim away. But it wasn't to be. No, he wasn't a murderer; she'd forced him to it. She wouldn't ever see the snow now, he thought, looking again into the fire. And that was too bad–regrettable. But he had to protect his investment. She would have told someone. He couldn't just let people steal what he'd worked so hard to find.

Mahler stared into the fire for a long time. He built it up again as the darkness came. He didn't notice the water streaming down his face; he was lost in his thoughts, weighing what he should do, calculating. He had tried to get Russell back here. They could have worked together and taken the Jaguar out together. But Russell was crazy. He'd gotten involved with politics. He would probably be killed. He was already as good as dead.

If something happened to Mahler now, what would become of the Jaguar, after all these hundreds of years? The jaguar was *his*. He'd found it. It belonged to him. It had taken his whole life to find it, and now he had. It was his to keep. He would get it back to Germany somehow. He would prove to all his father's friends that his father's son was the greatest archeologist of all time. He was the man who had found the famous Red Jaguar, after all, and it was bigger than anyone had dreamed it would be. He would have his picture in the paper. He would be famous for a thousand years. He would teach again.

He looked across the edge of the darkness past the firelight, the rain dripping off the brim of his rubber-covered cowboy hat as he stared at the temple. He finally got up and walked toward the temple entrance in the dark, with a torch from the fire. The rain hissed as it hit his torch. Here and there he saw the torch's yellow light reach out into the darkness, clawing at the night as he made his way. That night he slept in the temple, under the jaguar, and well out of the heavy rain.

• • •

"I haven't heard from Mahler. It's been three days," Russell said.

He'd brought a pistol. It was noontime, and the sun was intense. He'd barged through the front door of Carl Van Diemen's place in Antigua. The maid had tried to warn Carl he was coming, but he'd been right behind her, jogging past the fountain with the pistol. Russell pulled out his pistol as he ran; the maid saw it, and the gardener saw it, too.

Carl was in the shower. Russell had come right into the shower, past the maid and past the boyfriend, whose outline he'd seen under the sheets of the big canopy bed. Now he was staring at Carl's scarred face, water hitting him in the chest.

Russell yanked Carl out from under the shower and pushed him down on the toilet. Russell held the pistol down by his thigh. He was breathing hard, because he'd run all the way from the street.

Russell said it again.

"I haven't heard from Mahler in three days. Where is he?"

"I haven't heard from him either," Carl said. He was dripping wet. The maid, anxious and frightened, stood by the door.

"Tell her to go away. I want to talk in private," Russell said. Carl did as he was told, and the woman left them.

"Do you have any guns in the house?" Russell asked.

"No. Of course not. They scare me."

"Does your driver carry one?"

"No. Russell, what's wrong?"

"I want to know where the fucking jaguar is. Do you have it?"

"No. Of course not. How could I? Did you find it?"

"I think Mahler's taken it. And I want to know if he's given it to you. If you tell me the truth, I won't kill you. If you lie to me, I'll come back and kill you. Do you understand me?"

"Yes. I don't have it. I haven't spoken with Mahler in days. He was waiting for you at *Tres Rios*. I saw him here and gave him some money."

"You're sure about that?" Russell said.

"Yes. I didn't know he'd found it."

"Yes. I think he has. I think he's found it, and he's trying to cheat us."

"He can't sell it. He wouldn't know how. And he can't move it around the country like that, by himself," Carl said. His big white stomach was wet. His scarred face, just now healing, was red from the hot water. He was ugly, ugly and fat and afraid Russell might kill him.

"Yes, he can. This is Guatemala. You can do anything you want. He might already be gone. He might already have loaded it on a ship at Barrios!"

"No, he won't do that."

The door opened, and Carl's boyfriend–his arms straight out–was pointing a gun at Russell. It was a small woman's gun, and he was aiming it at his head. From the corner of his eye, Russell watched the kid move into the bathroom. The kid's gun hand was shaking; he was wearing lipstick and girl's panties, and he was scared.

"Put that down, or you'll get hurt," Carl told the boy. "We aren't fighting. Everything is okay."

"Put that fucking thing away or you'll be sorry," Russell said, without turning to look at the boyfriend. As soon as he said it, he felt the gun barrel press against the side of his head and stay there, resting by his ear. Russell was getting angrier and angrier.

He looked Carl in the eyes. The thought of the kid holding him at gunpoint was making his heart race.

The anger he'd been keeping at bay since he heard Blanco had appointed Selva president started to spill out. Beatrice had called him, to tell him again that she couldn't possibly leave the country. She was afraid of Carlos in a way she'd never been before. He would be president of the country by tomorrow, and more powerful than ever.

"No. You drop yours. It's your fault Carl looks like that," the kid said.

"You motherfucking punk. What did you say to me?"

"It's your fault the jaguar did that to him. To my Carl."

Russell knew then that the kid was going to kill him. He just understood it. He was still looking at Carl, at his face. He could see the scars on Van Diemen's face and the look in Carl's eyes. Carl *wanted* the kid to shoot him; it was in his eyes. Carl wouldn't stop him.

"Tell this punk of yours to put his fucking gun down, or I'm going to kill him," Russell said. He could barely speak. The rage was choking him. "Do you hear me, kid? I'm going to kill you."

As soon as he said it, Russell turned around, snapped his elbow up, and hit the kid's gun. It went off. The blast in the bathroom was loud. Russell grabbed the kid's arm and managed to slap his hand towards Carl. The gun went off again. By now Russell had his hand on the kid's wrist; he brought his knee up hard and snapped the kid's arm at the elbow. He felt the arm break, and heard the boy scream. The gun fell to the floor.

Russell looked up. Van Diemen had a bullet in his face and was jerking on the toilet, already dead. Russell's ears were ringing from the gunshots.

"*Ah, mi brazo! Ay... Ay mi brazo! Ahi, Poppi, mire que me ha hecho a mí brazo.*" The kid, screaming, hadn't yet seen what he'd done. He was in agony looking at his broken arm, the bones sticking out of the elbow. The arm pointed back in an ugly way.

"You killed him," was all Russell could say. "You dumb motherfucker!"

The kid picked his head up and looked at Carl's body on the toilet.

"You happy now, asshole?" Russell picked the kid up, carried him into the bedroom, and sat him on the bed. The kid's face was blank, as if he couldn't believe it.

"You're going to tell me where he sells his stuff. There must be a person in Europe–someone. A phone number. Something!" Russell said. The kid kept looking toward the bathroom. He hadn't said a word. He had to be in a lot of pain, but suddenly he wasn't saying a word; he wasn't even holding his mangled arm. He was just staring into the bathroom, at the body on the toilet.

268

"Listen to me, asshole. I want a name. I need to have that name or I'm going to break your other arm. Are you listening to me? I don't care, you understand? I don't care about your dead boyfriend, and I don't care about you. You understand that? I need a name."

The kid wasn't listening to him.

Russell reared back and slapped the kid in the face, knocking him back onto the bed. "Can you hear me now? You're going to give it to me. I've come too far to let a punk like you stop me. Do you understand me, kid?"

"His brother . . . Poppi's brother. He's the one. He buys everything from Carl," the kid said, looking up at him. "He's in Paris. He has a gallery in Paris."

"Get up and get me the fucking number," Russell said. "Go on. . . . Get the fuck up and get me that number."

"I can't," the kid said. "I can't."

"Yes, you can. Where is it? So help me, God, I'll break the other one."

"On the computer. He has it there," the kid said. He was going into shock. He was starting to shake, and he'd turned deathly white. Because of his arm, he couldn't push himself up off the bed.

"Where is it? His computer?"

"In the office," the kid said.

"It's your fault he's dead," Russell said. "We were just talking. Everything would have been fine. It's your fault."

He went outside to the courtyard and saw the fountain was on. The gardener and maid had run away. He went to Carl's study and found a laptop. Russell picked it up and took it with him. As he left, he could hear the kid sobbing.

TWENTY-NINE

Spring 1988

Love is a strange thing. It acts independently of reason, because all great and true love creates great and true pain—pain, because all love must end in death, disappointment, or both. The stronger the love, the less reason to it. Most people don't suffer from it, fortunately; most are indifferent types who see real love as a nuisance. It is a special kind of madness.

Olga had the madness and didn't know it. She loved Isabella, but never thought of it as love. To her, Isabella was simply part of her life, perhaps even more than a sister. They had, after all, shared a wondrous childhood, the kind that would never be seen again, in this country or anywhere else. Their childhood had been filled with nature and walks and running, the sky and the rain and the sound of people's voices working nearby. They had belonged to a place, and the place belonged to them. It had embraced them completely. They had been happy together as only children can be happy.

She went back to the central police station the next morning to ask for help because her mistress had not come home for the second night, nor had she sent a message. This had never happened before.

The new administrator had called from the plantation and asked for Isabella. Olga had said simply that her mistress hadn't come home. Stunned, the administrator said he would call Isabella's brother immediately in Paris. The administrator

270

called back in an hour and told Olga to go back to the police station and make inquires.

The sergeant she'd spoken to barely remembered her. Because she didn't have any more money, he didn't even bother looking up the missing person's form he'd filled out the day before. He told her, in a very curt way, that no white woman's body had been reported found. Then he continued his conversation with one of the other policemen at the counter.

This was a shock. Olga had not, until that moment, thought that Isabella could be dead. The idea of her mistress being dead was impossible to fathom.

She went back to the apartment, hoping against hope that when she entered Isabella would be there talking on the phone, or sitting at her desk working, and they would not have to speak about the last few days, as they had never spoken about the men who occasionally spent the night and left early —including, once, the President of the republic. But it wasn't to be. When she unlocked the door, the apartment was cold and the lights were still off.

She went to her mistress's office and sat on the edge of a club sofa that had been bought in San Francisco. She stared at the phone until it rang, hours later.

"*Sí, Don Roberto. Sí, entiendo, muy bien. Inmediatemente,*" Olga said.

Isabella's brother's voice was frightened, and he spoke loudly. He was conscious of being a disappointment to everyone who had ever known him. But he was successful in the movie business, finally producing two comedies that garnered some attention. An Italian movie star—a very young girl who would later become famous in the United States— was in the room with him, and he told her to get out while he spoke to Olga. He wanted to be alone while he spoke on the phone.

271

"I'll come home as soon as I can," he told Olga. "Everything will be fine. I'm sure my sister has just done something impulsive." Olga didn't understand the word "impulsive"; she thought it meant sick.

"She was fine when she left," Olga said, thinking that would help. "Not sick at all."

"Yes. Well, I'm sure she'll turn up. Where did she go?"

"I don't know," Olga said, and she was so sorry that was true. She didn't have any idea. "But she left with *Don* Antonio."

"De La Madrid? Have you called *Don* Antonio's house?" Roberto asked.

"*Sí, señor.* But they say he's away."

"Well, maybe she left with him?"

"She would have come home first, *Don* Roberto."

"You are very right, Olga. She wouldn't have gone without coming home to pack.

"No, *señor,* and I go with her when she goes *anywhere.* Even Mexico."

"Yes, of course," he said. "GET OUT," he snapped; the Italian girl, sensing bad news and thinking it was about a movie they were planning, had tried to come back into the room, and he'd had to shout at her. "Olga, I'll call Antonio's house. I want you to look everywhere for *Doña* Isabella. Will you promise me that? I can't come home for a day or two. I just can't. You understand."

"Yes, *señor.*"

"I want you to go see Cardinal Ignacio De La Tierra. I'll call him right now. I want you to go see him and tell him what's happened. He's Isabella's godfather. He'll help us find her."

"*Sí, Don Roberto.*"

The Indian men who picked Isabella's pockets didn't know her. They had all come from her part of the country; two, in fact—the two who found her—had worked a harvest for her once, without knowing it. But Isabella's face was bloated, and to them, she was just a dead white woman with fancy clothes whose face had gone strange. They could tell she'd been beautiful.

They dragged her out of the ditch and went through her things, then stripped her clothes off her, because they could be sold. The shoes alone were worth a fortune to these men. They fought over the shoes and the empty handbag. One man was hurt.

Drivers passed Isabella's naked body and didn't think to stop. Once a mother—a woman Isabella's age, who had known her—covered her daughter's eyes as they drove by. Because of the war it wasn't unusual to see dead bodies along the road, mostly the victims of death squads left out like trash to be collected in the morning.

Two young Indian women found Isabella's naked body on the way to church, after the men had left her. The sky had cleared, and was blue as it can be only in the highlands. Isabella's white skin shone in the sun like marble.

They took the body to the church nearby, covering it with their shawls. There was something very Christian and beautiful in the way they wrapped the body in their red shawls and then carried it, making sure they didn't drag her. There was something Christlike about the body as the two women bore it in the early morning sun, a few dogs looking on, past the houses of the miserable village. Along the way, an old man helped them.

The church was one of the oldest in Guatemala, founded in fact by one of Isabella's people, a Cruz from Andalusia. Once inside, the two Indian girls laid the body down in front of a bank of candles. The candles were lit in a large group on the great stone floor, itself stained dark from 500 years of worship and wax. A white Christ hung on the cross above the altar.

Sunlight illuminated the Conquistadors on the building's stained glass windows. One of the Indian girls went quickly to fetch the priest.

It was here that the spirit of Isabella Cruz finally left her body. In the ditch, she had been whole in that way that a dead person is whole until something leaves it and returns to what makes all the world. That thing left her now, and she was really gone; her spirit rose with the candle smoke, traveling and mixing.

People from the village started to enter for the noon Mass and, seeing the body, gathered around. The priest entered in his vestments; he pulled back the shawls and saw it was a European woman. He bent down and said two Our Fathers immediately, then rushed to call the police.

An hour later, the men who'd stolen Isabella's clothes sold her shoes to used clothing dealer. They got drunk. One of the men regretted what he'd done, and gave the money away.

Guatemala City woke up to ten more years of civil war. Many innocent people would be killed, some horribly. In the weeks that followed, many lies were told about Isabella, by men who regretted telling them. She wasn't married, so it was different. Had she been married, with a husband to look into things, perhaps it wouldn't have been that way.

The brother never came home. He did write Isabella's boy about what had happened. He thought the lie about a traffic accident would help. He hated himself for being a coward.

• • •

President Blanco was coming to the Camino Real at seven o'clock that evening to announce that he was leaving the country due to health problems. He planned to meet with the UN's human rights delegation just before he went down to the ballroom to make General Selva's appointment official.

Russell looked at his watch. The younger man from the IMF was saying that they were going to hold back a new loan, as they had just heard from the US ambassador that Blanco was going to resign. It would be best to wait until the political situation was more settled, he told Russell. The young man had eaten a good breakfast, and was anxious to go back to New York, get married, and take a better job with Citibank.

"We need the loan regardless. There's a debt payment due on Friday," Russell said, trying to sound reasonable. "We owe 500 million dollars. It has to be repaid, or it will be impossible for us to go to the credit markets."

"I'm sorry," the young man said. "The decision is final. We've lost track of what's going on in this damn country. How can we make a loan, if we don't even know who is going to be running the place tomorrow?" The young man from New York looked at his colleagues, a young woman and an older man in his thirties. None of the others said anything. But it was obvious to Russell the decision had been made by higher-ups, and they had sent these young people to the country for show. They had come with no power to change anything.

"There will be wholesale capital flight," Russell said, trying to keep the anger out of his voice. "It will be impossible for the banks here. They will have to shut down. You'll have chaos."

"There's a good chance I'll win the election," Antonio said. He'd come into the meeting a few minutes late, and that too had upset the kid from the IMF. This was a courtesy meeting the agency was giving all the serious presidential candidates. The fact that Antonio had been late pissed the kid off. "If my party wins, we will do everything to make sure there is transparency. We will work on the deficit. We will work on the human rights problem, I guarantee you. You are speaking to the man who will be our secretary of the treasury. He's

275

very competent," Antonio said, nodding to Russell.

"I understand that Mr. Cruz-Price is . . . well, that the constitution would bar him from serving in your government. He's an American," the kid said snidely.

"We will change that," Antonio said. "That is a technicality." The girl smiled at him from across the table.

"His mother was a Guatemalan. That means he has the right to dual citizenship. It will be the first piece of paper I sign. Problem solved," Antonio said. "As you can see, Mr. Price is very qualified to act as our minister of finance. He knows what should be done, and he will have my full support." Antonio smiled hopefully.

The IMF kid kept his game face on. He had already decided that Antonio De La Madrid wasn't going to win.

"I'm afraid that the present political situation makes it impossible. We can come back in a few months," the kid said. He put his pen in his pocket.

"Without the loan, there will be no political stability," Russell said.

"I'm sorry," the kid said. He looked at his watch, and then at Antonio.

They heard a burst of gunfire out in the street. Everyone froze. Protesters were demonstrating across the street. Depositors had been queuing up for two days, hoping the bank would reopen and allow them to withdraw their dollar accounts. Blanco had frozen the dollar accounts in a last-ditch effort to make Friday's bond payment, which was due in dollars. But dollars had been fleeing the country anyway. Only small depositors—like those in the street, without connections—were trapped by the banking holiday.

Russell got up and went to the window. He could see the mounted police below, wading into the crowd of teachers and clerks. An officer had shot his pistol into the air. Men were throwing rocks at the bank's plate glass windows. A

276

white puff from a tear gas canister burst into the air. The tear gas canister—shot from the other side of the street—tumbled under the horses. It all seemed so unnecessary, Russell thought. He didn't bother to turn around to say goodbye to the IMF people as they left.

"Rudy has been arrested," Antonio said. He'd walked up to the window, and was watching the crowd now, too. "It was Selva. Rudy won't be able to keep quiet. You know what they'll do. He'll be forced to tell them everything."

Russell was still watching the scene down on the street. Two men had managed to pull a policeman off his horse, and were stomping him. The policeman's horse was running riderless through the crowd. The crowd had smashed the bank's windows, and were running through the gaping holes into the building. It wouldn't do them any good; the bank had no dollars left.

"Then we have to act soon. Tonight," Russell said.

"We don't have anyone to do it. There's no one," Antonio said.

"I'll do it," Russell said. "I told you. Before Blanco makes the announcement."

"No," Antonio said.

Russell turned around. He looked at De La Madrid.

"Why not?"

"Because it's suicide. I won't have it. Besides, I need you."

"No. It has to be done," Russell said. "It might as well be me. I can get near him. I have access."

"Do you want to die? Is that it?"

"Of course not," Russell said.

"Then what is it? You don't owe this country your life. You're not even really one of us."

Russell grabbed Antonio by the collar and pushed him against the wall.

"Don't ever say that again. Do you understand? Never. My mother died here, for what? Do you want the filthy communists to win? Is that what you want, you gutless shit? They will, you know. They're just waiting out there, with their ignorant and stupid ideas, and as soon as it gets bad enough they'll come out of their holes and win what thirty years of war couldn't get them. Is that what you want?" Startled by what he'd done, he let go of Antonio. "I'm sorry. I didn't mean to . . . I'm sorry."

Antonio looked at him. He turned his collar back where it had been pulled up.

"No. I understand. I had no right to say what I did. You are one of us. I knew your mother. She would be proud of you. Very proud. Your grandfather would be proud of you, too." Antonio smiled at him. It was a strange smile, Russell thought. "You're like a son to me, you know that. That was the only reason I said what I did. I apologize."

"It's okay," Russell said.

"I promise you, you will have a place in the government."

"Thank you. But I'm leaving. As soon as this is done."

"I'll make sure you are . . . I'll make sure that if you want to come back some day, when this is over, that you'll have a place here. We will owe you that," Antonio said.

"I'm leaving with Carlos's wife. I thought you should know that. I don't want to keep anything from you. That's why I have to go. I can't stay here with her. It would be impossible."

"I understand," Antonio said. "You're right, he'll kill you if you stay here."

"I'm going to do it there. When Blanco comes in to meet with the UN. I'm going to do it there, at the meeting," Russell said.

"Do you want to see a priest?" Antonio said.

"No. I'm not going to die. He's going to die."

278

"God bless you," Antonio said. "I have to go. Will I see you again?"

"No. I don't think you should come tonight. Stay at home. If I fail, you'll know it soon enough. If he's dead, you have to move quickly and take power."

"Do you think we can really win?" It seemed a strange question.

"I don't know. Maybe. But you can't if Carlos gets in. He won't let go once he's in. I know him; why should he?"

"Of course he won't."

They shook hands. There was nothing more to say. It was obvious that Antonio thought he was going to die. Maybe he would be successful, or maybe he wouldn't, but nonetheless he was going to die.

"Let's hope Rudy can hold out until tonight," Antonio said.

"Yes. Let's hope so," Russell said.

• • •

Important people, lifelong friends of Rudy Valladolid, had been warned. They were doing everything they could to intervene with Carlos, but Rudy had gone too far this time. Even President Blanco, who played cards with Rudy at the Club Alemán every Sunday afternoon, said that he'd gone too far, and refused to stop the inevitable. It pained him, he said, as he and the senator had grown up together. Everyone liked Rudy Valladolid, because he was charming.

The first rule in the torturer's handbook is to leave the face alone, so that no photos can be leaked to the press. A beaten face says too much about what's gone on.

So they had worked on Rudy Valladolid from the waist down. They'd used sand-filled garden hoses, as the handbook recommends. But he hadn't cracked.

He'd come close. He'd lost control of his bodily functions at one point, but he held on, thinking about Isabella Cruz. It made him braver than he would have been otherwise. The men who beat him were surprised. He was an old man, after all, but he hadn't cracked. He wanted to give Russell time. He owed him that much. He was very aware, however, that he would crack soon, and tell them everything.

"I'm sorry it's come to this," Carlos said. "I didn't want this to happen."

Carlos sat down. He had come back, after dinner with Beatrice and the children, stopped the beating and had his uncle brought to his office. He had told his men to go easy and make sure that his uncle could walk.

The office was on the military base, on the third floor, and had a view of the parade ground, that now, in the dark, was lit by stadium lights. "I truly wish you could see our point of view, uncle. I'm in an impossible situation."

Rudy shook his head as if he were about to say something. His clothes were soiled, and he was shaking slightly. He had been given a glass of cognac, on Carlos's insistence.

Carlos watched his uncle take a drink. Then, very carefully, Rudy reached over and put the empty glass down on the desk. Carlos noticed his uncle's fingers had dried blood on them.

"The Americans are very concerned," Carlos said. "Can you see my problem? I have to tell them *something*."

"Could I have another? And would you mind pouring it for me? I'm afraid that would be beyond me." Rudy spoke in the soft voice of a man that's terrified and whose spirit has been damaged.

"Of course." Carlos stood up, unscrewed the bottle, and poured out four fingers of brandy. He handed his uncle the glass, then put the bottle down and returned to his chair.

"This is an impossible situation, Rudy. Why don't we find a solution?" Carlos said as Rudy drank the second drink.

Carlos looked out at the parade ground. A German shepherd ran across the grass with a sentry.

"They said there were riots. Is that true?" Rudy asked finally. There was brandy on his chin. He wiped it off.

"Yes, I'm afraid so. The banks. The people want their money," Carlos said. "It's natural."

"Did you get yours out okay?" Rudy asked.

"Yes, thank God. Did you?" Carlos asked.

"Yes. Weeks ago." Rudy smiled slightly. The second drink was doing its work. "Did Pablo do it for you? I mean, at the bank. He's my cousin, you know," Rudy said. He sounded very far away.

"Yes. It was him," Carlos said. "I want you to know I didn't want this." He looked at his uncle. "Why don't you tell me what you know, and I will personally put you on a plane for Miami. Then we can put this unpleasantness behind us."

"He's a good boy," Rudy said. "Pablo, I mean . . . I'd like to get this over with now."

"Good," Carlos said, smiling. He was relieved.

"No, you don't understand. I'd like to end this now."

"I would, too. If you could give me one or two minor names. People who are not important, but who might show up on the lists the Americans have. That would be enough, uncle."

"I cannot. They are all people you know. Some are people I've known since I was a boy. Anyway, I want you to leave that pistol you have on your belt. I'm asking as your uncle, your mother's brother. You cannot deny me this. You have a duty to your family," Rudy said. "No one will blame you. Everyone will understand that it was your uncle, and you had no choice."

"Perhaps," Carlos said. He knew immediately that he couldn't refuse. That was the code. It was that damn Latin code, the Americans would say later. They didn't like it, but they would understand, and they couldn't do anything about it. "But there's no reason. There must be a name you can give, one that doesn't matter," Carlos said.

"Everything matters, that's what I've learned after all these years of living. Now, are you going to honor my request, boy?" He knew he would break. Carlos could see the fear of breaking in his uncle's eyes. It was a look he'd never seen his uncle give before.

"Do you want to use the phone?" Carlos said, unholstering his pistol.

"No. I think if I spoke with anyone, I'd lose the courage. I can't waste the courage. I never had much anyway." He smiled, and his nephew smiled back. Carlos put his pistol on the desk.

For a moment the old man's spirit had returned, and it was as if none of this had happened.

"When you're President, you'll make sure your aunt is protected," Rudy said.

"Of course," Carlos said, standing up. "I will make sure. I promise you."

"Good. Well, that's it, then," Rudy said.

The two men looked at each other. Carlos came across the desk and the old man stood up and they gave each other the *abrazo*, the Latin embrace that goes back centuries. It was formal, yet warm. The old man sat down again.

"I'll go out for a moment then," Carlos said.

"Yes. Go out. It's a beautiful night," his uncle said. Carlos nodded and closed the door behind him.

He walked down the long corridor, with its trophies and green linoleum and photos of past commanders of the Army, when he heard the gunshot and stopped. He pulled out his cigarettes, took one out carefully, and then looked at his watch. It took several moments for a young lieutenant to come running. It was one o'clock in the morning, almost exactly.

He would be named President today, he thought, as the young man ran past him. He had always liked his uncle. He lit the cigarette and went home.

THIRTY

Russell had been calling Mahler at *Tres Rios,* but wasn't getting through. When he finally got an answer, Mahler told him his cell phone had been damaged and he'd been unable to call out.

"I've been hurt," Mahler said. "I can't move it–the jaguar–by myself."

"I'll be there tomorrow," Russell said.

"You're sure? We don't have much time. The news about the jaguar will get out, it always does."

"Yes. Tomorrow at the latest. Are you alone?" Russell asked. "Where are the men?"

"Yes. Alone," Mahler said. "I thought it best."

Russell held the phone a moment. The words were chilling.

"Carl's dead. I'll explain later," Russell said finally. "I've called his brother in Paris. It's all arranged. The brother is to meet us at Puerto Barrios in a week. He's flying in from Paris and making arrangements. He'll take delivery there at Barrios. He's arranging it all."

"What happened to Carl?" Mahler asked.

"I can't say now."

"Hurry up, then," Mahler said.

"Yes. I just have to finish up here in the capital. A few loose ends," Russell said.

"It's very big. Much bigger than I expected. But I can't move it," Mahler said again. "I don't know how the bloody

284

hell we can get it out of the temple. And it's too big for the river."

"We can take it through Bakta Halik," Russell said. He didn't want to talk so much on the phone. It was dangerous.

"Maybe. That's twelve kilometers of jungle. You haven't seen it. It's big. Taller than I am," Mahler said. Mahler sounded exhausted. "I guess it's four meters high."

"Jesus," Russell said, and they were suddenly cut off.

• • •

"Why are we here?" Katherine asked.

He looked at her. He'd rented the penthouse suite at the Camino Real. It had a fabulous view of the *Volcan de Fuego*.

"Because this is where you're going to meet with President Blanco."

"No, it isn't. The delegation is scheduled to meet him in the ballroom," she said.

"I want you to change that," Russell said.

"You want me to ask the President of the republic to come up here?"

"Yes," he said. "I do. It won't be difficult."

"Russell, what in God's name is going on?" she asked.

Katherine was wearing a blue pants suit. He'd never seen her in that kind of formal business wear. She looked the part of UN delegate now, almost severe-looking, he thought, and older.

"You're going to tell him that the delegation has special information about human rights abuses in the country. That Blanco has been named personally, and that you want to give him a chance to clear his name before the delegation goes to the press. That you are concerned for the delegation's safety if they leave the hotel, and that the delegation would appreciate it if he came here, in a more private setting," Russell said.

"That's absurd. There is no such report. And we aren't concerned about our safety. We have the UN Commissioner of Human Rights with us, for God's sake. No one would dare do anything to her."

"Do you want Carlos Selva to be president of the country?" he asked. He was sitting down in the huge living room. The maid had just opened the curtain, ignoring their conversation in English.

"Of course not. The man's a monster. And he *has* violated human rights as head of intelligence. I should know," she said.

"Well, if you don't help me, Carlos is going to assume the Presidency *tonight.* Blanco is leaving the country. He's had enough. He wants to go to Miami and appoint Carlos President. We can stop Carlos. But you'll have to help me."

Katherine came further into the huge room. The maid went to the servi-bar and started putting out soft drinks on the bar top. He'd ordered the bar to be stocked, and bottles of liquor to be arranged on the bar top. When he'd said the word Blanco, the maid had looked up at them for a moment

"I'm going to assassinate Blanco, and I want you to help me," he said calmly.

She looked at him a moment as if he had said something childish.

"You're out of your mind," she said finally.

"No, I'm not," he said. "You say that you want to change the world. You've said that since we first met. You said you've dedicated your life to it. Everything you do is about that, about helping people—about fighting back against evil. Well, here's your chance. You have a real chance to do something instead of just talking about it. If I kill Blanco, he can't appoint Selva.

"We're going to take over the government. Madrid's group. Antonio has promised to hold elections in 12 months. In the meantime, there's a plan to end the economic crisis. We're going to sell the national phone company and the oil company. Jose will be able to stabilize the balance of payments with the money.

"Carlos won't hold elections–*ever*," Russell continued. "You know that. And he won't do anything about the economy except what the fools at the IMF tell him to do. The country will end up like Argentina, only much worse.

"You're either with us or not. I promise you it will make a difference," he said. "Otherwise, the Communists will come back, and this time they'll win. Help me stop that from happening. We can stop all that suffering."

The maid walked by him and nodded. He took out a ten quetzal note and tipped the woman, and she left.

Katherine hadn't said a word. He got up, went to the bar, and took out a beer. He didn't know what she would do. If she said no, he knew he would probably die, because he would have to shoot Blanco in front of his bodyguards and the whole world. He poured himself the beer into a tall, elegant glass, went back and sat down on the couch. For a moment he just looked at the white head of beer in the glass. He wondered whether he had the balls to shoot Blanco in front of everyone.

Katherine sat on the edge of the couch, her knees together, her purse on the floor next to her.

He didn't want to die now. He wanted to take Beatrice and leave the country and be happy, have a family with her. He wanted to have a daughter. He wanted to see her grow into a woman. He wanted to be an old man.

"What's the world coming to?" she said. "Do you think killing people ever really works?"

"Yes. I do. What do you think the world would have been like if Hitler had been shot in 1936? Their side does it all the time. And that's why they win all the time. You see, they aren't like us, always wanting to be good. You can't be good all the time. Not with them. They don't respect anything but

287

power. That's all they respect," Russell said.

"You're sure he's going to appoint Carlos?"

"Yes."

"Do you really believe Madrid is any better? *Really?*"

"Yes, I do. He's different. You know that. He's modern."

"Why do you believe him?"

"Because he believes that it's time to stop listening to the embassy and to the IMF and to the whole lot of them. He wants to make the country independent and free and capitalist, and truly democratic. That means jobs and prosperity, and not just for the rich. It's as simple as that. Now I have to have an answer," he said. "Will you help me?"

She sat there across from him and didn't answer for a long time.

"Yes. I'll help you. Because Carlos is a monster. But not because I believe in Madrid, or any of them. I've learnt too much about the world. That's the irony. That's the truth. I've been a kind of liar. I don't believe, not really. I mean, that people are good. I don't know what I believe in. I'm completely lost. I love you. I believe in that. That's all I believe in, and you don't love me. So you see—nothing makes sense to me."

"You'll help me, then?" She nodded her head.

"We'll change things for the better," he said

"Will we? And the other side? Do you think they will let Madrid take power just like that?" He didn't answer. "They'll kill him later."

He took Katherine to her room, then went out to the pool off the lobby and dialed Selva's cell number.

"I've got the Red Jaguar," Russell said. There was a long pause.

"Good. Where?"

"It's big. Very big. So it's worth millions, only God knows how much," Russell said.

"What is it you want?" Selva asked.

"We need help in getting it out of the country."

"All right," Carlos said.

"We want to make you a partner."

"I want fifty percent."

"Fine. Blanco's coming to the Camino Real to talk to the UN people. Why don't you come with him? We'll talk here."

"Okay," Carlos said. "Good work."

• • •

Spring 1988

The Cardinal had gotten a call from Isabella's brother in Paris. They had been to school together. For a moment the cardinal thought that Roberto Cruz had called just to say hello, and was pleased. But then he heard the news of Isabella's disappearance.

He promised to help. Olga came to his office and was made to wait. The Cardinal would not meet with her, but he assigned a young priest to drive her to the hospitals, where they made inquiries.

The young priest, also an Indian from the highlands, spoke to her in Quiché and Spanish. They went to the public hospital in the Cardinal's brand new Chevy, with a driver. The young priest was sure they would find her mistress, he told Olga. Nothing escaped the knowledge of the church. Cardinal De La Tierra could move heaven and earth.

They searched the wards of the hospital, looking for people who were too ill to have given their names, or, for some reason, had been admitted without identification. They were all poor people, and Olga knew Isabella would not be there. She felt this with a certainty she couldn't describe. It was

289

unimaginable that her mistress could be here in these shabby, cold wards.

They tried the French hospital, which catered exclusively to the country's wealthy. They were told that there were no Jane Does, and no Isabella Cruz had been admitted either. The difference in the two hospitals was striking. Olga insisted, in a show of pique and anger, on walking all the halls. She was allowed to only because the young priest used the Cardinal's name. Olga had seen many of the people in this hospital pass through the apartment on the Reforma: young society women who'd just given birth, old men who'd known Isabella's father and who were dying. Some recognized Olga and made inquiries. Olga answered politely that she was searching for her mistress. Several showed real concern.

The head of the air force, who'd been a good friend of Isabella's mother and was dying from bladder cancer, said he would call his friend at X7, the Guatemalan equivalent of the CIA. He made a big show of it. He was in pain, but stayed on the phone, calling all afternoon to no avail. He died that evening, thinking of Isabella, about the day he first met her, how vivacious she was and how pretty. A military man all his life, he faced death well, but allowed himself to dream as he died of that afternoon on the plantation with Isabella's father and mother, when he'd been young and strapping. He'd met his wife that day. He died happily in a morphine dream.

They stopped for lunch at a cheap restaurant near the cathedral. Olga ate with the priest at a small square wooden table. Neither one spoke. He paid for the lunch, and she thanked him. They went back to the Cardinal's office and heard the news that a white woman's body was being held in a church on the outskirts of the city near Antigua. They went off immediately. Olga knew that God had taken her mistress. The priest, seeing her suffering, said that there was no telling that her mistress was the one they'd found. Olga felt she was there. He tried to hold her hand, but she didn't let him. She was mad at God. God was not fair or good. She was sure of that now.

The church near Antigua had steep stone steps. They walked quickly up them, passing the sitting Indians who'd come for market day. They entered the smoky anteroom littered with burning candles, then passed into the church itself. Afternoon light shone through the blue and yellow stained glass. Blue light fell on the empty crude wooden pews. Banks of candles lit the dark corners off the apse. There were many lit candles, as Ash Wednesday would be that week. Purple cloth had been draped over the saints.

The woman's body had been left where it had first been laid down. The police, overwhelmed by the war, would not come. They had called an ambulance, but it had not come either. There were so many deaths from the war that the army had requisitioned all the ambulances.

Olga began to sob. The priest tried to stop her, but she rushed to the body in front of the altar. She threw back the cloth that had been laid over it and screamed, a horrible sound.

The young priest would never forget it. It was an angry scream, he thought, a scream from a person who had been cheated. The scream dented his faith in God. Men suffered so. He wondered for the first time why it had to be. Later, when the war became unbearable, and the killings crueler and crueler, he decided that God was not a benevolent God, but rather a distant cruel man with little love for his charges. He left the priesthood and became a doctor, studying in France on a scholarship. He came to believe science was the only real god. And even that god wasn't benevolent, or even kind; at best, it was suitable.

He tried to pull Olga off the body, but it was impossible. She struck out at him. Her grief intimidated him. After a moment, he gave up. He bent down by the corpse on the cold stone floor and said an "Our Father," then crossed himself slowly and went to find the parish priest.

They called the Cardinal for instructions on what to do. Because of the lack of ambulances, they were forced to load the body in their car and take it to the undertakers. A doctor was called to perform an autopsy, only because Isabella's brother insisted on it.

THIRTY-ONE

It was raining lightly. The downtown traffic was heavy at noontime. Katherine Barkley, her hair slightly wet from the rain, crossed a quiet tree-lined street a few blocks from the Hotel Camino Real. It was a neighborhood of elegant older homes, built when Guatemala was still one of a handful of countries producing all the world's coffee.

She stopped in front of a large ranch-style house. The house, well off the street, was surrounded by a huge tropical garden. Katherine could see coconut palms and birds of paradise. A well dressed Guatemalan bodyguard was guarding the entrance.

Katherine gave the guard her name. He called someone inside the house on his cell phone, then pushed a button and the gate swung open. He smiled at her, but she didn't notice.

She was frightened now, certain that Russell would be killed. She'd sounded a mayday at the embassy and called for the meeting as soon as she'd found out about Russell's plan to assassinate Blanco.

She made her way through the lush garden to the front door of one of the CIA's many safe houses in the capital. Colonel Oliver North had used the house; some of the embassy's older CIA officers jokingly called the place "Ollie's house."

Iran-Contra, the Bay Of Pigs, the Contra wars—until today, Katherine's role in history seemed very vague. She'd joined the CIA, like many of her generation, on the heels of 9/11. She'd intended to go to medical school, but had joined the agency in a fit of anger and patriotism instead, because she wanted to help her country fight terrorism. Until she'd fallen in love with Russell, she'd been a fast-rising star in the agency's covert directorate.

That afternoon, her career seemed beside the point As she approached the safe house, everything suddenly was appallingly clear to her: It was a dirty world, and this was a dirty country. And now, she felt dirty too, for being part of it all.

She walked through the heavy front door and stood for a moment in the foyer, wondering what had happened to her after only three years in the agency. She'd been a naïve, fearless girl, and now she was something else altogether. Now she was afraid.

Crowley, the station head, was on a satellite phone. The other two men, much younger than Crowley, were sitting at a table. They glanced at her nervously as she came in, a thinly veiled suspicion in their expressions. How had she ended up here, in this room, she wondered, with men who didn't care about her, in love with someone their cables referred to as the "unpredictable American?"

Crowley nodded to her as she entered. The satellite phone's portable cone-shaped dish sat on the floor of the simple living room, pointing towards an open French window that looked out onto the garden. There was a patter of rain on the metal roof. The two younger officers with Crowley wore casual clothes, and sat at the dining room table just off the living room.

Crowley, in his sixties, was near retirement. He'd posed as an AID official all his career, and was the most innocuous-looking man Katherine had ever met. Quite small, almost tiny, Mr. Crowley, as he was called, was the last man in the world anyone would have thought could be an intelligence officer, much less Head of Station. He looked like a back office bank clerk. In fact he was very experienced, having started out as a young man in Vietnam and then Cambodia. Tonsured, his small bald head gleamed in the electric lights. Natty, he looked like one of those people who never allowed himself to get dirty. He wore golf clothes, but never golfed. It was rumored that he was bisexual. But looking at him now, Katherine didn't think so. There was something too square, and far too cunning for him to be caught up in sordidness like that.

Still on the phone, Crowley came and sat at the head of the table and motioned for her to sit down next to him.

The CIA had been using this house since the 1950s. It was still filled with bamboo furniture and mid-century touches bought years before. Watercolor paintings of scenes from the highlands decorated the wall.

The house had served as the military command center during the Bay Of Pigs invasion. This was the very living room that old American Coffee Pete had worked from forty years earlier, coordinating the air support the Cuban invaders had expected. The planes that would have carried the day, waiting on an air base in Nicaragua, were grounded by Kennedy himself at the eleventh hour.

"Now I want you to tell us again about Cruz-Price and what he's up to," Crowley said, looking at her and smiling, settling into his chair. He put the phone down on the polished table. She realized that it could still be on and that others might be listening. She took a breath.

"Cruz-Price is part of a group that's going to assassinate Blanco. They think that will incite a coup that will allow Antonio De La Madrid to seize power." She tried her best to sound indifferent, to keep the emotion out of her voice. Crowley reached over and made a show of turning the phone off. "They'll call back. You seem to have gotten everyone's attention, dear."

"And what do you think of young Cruz-Price and his band of merry men?" Crowley said after what seemed like an eternity. He'd been looking across the room, but suddenly turned and looked at her full on.

"I suppose they're desperate," she said quickly. She was frightened of him, and felt her heart start to race.

"Killing Blanco won't make a difference, you know. Not a bit. Only make it easier for our man to take over. Selva. Eye of the storm and all that. He'll rush in and bring stability to the chaos. Everyone wants a soldier at times like that, dear. No good at all killing Blanco, as far as that goes."

"We could stop it . . . Blanco's killing," she said. She was sorry she'd said it, and wanted to pull the words back.

Crowley stared at her for a moment. Each time he'd called her dear she wanted to slap him.

"*Dear.* You know very well we aren't allowed to interfere in the internal politics of sovereign nations. Isn't that right?" He said in a fatuous tone, finally bothering to look down the table at the others. The phone rang and he reached for it.

" . . .They'd like to speak to *you,*" Crowley said.

She took the phone from him. She told the head of the CIA's Central America desk exactly what she'd learned about the plot against President Blanco. When she finished, she was told to put Crowley back on the line.

Katherine glanced at her watch. It was almost four o'clock. Blanco was scheduled to come to the penthouse at 6:00. She'd arranged everything the way Russell had asked her to. Then she'd come here. She wanted to save Russell's life, and she still thought she could. She believed she'd done the right thing by telling Crowley. She didn't care about the mission anymore; she was in love, and desperate to save him. She'd only mentioned Russell once during the phone call to Virginia, making a point of calling him "the American."

"If they decide not to interfere, you'll have to stay out of it," Crowley said. "Up to a point, I suppose. We can't legally help him, but we can support Cruz-Price. He might be useful in the future. You can always use someone like that." Crowley looked at her evenly. It was obvious that he didn't care about Blanco one way or the other. His murder would be a policy decision.

"I've never *really* understood Cruz-Price. What do you think he wants, Katherine . . . just this *girl?*" Crowley said, leaning forward. "You seem to know him fairly well?" He dropped his gaze slightly as if he'd said something off color.

Does he know? Katherine wasn't sure what they knew about her and Russell. She supposed they might suspect she had gotten involved with him. It was something about the way they were all looking at her now, suspicion tinged with envy. She noticed one of the younger men wore a wedding ring.

"Have you told us everything about Cruz-Price's motivations?" Crowley asked. "It is crunch time. We wouldn't want to be taken by surprise."

"He simply believes Selva is wrong for the country and that the communists will take advantage of the chaotic economic situation. He hates the communists. I think it's something personal, something to do with his mother," she said. She stopped talking for a moment. Crowley's expression was passive. "He believes Madrid has a chance of winning, if they can get a fair election." She said it quickly, as if it were the key and she were betraying him again. She wanted so desperately to protect him, she felt insecure.

"I think he can be very useful in the future. If Madrid is elected, he'll be part of the government," she said. "I'm sure he'd cooperate with us. I'm sure of it." This was a lie, but she didn't care. In fact, she had no idea what Russell would do.

The satellite phone rang. It made her jump. Crowley took up the receiver and listened. He listened for quite a while.

Katherine felt the two younger officers in the room boring a hole in her. They both, she believed now, thought she'd "hooked up" with Cruz-Price. It was obvious to her, as she glanced at them. Neither one of them would look straight at her.

"I'm afraid there's nothing we can do," Crowley said finally, hanging up the phone. "We're to stay out of it."

Katherine was shocked. She'd been sure they would protect Blanco, stop it somehow.

"The important thing is to get Selva in place," Crowley said.

The two younger officers in the room were obviously surprised. They had nothing but contempt for Selva. They wanted De La Madrid to win the election, because he was a democrat and all their intelligence indicated that he wasn't hostile to the US in any serious way. But the officers were all young and for the most part still idealistic, if no longer naive. Selva, they knew, was predictable and completely compromised. He would take orders from the embassy, and that's all that mattered to Washington. Everyone knew Selva was a pig, but he would be their pig.

"The clandestine people are very concerned about your safety . . . under the circumstances. There's no reason for you to go back to the hotel. In fact, they'd like you to come home now," Crowley said. She'd gone pale. Crowley thought she was frightened because they might have asked her to be in the room when Russell Cruz-Price shot Blanco.

"I'd like to go back and get my things out of the hotel. Personal things," she said.

"Of course," he said. "We can have someone go with you if you like."

"No. That won't be necessary," she said. "I'll need an excuse to leave the commission . . . I'll tell them I've gotten a call from my mother... tell them that my father's gravely ill," she said. "How's that? No, I suppose not. That. . . ." She stood up. It was a silly suggestion, but she was upset.

It was raining hard outside now. She could see the rain bending the birds of paradise and battering the orange bougainvillea that grew along the garden wall.

"Langley has already arranged to have the NGO call you back to New York," Crowley said. "Do you want to take my umbrella?"

"No. No, thank you, sir."

She turned and left. She felt the doorknob in her hand and then she crossed the garden in the rain, warm on her face. She went to the garden gate and felt herself trembling. She'd never expected that Washington would go for Selva like that. She'd been wrong, and she didn't know what to do now but go back and try to stop it somehow.

She was two blocks from the hotel when they shot her from a passing car; she was dead before she hit the ground. They believed Katherine Barkley was a communist. She'd fooled everyone.

Most of the important European newspapers, including *Le Monde,* reported that a young American woman, part of a UN human rights delegation visiting Guatemala, was shot and killed, probably by a government-connected death squad, in Guatemala City. *Le Monde* reported that military elements were angry with the Commission's interference in the country's internal affairs. The head of the UN Human Rights Commission issued a formal complaint against the Blanco government in protest, and left the country immediately.

There was no mention of the killing in any of the American newspapers. The story had been quashed by someone at

Langley whose job was liaison with the *New York Times* and other major newspapers.

• • •

Russell waited in the enormous suite alone all afternoon, dressed in a blue suit and a black silk tie. He'd kept a pistol stuck between the pillows of the couch. But no one from the commission had showed up, and neither had Blanco.

When he'd tried to call Katherine's room, she hadn't answered. She didn't answer her cell phone, either.

He watched the sun start to set, the ice melting in the ice bucket in front of him. She had betrayed him, he supposed, or simply become frightened. He didn't really blame her. Strangely, he felt no anger towards her. It was his fate that things would end this way.

He'd taken off his jacket and tie, because the room was warm. He watched the rain come and go through the windows, with their view of the Volcanoes of Water and Fire. He walked to the balcony and watched the rain beat against the face of the hotel's pool 12 stories below, the pool's lights on now. The rain fell so hard and intense it seemed the world was ending.

There had been a tremendous silence in him as he listened to the beating of the rain on the window. He was going to have to kill Blanco when he came to give his speech in the hotel's ballroom, and that meant he was certainly going to die. He didn't want to die, not really, but he felt he had a duty. He would change history. It would be a little piece of history, but it would be his piece. It would do some small good.

He didn't feel lost anymore. He'd had an epiphany when he realized he was going to die. He felt, finally, as if it all had meant something. His life had a purpose. That terrible feeling he'd had since the day he'd heard about his mother's death was gone at last. In its place, for the first time, was a strange and cleansing resolve that he couldn't have explained to anyone. It would have sounded idiotic, since he had no more desire to die than anyone else, *now*.

And this was the great irony. He'd finally found himself. He wasn't sure whether it was a new self or a self he'd had as a child that was buried in the avalanche of his mother's death. Old or new, he welcomed it. He was certain to die because of this thing he had to do, and yet it was precisely this moment that was responsible for his finding himself. He had to kill Blanco. And there was nothing that would stop him.

He called Antonio and asked him to go to his mother's apartment on La Reforma and take away all his things. He didn't want there to be any connection with Beatrice or his family. He'd kept a book of Rilke's poems Beatrice had bought him in Antigua. She'd written "For my love" in the flap, and signed her name. He wanted nothing left that could hurt her. No connection with him. He'd been so sure that he was going to see her again. Now he was sure he would not.

"It's going to have to be tonight, then," Russell said to Antonio cryptically. They couldn't speak in too obvious a way.

"You are at the hotel?" Antonio asked. Madrid was in his car, leaving his office.

"Yes. At the hotel," Russell said. "I'll have to go down to the lobby. . . . He didn't come for the meeting. Something's happened."

"Are you sure? I mean, sure that you want to do it?" Antonio asked. He sounded upset.

"I want you to go get my things. They're at my mother's. I want you to pick them up and make sure that they are destroyed. There isn't much. On my mother's dresser. A book of poems. Can you do that for me? I want you to make *sure* that it is destroyed. Take all my things. The maid will help."

"Yes, of course," Antonio said. "But are you sure...?"

"Very sure," Russell said. "Goodbye. . . . Will you be there tonight, when he comes?"

"Yes," Antonio said. "Goodbye, then." Russell hung up; he didn't want to speak any more.

THIRTY-TWO

The bell rang twice.

It had been thirty years, or more—Antonio couldn't remember exactly how long it had been since he'd climbed the stairs to Isabella's apartment. He'd thought about Isabella every day of his life, but the memory was soft now, just their talking and their making love, nothing about her death.

He'd told no one about what had happened. He was proud that he'd kept his promise and helped her son until the boy had decided to do what he was going to do. And now Antonio didn't know what to do to stop him.

He hadn't expected Russell to ask him to come back to this apartment. He couldn't refuse the boy, of course; he was sure Russell would die. Antonio told himself again, as he waited for the door to open, that Russell had made his own decision to kill Blanco. It had just been so unexpected. Who can tell about a person, Antonio thought, breathing a little hard after climbing the stairs. Russell should never have come back here, that would have been better.

He was about to reach for the bell again when the door opened and Olga let him in.

"I'm here to collect some things for the young gentleman," he told Olga. She'd aged so much, and she was so stooped now, he hadn't recognized her. Then he saw the shoulder, and remembered. "Olga? Olga, is that you?"

"*Sí, señor,*" she said.

"Olga! My god! I thought you'd gone to the United States like everyone else. Where have you been all these years?"

She looked at him.

"*Don* Antonio?"

"Yes. Isabella's friend. Do you remember?"

"*Sí, Don* Antonio," Olga said.

He took her hand and held it a moment. "God, it's been so long, Olga."

"*Sí, Don* Antonio," the old woman said.

He looked at her for a moment longer, then let go of her hand. "You came to my parents' house after Isabella . . . after that awful time." He remembered now how Olga had searched for Isabella.

"*Sí, Don* Antonio."

"My family was beastly to you. I'm truly sorry. I was out of the country studying. I'm so sorry for what happened."

She shook her head in acknowledgement of the time she'd spent standing out in front of his house in the rain, coming back every day, trying to get an answer as to what had happened to her mistress. She'd collapsed out in front of the house and been taken to the public hospital, where she'd almost died of pneumonia. The war started in earnest right after that.

"*Pase Usted,*" Olga said, and led him down the dark hallway.

Antonio followed her. He remembered looking out the window once or twice at the silly Indian girl who'd stood in front of his parents' house in the rain. At the time, he thought she was mad or interested in blackmail. He'd gone to the university in Chicago soon afterward.

"*Don* Russell was using his mother's room," Olga stopped at the doorway. "Would you like a cup of coffee, *Don* Antonio?" she asked, her face expressionless.

304

"Yes. Thank you, Olga. Yes, please." He walked into Isabella's bedroom and back into his youth.

Olga watched him. He looked old, she thought, and fatter. He had been a handsome young man, very thin.

She turned around and went to the kitchen. She put the blue iron pot on the stove and turned up the gas. For a moment she saw herself standing in the rain. She listened to the water in the pot start to move and dance. She'd been pregnant then, but hadn't even known it.

She turned and looked at De La Madrid. Like all of his class, he'd taken it upon himself to sit at the dining room table and wait to be served. She closed the door to the kitchen, got out the rat poison and spooned it into the bottom of the cup. Then she filled the cup with essence of coffee, two teaspoons of sugar, and hot water.

She opened the door to the dining room and served De La Madrid. Afterwards, she went back into the kitchen, sat in the same chair she'd sat in years before, and waited.

1988
Guatemala City

Dearest Russell,

Antonio De La Madrid and I are getting married. I wanted to write to you as soon as he proposed, but I had to run to the plantation yesterday because of the harvest. I tried to call you from there, but the beastly Communists had cut the telephone wires <u>again</u>.

So, darling — I just wanted to say that you will be able to come back here and live with us, if that's what you want. I would like you to finish school there in the States, but you could come for a long, long visit. If you prefer, you can stay here. And there'll be a house here in the capital, as

Antonio wants me to find something for a new family. That means you'll finally have a brother or sister!

I want you to take a semester off and get to know Antonio. I know you will like him. I don't ever expect him to replace your father, that would be absurd. But I hope you and he can be great friends.

I'll finish this letter in the morning, as we are going to a party tonight. Good night, mí Capitan...

Antonio struggled against the rat poison. It had been violent and very painful. He'd run first into the bathroom; after he'd been sick, he'd staggered into Isabella's room trying to vomit the rest of it up, but it was too late. He'd screamed for Olga, but she'd disappeared. In the bedroom mirror he saw his mouth white with foam; he'd grabbed at the hair brushes and pulled the glass top off the counter. It was there that Isabella had slid the letter to her son before she'd gone out that last night. Olga had found the letter and picked it up, seeing her mistress's handwriting, but she couldn't read it; she'd never learned to read. She threw it into the fire.

• • •

"Where's Carlos?" Russell asked. Beatrice was in jeans and a T-shirt, and looked upset. There was something wild and desperate in her eyes when he'd pulled open the door to his hotel room.

"Here in the Hotel. But he doesn't know I'm here. He was to have a meeting with the Americans," she said.

When she'd knocked on the door, he thought it might be Katherine, with an explanation for why no one had shown up. Seeing Beatrice was completely unexpected.

He'd gone over a thousand times how he was going to shoot Blanco. He planned to shoot Blanco by the escalator as the president rode it up from the lobby to the ballroom. Russell had gone down and selected a place to stand. Then he'd come back to the suite to wait.

He looked at his watch. Blanco would be arriving in two hours. "I went to your mother's apartment looking for you," Beatrice said. "I've decided to leave him . . . Carlos. I don't care. I've taken the children . . . I've brought Olga," she said. "She's downstairs in the car park with the children now."

"What's wrong? Why are you looking at me like that?" he said.

"Russell . . . Olga's killed Antonio," she said.

"What are you talking about?" He glanced again at his watch. It was a quarter to six. He had to go downstairs soon, if he wanted his place, before the crowds got too big.

"Antonio is dead, Russell. I saw him. . . . She begged me to take her away. She's killed him, and she's terrified. She begged me to take her home to your mother's plantation. I didn't know what to do. She said you were here at the hotel, that Antonio told her.

"I've taken the children," she said again. "They can't grow up with Carlos. I won't have it. I want to be with you. I can't stand it anymore."

What she'd said seemed crazy, and he wasn't sure she hadn't gone mad. He slapped her. It was involuntary; all the tension of waiting for nothing made him do it.

"You're lying." He held her by the shoulders and shook her. "I just spoke to him. You lying bitch." Her face was red where he'd slapped her.

"No. He's dead."

"Why are you lying?" He let her go.

"I'm not." She was holding her face.

"I'll call him right now. You'll be sorry you did this," he said. "Did they put you up to it?" He went to the couch, picked up his cell phone and dialed Antonio's cell number. He got the voice mail message.

307

She hadn't moved.

"I'm sorry," she said. "I'm not lying. He's dead. I'm sorry, but it's the truth."

"You are lying and I don't know why, but I can't forgive you. Not for lying to me about this. They sent you, didn't they? Carlos. You're working for them now. Is that it?"

She shook her head. He closed his phone. He had a horrible desire to hit her again, but stopped himself.

"I came because I love you. Please don't hit me again. I've left Carlos. I wrote him a note. He's going to know about us when he gets home. I couldn't stand it anymore. Any of it. I want to be your wife. I want you to take me and the children away from here."

"If you're lying . . . I'll. . . ." He reached for the pistol he'd shoved into the couch pillows, pulled it out and walked towards her. She didn't move.

"You told Carlos. That you've left him?" She shook her head yes. "Are you working for them? Is that why you're lying about Antonio?"

"No! Stop it. You're scaring me, Russell. I've got the children downstairs, for God's sake! We have to go *now*. We have to leave. We can be in Mexico before the announcement. Antonio's dead, and I'm not lying about that. Why in God's name would I lie to you?

"Are you listening to me? We don't have much time. Carlos will be President in a few hours. I'll never get the children away from him then." He was standing there staring at her, the gun in his hand. "He'll never let me leave with the children once he's been named President. You know that."

He saw suddenly that she wasn't lying.

"Why did she do it?" he said. *"Why?"*

"Russell, I don't know why. But we have to go. Now. We can take Olga with us if you like. You know what they'll do to her if they arrest her. She's an old woman. I couldn't leave her there. She was pathetic, just sitting in the kitchen staring at the wall."

"I can't go with you. Not now," he said. "It's too late."

"What do you mean? It's two hours to Mexico. He won't notice I've gone until late tonight."

"I have to kill Blanco. Now. In a few minutes."

"What?"

"I have to. You don't understand. If Blanco makes that announcement, Carlos will be President," he said.

"What difference does it make who's President? We *have* to go now. It's our only chance to take the children. *Please.* Russell, I'm begging you."

"Don't, because I can't. Not now. You don't understand. It doesn't matter about Antonio. There'll be someone else... anyone but Carlos," he said.

"I won't let you do it. They'll kill you," she said. She took her cell phone out of her coat pocket and began to dial. "I'll tell Carlos what you're planning."

He grabbed her phone away from her and threw it across the room, against the door of the bathroom, smashing it. She collapsed in a heap on the floor, and was crying. He bent over and lifted her up. "I want you and the children to go to the hotel Lago in Puerto Barrios. Register under the name of Molly Jones. Take the children, and take Olga. I'll meet you there in three days. Do you understand?"

"But they'll kill you."

"Maybe. You'll know soon enough if they do," he said. "If they do, you can take the children to Honduras from there. There's a British consulate office in Tegucigalpa. They'll help you get to England."

"You *promise* me you'll come?" she said.

"Yes," he said. "I'll come in three days. But Carlos will have to die now, too. I can get close to him. I'll have a chance." He looked at her. "Can you live with that? If I make it, they'll have to grow up with the man that killed their father."

"I don't care," she said. "As long as you come to Barrios in three days." She threw her arms around him. "I don't care about Carlos, just come to Barrios. Please."

• • •

"I've got the Jaguar. Here," Russell said. He'd dialed the general's cell phone. "Where are you?"

"I'm at the Camino Real," Carlos said. "I thought you said Mahler had it."

"He did. He's brought it out. It's at *Tres Rios*. We'll sell it to you for two hundred thousand dollars cash. . . . In an hour."

"Wait a minute, I can't speak here," Carlos said. Russell heard the sound of voices, and he guessed that the general was in the café downstairs. "Why so cheap?" Carlos asked finally.

"Because we can't sell it, and you can. You'll be President. It shouldn't be a problem, should it? You can sell it back to the state, right?"

"You're very clever. All right, I'll get the money," Carlos said.

"I want you to fly me to *Tres Rios* in your helicopter. You can have the whole thing, the plantation and the Jaguar. You will be back in time for the ceremony. By the way—congratulations, Mr. President.

"I'll meet you in the lobby in—" Russell glanced at his watch "—in half an hour."

"Fine. Is it big? The Jaguar?" Carlos asked.

"It's huge. You'll see," Russell said.

Exactly ten minutes later he managed to shoot President Blanco dead as Blanco was riding up the escalator. His body guards did nothing; the Americans had paid them off and told them not to interfere. Russell had simply stepped on the escalator and ridden right past the smiling Blanco, who thought he recognized the kid from somewhere.

310

THIRTY-THREE

Sitting above the jungle canopy on a hill, the temple's stone face was hit by the last of the slanting afternoon sunlight. It was both frightening and beautiful. And, Russell thought, there was something clearly defiant about the way it sat alone facing the river, forever a silent epitaph of empire. *Was it the start of a Mayan city? Or was it something else?* Finding no one at the camp site, he made his way along the track towards the site. *Was it only the last moments of a defeated culture?* he wondered. *Had the temple been only a hiding place, as it was for him now? Had Mayan soldiers huddled here with their wives and children, praying to their Gods, waiting for a last great battle?*

It started to rain as he trotted up the track past discarded boxes of equipment. A cloud blocked the sun and the jungle darkened the finishes duller. Further along, he found Mahler's horse lying dead at the foot of the temple. Its saddle had been torn off and lay nearby. High above, at the top of the site, he could see Mahler sitting by the entrance, waving to him excitedly.

Unable to walk, Mahler had crawled out when he heard the jeep cross the river. It must have hurt him to crawl, Russell thought, because he looked like he was in a lot of pain.

"How did you get here?" Mahler asked him. He was sitting in the dirt, a kerosene lamp at his side. Filthy and gaunt, he had wound a piece of torn rain slicker over his injured leg.

311

"Bakta Halik. I've brought your jeep," Russell said. A bad smell hit him as he stepped closer to Mahler. "What happened? Where is everyone?"

"I tried to move the Jaguar. I think something scared my horse. I'm not sure. But it fell on the steps," Mahler said. A few bats flew out into the twilight past them. Russell saw a colony of them clustered on the ceiling, their upside-down bodies twisting slightly.

"I've broken my leg. It's pretty bad," Mahler said.

"Can you walk?"

"No. Can you smell it? The leg."

"Yes," Russell said.

"Septicemia," Mahler said. "The bone came through the skin. I managed to shove it back down." Mahler looked down at his leg, then up at Russell. "But my hands were dirty from all this bat shit. I couldn't get down the steps to the medical bag."

Russell could see flies sitting on Mahler's leg. "You hold the lamp," Mahler said. "I show you." Russell took the kerosene lamp and held it over him. Mahler rolled back the bloody slicker. "What do you think? Not so bad?"

He could clearly see where the femur had snapped, leaving a sharp glossy end. The wound looked badly infected, and he could see hideous clusters of fat maggots.

"It's infected," Russell said. He didn't use the word gangrene, but he thought it. Mahler slipped the dirty slicker back over the hole in his leg.

"Bad luck, huh," Mahler said absently. He looked down towards the camp. The mist had turned to rain, the dusk-colored jungle canopy an ocean of tree tops that went on for as far as the eye could see. "I couldn't get down the steps. I could see the camp and the medical bag. . . ."

"Yes," Russell said. "Bad luck."

"Maybe they were wet. The steps. It was raining pretty hard."

"Maybe," Russell said.

"There it is. I told you I'd find it." Mahler smiled. He grabbed the lamp out of Russell's hand and held it up. Its yellow light opened a passage in the darkness. Russell could see the Red Jaguar standing in the middle of the temple, the rope Mahler had used to drag it around its neck. "Fucking huge. . . . Can you see it? It's getting pretty dark." Mahler turned the lamp back toward Russell. There was nothing he could do for him, Russell thought. Mahler was going to die, and he knew it.

"I remember when I was a boy in Germany, we had a view of the wall. . . . The wall, remember?"

"The Berlin wall?" Russell said.

"Yes. The Wall. We had a garden right on the wall. You could hear the guard dogs barking. . . . My mother hated it. I'd like to call my mother," Mahler said. "I think she should know I've found it. . . . Do you have your phone?"

"Yes," Russell said. "But from in here, you. . . ."

"I thought maybe if I crawled outside into the open," Mahler said. His face was very pale, his eyes reflecting the yellow lamplight.

"You shouldn't, it's raining pretty hard," Russell said.

"Could you get me some brandy from the camp, and your phone? I want to call my *mother*," Mahler asked, as if he hadn't heard what Russell had just said.

Russell took the lamp and went and got the brandy and the medical bag from the camp. He passed Mahler's horse again on the way back.

"No more will my green sea go turn a deeper blue. . . ."

Mahler was singing in a soft voice, drinking from a cup Russell had brought him. The metal cup fell from his hand suddenly, but he didn't seem to notice at first. The sound of the falling cup echoed on the temple's stone floor. Mahler seemed to be somewhere else. "I could not foresee this thing happening to you. I want to see the sun blotted out from the sky. I see no red doors . . . go ahead and turn them black." Mahler was singing and rocking a little, maybe because of the pain. His lips were wet. Outside it was pitch black now.

"I'd like more," Mahler said suddenly. "I can't hold the cup. Why not?"

Russell didn't know what to say. It was hard to watch someone die, even someone he didn't like. He'd cleaned and dressed the wound as best he could.

"What happened to everyone? Where's Gloria?" Russell asked. He bent down and helped Mahler drink straight from the bottle.

"I killed them," Mahler said, swallowing weakly. The brandy spilled out of his mouth as he spoke, onto his stomach and bad leg. He drank a lot of brandy and spilled a lot. "It's a ton at least, isn't it?" Mahler said when he'd drunk his fill. "Will you put the light on its face? I want to see it again."

"Sure," Russell said. "If you want." Russell picked up the lamp and walked into the darkness. It smelled better away from Mahler's leg. The yellow lamp light caught the face of the Red Jaguar. Its eyes were gold nuggets; its teeth were white bone. The body was a red jade that looked almost translucent. The face, jewel-encrusted, was frightening. He'd never seen anything like it. *Was it a talisman against the Spanish?* He reached out and touched its face. If it had been, it had failed them.

"Mayans. They were fucking good, man. Make something like that. Fucking good, man. I just wanted to pull it out of here so I could see it better. I wasn't going to try and steal it from you," Mahler said. Russell didn't believe him, but it didn't matter now. "The horse slipped . . . on the steps. Or something scared it. Bad luck," Mahler said again, like he couldn't believe it had happened.

"Could you move it?" Russell asked, coming back towards him.

"Yes. I moved it. I had to dig it out myself. You won't have to do that. It took me two days," Mahler laughed. "That's why I'm so dirty. It's filthy in here. Will you give me your phone now? Please. I want to try to call Germany."

"Sure," Russell said. Mahler took his cell phone and tried to dial.

"I can't see," he said. He was dying, and his eyes were going, Russell thought. He held the lamp over Mahler's head to help him see the phone.

"Mutti," Mahler said. "Mutti, why don't you answer?" He was losing his guts now. "Why can't I talk to my mother?" Mahler asked. "I'll go outside. It will work outside. Will you help me? I want to speak to my mother." He started to crawl towards the door frantically.

Russell tried to help him, but Mahler screamed in pain and they had to stop. There was a frightened look on Mahler's face now. He started to cry from the pain. Russell suddenly felt sorry for him, because he knew Mahler was going to die like that, in pain and alone. There was no way he could take riding in the jeep.

"Fucking horse," Mahler said when he could finally speak again.

"I've brought your jeep," Russell said. "I can try and take you out."

"How? You told me, but I've forgotten."

"I came through Bakta Halik. It took eight hours."

"Yes. I suppose you could. It will be dangerous on the way back, with the Jaguar."

"Do you think we can get it out?" Russell asked. He got closer, bending down over Mahler.

"Maybe. I don't know. Maybe. You could take me to the doctor, maybe, too."

"I'll take you. It would be very painful, in the jeep. But if you want I will try."

"No, I don't think so. Maybe you could send someone back for me? Maybe that's better."

"I've killed the President of the republic. So I don't know if you want to be traveling with me anyway. But I'll send someone. I promise," Russell said.

"Fucking hell! Really? Blanco? That tub of shit."

"Yeah," Russell said. "And Selva. He's dead, too." He picked Mahler up and dragged him back over to the wall so he could sit up.

"You're crazy," Mahler said. "I always said so. What happened?"

"I had Selva bring me to *Tres Rios* in his helicopter."

Mahler looked at him. "You fucking crazy."

"I told him we were going to sell him the Jaguar. I also told some people who had a score to settle with Carlos that he'd be there. They killed his pilot and bodyguards, and then they took Carlos away. He's dead by now," Russell said. "I'm sure of that."

"Fuck him. He would have made a lousy President," Mahler said. "You brought *my* jeep?"

"Yes."

"There's a winch in the back. I hid it so that it wouldn't be stolen. You can use that to drag it out of here. I want my cut. When you get it sold," he said. He was sucking on his lip now because of the pain.

"Okay," Russell said. "I'm meeting Carl's brother at Puerto Barrios. Tomorrow."

"Then you take the luggage rack off the top and you drag it on that," Mahler said. He was a genius, it was true. Russell knew he would never have thought of that.

316

"That's a good idea," Russell said. "It might work."

"Fucking right it is. How do you think I found the Red Jaguar? I want my cut," Mahler said again. He was a little drunk now. "I found it, didn't I?"

"Yes. You found it. And you'll get your cut," Russell said. He wasn't smelling the leg so much now; the rain was blowing fresh air through the temple door.

"I'm smart, aren't I?" Mahler asked.

"Yeah," Russell said. "You're smart."

"Fucking right," Mahler said, looking at him.

There was a shot; the bullet hit Mahler in the forehead. Mahler's body twitched violently for a moment, as if he were trying to get up.

"Now, *amigo,* I don't want to kill you, too. But I will," Coffee Pete said. He was standing in the entrance of the temple, wearing a black rain poncho and a cowboy hat. His .45 was pointed at Russell.

"Now that's what I call a stinking kraut," Pete said. He walked over and gave Mahler's chest a hard kick. "I heard that last part about dragging it. I just don't know what the fuck you boys are up to. But I guess it's in here. Right? What is it?"

Russell had been crouching very close to Mahler, his hand on the lamp. He could smell the acridness of the gun shot. Mahler was staring at him.

"Well, lift it up! The light, asshole, so I can see what you got in here!" Russell didn't move. "Listen, kid, I don't have a lot of time here. You got half the Guatemalan army out looking for that General, and they'll get here sooner than later. So lift the motherfucking LAMP!"

"He was dying anyway," Russell said finally. "You didn't have to shoot him."

"Yeah, well, I spared him the wait," Pete said. "Now, *amigo,* lift the lamp." Russell did what he asked. "That's right; why

317

don't you stand up, too. Are you carrying a gun?"

"No," Russell said.

"I bet you're lying. Drop your pants. And take your shirt off," Pete said. "Go on, don't be bashful." Russell put down the lamp and took off his shirt, then dropped his pants. "Okay. I hope that was as good for you as it was for me," Pete said. "Now pick up the lamp."

Russell didn't say anything. He pulled his pants up and lifted the lamp as Pete asked.

"Jesus. Fuck *me*, boy. I got to see that a little better. Get closer. What is that down there?"

"What's it look like," Russell said. He had hoped Pete wouldn't see it.

"Fucking giant pot of money, is what it looks like to me. That's what you two have been up to, then?"

"That's right," Russell said.

"And what about the sack of money in the jeep? What's that about?" Carlos had paid him for the Jaguar in cash and he'd brought the money with him. "I was going to leave with that, but then I saw the light up here. The girl at *Tres Rios,* she'd said something about digging out here, and I thought fuck it. I had to know what was up here. For all I knew, you two had found the fucking lost Dutchman mine," Pete said.

"What girl?" Russell asked. He thought of throwing the lamp at him but he decided against it.

"The girl the kraut here tried to send to her maker a couple of days ago. See, I've been staying in the village next to *Tres Rios* since I met you. I started thinking about it. Why would anyone buy a coffee plantation nowadays? It didn't make any sense. I started wondering what was going on. So I went back to the village and put my ear to the ground.

"That girl had to walk all the way out of here with buckshot in her ass, but she lived. I heard about it yesterday. Then today, I heard Selva had been kidnapped by a lot of ex-

318

guerrillas when he landed at *Tres Rios.* You're a busy mother-fucker, kid, I'll say that. I'm just guessing now, but I guess that's the general's money in the jeep. But it don't matter to me whose it is now," the old man said.

"You're awfully quiet, Price. You must be trying to figure out how to kill me. I'm seventy years old, son, and there's a lot of men that's tried, and I'm still here. You best figure out another plan."

"All right," Russell said. "Help me get the Jaguar out to the asphalt and you can keep the money in the jeep."

"How about you help me get the Jaguar out of here, and I don't kill you. That's what's on the menu today. Take it or leave it." The old man raised his pistol.

"I'll take it," Russell said.

"Good. I thought you might. You won't mind if I don't shake your hand," Pete said. "I think that might not be such a good idea. Now, drag that dead motherfucker out of here, because he stinks."

THIRTY-FOUR

Two jaguars had been watching Russell from the edge of the clearing. Sometimes they would move, but he knew they were jaguars and he knew there were two. Coffee Pete had left him chained to a ceiba tree. Pete hadn't killed him, he said, because he liked him. He told Russell that the army might find him, or someone might happen along before he starved to death. The old man said he thought Russell had a fifty-fifty chance of living. He'd promised to let someone at *Tres Rios* know where Russell was, and then he'd driven off in Mahler's jeep, dragging the Red Jaguar behind him, covered with a canvas. Russell thought that was two days ago.

The jaguars entered the clearing on the evening of the second day. Russell yelled something to try to scare them, and one of them had jumped in the air like an electric current had passed through it. It landed on the run and both animals tore into the jungle again, but he knew they would be back. It was only a matter of time.

His arms tied behind him, he looked up into the sky and saw the blue tint of afternoon. The huge limbs of the ceiba tree waved above him. He wanted to climb the tree, see the river, and see Beatrice again, but he knew he would probably never do any of those things, now. In sudden fury he struggled against the chain. Finally, exhausted, he stopped.

He dropped his head and searched the clearing for the jaguars. They'll come back at full dark, he thought. They'll come then, and I might not see them until. . . . He stopped thinking about that, because it terrified him. He closed his eyes.

No one ever believes they're lost until it's too late, he thought. No one finds that one important map that will make their life clear, the map that would show you where you really stand in the world.

He had been a fool. He knew that now, but it was too late to change anything. He'd tried to find one thing, just one thing, to make it all better. That's all he'd done. Something to make him forget that life was the joke it was. Everyone searches for that one thing that will fix it all. A love affair, a coffee plantation. Something else that becomes a reason for living. Maybe you find it, and maybe you suffer as a result. He certainly had.

He opened his eyes and looked at the temple entrance on the cleared hillock above him. It was getting darker. The muddy track left by the dragging of the Red Jaguar was disappearing in the gray-green twilight.

He'd been lost in so many ways for so long that he was glad that he recognized the road before him now. He supposed that being alive, really alive, was allowing yourself to become completely lost. That was the irony. He would have liked to tell Beatrice that all his fear of being lost was gone now. He would have liked to have told her that. He wished she was there with him. They were two of a kind, she and he, he realized. He wondered if she'd gone to Barrios. He'd asked Coffee Pete to let him use his phone so he could tell her not to wait for him but to go on to Honduras—but Coffee Pete didn't have a cell phone, and he'd destroyed Russell's. He wondered what would happen to Beatrice and the children.

He looked again and saw that one of the jaguars had gone up the steps to the temple. It turned and looked at him, then sprinted up the stairs and disappeared inside.

He checked on the sky through the canopy of the ceiba tree. He could still see bits of red-stained clouds, but it would be dark soon. It hurt his shoulders to look up, but he wanted to. He wanted to see the sky for the last time. He would never see her again, nor would he be able to tell Beatrice what he had finally discovered about life: when you are most lost is precisely when you are the most alive. He understood that now. He hadn't expected that, but it was true. He nodded off and dreamed.

He and Beatrice had been on the beach together one sunset at the height of their affair. It was a painful memory, because it was so good—painful, because he was afraid. Death hadn't been there then. The mother of pearl-colored, deserted, shack-strewn beach at sunset, that's what they had. The memory was so clear, so beautiful—of her naked, standing alone on the beach, him coming out of the surf, looking at her, knowing she was his, the rush of knowing. The taste of the salt on his lips. The way her voice came to him over the surf, with the Englishness that he loved so much, the lilting of it. He couldn't describe exactly what was in Beatrice's voice—just youth, perhaps—but everything about her was in it. It was so full of that sparkling intelligence, so full.

He didn't feel tied to the tree anymore. He'd left the tree behind him and was free, walking out of the surf. Bits of dark driftwood glided past him. He looked at Beatrice standing there, waiting for him. Nothing was better than seeing her like that, and being in love with her. Nothing. Death? So what?

I don't care. *I killed for her,* he thought. That was Beatrice's effect on him. That was the nature of his passion for her. But passions have their price, and now he would pay the full amount. So be it.

I only fear never having met her.

He let the half-dream end and forced himself to open his eyes.

A purple darkness had taken over the jungle sky. The camp had turned a soft blue color, and Russell could see just the outline of it. Night was finally collapsing the camp. He thought he saw something to his right, and screamed; he turned his head, but it was just a bird that had landed near him. He started to shake with fear. He tried to stop but couldn't until he let something go, something he'd carried with him all those years since his mother's death.

It was all over now, he told himself, finally controlling his shaking—but it had been worth it. All of it.

He closed his eyes again. He imagined Beatrice and the children waiting for him. They were in a restaurant, a very clean one with white walls and air-conditioning. He was parking the jeep, and they were waving to him from inside. *I would do it again,* he thought, no longer frightened. He would do it again, knowing that in the end it would come to this.

He heard the jaguar inside the temple growl, its growl amplified by the temple walls. He tried hard to make out the temple's entrance, but couldn't anymore.

They'll come now, he thought.

• • •

Olga Monte de Oro stepped off the bus at Colomba. It was market day and the streets were busy, the rain clouds pearly smooth and gigantic. Indians in traditional garb filled the narrow street as she passed. They called to each other in their language. There was a timeless, sad mute quality to the town's narrow streets; the tiny shops painted in shabby blues. On the square, Olga passed market stalls, hung with worn tarpaulins, their fruits and vegetables piled high.

Olga stopped and bought tortillas from a woman her age with bad legs, who was making them out on the square for a penny apiece, the woman's kind face horribly wrinkled. Beatrice Selva had given her a hundred dollar bill when she put her on the bus. The bill was too big to use here. Olga found a few pennies in her pocket and paid for the tortillas. She had the old woman wrap them in a banana leaf.

"Where are you headed, sister?" the old woman asked her in their language.

"Plantation *Las Flores*," Olga told her. "I've been away. But I'm going home now."

"God bless you," the woman said. "And keep you safe. The world out there is no place for us."

"And may God be with you," Olga said to the woman. She went on along the street, past the little shops with their corrugated metal roofs and open fronts. A young plantation owner's wife was shopping with her maid. Olga stopped to stare at the young girl, the only white person on the street.

"*Doña* Isabella, I'm sorry. I went to buy tortillas," Olga said. The young woman looked at her.

"Excuse me?" the girl said in Spanish.

"I'm ready to go home now," Olga said. "We need vegetables. I know where we should go. I know. Where the best ones are, *Doña* Isabella. And those sweet breads the child likes so much. I'm so glad I found you, my lady," Olga said. She grabbed the young woman's hand and held it.

That afternoon in Colomba, no one would have noticed anything unusual—just the brightly painted chicken buses passing and Indians hurrying to catch them on their way back to the mountains.

"I'm so glad that you're all right, *señora*. I've been so worried," Olga said. "I looked for you. I did."

The young woman and her maid gave Olga a ride to *Las Flores* in their jeep. The young girl was kind. She knew nothing about war or death yet. They watched Olga walk up the narrow road and through the gate to the plantation.

• • •

Russell Cruz-Price opened his eyes and saw the eyes of the jaguar in the night. There were two of them, a female and a male, and they weren't afraid of him anymore.

Then he heard voices and saw a light, carried by a party of Indians coming from the river in single file. He was sure it was a dream, until he saw one of the jaguars turn and sprint away into the jungle. The other one, the female, looked at him a moment longer, a straight, level gaze. Something seemed to pass between them, that perfect understanding beyond language that all living things share. Then she, too, was gone.